THE ERA OF THE END

OMEGA PLAN

VOLUME TWO

JONATHON KARAGIANNIS

ESCARPMENT PUBLISHING

Omega Plan, Volume 2
Jonathon Karagiannis
Copyright © 2025
Published by Escarpment Publishing
ABN: 32736122056
http://www.escarpmentpublishing.com.au

Paperback ISBN: 978-1-922329-88-2
Hardback ISBN: 978-1-922329-89-9

FOREWORD

Welcome to Volume 2 of *Omega Plan*. This volume is a direct continuation of Volume 1 of the first book of the series *The Era of the End*.

Because of the content, themes, characters and the foreshadowing that I wish to present in this book is on an epic scale, a short book would fail to convey what I want for this series. It needed to be this long and in fact, I mean future instalments to be longer. Publishing *Omega Plan* in one massive thousand-page volume would not only be extremely expensive (to print and for customers to buy), but it would also be quite intimidating and therefore, lose potential for success. Especially for a debut author in a very competitive publishing industry, this wouldn't be wise.

I hope you get what I mean.

Due to this, I selected the breaking point myself, where I saw fit. It could have been easier to break at the end of each of the three parts (or acts) and create a trilogy, however, this didn't feel right. Firstly, the three parts in this book are like three acts, the end of one sequence and the beginning of a new one. They couldn't serve as satisfying ends in themselves. Secondly, splitting *Omega Plan* into three volumes would create the impression to readers that it is a complete series, not a single book.

So, I've broken the book in the middle after chapter 43, for this scene is extremely pivotal for not just the book, but for the entire series as a whole. It fulfills several plot cycles as well as anticipating future conflicts and answers. I want you to understand, however, that *Omega Plan* Volumes 1 and 2 are a *single* novel. They are *not* two separate novels. I encourage you to read them as a cohesive whole, as it was intended to be.

I felt this would be necessary when I began my publishing journey and hearing advice from professional publishers to split it. Once again, thank you so much to everyone who has supported me on this writing journey. It's only just begun.

If you haven't read *Omega Plan* Volume 1 yet, I highly advise you do so first.

PART II

CALL FOR HOPE AND JUSTICE
(CONTINUED)

44

THE FOURTH REALITY

"The misfortunes of the Book of Balaam, son of Beor. And he beheld a vision in accordance with El's utterance …
The gods came to him at night …
They said to Balaam, son of Beor: 'So will it be done, with naught surviving.
No one has seen the likes of what you have heard!
The gods have banded together;
the Shaddai-gods have established a council.
And they have said to [the goddess] Shagar,
'Sew up, close up the heavens with dense cloud.
That darkness exist there, not brilliance.
Obscurity and not clarity;
So that you instil dread in dense darkness.
And — never utter a sound again!
Heed the admonition, adversaries of Sha[gar-and-Ishtar]!'"
—From The Deir Alla Inscription, Jordan, 8th Century BCE. Translation by Baruch A. Levine, from *The Context of Scripture Volume Two: Monumental Inscriptions from the Biblical World*, William W. Halo, Leiden; New York: Brill, 2001, pg 140-145.

All Brianna could see was red. She almost lost control, speeding back to the reservation, her heart pounding with fury, hands shaking. Orange dust billowed in outrage across her windscreen. Tyres grinding gravel, bumping precariously, the only thing she could think about in this emergency was that helicopter and Alfred Bonner.

Brianna made a sharp right turn off the gravelled road and onto the main, skidding. Gripping the wheel, she raced right back down to the Navajo property, towards the central building, where the black helicopter had landed in front of the main yard.

They're going for the CD, Brianna thought as she ran into a file of soldiers pouring out of the doors of the helicopter, storming into the building.

Knots forming in her stomach, Brianna dashed towards the building, raising one hand to block the swirling dust. The thrumming helicopter pierced her ears; she charged into the reservation, and immediately someone tackled her. Yelping, she struggled impulsively from the hand grabbing her body. She elbowed and kicked, but to no avail; the man's hands on her body were like iron. Another soldier pinned her down, driving her head to the floor. Something hard jabbed into her upper back.

Gun!

"Go! Get out! Move it!" More voices shouted from the din.

An unruly powerful hand yanked Brianna up by the collar. She tensed as the soldier carried her into the waiting room, where soldiers stood over an old Navajo with wisdom behind his eyes, slowly lowering to his knees. The old man's carved face remained completely peaceful, in contrast to the distressed lady next to him.

"Easy! Come on! Why, Jason, why have you created a hostage situation? This is not going to look good for the Alliance." Though Bonner's voice was even and calm, Brianna could hear frustration in it.

"Sorry, Arhat," Jason said, lowering his head. "I …"

"You idle Aes Sidhe!" Bonner snapped, stalking into the hostage circle, raising a hand. "This will be very quick. Albert has classified documents that I must secure. No harm shall be done to his family or his property. None of you are to be arrested or detained. I apologise for my brash men."

As Bonner went away to take the CD, Brianna wondered about the sinister conspiracy that drove these people, keeping crucial secrets from her. She dwelt on the uncertainty of what she didn't know and of what Ben had embroiled himself in. It made her want to throw up.

It wasn't long for Bonner to return down the hall with the CD in his hands inside its packet. He ground his teeth, scanning the room briskly, the soldiers poking their guns down upon the Navajo man.

"There are various expectations for a Chief of the First Nation peoples, Albert," Bonner said. "But to hide away a piece of important information is cowardly …" The man blinked as his voice dithered. "You'll thank me one day. The Cabal would not deal with you as kindly as I have. Be grateful."

A whole dozen of Navajo people had gathered with wondering faces at the commotion, the large soldiers and the helicopter outside.

"All right, Indians, my job here is done. You're free to roam about this country." He met the Navajo bystanders' gazes. "Thank you, and apologies for the inconvenience." And with that, the soldiers disbanded into their helicopter, leaving the Navajo and Brianna alone.

—

Joshua loved being around momentous events. It invigorated his knowledge, that he was living in history.

But he *hated* being around events that made his insides feel like they were being liquefied and the Holy Spirit within him grieve. He could feel an awful ravenous atmosphere in this city of Phoenix weighing heavily on him.

It was nighttime when Judd Pounders got a call from Keller Butcher and the Phoenix police department for a meeting regarding Ben's disappearance, and by then Joshua's mind was aflame.

Ben is gone too? What's happening to this world?

Crossing his arms, Keller Butcher stepped forward to face Brianna after recording her testimony of the day's extraordinary events in the Grand Canyon in the interrogation room. "Is that all that happened to you?" Keller intoned. "You're saying the Alliance knows about Mastemah and the kidnapping of Veronica and Zoe are linked?"

"That's what they claim, but I'm not betting my money on it," Brianna said. "The Alliance has the CD – which is the least of our problems. But now, because of the CD, Ben's gone. And as far as I know, Ben could be dead. We need to find him."

Joshua's fists blanched. "Who are these people? They were behind the looting of Uruk, the Shinar Mission and now this?"

Bonner – the Liberal Lamb who spoke as a Draconian Dragon – *never* asked for consent from the soldiers who enlisted in the Marine Corps in the Shinar Unit. According to Marcus Theis, Bonner swooped in for the coffin, leaving for the States perfunctorily. And now he had just stolen another cultural artefact: guarded holy knowledge from the Navajo. Perhaps what justified this in his mind was that looting remained a chronic issue in all countries, so he needed to come to protect the artefacts *from* looters.

Keller placed a hand on Joshua's back and said to Brianna, "The Alliance is simply doing their jobs, following protocol. We're not sure yet if they're behind any of these terrible cases on your family, Brianna."

"These people have a *foul* protocol to follow," Pounders added in a disciplined, firm voice. "I need to speak to Bonner himself if we're to get to the bottom of this."

"What about those people who assassinated Ben's father? Whose protocol was that?" Joshua said.

"It …" Pounders swerved his head, hesitating. "Joshua, don't think like Ben. You have no reason to get yourself involved in this. Leave the investigation to the FBI."

"I think you are right," Joshua said, feeling exhausted. "I will leave them to do what they do, but … Yeah, I want nothing to do with this anymore." This situation was dangerous. Irrelevant for him, and even worse for his growing reputation as a future scholar in academia – a reputation that was already extremely problematic. Ben was a blind, deceived fool, a violent man who valued pride from his fame. Any affiliation with him would put Joshua's track record in jeopardy. *Not surprising that Ben fell into sin so awfully. I just need to get away from here. I cannot stand thinking about Ben and all of the toxicity of the Southwest. It is not good for my research. Not good for my brain.*

Brianna spoke up, saying, "Kala and her agents are making headway in tracking down Ian Mastemah and his terrorist group, the Manicheans of Light. But what is paramount is that we change our focus and search for Ben as well."

Keller nodded. "And I will continue the hunt for Veronica and Zoe."

"Can you do me a favour?" Judd Pounders said, handing Joshua his car keys. "Can you please wait for me outside?"

Upon retrospect, Joshua thought in his mind as he left the office room, departing to wait for Pounders in his car, *I'm sick of the south states. I'm going to listen to you, Pounders, and I'm going to take your leave and go and start a new life in Oregon! Portland, Oregon! I heard they have good biblical studies and ancient history courses at Willamette University. I'm going there! It's not right that I dwell here, as Ben's crisis plagues me. This whole time, Pounders has given me a new head start, so I will not ruin this only chance by cutting off my hand, trying to get involved in other people's problems. I need to live my own life the way I want – according to God's will. Ben's crisis is not my own. Ben's mad, and may God bless his heart, I want nothing to do with him.*

And Joshua wanted nothing to do with Ben, because it was as if he'd encountered the wretched con man he had once been.

———

Camelback Mountain overlooked the city – webbed with roads and buildings across the valley floor.

But in the Spiritual World, Phoenix hung in a metaphysical shadow, spasming with yellow and red vapours of spirits, slithering lacy wisps of light and darkness, distorting things that were material and made of matter into a wispy black oceanic abyss. The land was formless and void. But bodies of water were solid islands of flaky navy crystal. In the Spiritual World, everything was upside down.

The sky was midnight, without any stars; though some floating orbs of liquid light, small and the size of a melon, zoomed by, up into the heavens. The sun seemed too distant, too frail, to properly illuminate the Otherworld. It did not need a sun, as all beings that had not taken a carbon-based body had their own photon radiation of hydrogen and helium light imbuing them from within.

Wings flapping, Ashur skimmed towards the pyramidal Camelback Mountain. He was in a desert, a familiar place to him. The dry air made his skin, even his feathery body, feel like paper.

This was his new home. The desert of the Westerners. The land of the dead. His kingdom. Here he would plot his revenge against El – the Creator – who had waged war against him, denying him a seat amongst the Elohim gods in his council on high.

"Ohhh!" gagged an angry buzz from the rocks made of smoke. It sounded female, but not human. "Welcome, sweet traveller. Welcome to the Southwest." Out of a cleft of the rock-smoke, swift and scuttling, was a gigantic hairy black tarantula – gold, brown and black. Jointed legs trembling, gripping the rock, the great arachnid made Ashur diminutive in comparison. "Welcome, Chicken. Ohhh." She sounded pleased; a humming groan came from the chaos creature. "Hmmm. I want to say, I cannot resist birds. You are an adorable young man. Have you come to seek my wisdom?" The spider woman got so close, her legs brushed Ashur's face. He remained calm and still. *She will not eat me. I'm not a chicken, I'm only in my* ba *form.*

Ashur turned, folding his wings at his sides. He could feel he had a face of a man, but his body resembled a kite with white, blue and green feathers. In lieu of arms, he had wings, and instead of human legs, backward reptile legs.

The *ba* – what was immanent – was his personality, his identity. Like a doppelgänger or twin, it was the force that animated the individual. There were four other parts of his soul and the *ba* was one, constituting five parts.

"What are you called, and what do you want?" the woman groaned, torn between lust and fear. She had a body of a monstrous spider so big and hideous, Ashur was afraid. Her abdomen was swollen, and her body belched forth black vapours.

She circled Ashur, her eight legs bristling with hairs, clawing and clinging along the rocks made of smoke and black water. Her upper body resembled a congealed human female with an hourglass body, melting into the spider. She had no skin, but shadows shrouded her form with unlight. Her hands were her front legs, which erected and gestured as she spoke. Her face was skeletal, covered completely in mottled hair, and eight jet-black eyes – two jutting out of her temples, front tiny eyes dotting the face and a massive globular pair on her flat forehead – lidless and black. Large hairy fangs hung from her mouth, and they paddled like two tiny hands as she spoke.

"I am Lugal of Kiengi and Kiuri!" Ashur trumpeted. "Ruler of the Four Corners of the land, the Anointed One. Do as I bid, and I will give you whatsoever your lusts may demand."

"Oh …" The great spider rose her body, vibrating. "Dark Lord Abaddon, I will obey you. But Sinnhu, Chief of the Hohokam, wishes to speak to you first."

"What is your name, creature?" Ashur boomed.

The spider woman's mouth gaped open as if she were screaming, but in silence. Her fangs dripped with venom, thick like tar. "My Lugal Abaddon! I am Koyangwuti. The Anaye, Mother of the Azag and Girtablilu – the Sleepless creatures."

Impatiently, Ashur followed the crawling Koyangwuti up the ochre mountain. Higher up on the peak, a light source less vibrant emitted a crimson glow – so red, it made the entire mountain from inside the crust seethe with a deep glow. In the Spiritual Realm, human settlements were thin smoke structures resembling spangled webs emitting radiance, resplendent and brilliant. They surrounded the red pyramid peak, *swarming* with emotion sprites taking on bizarre shapes, organic and beastly. They flew, crawled, climbed and slithered through the settlements like a hive.

Sprites appeared when something changed – when fear came about, or when it began to rain, or when an animal died or was born, or when humans made a decision. The tissue that connected the universal ontology, sprites were fragments of creation that had pre-existed humans for billions of years.

Ashur could see the rock of the mountain as if it were a transparent veil, looking down right into its centre. Streaks of dark light, like dormant snakes or worms, palpitating veins of the mountain, dwelt inside caves, clefts and hollows in the void.

Mutual disdain stained this peak. The spiritual forces had a strict hierarchy. Frustrated by others' selfishness, suffering unbearable tantrums, territorial spirits with a slim bit of intelligence could either be slighted, persecuted or walked upon by anyone higher up who wanted to be exalted above all. During his time ruling the Two Rivers, Ashur dealt with many spirits – they were relentless, unpredictable, unreliable beings, doing what was right in their own eyes. They couldn't be trusted unless they were enslaved. Only one could wield dominance. Everyone else grovelled.

But that's what the Chiefs or Patrons of regions were for. The Chiefs or Patrons were the Principalities and Powers of geographical locations and, above all, human culture that worshipped these beings. Chiefs and Patrons kept regional spirits in order as restrainers. They may contend against one another, if they so wished, but that often had to be dictated by human behaviour, which drove all spiritual powers to action. By the noise of the god's footsteps stamping, triggering nations to war, the Chiefs would bustle fiercely, taking sides.

Ashur was Marduk and Nintura – as an Anunna, he was a Patron of Principalities and Powers. Yet in this new land of the Pueblo, he did not know how the local spirits worked.

Koyangwuti led Ashur towards the highest point of Camelback Mountain and saw three powerful beings, giant with an imposing air. The Spiritual Realm gave Ashur all the basic information he needed to know about these three Chiefs before coming into their presence. Their power was impressive.

Achiyalatopa – Chief Principality and Power of the Zuni – stood in a visible aura of pride and arrogance. Once a human hero, he took up the identity of the spiritual power and ascended. His zoomorphic face resembled a bald eagle, beaked, with large golden eyes, and the horns of a buffalo rising from his head. His clothes were the hide of a bear, with a pair of glassy eagle's wings folded at his sides, feathers resembling flint knives. He leaned on an alabaster staff, its tip the shape of an infinitesimal shell spiral. He did not have a bird's body as Ashur did; rather, Achiyalatopa was humanoid from the elbows and knees down, his feathers blending into various yellow-orange cracks webbing his rocky skin.

The second, Tawa – Chief Principality and Power of the Hopi – was rather corpulent; he had more of a human appearance, but his lower body appeared as if he were a bright green-and-white slug, with white horns jutting out of his slimy body. His hands were human and muscular; he held a bow and arrow in one hand and a shield in the other. Floppy layers of fat covered him, and he throbbed with greed, odium and dominion. Around his stern, imperious face – blue as turquoise and hard as a gemstone tattooed with yellow and white glyphs – was a white halo. A halo with petals shining dazzling rays of light.

And the third, Sinnhu – Chief of the Hohokam – was a woman, with prominent breasts and hips, floating in midair, emitting visible sprites of conceit, pride and selfishness. She was white and orange, her face a triangular mask covering her mouth embossed with shell-like patterns, and her eyes glowed in even green blotches. Three white protrusions grew out of her head – two were elongated horns, and the other, a flat disc in the middle. Her shoulders were rectangles, and in her chest was a glowing gem heart in a circular cavity. Sinnhu had tapering legs, segmented by a vertical blue stripe forming into spikes on her knees. Her arms were four long whiplike tentacles with pointed tips, twirling and whirling around each other in the pelagic current of the Spiritual Realm. She was weightless, floating as everything in this Realm did.

The Chiefs, in unison, raised a powerful surge of power, channelling a whirlwind of orbs, swirling around them, forming into a large gathering of monstrous forms.

Sinnhu, Chief of the Hohokam, spoke up. Her thundering voice declared, "Gods without hosts! Gods without temple houses, come!"

"The humans cannot stand again with the dangerous Powers," Tawa boomed capriciously. "Then why must we be subject to them? If the Tyrant wanted it this way, he will suffer loss. For too long, he has been too dependent upon humans – those mud toys. If they forget us, we must be prepared to gain our freedom and immortal power independently to rule the universe without them."

The petty spirits cheered – a wild wind buzzing with frenzy to conquer and rule the cosmos beyond Earth.

Achiyalatopa turned his zoomorphic horned eagle face towards the glowing orbs. "Tell us, scouts, what you have learnt from your travels on the winds? What is Awonawilona planning?"

"My Chief," a pink-white spirit orb pulsated with a metallic buzz. "There are no enemies against your sublime whims. Joshua – the pretender – has left for the Pacific Northwest."

"Good," Tawa said. "We must keep the enemy's forces scattered."

"Benjamin DePaula still hasn't perished," Achiyalatopa intoned. "He lives – both for the good and for the ill."

"What more must we do to destroy his family?" a dark blue orb growled. "What more? The destruction has been extremely great, Chief."

"What more?" Sinnhu mused fatalistically. "Much more. Ben will surely return. I want you all to wait for him. He will guide you to his own destruction. The Thomas Jones decoy is working. We cannot do anything to bring about a collapse in Ben's life, but wait and watch as Ben becomes one of us. Our aim is to absorb his will into ours, increasing our own power at the expense of his."

The swarm of orbs buzzed and cooed in awe.

Well, if we cannot do anything, Ashur thought, *at least I could share this land and culture with other beings. If Arhat Alfred Bonner brought my* ba *here, then my devotion is being revived. My power to rule and establish order to this chaos.*

"And what about you, Gilgamesh, Lugal of Sumer and Akkad?" Sinnhu turned her unearthly head towards Ashur's *ba*. Fear sprites flashed around her form. Ashur smiled. "You're not what you once were. You're half formed. Half asleep."

"I will not rest until I have gathered the power I need," Ashur intoned.

"We will be there for you to rebuild your empire," Sinnhu said with heaviness. Her arms undulated, tentacles twisting together, forming into arms – distinct hands that shimmered. "You are the Chief of the Anunna Sky Beings. This world is destined to be yours and yours to rule, to wage war against the Tyrant. The Great Spirit wants to create a false humility in people – a great value that contains the truth – of everything sorted out. Nihitaa' wants humans to be replicas of himself. But most of all, our Tyrant is selfishly blinded by jealously for the Homo above all else. It's hypocritical. He gives to them with his right hand and takes away with his left. You, Ashur, are empty and want to suck in, while the Tyrant – overflowing – wants to give out. This is why you have become the hero of the ages."

"The world is yours to rule, mighty hunter, and we will rule jointly in the prosperity you bring," Tawa confirmed. "Every god knows of your awesome destiny. Hero of the ages."

Mine? The universe to rule? He had just been given confirmation. He'd attained this legitimacy after being immortalised by humanity, to rule the world and to *save* the human world. From death, to promise eternal life, judging men, satisfying the gods, realising Ma'at, annihilating Isfet – chaos – threat of the gods, rival of Creation. In that, Ashur remembered his innate desire to overcome death – yes, he'd feared dying for this reason – he still had to save those he loved – himself and those associated with himself. But chaos had embraced him, and he embraced chaos, brandishing it for what it was, to destroy the enemies of his purposes.

But ironically, Ashur *needed* humans to create meaning for his purposes to flourish. Humans shall save him first – as Alfred Bonner had admirably done – so he could rise again, providing salvation from the Galactic Tyrant.

My coffin is the key to the Bottomless. The Light Alliance has my coffin, and they shall amend me to save the world from the Galactic Tyrant.

He hoped his *ka* (the animating spiritual lifeforce) could come soon. Kings had multiple *kas*, at least seven. When the *ka* and the *ba* reunited, they became the *akh* – his glorified spirit – and then Alfred Bonner would know what to do. He will evoke Ashur's *akh* and bond with his *ka*, becoming a suitable avatar.

"Justice comes," Tawa said metallically, raising his bow as the orbs settled down on the slopes of the crimson summit like flies.

Ashur could feel the presence of the Black Rider before he saw her. She skimmed through the weightless water. The beast was prancing – swimming – with six legs. Mounted on the beast was a body of a woman. Ashur noticed her dark purple-and-grey stola with a high neckline with an oval cut-out that exposed the tops of her breasts, wearing a peculiar encrusted necklace. Her cloak draped and flowed in the water current. One hand held onto the reins, and in the other hand, she held a pair of creaking scales to determine weights and balances.

The Black Rider's steed had six finned flippers moving like a great fish, and a thin, long-barbed tail whipping back and forth. It had grey-black skin, and its large, finned wings flapped at its sides with three red thorns protruding out of them. Its body glowed with an internal pink energy – a body that consisted of crystal protrusions, a remarkably bizarre unearthly form. Its head branched out with a slender reptilian skull with no eyes that Ashur could see, and it had terrible mandibles.

This goddess on the strange mountain donkey's back had subtle power that Ashur could feel. Not an American god allotted to this country. The goddess was from the old world, where Ashur had come from. Far, far away.

"Dike Iustitia, the daughter of goddess Themis and the god Zeus," the Chiefs welcomed. "And Kokopelli, the Aztec merchant."

"Noble Powers and Principalities of Pueblo lands," deep-bosomed Dike said, her voice a tremor in the waters. Her cowl flew back, revealing the countenance of a handsome woman with olive skin and grey eyes, one darker than the other. Her dark hair flowed in the water, wearing a *stephane* crown – a metal decorative wreath worn on the head.

Next to Dike, a form coalesced from dark smoke, becoming Kokopelli. His hair bristled with needle-like spines. He had a thin beak protruding from his nose and wore baggy clothes with a prominent hump rising from his back. He held a pipe instrument in his hands.

"What do you report, Dike?" boomed Tawa.

The goddess' mouth contorted smugly. "I'm fed up with how awful humans are." She raised her scales and placed them on her lap securely. "They set for themselves a precedent, an order. But as famine strikes, their order becomes the very means of their undoing. Inflation. Disease. Our impish human slaves deserve their own death. They were made to be our servants, but they have become our enemies. Insects and beasts. Darkness and violence. Vile apathy, scorning us, disrespecting the authority from of old. We have become irrelevant to them. Those apathic fools must be destroyed, one by one."

Dike's scornful speech became a loud, boastful proclamation. "The world is mad, and at this rate, it will kill itself if nothing is done about it. Justice used to be life and truth. Now, human destiny and meaning are death. Like the Seven fallen Sages, humans are trapped in their nugatory prison of their sensual desires. They progressed and forgot about us. Good. Then we can *judge them* with a mighty hand, because they do not listen to God's Law!"

The spirits cried in concord. The three Chiefs nodded, enthralled.

"These sinners have ruined our days," Dike shouted passionately, to the tone of judgment. "More and more, the human slaves are becoming obnoxious, parasites on our lands. They keep on killing, multiplying, thwarting our plans, while we hold up a dead sky, preventing the fiery sea from drowning us all. We are dead in their eyes, and so their extinction is inevitable. The judgment is adequate. The penalties irrevocable!"

"Let it be!" Achiyalatopa cawed. His beak clacked as he spoke, his staff pointing at Ashur's *ba*. Ashur listened. He relaxed when strangers spoke so well of him. No challenge. "However, no matter the state of the human disaster, the gods restrained by Awonawilona's viceregent in the Abyss will be freed. Only until the Restrainer is removed from authority can the old powers locked away in the Void rise."

Yes, Ashur thought with pride. *My power, the power Marduk Abaddon, is in the Abyss.*

"But the Principalities and Powers assigned geography and regions, they are not prepared for the Return," Dike said. "They all have their own plans.

Yet, the gods trapped in the Deep all have one accord. They are a hive mind, purely bred for dominion. Someone must unite the Powers and Principalities. Someone lord over the Abyss." Dike's imperial eyes sighted Ashur. "Someone must persuade them that we all have chosen to rule this world ourselves. And if we should rule, we have a common enemy trying to buffet us."

Ashur smiled smugly, wondering what power awaited him there, in the Deep, where parts of his soul still ruled, preparing the gods in prison in the Galactic Tyrant's thraldom to unleash great armies to conquer the world that was rightfully his. The people – human, Lahmu and asura – were already deceived, ready to accept him as their lugal. King.

"Humans have destroyed me! Such horrid monsters!" Tawa snarled, undulating his thick blue body. "Stand aside and let me smite them all!"

"Not so fast, Tawa." Sinnhu raised her tenacles. "It is not that simple. There are humans, a remnant, who try to understand us. The Alliance's leaders are such people."

"But Judd Pounders will fight against the Alliance with justice," the goddess Dike said measuredly, examining her pair of scales. "But whatever the outcome of these events, the marines are no longer important for Alfred Bonner. Out of the Alliance and the Cabal's many factions, only one must rule. This is a natural law. What is important now is that the right and worthy ruler of the cosmos can bring humans to Ascension. The Aes Sidhe are finding ways to do this. So is the Tyrant. For too long, the Tyrant has ruled, but he has grown senile and weak." Dike cast another approving glance at Ashur. "Our best candidate to unite the forces of the Abyss and the Powers and Principalities is Ashur. Marduk himself."

"Yes, indeed. He is our only hope," Sinnhu said. "You will destroy the humans and remake them to worship us, no?"

Ashur nodded at the suggestion. "I will do it. They will rally behind me, and by worshipping me, they will worship you all who submit to me."

Sinnhu relaxed slightly. "I don't know what the Tyrant sees in humans."

Dike nodded. "His filthy value on humans makes justice bankrupt. He asks humans to abandon their self-will, only for him to conform them, and give back all their desires as gifts, turning them into liars. Obedient slaves they are, selfish, wanting to be petted and admired, to take advantage of others and rule the whole universe. This *outrageous principle* is worthy of retribution."

"Humans like Ben think they have it all figured out," Sinnhu said, tentacles spinning as she wove her speech of hate. "The humans are the representatives of death, not the Tyrant's images. We can harness their erudite ignorance to wage war against the Galactic Tyrant. So meticulous, even when he sends agents of the Satan out to curse and destroy, he uses us all as means to an end. And an end where gods are *nothing* and dirtlings are *exalted*." The demon beings roared in wild outrage. "To this frail form of care, our enemy shows his greatest weakness: generosity. How can he truly love, when exalting humans, he forgets his other glorious children were also made in his image when time began?"

At that speech, Kokopelli and all the orbs pulsated sporadically, bursting out laughing as if everything – the spiritual functioning of the cosmos – were a total farce.

Ashur listened, engrossed. *Ma'at … You are Ma'at Ashur. Kittum u misharum – a disposition of justice. The restorer of order is thrown to the outer edges of the world. Isfet that threatened to encroach the world. Calamity can only be averted by the right functioning of gods and men, both working together to maintain order. Unite the Powers. Raise the Anunna. Free the Rephaim. Rally the Sleepless hives. Bring back your loved ones and transform humans in your image. Establish the equilibrium of the universe.*

Ashur – or in a real sense, Marduk and Nintura – *knew* his purpose. He studied the scales of Dike dangling in her hands like chains – they were the weights of economic measure and societal value. "Ma'at," he whispered, determining the truth with discernment. He gazed down at his feathery breast. His heart was light. Rotating his head, he gazed at Koyangwuti. A Beast. "Isfet."

"I must go out now," Dike intoned, preparing her mount.

"Good. Go out," Sinnhu confided. There was a stir among the dark powers, crying in shrills, cheering, swellings, groanings.

Ashur felt the familiar and irksome tugging on his spirit. His *ba* now had to return to his coffin every morning as the sun rose from the east. His parts could only become one by no other power but the concentrated power of the Dragon – the Pearls. And Alfred Bonner sought to recover them. Ashur told him he had to, so their plan could work. To regather the Five Pearls of Power from the four corners and the heart of the Earth so Alfred could resurrect Ashur in bodily avatar, to save the world. To set the universe in perfect order and peace.

Unite the Powers. Raise the Anunna. Free the Rephaim. Rally the Sleepless hives. Bring back your loved ones and transform humans in your image. This was his intent to destroy the Tyrant.

But for now, his time had not yet come. He must plot. Abide his time.

Alfred Bonner had the key. The coffin was the anchor that kept Ashur's *ba* alive and humanity's the only hope to salvation.

45

THE HOLYWAY

"Your body is your soul, and your body is your identity.

This is what I tell a lot of young people who come back to the traditional teachings of our people. They say that their body and their relationships are not important, but their inner spiritual life is. I have to lovingly rebuke them that this attitude is self-defeating and harmful.

No. This is not what being spiritual is about. Being spiritual requires the fullness of being. Everything is whole, working towards a greater purpose.

Your soul is the life of the body. Your true identity is not an inward thing, but who you are in the relationships you have. Your identity is your life, it is evolving, spread out over time. You when you were fifteen is the same you when you are eighty. Our bonds with loved ones, our things, our work and our achievements will continue to exist. The life in this age will continue in the age to come. God will preserve and complete your life now. The life in the age to come is triumphant joy, putting to death all the pains and sorrow. All the experiences of joy we experienced in life, those become eternal. Everything else is burned away by the Great Fire.

Who we are and what we become in this life, in this body, will become eternal. You only have one shot at this."

—Chief Albert Tobadzistsini at the Turtle Island First Nations Gathering, Oklahoma, 2002.

The wind was calm, and the sky was bronze and purple over the Grand Canyon as Albert spoke to the Great Spirit, saying, "Where the land stands, the sky is upheld. The sky and the land were placed after the people emerged from the four worlds. Four Holy People – First Man, First Woman,

Salt Woman and Black God planned the conditions of life on the surface of the land, by your will. Jóhonaa'éi Nihitaa'."

Before him was the secret shrine mountain of the west. The cave, the slot canyon, nestled by pines and bushes, sealed by rosy escarpments not formed by hands.

His awareness of this place was not brief and unselfconscious, not a fleeting moment, not a flash of recognition, nor a trace of memory, that was swiftly replaced by an awareness of something else. But now and again, and sometimes without apparent cause, his awareness was seized – arrested – and this place on which he dwelt became an object of spontaneous reflection and resonating sentiment.

The old sun in the azure sky sunk under the vast canyons and the thick blazing clouds. Insects chirped, adamant to bathe in the last winds of day, readying for the nocturnal. The fresh wind blew far, keening like the sound of the trumpet, pensive with a scent that would change the world.

Albert inhaled the desert pines and scents as he thought of what he must do. Mother Earth had helped young Albert guard the Pearl of Power until today. Now he had given it over to the wicked for Ben's sake. Yet Great Spirit had selected him as a Shepherd. Albert had no reason to know why. He'd simply taken on the cause of restoring Ben, for Ben, on his behalf. Ben was afflicted, vulnerable. He had lost everything; with no parents, no children and a wife who did not pray for him.

"The first humans lived underground as lizards," Albert exclaimed to the Great Spirit, his voice forthright and determined. "Just as Ben is buried underground, so must Ben rise up to be recreated."

Albert began gingerly, staggering down a rocky slope. The wall, sinuous and fleshy, resembled the red lithe muscles of a living being. Strata of ochre and white bands swirling in marbled patterns through the wavy sinuous canyon of Tsé Bíghanílíní. Great Spirit guided him. "Forgiveness must be attained," Albert chanted.

As he hiked, he hummed the song of the Holyway. Of reconciliation. Of the formation of humanity. He travelled down the slot canyon as the words echoed, down rosy gorges and caves, down towards the Colorado River.

Welcomed by the darkening violet sky, Albert rested his jaded legs and body, sitting on a rock overlooking the sunset. He straightened his back, looked up and saw buzzards. Black vulture persons, unfurling. Four of them.

"These carrion eaters wait for death patiently," Albert meditated, strolling towards the red gorge directly below the flock, not too far away downhill.

"Jóhonaa'éi Nihitaa' – you use death to make life epistemically more valuable. Your will be done – not my will, but your will be done – on the land as it is in the sky."

Albert walked under the birds in the sky until he could walk no more. Albert's legs twisted, and he collapsed under a thorn bush, grunting, rocks clattering from his fall.

He exhaled, immobile. As he went further to the bottom, he felt crushed, clasped shut by the wondering rock monster Tsé'nagahi, who watered this canyon with the Colorado, shaping this narrow chasm.

The night, as it descended into darkness, became freezing cold, but in the skyless chasm, heat still held absolute sway, rising up. Thirst became an itch, then it ached, rendering his mouth raw and sticky. Visions came swift and relentless. There was no rest from them. They spun in the star-encrusted sky, murmurs in the dank breath of the wind and shadows of the water-shaped sandstone. Albert followed the star trails in the crack of sky above, their tails luminous.

Visions were objective omens, selected by Nihitaa' to instruct a human with the vision quest in the fight against the sky monster, the Dragon.

The message was clear. *Gather them. The repentant Church. Scattered. Exiled. Unite my body. The Great Chief Cornerstone is laid.*

To gather ethnic groups, to heal the schisms between cultures, ethnicities, families and marriages. To remove the root of bitterness in all indigenous cultures harmed by white Christian men.

Prepare the world for the return of God.

This was the great plan of Nihitaa' for this era.

But one thing perplexed Albert. How could one speak of one body if all the body parts were completely dismembered and different? This was the blessed dream, the reconciliation between God's children. Israel's old vocation. One body, many diversities, a new human, functioning optimally. City lights on a mountain. Harmonising flesh and spirit. Rectifying the Khesed Bond.

Albert's breaths of wisdom, insight, counsel, valour and knowledge helped him sniff out, helped him gain the worth to prove himself to pass the test. He sensed not what his eyes saw, but with faith, to overcome the test of the Pearl's allure. A power that so easily corrupted men.

Albert sniffed. Ben failed. Like all typical men.

Then why do you want him, Jóhonaa'éi Nihitaa'?

By the caw of the buzzards, Albert got to his feet, his hands feeling the sandy ground. They came upon a fissure, touching something fleshy.

The moon cast a sheen over the shadows, so Albert could see, mingled under loose rubble, a human arm. The hand clawed motionlessly; its last known movement had been a desperate strain for deliverance.

Albert held on to that hand and pulled up Ben's body. He checked his pulse and found it feeble.

———

As the dirges of crickets and cicadas pierced through the icy night, Albert followed the procession of four male youths carrying Ben's moribund body wrapped in a patterned rug on a stretcher. Shadows danced in the moonlight from the bobbing tresses of fire from stick torches held by the youths. They crept through the gnarly trees towards the sacred dwelling space.

The conical winter hooghan stood to represent the four quarters of the Earth – it was a cave hut of mud and leaves with a low ceiling. It only had one doorway, facing east – representing birth, dawn and purity. Over the doorway hung a draping curtain decorated with two symmetrical coyotes. One only entered the hooghan this way – past the coyotes, coming from the east into the warm womb. A cross-piece, forming a lintel, connecting to the jambs, created a hole for the smoke to escape into the air like a chimney.

Before entering the hooghan, the participants and Ben were sprinkled with water by the guardian holding a ceramic jug. For Albert, he'd already cleansed himself in the sweat lodge four times, singing four songs to prepare himself to draw near to the Holy People for this ceremony.

Albert gazed at the hooghan, reminded of the beautiful principles of Nihitaa'. The Diné and all humans were co-rulers on Earth; they had to subdue the land with full recognition that they were caretakers. Whatever humanity did, being truly human was directed towards bringing order out of non-order. Exploiting things, taking power, humans always led the environment into disorder. This hooghan wasn't just a temporary hut for ceremonies, it was Earth in miniature; a divinely gifted home, a sacred precinct for humans to care for and maintain other humans.

Albert parted the curtain at the door to the hooghan. Thick pungent earth smells filled the interior. The stern youths adjusted themselves to the side as a servant woman came to lay down a bundle of pine leaves over the raised clay bed at the far end of the hut. A single torch burned on the wall, casting both light and shadows in an effervescent dance over the ochre wall and wooden beams of the roof. Once Albert got the fire of incense prayer ready, there would be no need for this torch on the wall.

Also on the wall was a yellow, red, black and white wheel divided into quarters by a cross with a single smaller green circle in the centre. The Sacred Hoop without beginning or end was said to break when forgiveness and love departed from the Earth.

The lady tending the pine leaves carried the body to the end of the hooghan, ensconcing it, covering Ben in a shroud on the bed of fluttering pine leaves.

Albert sat at the north, facing Ben. The north meant faith.

The preparations were made in steady haste. Servants came, carrying the ritual tasselled clothing, the eagle headdress and the pigments of rainbow clay with a cloth tarpaulin, setting them on the ground before Albert. He said to them, *"Ahéhee"* (thank you) as they laid down these wonderful gifts for the healing. As the servants served the servant, the servant can serve the servants more. *As it should be.*

The reverent Navajo made a susurration and, as Albert collected twigs, lighting the fire, he heard a rustle. Sweeping his head, his twenty-one-year-old grandson Declan arrived with a tentative stroll, his blue-and-white tassels swaying at his pants, looking about warily. Behind him was his father, the Cherokee, Summerhill – Albert's son-in-law. The marriage between his daughter Haseya and Summerhill had been the bridge that had bound the Navajo and Cherokee together, their marriage united by belief in the Great Creator Spirit.

Albert glanced down at the body that lay on the bed of leaves. "The apocalypse of the overlapping of Earth and Spirit," Albert said. The fire crackled and spat rosin. "It requires a transformation. A reconciliation of one with the many." Smiling absently, Albert welcomed Summerhill and Declan in. "Has your son found his calling yet?" Albert asked.

Summerhill shook his head. "He's still unsure." He gazed at Ben in the south, which meant planning. Potential. Normally, Summerhill's voice during powwows was so loud and booming with perkiness, it almost seemed he was singing in normal speech. Tonight, he sounded subdued.

Hovering pieces of bound-up twigs over the orange hearth fire, Albert twirled it around. "The fire is good," he said with a peaceful smile, thinking of how the Creator formed the fire, making it alive and innovative. The fire wasn't too big and loud; neither was it so smoky that one suffocated. A good fire was built with enough warmth, with minimal effort to stoke. He met his grandson's eyes, which stared at the fire, gleaming like tiny candle lights – little fires in his soul – ready to ignite. "To stay at home is to stay around fire."

"I wanted to raise Declan like this, Chief," Summerhill said, brow creasing. "To keep the fire burning." Summerhill met Albert's gaze, and with surprise, he saw gleaming tears brimming them.

"And when the Great Fire cleanses the land," Albert intoned, "everything will become clear."

Summerhill nodded lugubriously. Albert's friend Harold approached from the curtain of the east – which meant thinking – carrying a drumstick and drum, the scent of buffalo hide pungent in Albert's chest. So euphoric, it made him beam that, after so many years, he was healing a patient once again.

No sickness or infirmity was too much for Albert. The Navajo believed a hooghan medicine hut to be haunted when a human being died within it. They would never enter it again, usually destroying it. Such ideas of purity could explain these onlookers' nervousness and Summerhill's uncertainty.

"When do you think this man will be healed?" Summerhill said, tension seething in his expression.

Albert blew at the fire, tending it gently, shifting on his mat. He then got out a large grey feather, waving the hearth, stirring the flames gracefully. "Three to four days."

"Chief? Did you happen to find him lost in the canyon? You don't even know this man." He examined Ben, and pain bubbled from his mouth. "After all the lies and massacres of our people, you bring him in for healing? Chief, he's one of them! Those that don't care!"

"One of what?"

Summerhill groaned. "Stop playing dumb with me! You know!"

"Summerhill, if you were found in this white man's position, lost and broken, would you like somebody strange to help you or leave you?"

Silence. Summerhill sighed protractedly, slumping, eyes closed in shame. "Forgive me."

"It's time for the First Nations to uproot the root of bitterness in their hearts towards the colonisers. This *is* the fire – the calling – you'll pass to Declan."

Albert undressed, only removing his shirt, so his friend could clothe him in the medicine attire – a filmy white shirt adorned with a red bandana around his head and crowned with his bonnet of eagle feathers, small in comparison to his regular war bonnet of extravagant plumed crests and long draping feather tails.

Albert closed his eyes, and he prepared his soul to reknit Ben's soul.

He inhaled and took on the Holy Wind, the invisible personal Presence of the Creative Creator. When infused by it, his body glowed faintly like a fire, orange smoke rising from his radiant skin. The energy sharpened his physical and mental faculties, pulsating to many cohesive rhythms of compassion and passion. Albert, when working with God, became the most powerful version of himself he had ever been.

It is time to create my beloved brother, the Spirit said, gently invigorating him. Albert smirked.

It is time, old friend.

He washed his hands in cold, living water in the basin. Then, reaching over for the flat sand-coloured cloth tarpaulin, arranging the assortment of coloured pigments, Albert took a deep intake of the incense, of the pine, of the dust, of the animal furs, and blew upon the blank tarpaulin.

The *'iikááh* – sand paintings – were the first step to restoring a right and proper relationship with the Great Spirit. They were patterned in four groups of four, creating a symmetrical order in the four Realms.

Albert's hand dipped into the cup of mineral powder. It had been formed from Tsé'nagahi – the Wondering Rock – as his bones became white rock, his flesh became blue pigment, his hair black pigment, his mouth and blood red pigment, and his intestines yellow ochre.

Albert began to paint.

Art, in essence, was creation. Just as order and value came out of chaos and nothingness – a parched desert, a stormy sea – so did sand painting. Out of this wild nonexistence, one gathered, comprehending it, making it understandable, and by giving it existence – a role, a purpose. Uniting large amounts of chaos into something ordered, something coherent. The sacred was order, diversity, sublimity, complexity. This was art. Not novelty, but variety. Expression. Function. Fulfillment.

Eccentric Albert hushed under his breath a puffing song of elegant flight, splaying across the face of the Deep. For creative healing and harmony, the Holy Wind drove him on with each finger stroke.

Ben was a child, weak, and no one cared for him. Albert crawled on the ground, furiously dipping his hand into the pigment. He tried imagining himself lying there in the bed of leaves in place of Ben. There was something moving about envisioning and looking upon the past and the younger.

Albert's attendants gathered around, watching in awe. Some young women handed over more jars of pigment as he continued creating, drawing his prayer for Ben on the ground. It had turned out larger than he thought, but it came naturally, the Spirit working in harmony with him.

Tears mixed with the azure light-blue pigment as he went through the jars, smearing the powder on his cheeks when he wiped his tears. When he had finally finished, he knelt back before an *'iikááh* with equal dimensions, stretching across the diameter of the hooghan, barely leaving room for singers huddling against the wall. The sand painting was circular and symmetrical. A living, sacred story of colours, lying before Ben's bed – an altar.

Albert gasped in silence, feeling his whole body quiver from the exercise. Then he grinned, as the Holyway song sprung out of him naturally.

There were nearly a hundred Navajo songs of varying range and intricacy. Originating from the Creator's heart for creation, they were so nuanced and complex that a medicine man learned only one or two Ways over many years of apprenticeship.

After Harold blessed the sand painting by sprinkling pollen, two silent servants entered, carrying Ben off the bed, bundling him in the cloth and branches, laying him on top of the dried painting.

The assistant first pressed the figures of the painting with his finger, then rubbed the brown pigment onto Ben's forehead into dots over each of his eyebrows.

"His soul wants to return, Father Mother," Albert found himself uttering with a croaky sound.

Harold blew the seven notes of the *chanupa* sacred pipe, vaping smoke of intercessory prayer to drift skywards. The smoke smelled of sweet grass, herbs, pine and cedar. Albert took a pinch of pollen, sprinkling it over Ben.

Placing down his pipe, Harold grabbed his buffalo-hide drum and began to tap it with a swift single note. As he played, his eyes remained fixed on Ben, never altering the rhythm, maintaining the rapid beating of the deity's heart in distress for his children.

Rum, rum, rum, rum, rum, rum, rum, rum, rum, rum, rum, rum.

—

The beatings thundered within the everlasting space between spaces. It awoke Ben's spirit sleeping in a sea of stars on the face of the Deep. He could somehow sense he was lying in a bed of leaves, lying on something. Yet he sensed he floated on water, swaying with the swells.

The beats of the drum throbbed the universe. The beating of his daughter's heart.

In this delicate place between spaces, Ben remained afloat, unmoving, swimming without fixity.

A figure of hovering vagueness took a form. It had long hair around the head.

Mother. She had come running to him with welcoming hands.

Ben sensed the nascent entity, a dark hiddenness coming towards him, shrouded in a smoky veil.

You are filled with jealousy for your child, son. You strike the heel of the weak. That sound … it was riddled with cold indifference. Observing. Input. Output. The universe hung in the ambivalence of the verbal syllables.

Ben tried to cognitively make shape and meaning out of this sound. His mother? His own mind? But the source of the voice was indifferent as a black hole, collapsing all things and all elements.

You've embraced your de-creation, Ben, the voice intoned.

Ben felt that the monotonic sound had come from everywhere. And even being surrounded by stars, he could feel they vibrated, emanating disappointment and long suffering.

Ben's body was incapacitated by dark shadows. Coruscating stars shone above, red, green, purple, blue, white.

Devouring ashes, you've swollen with rashness and deceit. It has made you obsolete from the truth. The voice continued sending feelings rather than just vibrations of sound into his ears. Ben only felt the devastating impact of the sounds. *The risk is the gift. It is both bound in you to receive it or otherwise pervert it. What you do, Ben, is all that matters. And what one foreknows cannot propel what another would do otherwise.*

The Presence departed.

46

A NEW MENACE

"What you base your identity on will determine if you are going to live in eternity with God in joy or eternity with God in shame. Because when the End comes, the righteous will be resurrected before God. Will you be set free from evil? Or will you choose evil?

All human beings have the gift of free will and responsibility over their moral decisions. It is a great power given to us by the Holy People. Do with this gift as you wish. You may risk destroying yourself by choosing resentment, rebelling against God's will, or you may choose to be wise and be loving. None of our free decisions can threaten God's ultimate purpose in the world."

—Chief Albert Tobadzistsini at the Turtle Island First Nations Gathering, Oklahoma, 2002.

The candlelight vigil for Veronica DePaula and Zoe O'Leary was on 15th Ave on the slopes of North Mountain, late in the evening on the seventh night since the kidnapping. Despite the chilly night, all these people, loved ones and members of the community, gathered in a large crowd in their hundreds to support Brianna's and Patricia's families – most, of course, to Brianna's umbrage – had come on the basis of her husband's great fame as an actor, who were saddened by the loss of his daughter and ultimately grieved by his self-ostracism. As she stood with unease with Dominic, Morgan, Patricia and their parents, Brianna couldn't feel alleviated from uncertainty, despite the affections from all these people.

Joining Brianna at the vigil were Keller Butcher and local state police, who were asking that anyone with information report to the news authorities filming the vigil outside, in front of her house. They broadcast the candlelight vigil to the world – hundreds of lights together as a star cluster in the vast darkness of space.

Brianna watched Dominic, walking with his hands in his pockets towards her, staring at nothing, without any sense of awareness. Patty gave him a long, big bear hug to soothe him. Brianna leered at them; she felt a pang of jealousy and great envy for Patty. *Why can't I show my affections towards my own husband! Where the hell is Ben? He can't be dead!*

"Are you okay?" Keller whispered behind her shoulder.

Brianna blinked, melted wax and the sweet aroma of smoke infusing her nostrils. "I–I'm worried about Ben."

"I am too." He detached his gaze from hers, studying the roadside vigil with hundreds of candles, many bearing images of Jesus Christ in blue and crimson garments, as well as angels, saints and the Virgin Mary. Most were plain, others decorated in creative ways with pink ribbons, fairies, marbles, love hearts and beloved characters from Disney movies, all adorning the grassy island on the road. Flowers – tropical bouquets – were votively deposited around the candles and lanterns, as well as toys and other children's drawings, sowing hope into the forlorn hearts of the adults. The warmth from all those orange and yellow candles was a relief – perhaps that had been why candles were symbols of hope. They were small, insignificant, and yet resembled that small light of life.

Brianna held a candle – a candle that glowed with a warmth that seemed to prickle her cold cheeks, encapsulating the entire world on a single wick. Around the flame, protecting it, was a plastic red cup, catching the melting oily wax.

Dominic was struggling to stand up, his breathing uneasy, hands feeling for the brick fence. Patty and Morgan and Dominic's mother gathered around, trying to support him, holding him up. Weighted down by distress – a loss that felt like a part of himself had died – Dominic knelt on the ground. Patty clung to him, weeping. Then Dominic, after holding it all in, began to sob and whine in shame, shaking his head.

Brianna shivered. She watched in silence at Keller's side as Patty and her mother-in-law escorted a broken Dominic inside so they could rest. Brianna shivered some more, her throat tightening. She clenched her fist tightly around the candle. *Where the hell are you, Ben?* The time she spent with Keller solving cases rather than living with her husband would make everyone think that Keller *was* her husband. It was ridiculous – the man practically acted asexually – he had no experience with relationships whatsoever. Cases and being an elite police agent were his priorities.

Keller walked towards the votive grassy patch, and Brianna followed. Spring nights in the arid regions of the southern states, like Arizona, resembled the winter in the northern states. Brianna wore her coat and still felt the slight bite of the cold.

Idly, Brianna snuggled up to Keller's side, her gaze sliding towards a man with a long moustache kneeling to place his teddy bear from his gloved hand by the candle votive. Odd how a grown man would own a teddy bear, unless … Brianna looked the man in the eyes. They were turquoise-green in the firelight, and immediately they slid downwards as he saw Brianna. She turned to look at Keller; he was also studying the man.

The man, rigid, his cheeks tensing, slowly stood up. Brianna felt uneasy by the way the man held himself shyly. The man with the brown moustache knew well who Brianna and Keller were.

Brianna watched him turn slowly, holding his hands, slipping away into the crowd. She exchanged looks with Keller, nodding. *Follow that man.*

Prowling through the crowd, Brianna and Keller parted their way slowly, prompting gasps and turning heads, but they paid no heed, keeping their eyes on the man with the grey hoodie, unwilling to lose him.

It was difficult work. Brianna lost sight of the man immediately, but Keller, determination carving his calm, dangerous face, kept on going down the street until they were out of the crowd. The man had vanished into the darkness.

A ruckus sounded down the neighbourhood block on 15th Ave.

Brianna stared at the source of the sound. An automatic motion-sensor light flashed on two blocks down the street, exposing a solitary man running for his life.

Brianna and Keller bolted after him, scrambling down the small incline into the backyard of the first house. Keller surged on ahead, sprinting, weaving around the corner into a driveway and out into the backyard of the second house. Down ahead, at the third house, another motion-sensor light turned on, prompting a dog to bark. Suddenly, Keller stopped, getting low, Brianna shadowing him. The dog's barking was fierce, high pitched and exasperating, doing in Brianna's head as her ears starved for any sign of the runner, but the dog's barking …

Then the dog's barking stopped. Brianna crept at Keller's side as the sensory light switched off, casting them into darkness. Yet even as Brianna's eyes adjusted, she could hardly see, except to estimate shapes and fences.

No sign of the runner. An eerie sensation coalesced in her mind, and she found herself battling an instinctive sense of terror – were she to try to run back, she would only encounter the runner, who could be hiding … right behind her.

Heart thundering, she tried breathing through her mouth. As they skulked past trash cans, her own breath quaked like strong winds. Brianna had enough training and experience to know this was what adrenaline did, but that did not stop her unconsciously gripping her pistol holster.

As if responding to her thoughts, Keller turned around, whispering, "Are you okay?"

She nodded curtly.

He covered a hand over his mouth, signalling Brianna to ease her breathing. *I'm all alone, surrounded by nothing. I am falling, and Ben will not be there to– What's wrong with you?*

Brianna's eyes popped open. Recognising her huge mistake, with a shootout that may occur at any moment, she had to be on her toes. Yet something about the darkness, the evil, tore at her sanity. A beast lurking in the dark.

"*Stop! Hey!*" Keller's holler had Brianna issuing a gasping yelp. Her chest hurt from her overwhelmed heart. Bounding, Keller took off at a full sprint, Brianna blundering after him. They hurdled a metal fence onto a lawn, turning into a wooded area. There, Brianna thought she saw a wraith vanish behind a shed swathed by large tree bushes with bare pinyon branches.

Both Brianna and Keller whipped out their pistols, slowly approaching the shed, aiming, scanning. Brianna's boots kicked pinyon nuts hard as small stones. Blood pounding in her ears, Brianna thought she could not tolerate the tension any longer, as a body dropped out of the tree.

Brianna fired her gun, the sound cracking the air, causing more dogs to go off in the distance. She missed, hitting the grass. The body slammed on top of Keller. Two men, grunting and swearing, fought in a frantic brawl, fighting to get the upper hand. Sprawled on the lawn, Brianna, scrabbling on her feet, saw the hooded man on top of Keller.

"Get off me!" Keller hollered. The man kicked Keller, who tried to trip him with his own feet, but he bounded over Keller, and without pause, dashed away spryly.

Hissing in frustration, Brianna ran after the man as hard as she could, her face numb from the cold air.

"Hey! FBI!" Brianna shouted, but the man didn't stop. He flew over fences like a professional stuntman.

I'm losing him! Come on! Run!

She pushed and pushed until her thighs were sore. She sprinted and climbed fences, whipping around corners up until the point where she was breathing laboriously, desperately tired. Her lungs were on fire, and she struggled to breathe.

Brianna rushed through into her own dark backyard, legs making long strides, with no signs of the runner. Her window was open – odd – noted that, and dashed down the rest of the way towards the woods that opened up to the highway.

The runner had clearly gotten away. Brianna could glean no sign of him.

"Okay," she panted, hands on her knees. "Okay. Where are you?"

Trotting to the roadside, she noticed a car screech out from one of the conjoining streets, and instantly pulling out a small notepad, she got her pen, chasing after the car to see the number plate, white on black.

K1407.

Heaving out a deep breath, Brianna made her way back to the candlelight vigil to report back to the news reporters about the interesting character who had attacked police and fled.

And yet, as she passed her house, she took a moment to stare at Veronica's bedroom window, wondering if she had locked it, or if she'd forgotten altogether.

She scribbled down a note about it in case it came in handy.

—

In a dark red room, with a bed with white satin-style sheets and an oxblood bedspread and a statue on the wardrobe, Tara lay on a couch, her legs propped on the arm, tipping off her high heels.

She gazed out the window of The Pageant Queen, where a white van – old and yellowed – parked outside the brothel.

After landing back in Los Angeles from Baghdad, humiliated and fearful, she ditched Airgetlám – he took all the artefacts, called her a failure, and said that she was good for nothing, then he made his way to Pennsylvania to report back to Barbelo and Abraxas. Tara, in indignation and in shame, had fled down to Arizona – without a car, without any possessions but a few changes of clothes, a bag, a fake passport and a knife, trying desperately to scavenge food and hitchhiking her way. She had no home there; she only found herself going there naturally.

And that was when Tara stumbled upon The Pageant Queen brothel in Phoenix. She had no idea why she was staying here for this last month, but she had nothing and no other option. The best and only asset she had was her body. As it had always been when life went south, this was how she survived her early teenage years when she was enslaved, getting around with sex traffickers and prostitution for pornographers. Tara was the youngest girl here, and it made her proud. The people of The Pageant Queen were sympathetic to her. They didn't infantilise like the porn sex traffickers. Here, she could sell her body and gain adult respect, exhilaration and good money.

This brothel offered refuge for the unfortunate – those suffering the Bleakness – women of abject condition who were formally excluded from respectable life and any legal privileges that went with it. They sold their bodies for people with needs that were not being met in embodied relationships. The Pageant Queen also offered luxurious quarters like this one, and Tara capitalised on it. They gave her full autonomy to manipulate her clients.

Men.

She used them. She needed them.

That, Tara guessed, was why she decided to stay here. She found purpose in having control over men's bodies for a change.

She heard the sliding doors slam shut as a new client arrived, making his way to meet a prostitute. As the newcomer arrived downstairs, Tara examined the statue across the room. It was a white marble Greek statue of a woman with a bun, in a dress, cross armed, holding a knife in one hand, deep in irascible thought, gazing at a glass tank containing a pet Honduran Curly Hair. The Greek woman had vitriolic eyes – a look that she'd had been betrayed by a man she trusted. For some reason, the statue reminded Tara of her mom.

Her eyes fell to the dark-crimson liquid of her wine, the glass's neck lodging in her hand.

Then a man with an olive t-shirt and expensive blue jeans entered her room.

Tara licked her lips – tongue rolling across her lipstick, absorbing the wine juice. This man, the head of the Manicheans of Light, had a wealth of money and information. He'd come right for her for an "exchange".

"Tara," the man said with a sigh, locking the door.

"You look like a man with insider knowledge," Tara said apprehensively. She wasn't willing to give herself over; she knew this man was no ordinary person. If this man tried to attack her, it was against the bargain. Tara had her knife in her hand, and he would suffer a loss of manhood if he dared.

No longer shall I be abused.

"When I first saw you on the modelling advertisements, I thought you were a man with those intense eyes," he said with an oily voice.

"You don't seem to like that?" Tara whispered, flirting.

The man shrugged, taking out his wallet. He dropped a card, and Tara saw for a moment that it was a CIA ID. "I'm only attracted to women who are women," the man said, picking up his ID. "I'm glad I found you, Tara."

Yes, he has no idea where I came from. From the Cabal. "I'm flattered," Tara cooed.

Tara was dressed in dark Victoria's Secret lace lingerie in too-tight silk shorts, her breasts pulled up and pushed forward in a considerable cleavage that impressed her as much as it impressed the fashion people in the photoshoot. She even had the white blouse tied beneath them, exposing her naked belly and lower back. Her brown hair was piled high and knotted on top of her head, making it look short. But despite her horse prance, she was a cobra ready to strike if anything went amiss. *Have pride over your sexy body,* the fashion people told her. *You're young, lean and mean, girl.*

"So, what are you going to tell me?" Tara whispered with a languid hauteur. "What exchange do you offer me for sex?"

"Complicated cases going around about the DePaulas – the disaster of the Actionman's life. Everyone is talking about it across America and around the world. Rumours abound, and outright lies. But I have insider information nobody knows about yet. It is all linked to James Casbolt, as a matter of fact."

Ahhh. Men who were honest, wise and with valuable knowledge were the only men she respected.

She twitched vigorously but kept her chin up.

"Tara. An Aes Sidhe lady …" the man purred, gazing into her light eyes, and moved to kiss her on the lips.

Tara mounted the man – this stranger's nails clawed her back, tugging at his olive shirt, lips pressing against lips. She slithered into his embrace, closing her eyes. It was gradual; they undressed one another slowly. All bodily contact was part of guaranteeing the most arousing experience. Erotic playacting was good for business. It brought clients to return again and again for more.

"Goddess," the man sighed, taking a deep breath, inches from her face after the kiss, smelling of aftershave.

She looked into his hazel eyes; she could feel his horniness. "Oh yes. I'll do anything for you." Tara hated worthless sex, but she took risks because they would grant her opportunities to get by in this bleak life.

It was what the Cabal taught her by principle. Too many times had she let men penetrate her, but she would *penetrate* them first. She was strong, not weak. She was a success, not a failure. She could use this man – his elite knowledge – for herself.

"What is your name, honey?"

"Ian."

"Last name?"

"Mastemah." The man hesitated in his reply. He placed two hundred bucks on the table at the feet of the Greek statue. Her money.

"Now, come, honey," Tara accepted, giving Ian an oeillade trick with the eyes she knew lustfully enticed. Good models for clothing, beauty and fashion advertisements knew this trick of the eyes, the tilt of the head, the pose of the body. As they posed, they were trained to imagine having a sexual encounter with a sexy man. And it worked. It helped seduce customers.

Ian's hand rubbed her thigh pressed against his own. "What is it that you would like to show me about Ben DePaula and James Casbolt?" she said languidly.

Ian levitated his head from looking in between her breasts. "The Actionman still lives. I know where he could be now. He has an old house on West Jomax Road. He's been going there every night, ever since Thomas Jones – the James Casbolt doppelgänger – went missing." He smiled pointedly. "I've been watching him."

Tara cocked her head and twitched, saying, "Thomas Jones is a doppelgänger?"

"Yeah," Ian said. "That is still a mystery."

"Does James Casbolt, the Chief of the Aes Sidhe, know about Thomas Jones?" That was the information Tara wanted to know. A doppelgänger? What could that entail, then, for Casbolt and the Aes Sidhe of the Alliance in Antarctica?

"I'm not sure, Tara. But it will only be a matter of time until he finds out."

"And when he does?"

"Then the Chief will be vulnerable. He will become distracted, and Max Spiers will have to ostracise him for good and elect Vercingetorix as the next Chief Agaid."

All Tara knew about James Casbolt was that he was a bloodthirsty, vile man who abused women and children to get his way. Tara *hated* him – James Casbolt was a liar. He had been the one who had destroyed the society of the Carnutes Aes Sidhe in Antarctica. He had cut off Airgetlám's arm, slaying his family. Tara felt sorry for the honourable Maximilian Spiers, who did all he could to put sanctions on the Cabal human trafficking network while living with a dangerous blood brother such as Casbolt.

"From what we can deduce," Ian continued, "Ben's been torturing Thomas Jones to the edge of his life to find out the information on the CD known as Metatron's Golem. Metatron's Golem is a place I work for. They make robots and build machines for tech companies, engineers, the Goibniuium for Aes Sidhe, you name it. And of course, Metatron is a child of Inshushinak's Golem industry. That's based in the Underworld. The CD actually tells you some of the locations of Gateways into the Underworld. Danavas who live in the Underworld love human trafficking, and Danavas who work for Inshushinak use child slaves and machines to create Golems. Don't ask me what Golems are. That is a secret I do not know. But my point is, everything is connected. Robots, Patala, child sex trafficking. There is always another secret. Always another plan. My bet is that Veronica and Zoe have been sent to the Danavas of Duzakh for trade and are likely to become slaves mining and smelting voidstone for Inshushinak." Ian chuckled, his grin despicably smug. "I can bet a million bucks on all this and win."

"Really, honey?" Tara marvelled. Inshushinak? Danavas? Robots and child sex trafficking in the Underworld? *What the hell am I hearing?*

"Yes ... Ben is the threat to us," Ian said. "His antisemitic father is dead, his daughter is taken. You see, when pushed to the limits, people do very disturbing things. You know this very well from when you were deceived by Ghislaine and taken on the boat."

Tara twitched, her skin creeping.

Death ... *No! Don't fall away! Focus!*

"You hate the sexist men who abused you," Ian went on, unaware that he'd triggered her. "Ben is the most misogynistic of them all. Worse than a man from ancient Athens, tainted by the patriarchy. It's due to his conservative Catholic father and his Catholic upbringing that Ben has become what he has become. Ben's full of testosterone, Tara. Don't be deceived by his looks."

Tara gripped the sheets, her distress seething. She took calming breaths. "I can make *any man* bend to my wishes, Ian. Even if they are worse than an Athenian. But Ben ..." She could totally understand why forlorn girls and women were led into pornography nowadays because of Ben DePaula's Bonds underwear photoshoots. They were *extremely* sexy, and she could understand how addictive and comfortable that desire could be, because she had been addicted to them ... Once. "Ben makes me sick."

"Pretty, isn't he?" Ian chuckled wildly.

Tara smirked – a mangled, distorted smirk to cover up her shame. *I want to die inside! Stop! Stop talking on about male pornography, Ian!* "Is he an Aes Sidhe too?"

"No, no, Tara. Ben is a pleb. But his father knew all about your kind. Ben also had James Casbolt enlist in the Marines, which means Ben knows about the secret societies. Ben's a hard man to kill. He's got skill and experience from the movies."

Tara was not convinced. "I've killed men before. Strong men. They cannot escape the spider once they are caught in its web, you know what I am saying?"

"I understand," Ian said, his hand slowly creeping up Tara's body, stroking her breasts. His other hand gently cupped her temple and hair. He smiled warmly. "That's all. You're off the hook." He pressed his lips against hers, and Tara held her breath, grasping his body passionately.

After Ian and Tara had their fill of love, they lay together undressed under the bed covers, flushed and sweaty.

"I have something else to tell you about," Ian said.

"Go ahead, honey. Take your time."

Ian leaned over to the table, grabbing a roll of newspaper left by housekeeping every morning. "Here's something you do not know." He unrolled the front page, showing her the image.

Tara blinked, not gasping, but staring indifferently.

On the front cover of the *Arizona Republic* under the headlines – SEARCH FOR VERONICA DEPAULA CONTINUES – was an artist's drawing of Airgetlám! A divine, handsome man with a youthful face, a moustache and godlike eyes – perfect turquoise eyes – a pure blue-blood Aes Sidhe Indigo Child. Unmistakably Airgetlám.

"This man's real name is Gladius Huyard," Ian explained. "You didn't know that? Well, he was raised Swartzentruber Amish in Pennsylvania and is an Aes Sidhe. He's part of an ultra-conservative Mennonite mafia called Thelema that seeks power by whatever means to generate prestige and secrecy. They operate in the shadows of the isolated Amish community. The Aeons rule the Thelema cult, and you, bound to it, are obligated to serve Thelema."

"How …? How do you know about the Aeons? How do you know so much about me?"

Ian's oily voice and hawkish face were unsettling. "People talk. The Aeons are heads of an intricate network of cults and child trafficking rings worldwide, hiding in plain sight. The Carnutes is only one branch. The Thelema are another in Amish country."

Amish … Thelema … Aeons … How did the leader of the Manicheans of Light know so much insider information? It was *inhuman* of him to be an expert on the Cabal's human trafficking networks.

Only then did Tara tremble – her neck and shoulders hunching in twitching fits. Her mind went blank. Suddenly, all the sex that brought her so much pleasure faded away – and she felt *awful*.

"Why? Why have you done this?" Tara whispered, her mouth feeling full, tears brimming her eyes, her fingers creasing the newspaper. "*Why?*"

Ian looked shocked, and defensively he said, "I've done nothing but what you have wanted, goddess. Only what you have asked."

Ogling, Tara skimmed the article. Airgetlám – Gladius Huyard – was framed for stealing Ben DePaula's daughter.

"Get out," Tara intoned.

"Oh, perhaps—"

"I need time to myself, Ian. Thank you for your exchange. You may leave now. Leave! Please!"

"All right." The man obeyed her, standing up. He looked disappointed as he paid her another two hundred dollars. "I shall make sure that your needs are adequately taken care of. Be at ease, my goddess. I'll leave now. I'm paying you more, because I have a better job for you."

"You're hustling me," Tara said gingerly, staring at the paper dollars as she took them.

Ian winked. "I'm a hustler. You will now have a real job. Meet me at West Jomax Road tomorrow night at Ben's mother's house. Good night, until then." Ian gave her a plump smile, chuckling. He got himself dressed again, grabbed his belongings, then left The Pageant Queen.

Tara sat under the covers, reading the antic article entry carefully as soon as the door shut. She bounded out of the bed, zipped on her shirt and shorts – why did she have to go so tight? She paced, tossing the newspaper across the room.

"Grrr! Airgetlám, what are you doing? What have you—"

Buzzing pain racked her. The mark on her forehead – her skull felt as if it had been bashed by a hammer.

All she remembered was her jaw gaping wide, falling onto her knees and her eyes skewering shut.

She gasped. Her bones felt like jelly, her hands grasping her skull so hard that she left marks on her skin. She convulsed violently, struggling for breath.

"Ohhhh!" she whined through gritted teeth. "OHHHH!"

Hyperventilating, flapping her arms, twitching violently, she hit the floor, the buzzing demonic power pushing through her, molesting her.

Everything rang with tension. Violent strikes attacked her. Strikes that destroyed her ability to love, to feel wholeness.

The boat. A container ship. Thrown into the van. *Shut up or you will get a beating!* Plump man, curly hair, grotesque breath. Fish smell, nets, crates. The dark shadow men hauling her out of the van with the screaming children. *Where are you taking us? Take us home! Please!* She panicked and thrashed. There was an aching pressure between her legs, between her thighs. She squirmed and screamed, screaming until she coughed. A fist smashed her face, silencing her. Blood blinding, she reeled. But she fought on, as the men held her down, their strength too great … Trembling breaths … A searing pain, a tear of flesh. Hard thrusts, and it was over.

Her body ran warm and then cold, as the person over her shuddered, panting. She spasmed, her soul shattering with shame and damnation.

God is the tyrant. The Shaitan is the saviour.

She keened, retching. She wanted mommy, but the men were not done.

They turned her over, face on the ground, grabbing her hips, wrapping her hair in their fists, pulling, arching her back. She was a quivering thing of fear and pain. A hard stream of hot liquid showered upon her, pressure paralysed her, brief bursts of light, and she was dragged, whimpering wordlessly, deeper into the ship.

I'm sorry. There is nothing we can do.

Tara stood outside on the porch of the mental health counselling centre across the St Catherine open campus. They told her that she couldn't be fixed, couldn't be counselled. Her brain broke. It was snowing outside. The sunless sky faded to a lacklustre, cadaverous, grey-black. Her bones were numbed, weak. It had just been confirmed: Tara didn't exist, she was invisible.

Tara's soul felt like shards of glass splintering. All this wasted time getting help always ended badly. So why try? She sunk below the tsunami of pain that she'd endured all her life. She reached the bottom, where there were no more waves, still and silent. Nothing could be lower than this. She was a walking ball of nothing.

Pain, anger and revenge destroyed the world, cracking it with calamity and terror. Shooting up a school … Tara already had a detailed plan to kill everyone in the St Catherine food court. She'd stolen a gun. Cause as much damage as possible to the world.

She didn't.

The utility knife sliced her forearm, the pink lacerated flesh tearing, peeling, oozing a bright bloody path. The hand holding her knife trembled slightly, but as she cut, Tara kept her muscles slack; if she tensed, the wound would hurt all the more. She made herself apathetic, knowing such a catharsis would satisfy her.

The knife was cold as ice. She slowly cut another gash. Frantic streams of blood ran across her wrists and down her fingers, splashing in a thick pool by her feet.

She'd offered herself up, *everything she had*, not just to calm herself down from the anguish of making promises to shoot the school and not committing to them. No, she had to shed her blood, because bloodletting satisfied her volcanic resentment. She'd stirred up her vengeance towards the Cabal for months; she had no choice but to release it somewhere. It was, ultimately, her self-sacrifice. An atonement to the demon of the emotional storm.

She made another cut. She offered up a wordless cry to the darkness above the broken shack roof. Her left arm twitched, and the knife swerved as a result, leaving her with a long, jagged laceration twice as deep as the others. Her breath stopped. She dropped the knife and writhed in agony. Her entire left arm felt numb, the throbbing becoming unbearable.

Why ... *Why* did Barbelo have to torture her with the past? Why did Tara have to align herself with evil men? She'd be better off dead. Tara never feared death.

"Please," Tara grovelled, words incoherent. No one heard her sobs. She wanted the guilt and shame to stop *so bad*. She trembled so violently, her eyes, her body twitched so much that she could hardly breathe.

She must have blacked out, for when she blinked, Tara found herself hanging by her aching arm on the couch limply. Everything was still. The throbbing agony subsided, but it left her with a terrible migraine, cheeks wet with tears.

Tara then lay drenched in cold sweat. Her breathing was unstable, feverish.

She had been smitten. Something spiritual had assaulted her that made her retch. An astral projection or a hex? Dark magic from the Aeons cursing her for failing in her Baghdad mission? No human being could ever endure such death again and live. Tara felt the embarrassment of the *insufferable* amounts of self-loathing she endured after every episode of remembering. Because if she had to be the only one in this world to endure such impossible dread, why live?

"Why?" she whimpered. She could find no way forward. "*Why?*"

Tara then thought of a way she could end this. The balcony was high enough outside … A kitchen knife would do well … The bath … It would only be a matter of time …

No. NO. She *had* to find this Thomas Jones. She lay there for a long time, blinking, waiting for the mental and physical exhaustion to subside; she *refused* to let it return. She had two options: go and sedate herself and escape her inevitable bondage to the Aeons, or join the hunt for Ben DePaula.

But suicide from the Bleakness still lingered in her mind as a third option to fall onto in case everything failed.

"One more chance …" she whispered. "One more chance, Tara. Come on, Marcell. You're a good boy."

Tara slowly got up, rubbing her forehead. She gritted her teeth, and saw …

The Honduran Curly Hair on the glass tank wall, all eight legs splayed outwards. Tara jumped, flinching, facing an eight-spoked star of hairy darkness. Her skin crawled.

"Yeah," she smiled sinisterly. "Go to hell, Barbelo!" she spat at the spider. "I am a master of my own fate!"

West Jomax Road, Union Peak … After she rested herself and finished ablutions, she would go down the dark, dingy, inconspicuous streets of ill repute to the closest bus stop to take her to the other side of the city of Phoenix.

47

BREATH OF DAWN. DUSK OF DESPAIR

"He had no form or majesty that we should see him,
and no beauty that we should desire him.
He was despised and forsaken by men,
a man of pain, and acquainted with sickness,
and like one who others are hiding of face from him.
He was despised, and we did not hold him in high regard.
However, he was the one who borne our griefs,
and he carried our pain,
yet we ourselves assumed him stricken,
struck down by God and afflicted."
—From the Scroll of Isaiah, the prophet's disciples, c. 740 – c. 540 BCE. The Suffering Servant Poem.

Facing east at dawn, Albert sent his prayer of gratitude like sweet smoke to Nihitaa'.

He raised up in both hands a sack of corn pollen as an offering. He wore his elaborate turquoise and shell necklace for the third day of the Holyway ceremony. He gave thanks to Nihitaa' for the sunlight's warmth and light. He gave thanks for Mother Earth, holding up his feet. He gave thanks for water – the rain, snow, hail and dew. He gave thanks for the oxygen that gave spirit and life to all creatures.

He gave thanks for Nihitaa's healed and performed wonders.

The first beams of sunlight blessings stretched forth into the entrance of the hooghan. It was deep dawn when Albert heard a faint noise from within.

Pushing aside the curtain into the sanctuary, he stood still in the entrance to listen. Within the flickering dimness, the talking of the rosin crackling, occasional faint creaks and chirps from insects afar could be heard.

Albert untied the knots of woollen cords pressed around Ben's body, cords tied for restoration. Once the sun was up, the bathing ritual for Ben came, washing and cleansing from impurity.

—

Violet light seeped through Ben's closed eyelids, and he awoke inside a clay hut domed with wooden beams, clothed in a simple grey-and-black robe, and surrounded by the merriment on the faces of the Navajo dressed in buckskin clothing.

He blinked many times. There was light from overhead, streaming in from the boarded ceiling in barred motes, layers of incense infused with a sweet aroma, coalescing the light upwards and through the small cross-piece smoke-hole. The amount of smoke in the room was so overwhelming that he wanted to rush outside to breathe. However, the smiles on the Native Americans did not seem to indicate they were at all bothered by the thick incense air of the hut.

But lodged in the back of Ben's mind was his daughter – hunting him. Controlling him.

How long had he been here?

Suddenly, Ben rose out of his mat bed. "How long have I been here?"

The medicine man who cracked the CD code, wearing a red bandana and an aqua-and-white striped cardigan, placed a friendly hand on his shoulder, easing him down. His face cracked into a wrinkled smile. Joseph's gleeful smile. An expression that would have made the Navajo Chief handsome in his younger years.

"Three days, Ben," the resilient old medicine man said. Ben blinked and knew he recognised the man, but his name escaped him altogether. "Now, you must be cautious to conclude the ceremony properly. When you leave, you must not do any work, change those clothes, nor bathe for four days."

Ben widened his eyes and nodded, but inside, he was screaming. Castigating himself for not being good enough. A father was a failure if his daughter ended up like Veronica. If she died, Ben would die.

"Well, that's the end of my social life." Ben grinned with a tinge of his humour – he naturally acted, lying, putting on a mask, surprising himself that he could even pretend to smile. He was before an audience and a wise man – he couldn't help acting. He made the Native Americans happy, and they thought he was glad and thankful. *Let's keep it that way! What more torture do I need? More people to think that I am mad?*

"Oh! I almost forgot," the medicine man said. "My grandson, Declan, has a gift for you."

From the group of boys, a youth in his mid-twenties got up, carrying a small cardboard box, handing it to Ben. Looking upon the gift and taking it, Ben felt the warmth in his hands. Curious, he opened the lid, and the *sweet* steam of a wonderful aroma of sweet potatoes enveloped his nostrils. He closed his eyes, relaxing his shoulders, overwhelmed with thankfulness.

Oh, sweet, *sweet* potatoes. His mouth began to water, for all he could think about was the food. He was so tempted to devour it right away, so he grabbed an orange wedge to put in his mouth and almost forgot politeness.

"How ... did you know?" Ben managed.

"You asked for them during your worst fevers," the medicine man said, smiling benevolently. "Declan's mother made them for you. Grown from her garden and freshly made."

"Thank you ... Thank you so much," Ben said, bowing his head in a reverent gesture of admiration. He gestured for permission, and with a nod of approval, Ben indulged.

His screaming stomach made him sigh; his mouth loosened from tension as he munched. Soon he ate two chips at once. Then three. For a second, all the watching Navajo seemed to disappear out the door. He had experienced the astonishing hospitality of these people, which he had never seen anyone provide before in his life. They had saved him and blessed him along the way. As Ben ate the tastiest sweet potato chips in the world, he pondered these things.

How lucky was he to be in the graces of these simple people? He had to give back to them somehow, but Ben did not know how. If anything, how could he even pay back their incredible kindness, when Ben showed none of it to anyone and when most of the world was venal? They were from another world, another culture. They had offered something beyond measure – a remarkable precious gift of grace. They treated him as kin; they treated *everyone* with respect and unconditional love. How could oppressed humans do that? All the men, the women and the children – they looked untainted, purified, and washed clean in morality and spirit. They almost seemed to glow, the gleam on their olive skin dwelling in the smoke – they appeared angelic.

Godlike. And for that reason, Ben felt a melancholy grip him. He could *never* attain that perfection. He had to be a perfect model, but he simply *couldn't*.

If I lose family, I can come back to these people, Ben thought. *Remake my identity and purpose to sedate the pain of guilt.* Magic or miracle, they healed his hip, but they had not healed his crisis.

Ben's eyes widened as he felt his hip – as if it had never been broken and bruised at all. The horrific bolting pain and fatigue that almost killed him, aches and sores ebbed to dim memories and vanished. Consequently, the medicine man followed his hands as he felt his side.

"For Nihitaa' makes sore and binds up. He wounds, and his hands make whole. Your hip was able to be massaged with essential oils each night, fasted and prayed over while binding it with the cords of restoration. It is not completely healed, but the pain had been taken away so you can walk on it. Just promise me that you do not fall on it again. Okay?"

Ben could not fathom the infinite kindness of these saints. "You … healed *me*?" Ben wanted to laugh. Freedom. Progression. Ben got up and walked outside the hut.

"You know, Benjamin," the old man sighed, following him. He placed a leathery hand on his shoulder. "The truth is something you don't want to believe. It will only convict you and will never submit to your prideful self-assumption. Be careful, for what you want to believe might deceive you from the truth that is in plain sight."

Was that a warning, preparing him for something? For did that mean the truth was something he didn't want to believe? Ben *would* believe it if he saw it, and that had to mean one thing clearly: the truth was in Thomas Casbolt – in his mother's bathroom trapped and crumpled up in a shower.

In the hot dusty day, a modest number of Navajo were having morning tea on picnic blankets, families and friends all getting together under pine trees in the red sand. Ben was surprised that he was shocked. Yes, Ben the Actionman knew many people were aware of his fame, but this had nothing to do with his honour. The Navajo women were yodelling, and men were praising their God with elation.

Ben pulled his lips in a taut line as people surrounded him, giving him greetings. He did not utter a word, but smiled dishonestly. No one noticed his daughter, who haunted his mind. It was not a time for celebration. Dread was at hand.

Never before had Ben felt so inwardly drawn, felt so lonely among a crowd of people. The monkey on his back could not stop hollering in his mind. He had to escape this place, to go back, back to his mother's house and find Veronica, quickly, before the monkey became Bigfoot about to break him. Brianna was right. The CD was *irrelevant*.

Sooner than he could even comprehend, in a blur, Ben sat back in his truck departing the Navajo reservation, down back south to Phoenix.

Ben's mind burned, scorching him like the early summer air with broken shards of disjointed desire. The medicine man's steadiness of mind condemned Ben. He needed to get back to his mother's house fast, escape his guilt, to torture James Casbolt.

All that I learnt, Ben thought, *was that no one, except for the Native Americans, can be trusted.*

—

Arriving at his mother's dilapidated house to check on Thomas Jones, Ben barged inside, feeling regenerated and powerful.

"I'm back, you bastard! Wakey, wakey!" He knocked on the door of the wooden shower. "I told yah I'd come back!"

Ben opened the wooden door, and Casbolt roared out a gasp as Ben hauled him out of the shower and tossed him into the wall. Groaning, mouth open in excruciating pain, the only sounds escaping his mouth were weak gasps. "Oh yeah, baby! My strength is back! I've got my hip healed, and now I can walk again, only I have a stupid limp. Doesn't matter, though."

Casbolt roved his bloody swollen face at Ben, who squatted before him. "What do you want?" Casbolt rasped. "I'm hungry."

"You know," Ben said. "You know where Veronica is. You heard them cry when you left them. So where did you leave them?"

Casbolt stared at Ben blankly. Those blue bloodshot eyes drained away all of Ben's previously enraptured state of mind.

"Screw this crap!" Ben shot to his feet, turning around, hands on his hips. Burning in his mind, insufferable grief and anguish threatened his new order. Boiling up inside of him, all his kindness burned away.

Turning back around, Ben threw an axe kick into Casbolt's face. The man hit the floor, body heaving and struggling to breathe.

"Bastard! You seriously – *seriously* … We're not playing this game again! Are we?"

Ben front-kicked Casbolt. The wretch gargled.

"Why aren't you speaking to me? How long do we have to do this? How – long?" He kicked again. "Come on!" He kicked again. "Tell me!"

It wasn't long before Ben got bored. His order had become disorder – and so fast! – the healing by the medicine man became nothing. He'd made no progress. He'd run winged-footed to the Grand Canyon to crack the code of the CD for … nothing.

"I hate myself," Ben muttered, trembling. "Hahaha. Brianna was right. I am a moral pit. This is what you have done to me, Casbolt. You have done this to me!"

He grabbed Thomas by the neck and threw him back into the shower, locking the wooden wall. As his hand reached the tap, he froze.

With an intake of breath, Ben closed his eyes. *Was this worth it?* Brianna had said to him. *Is this going to bring your dad or Veronica back? Ben, Thomas is innocent.*

It was beyond question: no doubt it had to be worth it. There was no other way – Casbolt said the girls cried when he left them. His van was in front of the house when Veronica vanished without a trace. Casbolt *knew* Ben; the man had an antagonistic bias towards Ben when he first met him at San Juan, Puerto Rico, at Julian's place and at the airport. He *knew* about Joseph and the dangerous conspiracy theories. Casbolt was a super soldier – a toy of the Light Alliance and the elite secret societies. Casbolt was a paedophile. Casbolt was a centre of bad ideas. Casbolt was …

Ben gazed at his boots – blotched with crimson smears.

Was James Casbolt guilty?

Veronica's screams pierced his soul when Ian dragged her out from underneath the bed. A hammering blow that rendered him into shards.

Ben turned the tap to ice cold. The inhuman bleating and mewling that disgorged out of the shower fluttered Ben's eyes open.

So, I let this run until he can no longer stand it. Until I can get out of this prison once more to gain some momentum. Enclosed inside his own mother's bathroom, all four hostile walls suffocated Ben.

The screams trapped Ben, enclosing him in a sort of metaphysical inactivity that made his eyes pop from his skull. His chest being eviscerated. *Enough! He's in too much pain! Stop it!*

No, *no,* Ben *mustn't* feel sorry for this evil beast – it refused to tell the truth. Gazing at the photo of Veronica and Zoe playing in the go-cart, nostalgia – intoxicating and powerful – filled his veins, filling his soul. Nostalgia and love – they reacted together violently.

Retribution had to come one way or another.

And the cycle – nauseating and hateful – Ben endured again. From pure nostalgia transforming into passion and anger and then, when the anger was exhausted, it deflated to depression, then into sympathy for Thomas, and then to self-pity for himself, until he thought what his daughter might be thinking of him now. And so, the nostalgia rushed back again like a firestorm, and Ben could not stop it.

The screams! He was trapped. Imprisoned in the regressive cycle of … death.

His hand, quivering from the effort to lock it tight, turned the tap off as he gave a deep groan. Casbolt whined and sobbed in the wooden shower.

But what other way could there be? The answers – the truth – were right in Ben's grasp – but it kept on slipping out of his hands like water between his fingers.

Is what happened to Veronica God's judgement for what I did to my own dad? Ben thought. *I will never be virtuous like the Navajo. I'm a wretch.*

Oh, his daughter – little Ronnie – was hoping, *hoping* for him to come and save her. Waiting for her hero.

"I'm not Casbolt," came a trembling small voice. A mere whisper, barely audible.

Ben opened his eyes, brimmed with tears.

"I'm not Casbolt."

Enmeshed by optimism, Ben slid down, crawling, pressing his ear to the peephole, heart thundering madly. "Wh–what? What are you saying?"

"I'm … not James Casbolt."

A single tear dripped down Ben's chin. "What? You're not Casbolt?"

"I'm not Casbolt." His voice was husky, riddled with anguish. "I'm not …"

Ben jerked his head from a spike to irritation. Come on! *Something* to pay off all this time clogged up in a bathroom night and day! Nine days! Veronica would be wondering … where he was. She'd give up if Ben wasted another day. "I don't understand. Just talk to me."

Shuddering weak breaths. "Daddy, I waited … I waited for Daddy."

"Come on, no. No more riddles, just freakin' talk."

"I just wanted … to play. Why? I just want …" Icy, oblique hisses.

"I'll let you go home if you tell me where they are."

"He never came. He never came."

Ben's ears starved for a coherent answer. He felt he had to be getting somewhere. "Don't make me do this to you."

"And he never came to save me. Daddy never came."

"What were you doing?" Ben waited for a reply. They were coming so fast, but they stopped suddenly. No. The boy was breathing hard. No! Frothing to gain this new information, pressing his forehead against the wood, Ben grimaced, his body cramping. *No, this has to be it! This has to be Thomas recounting what he heard Veronica saying.* "Answer me! Please!"

His chance … like water slipping past his fingers.

"Why are you making me do this?" Ben whimpered, feeling a lump form in his throat. He couldn't breathe. More tears ran down his face, but he felt too shallow inside to sob aloud.

Slowly, he closed his eyes, hand seeking for the tap blindly. He would strike again to get more answers when he was so … close.

Veronica was wondering why he wasn't there …

His hand slipped from the tap, and Ben fell to his knees, hands to his head. He bowed, completely willing for anything, for *anything* to help him now. His brain buzzed, hissing with flames of fire. Burning and raging for eternity.

He thought of his Christian father then – of Joseph – the things he'd spoken about God, the scapegoating mechanism, divine wrath, reminded Ben of what he had learnt about God in grade school. They *all burned him.*

"Oh God," Ben sniffed, weakly shutting his eyes. The Native American songs were in his head – the songs of pure freedom. Ben wondered jealously, how could anyone be so glad and free?

Ben exhaled. The tightness around his chest felt like the constriction of a giant boa slithering around his body. "God … Where are you? Why are you doing this to me? Why?" Ben could not come to raise his head. He felt guilty, unworthy to be praying. He'd tortured a man.

Scalding emotion boiled in Ben's throat like acid, causing him to thrash his head from side to side. He held his breath, but the boa only constricted him tighter, causing more tears to drip profusely, wetting the tiles and his cheeks.

"Why … God, are you silent? Why are you silent, when I … when I'm in anguish? Please, I'm relying on your infinite mercies. Pardon me for my sins. I've lost … Forgive me, because I'm lost."

Ben lay there in a ball, enduring the worst hell – everything in the world became centred on Ben and his pain. The self-inflicted torture of unsatisfaction. It convinced him that he wanted this pain above all else; he wanted the hell of never finding his daughter ever again.

Because he was ready to accept this as his new normal.

He had to gather himself up. He had to start gathering …

Gather them.

"I'm sorry, Thomas," Ben whimpered. "I don't know what to do. I don't know what to do anymore. You know what I've done is completely messed up, and I know you know where they are. For the sake of both of us – *please* tell me *something*. I'm not going to torture you anymore. We're done." Ben leaned back against the wooden door, heaving out a sigh.

Gather them. The First Fruits. Prepare for the Nephilim.

"They're … in the maze." Ben heard Thomas' still-small voice coherently. "They're in Patala. That's where you will find them."

"What?" Ben could not believe he'd come to an answer. "What did you say?" He excitedly pressed his eye against the peek hole.

"In the maze."

"W–what maze? Where is it?"

"Patala."

"Where do I find Patala?" No answer. "Thomas, listen to me, please. I'm going to get you out of here, but please be specific – what is this maze? Tell me what it is. Just tell me, man. Where is the maze? Come on, tell me."

"Patala."

"What?"

"Patala."

"What *is* Patala? The maze?" Silence. Insufferable silence. Ben trembled. "Come on, don't mess with me! Don't mess with me, man!" He smacked the wooden door, thumping it with each futile exclamation. "Goddamn it! Tell me where they are! Tell me! Tell me! Tell me! Tell me!" And finally, his heart exploded like a flash flood.

Ben leapt out of the bathroom with a soul-shredding yell, throwing the yellow construction lamp to the floor, shattering the pieces of wood on the workshop table, tossing tools across the room. His anger gave way to pain and a fresh wave of sorrow mixing with confusion.

Tears began to well up in his eyes as Ben laughed with madness. "Awww. You're going *to really* get it, man! You're going *to really* get it! Where is Patala?"

—

Undercover, Keller chewed on mint gum as he sat in his car, air con blasting on high, in the heat of the day, under the angry sun. He sat by the road, watching Ben DePaula blithely walking with a peculiar limp towards the wine and spirits' store.

He'd knew Ben had only gone to decode the CD, but what had all the fuss been about Ben dying in the Grand Canyon? He was right here; the only problem was, why didn't he have his crutches anymore?

Bizarre. This is not right, Keller thought, stroking his chin.

A truck driver beeped at a lousy driver, and Keller watched as Ben rubbernecked, and vitriolic eyes found Keller staring through the windscreen.

Cursing, as the moron skidded away around the corner, Keller watched Ben, eyes like a hawk, glancing at him. Then he slipped inside the store.

"Come, DePaula," Keller muttered, shifting in his seat. It took a few minutes for Ben to return with a bottle of whisky in his hand, walking towards Keller's car.

Keller cursed under his breath. This body builder of a man without his crutches could be dangerous, and if he'd been drinking all this time … Keller shook his head, gawking as Ben strode right up to his car, scowling, ripping the cork off the bottle, and swung back his head, pressing the bottle to his lips. He reached Keller's side after his long shameless scull. Keller rolled down his window, not meeting Ben's forceful eyes, the man's raw breath reeking of alcohol and bile.

"Why are you following me?" Ben retorted croakily.

And Keller replied tartly, "Get in the car," while chewing on his mint gum.

Ben complied, but Keller laid eyes on him then, following him as he rounded the car to the passenger seat. The man also reeked of violence, as well as sweat.

"Why are you following me?" Ben said again.

"Your hip is healed," Keller said. "Good. I've just come to check up on you, to see how you're going."

Ben nodded.

"What are you doing at a liquor store?"

Ben stared at him, bewildered. "I'm thirsty. You're a detective, so figure it out." Ben took a short swig, leaning his head on the seat, smacking his lips.

Keller did not have to be a detective to glean that Ben was self-sedating himself with alcohol because of the high stress of his daughter being missing and the criminal was not yet in custody.

"Why were you not at the candlelight vigil, Ben?"

Ben sighed. "Well, I'm too bogged down, you know."

"You went on a trip to the Grand Canyon, didn't you?"

"Yeah. To help clear my mind. It's a sacred place for the Navajo. A lot of them know me. Wonderful people."

"You went there to crack the code of the CD," Keller said sternly. He was not going to play games with this man. "Did you find anything useful while you were at it?"

Ben scowled, shaking his head. "Nah."

"Was that what you were doing in your truck Saturday night?"

Ben turned and stared at Keller, studying him. His eyes were intense underneath a knuckled brow. "Where's Brianna?"

"She's hunting down Gladius Huyard. The suspect that attacked me two nights ago at the candlelight vigil. So what were you doing when Thomas Jones went missing?"

"What? Am I a suspect?" Ben said with a hint of fierceness.

"No. I am just asking because when the FBI investigated Thomas' house, they found it empty."

Ben stared at Keller. "I heard about that. What happened? I thought you had him under surveillance."

"We did."

"If he's guilty, I don't think it is something he'd get away with, right?" Ben turned the other cheek, sniffing in derision.

But what Keller really knew was that Ben denied his capability to solve this case – he was like a libertarian – they did not care for law enforcement and the police, they all thought they knew better. Keller believed that his willpower and strength to bring justice helped others without hope to see that authority, professionals and expertise mattered. Keller was somebody who *did* care to protect lives, save lives. That Keller never failed in a single case proved this, and Ben needed to see that, or else there would be serious consequences. *I would hate to arrest you, Ben, if you keep on baulking from Brianna and me, but I could if you don't stop acting like a pain!* Keller had no time for uneducated unprofessionals getting in the way of his investigations.

"Ben."

Ben didn't reply.

"*Ben.*"

"What?"

"You need to take care of yourself *and* your wife," Keller pressed. "That is the *best* thing you can do right now. You got to listen to me. Chasing down this CD, going on vacation to the Grand Canyon, didn't do you any good." Keller paused, the strain in his voice, he imagined, acted as a hand to grasp this stubborn moron out of his pit, but Ben kept on slipping, refusing to commit to pulling himself up. *Bastard. The government justice system is meant to help you, not oppress you! Just – comply and obey!* Keller tried one last tactic and said with gravity in his voice, "That little girl is going to need you right now." Ben winced. "She is going to *need* you when she comes back home."

Ben's entire body clenched, drawing his lips to a thin line. His eyes were ringed with shadows, filmed with uncertainty and distress. Such a contrast to the movie posters and the glamour of Hollywood. Keller witnessed the true DePaula – a deprived, broken man with no love. Though Keller did not know what it was like to have a daughter – he did not know what it was like to love a woman – let alone have a child taken from him, but he *tried* to imagine it, like having a part of one's self ripped from you. He *tried* to imagine. God, he *tried* to!

"She's been gone for a week," Ben said, his voice quavering with passion. "Kids gone for more than that are less likely to come home or to survive. And after a month, most are not alive. All right, so please, forgive me for trying to be a father, doing *everything* I can! Every day, she's in some dark place, wondering why I'm not there to rescue her!"

Keller twitched, sympathetic to Ben's outburst.

"You *understand* that?" Ben exclaimed.

"Yeah," Keller whispered, shaking his head. *This man needs to calm down, or screw any civilised talk!*

"No, you don't understand!" Ben beat his chest, foam gathering at the corners of his mouth. "Me! Only I understand! Me! Not you! She wants *me* to save her! Just me! *All the time!* So, *forgive me* for not going home to have a good night's sleep! To pretend as if nothing has ever happened!" Ben paused, sucking his lower lip. "So why don't you freakin' get off your ass and fight to look for my freakin' daughter? Why aren't you freakin' – Argh!" Ben lost it and began to beat the dashboard with his leg and hand, shaking the car.

"Hey," Keller said. "Hey. Hey. Calm down."

"Don't follow me," Ben roared, pointing. "Don't you *ever* follow me! Or I swear to God, I'll ..."

Keller raised a hand. "Mr DePaula! Hey! Easy!" Back of his head facing Keller, Ben opened the door, and Keller said, "Ben, I don't think I'd let you go behind the wheel after drinking, do you?"

Ben glared at Keller with eyes that radiated resentment, betrayal and mistrust. His voice was on the verge of tears. "I'll walk. Promise me you will leave me alone. Can't you see I've been through enough crap?" And with that, he slammed the door, hobbling away, half jogging, half a bottle of whisky in his hand.

Keller took a deep breath, stroking his face – cold as a summer night from the full blast of the air conditioner in the cabin of his car. He used his tongue to dislodge his stale gum from his teeth and chewed.

Then, resolving to himself, Keller decided to follow Ben under the cover of night. To keep surveillance on him. It was for public safety's sake, and he did not care what Ben or anyone else thought of him – or if he infringed on Ben's rights. The man needed a restraining order. He was dangerous – Keller could discern it in Ben's eyes. *But not* yet *a threat.*

48

TOO LATE

"But he was pierced for our transgressions;
    he was crushed for our iniquities;
upon him was the chastisement that brought us peace,
    and with his wounds we are healed …
He was oppressed, and he was afflicted,
    yet he opened not his mouth;
like a lamb that is led to the slaughter,
    and like a sheep that is before its shearers is silent,
so he opened not his mouth …
    By oppression and judgment, he was taken away;
and as for his generation, who considered
    that he was cut off out of the land of the living,
stricken for the transgression of my people?
    And they made his grave with the wicked
and with a rich man in his death,
    although he had done no violence,
and there was no deceit in his mouth."

—From the Scroll of Isaiah, the prophet's disciples, c. 740 – c. 540 BCE. The Suffering Servant Poem.

Glum and lethargic, Ben DePaula, not sober, but not entirely drunk, walked all the way back home to his house.

The truth is something you don't want to believe. Be careful, for what you want to believe might deceive you from the truth that is in plain sight.

He'd hardly drunk that much alcohol in … what? A decade? Compromises had to be made – his heart was cold hard with personal guilt, his stiff limp gave him constant anxiety, and it slowed him down still, even with the throbbing now healed.

He passed the outdoor cacti farm; the succulents marching alongside him opposingly with needle-like spears. Their fat, bulbous pads, carcasses planted upright, hands and legs dangling upwards, odious – rotten green – corpses. Green and visceral – their spikes pointing at Ben.

He'd been pricked by those giant succulents once – a long time ago.

Ben looked on ahead, simply pushing on down the road, squinting. Concurrently, the burning through his shoes, and the sky, flat and leaden, for all the lack of clouds, the sun hung above him like a swollen fiery eye, smiting him from on high. His tongue cleaved to the roof of his mouth, his lips flaky and pallid. He thirsted. He hungered. The back of his neck stung – he'd been sunburnt, and sunburns caused skin cancer – but that was the least of Ben's worries. He could still feel his hands around Thomas Jones' throat, yet only in his mind, as he still walked.

Step by step, with a little limp there, he pushed inexorably onwards. The journey of his Flesh. The path of his Flesh. Where it had ultimately gotten him was back where he had started.

Devouring ashes, you're swollen with rashness and deceit. It has made you obsolete from the truth.

Strange, during the last week, Ben had totally forgotten about the cosmic war. It was waged for souls, between unseen forces. The War on Terror. Native Americans and the giant Nephilim. The Galactic Tyranny. The super-soldier programme. The Cabal and the Alliance secret societies. The so-called "Omega Plan". Once upon a time, when he had given that grave, fatalistic conspiracy some thought – when it mattered – it had been when his dad was alive and Veronica all safe. The apocalypse had meaning, because Ben knew if he had to face it, he had something to fight for. But now … that was a dead belief. Ben felt like he'd fought *one hundred* wars in less than ten days!

At long last, Ben arrived at home. He reached the door and hated himself – hated the house. He dropped his keys, hating himself even more.

The door opened. It was dark inside the house.

Your goodbye to me is perfect when you leave me and never look back. It's an unpleasant thing to miss someone still here.

His father Joseph … Ben missed him, because he missed the part of him that loved Ben in his loneliness, despite being at odds. Ben missed him, because

Joseph was the only man – the only member of his family who had lived long enough – just long enough – for Ben to renew his love. The last parent, after his mother died, he remembered for as long as he could remember. Joseph would look after him, and occasionally, his aunt Veronica – his daughter's namesake – who was an angelic mother Ben remembered. He choked up when he thought of her.

And Aunt Veronica had gone too, like his mother. Breast cancer. Four years ago. When Ben married Brianna.

His own house made him bilious, and he unconsciously found himself inside Veronica's bedroom.

Her window, still open, let in a slow-moving boiling breeze. The sheets were still folded open from how Veronica had gotten out of bed. For a moment, Ben thought the pillow still bore the imprint of her small head. After all, it lay unmoved at this time, no one home to make it. The sheet impression of her body formed the diagonal way Veronica used to sleep; legs folded at either side to hug them, and so that they could hug her back. She stopped sucking her thumb when she was five, and Ben couldn't recall when in the past she had matured.

Ben slumped against the door frame. Out of the corner of his eyes, he glimpsed movement. He turned around and saw his dark silhouette gazing right back at himself, an image, an idol, distorted on the flyscreen. Not really a reflection, but his own dark shadow.

The window next to it was open – wide open – enough for someone to slip inside.

Ben stared at his dark reflection on the flyscreen, studying the face. Why would he waste time jumping at his own shadows? His heart yearned that Veronica could have slipped through the open window … His reflection of the flyscreen had no facial expression, no features, no identity. It was a void in his shape and likeness. Unmade Ben DePaula.

The window was open! The bed was unmade! Where the hell was Brianna? Where was the woman in his life who he needed most to comfort him? Why did she have to be an FBI agent running around with men when she had more important *domestic* jobs to do?

Then Ben vainly searched the house. He hoped that Veronica could have slipped through her window to come back home. He found nothing.

A few minutes later, Ben considered having a shower, for he felt both physically and spiritually filthy again, but he stopped, recalling the medicine man's commands about not having a shower for four days. Ben felt superstitious fear lace through him. He didn't want another curse, let alone a witchdoctor's curse, so instead, he collapsed on the couch, lying on his back, his weakness almost painful.

Sleep came unaccounted for.

—

Ben dreamed he was flying.

He raged into the sky alongside a colossal arcus cloud hanging low on the horizon. It rose thousands of feet into the air, a mushroom dome of wool dipped in black ink, smoothed off by vicious crosswinds that swept east to west, threatening to topple Ben. The clouds in the heavens were milky and luminous, as if lit from within.

In the midst of the chaos, a sonorous voice, exhaling in the sky, sighed like Niagara Falls.

"I'M GRIEVED EPHRAIM."

"I don't understand!" Ben screamed into the tempest.

"A GREAT OUTCRY HAS ARISEN. I HAVE SEEN HUMANITY MULTIPLY CONTINUOUS EVIL IN THE LAND. MY HEART IS GRIEVED FOR HUMANITY. THE END OF ALL FLESH HAS COME BEFORE ME; FOR THE EARTH IS FILLED WITH VIOLENCE; AND BEHOLD, I WILL DESTROY ALL FLESH WITH THE LAND."

Stiff winds battered Ben. "What?"

The storm rumbled like a considerate aged father. Lightning flashed and the thunderhead disappeared.

The scene shifted, and even before the primordial storm became distant, the smell of sawdust and burning bitumen filled Ben's nose. The air rang with the sound of commands, hammering and sawing, the blows of axes and the rasping of adzes; ceramic pots of pitch bubbling, reeking like burned tar and rubber; fires glowing, elephants roaming and hauling.

The air was hot and humid, the sky overcast and the ground damp. Ben gawked upwards, almost stumbling over his own feet.

He saw a skeletal ribcage of wood penetrating the cloudy heights, set within a large valley, a dense rainforest of tropical trees. The frame was linked with reed fibres like a colossal basket – a coracle made of reeds. Over the double insulating wooden frames was a reed reinforcement in place like scaffolding.

Hundreds of humans tirelessly worked on the giant coracle. Some were on the ground, hefting lengthy beams of timber, Asian brown-skinned men wearing gritty faces and leather jerkins, hauling massive planks led by a foreman carrying a clay tablet of blueprints and instructions. The foreman worked them hard. Women and children darted around with pet dogs and herds of many animals, carrying food baskets others brought in from the jungle with the baskets balanced on their heads and from the nearby logging yard, where temporary markets were built, and from their terrace farms in the distance.

Ben turned around, taking in the din of activity, seeing people dangling feet in the air from craned scaffolding inside the structure. Inside, workers maintained tightly wrapped reed-like bundles as caulks between the timber, covering them with pitch. Most of the workers laboured on the top section of the building – a massive nest, as if it were an aviary for colossal birds.

"Hey, man, where's your axe?" The curt, authoritative voice startled Ben, making him spin around pathetically, tripping over a discarded chunk of wood.

"Oh, I got you, friend," the man said, perkily pulling him up, his hand as coarse as sandpaper.

Ben wet his dry mouth. *It's one of these dreams again?* he thought. *Like the King David dream. I'm in someone's body and acting as myself in the vision?*

The tall brawny man held himself with the bubbly radiance of his prime. He was south-east Asian – due to his eyes, skin and the climate, but his height was remarkable – he was as tall as Ben, just over six feet. The majority of the workers, herders and builders were interestingly athletic, healthy and slender, and much more well fed than rural south-east Asian farmers in the modern world. Ben was speechless. It felt so real: the smells, the senses, the air and the ground. He almost wanted to convince himself that this could not possibly be a dream. *I am in another world!* And he wanted to remain so forever.

The man had to be in his twenties. He wore a leather jerkin with a light-blue robe underneath, torn and sun-bleached. A couple of ripped threads swathed his glistening shoulders and thighs. Around his neck, he wore a modest necklace, a simple black cord with a square ivory seal etched with glyphs and a bull. He wore a tool belt wrapped tightly around his waist. "Come along," he said with a spring to his stride. "You need an adze? Pitch tools?"

"Ugh." Ben's eyes rapidly scanned the man's warm-brown eyes, thinned with an epicanthic fold. "Uhm ..." Ben shrugged, getting into character, improvising. "Lost. Sorry, man. Sorry. I'm new here."

The worker's face blossomed with a lovely ear-to-ear smile. He chuckled with mirth, tugging at the glove on his hand. "Ah, friend, you don't worry.

U-Blei is good. You from the Indus Valley? Meghalaya? Or from the Far West?"

Ben stared at him blankly.

"Oh! Here, I'll get you something to do. Everything is free – no barter needed to collaborate with us. We barter for *you*." Ben smiled. A good deal indeed! "What would you like?"

"What do I like?" He looked down. His feet were inside sandals. He wore rugged shorts, and he was topless.

The man rubbed his chin in thought. "Let's see. Ah, you may like to … portion some pitch for the workers? Or maybe even climb up the coracle to smear it – if you like heights, that is."

"I can help with the pitch. That is awfully nice of you," Ben said, smiling. *Such an immersive world.*

"Right, let's go. Follow me."

Ben did so, weaving through the throng.

Everyone here was diverse in ethnicity. They pulsed with the joy and contentedness of their hard labour. He saw sweating male and female lumberjacks in minimal clothing sawing, clomping and hacking down thick, monstrous trees, putting all their effort into the work. The air had a muggy humidity, like a greenhouse, with the smoke of burning bitumen and sawdust ridding the atmosphere. It allowed Ben to relax, his muscles surging with firm renewal.

From the right came a wailing horn in the air. Ben swallowed hard, his throat prickling as the thin sound floated out of the north, freezing the bustling labour. Even the man leading him strode forward with a concerned face, and Ben knew something was wrong. Another horn blast, much louder this time. Ben's ears pricked as distant bellows and warbling womanlike screams rattled his very bones. Shrilling cries, cawing whoops, deep long insidious howls like sirens; they sounded familiar, bellowing surreally in a cacophonous dirge, carried on by an ominous rumble.

"*Nephilim!*" the man bellowed, awakening everyone locked in consternation. "Protect the Ark!"

Ben ran into the lumberyard and saw women and men shouting, leaving their jobs, arming themselves with anything – from tools to stones – items that they had on them.

The screaming nonhuman hollers persisted. Heart thumping, Ben broke into a jog, and in the stampede, he acquired for himself an axe leaning on curtailed tree trucks – curved and sharp, yet chipped and hardened blunt. A good-enough weapon, even though the crescent axe was made of copper on a wooden shaft.

Ben warily eyed the building, seeing floods of dark people rushing around him. *Is it a battle? A raid?* Ben thought.

Somewhere ahead in the frenzy of dust and confusion, dark shapes – arms, legs and conical heads – bobbed above men, some bounding and smashing their arms upon the defenders in the front line. It was carnage; there wasn't even a charge. Women screamed. Women fought with the men, and children cried, scrambling away from the riot of people bludgeoning and thrashing. Some bold men rode on the backs of elephants, trumpeting into the front lines, whooping.

The sounds beat at Ben as much as the stampede. He could barely see in front of him, pressed against bodies, tightly packed. Everyone was so bloody tall and sweaty. He saw mingled with the grimy faces of men, the Nephilim – black and brown wolfish faces, neckless, long solid hairy arms, roaring crackling snarls. The giant hairy Nephilim clubbed heads, bashing through the wall of screaming, angry humans.

Most humans were lynched in the rioting. A difference between a directed movie set was that there was the art. But this was chaos unleashed – human versus Nephilim. These workers were not well trained, but whatever these Nephilim were, they were powerful and coordinated.

Ancient and medieval battles were messy, hot, fast set-piece fights. The outcome in the chaos was unpredictable, so one had to retreat often. Ben found himself in the middle of this set-piece battle, clutching his axe, hot bodies slamming shoulder to shoulder around him, heat, dust and matted hair smothering him. Two things went wrong: first, nobody supported him or anyone else from being surrounded. Second, the Nephilim were giants, a head above all men and women; they ploughed through them, cleaving their way towards Ben.

There was no room to even lift his axe! Prancing for sight above heads and breathing hard, Ben saw the hulks, almost-men, black skin, large mouths, square heads, carrying spears and bows and arrows, eyes beady and black. Stressful, wailing chimpanzees came from the bestial hordes, clambering up the roofs of houses, massive feet thundering, setting fire to everything in sight.

Nephilim … They looked like … intelligent primates from the *Planet of the Apes*. Bipedal gorillas. Bigfoot in the Grand Canyon.

Suddenly, a deep rumbling growl crackled, a shadow looming over Ben and the Nephilim. A charging grey elephant with long curved tusks smashed right through the Nephilim lines, swinging its titanic head, knocking and stomping over the foe. Nephilim scattered, bounding away on all fours, screaming demonically. Ben had been spared, and he thought, *What if I die in this vision?*

"Stop fighting! No!" a voice cracked over the battle like thunder in a storm.

Stop fighting … Stop … fighting. Those words sounded from an old, worn-out soul that had seen scathing warfare. Ben roared as he attacked a hairy brown hominid, his axe breaking its face. He thought of Brianna as he struck. He thought of his father and Veronica.

The scene shifted. Or so it seemed. Ben was standing in the same area with the slain Sasquatch – seven feet tall and muscular – as stone walls coated in brambles of thorns and thistles rose on either side of him, twice as tall as he was.

A fire roared somewhere off in the distance. The battle in the lumberyard still raged, but Ben couldn't see any of it.

Ben went on, straight through more passages that looked undistinguishable from each other and presently came to a fork in the path. Ben ground his teeth. Mazes – he'd remembered as a child playing in hedge mazes in a garden that there had been a trick to finding his way out, but he struggled to bring it to mind.

Mazes … Thomas Jones mentioned a maze …

My daughter is in the maze!

Ben took a right, proceeded, and hit a dead end. Susurrations molested him, the sound of burning fire crackling. He could smell and feel the fire roasting his skin, but he couldn't see it – only the hazy smoke.

Heart thundering, Ben ran back to take the left path. This time, it took four right turns to bring him to another dead end. Ben tensed, hissing grimly.

Then he heard a girl crying from somewhere in the maze, over the wall. It struck his heart.

"Veronica!" Ben bellowed.

As if time itself were ending, Ben ran. This was it. *The* maze held Veronica; she could finally be found. Sounds followed Ben – sounds like a human chorus of chanting beats. A tribal war cry of beating chests beyond human.

He whipped around a corner and heard the screams again.

Oh God! Veronica! I'm coming!

Ben sped back around and turned right through a zigzagging passageway. He was sure there was a trick to the maze. The tribal chanting escalated as he doggedly navigated. At the last fork, he went right, then left, then right determinedly.

Veronica's screams. They sounded close. Ben hadn't yet hit a dead end. He was doing it!

The smoke was becoming thick and intense. The chanting persisted. Increasingly, Ben's breathing rent his throat.

Left, right, then straight, until he came to a fork. Left, then right. Straight, he came to a fork. Right, left, left, left and right, left. Then a long corridor and a fork. Ben took a right, then a left.

The maze never ended.

"Daddy! Daddy!" The chants were sonorous.

"Veronica!" Ben could not help screaming. He craned his neck, wishing he could find some vines to climb over and run on top of the maze. "I'm coming, darling!"

He turned right, and above, he saw the flame.

Of fire leaping over stone. Of scorching heat that burned bare bones to ashes. Ben ran right through the smoke, growling.

Left, right, straight, fork, right, left, right, right, dead end. Ben bellowed, throwing his axe at the wall. Picking it up, he ran back. Left, left, right, left, fork, left, right, a wall of fire, back around, turned, left, straight, right. Fire licking from above, chants raging all around him, he went left, straight. At a threefold fork, he went straight, left—

"Wombat!"

Stumbling to a stop, Ben saw a little girl huddled on the ground, holding her legs, facing a large hairy four-legged bear, but its hands and feet were … squatted low, in a push-up pose, its limbs spread out wide, grasping the ground like a spider.

Ben's heart almost leapt out of his chest. His legs seemed to work before his mouth. "Veronica!"

"Daddy!" she shouted with glee. "Daddy! Look! Look at the enormous wombat!"

Ben raised his axe. Almighty, but it was wonderful to see his daughter's face again! He quivered, saying, "Darling, get away! That's not a wombat!"

Ben did not know what it was. The brown bipedal Nephilim grunted, rising onto two legs, scowling. It had intelligence, had an intimidating vitriolic nature to it; it knew very well what Ben was, and thoughts worked in its mind.

Locking eyes, Ben felt wild fear course through him. The Bigfoot, though extremely humanlike, its body mass was incredible, dwarfing Ben by three feet. Its head shrunk into its shoulders – a mass of muscle – hair grew long and matted, a brushy beard rounding its face. It towered over his daughter.

Its eyes – angry intelligent black eyes – paralysed Ben; it took effort to keep his knees from trembling. There was no facing this beast. This Chewbacca.

"Daddy!" Veronica called. "Play with wombat! Come!"

"Come," the giant repeated. Its guttural voice resounded so deeply, it took Ben a second to realise that it had uttered the English verb. The ground vibrated from the sound of its voice.

The Bigfoot hauled Veronica up in its arms like a toy, making her squeal. Fire danced before Ben's vision. The chants were roaring.

"No!"

Ben lunged to take his daughter. The Bigfoot raised his left hand, leathery black and callused, palm patched with pink pigmentation.

Screams tore out of Ben's throat as the Bigfoot shoved him, sending him flying backwards.

Too late.

———

Crushed by despair, Ben jolted awake. Hands pinned him down. He realised both Dominic and Patty were holding him, their expressions sliding from fear to discomfort to concern, glancing at one another.

Ben grew still, his mouth open. He had been yelling. Perhaps yelling out his role in the vision, speaking gibberish, flailing around.

"Ben!" Patty's voice sounded. "Ben! What happened?"

"I had a nightmare," Ben said. "You can let me go now."

They let him go, and Ben sat upright on the couch, wanting to breathe in and out, to think.

Did a Bigfoot take my daughter? That thought wasn't out of the possibility. He'd had two encounters with the Nephilim this year. It made sense to him, the Native American message to prepare for the giants and gather the First Fruits, and the only objections that arose were the same: impossible. Bigfoot didn't exist, and if they did, Ben had no hope of finding her if no one could find Bigfoot …

And yet, Thomas Jones – James Casbolt – had taken her into the maze. Not a Bigfoot. *It's just my troubled mind processing trash information,* he justified. *That's all!*

But, of course, both Patty and Dominic would pressure him now for answers.

"Where the hell have you been?" Patty snapped, drawing Ben out of his thoughts.

"He's been staying at his mother's old house, that's where," Dominic replied.

"No! You told her?" Ben blurted, jumping to his feet. He glared at Dominic. "Crap!"

"Jesus, Ben! Easy," Dominic said. "You need to tell me what's up. Keller's been saying that you've been spending time at your mother's house. Why?"

Crap! Keller had lied to him! He'd been following Ben! Did he really have to tell his sister and brother-in-law that he'd been torturing a guilty person? He refrained from the explicit truth – it was impossible to say it outright. Seized with action, he said, "Dominic, you tell anyone?"

His forehead contorted. "Tell what?" he hissed.

"My mom's house. You tell anyone?"

"No."

"Good."

"You've been doing something with Thomas Jones, haven't you?" Patty said, staring at Ben bleakly, one side of her lip almost a snarl. Eyes like ice, she expected the worst. "What have you been up to? It is no coincidence that Thomas disappeared while you've been out driving at Union Peak."

Ben felt his body clench, panic overcoming him, pursuing him on the heels. Feverously, like a sort of addiction unable to bend, Ben had one thing on his mind: his mother's house.

Veronica was waiting for him. That's what that dream meant. And if these people wanted to stop him …

"How did you find out?" Ben lashed out.

"I told you – Keller has seen your truck going to West Jomax Road. There is no other reason for you to be going there unless you have Thomas Jones. And you started going there on the same night Keller Butcher said that Thomas Jones went missing. So, I figured …"

"The government authorities have been watching me, robbing me of my privacy."

"I want to see Thomas Jones," Dominic said forthrightly, angry with Ben, arms crossed. "Is he held captive?"

Ben ground his jaw, lowering his gaze. *How the hell did he guess?*

"You have been torturing him for information, have you?" Dominic said.

Ben hesitated, shocked. "So now I will be disallowed! Don't say a word!"

"But—" Dominic began.

"Don't say a *freakin'* word, all right!" Ben shouted.

So then, Ben had been reduced to two options: either leave this leak and risk the word gushing out, spreading that Thomas Jones had been found by Keller and worse, the whole world discovering the final nail in the coffin to the Actionman's legacy. Or he showed Dominic and Patty, letting them see for themselves, then telling them over again to shut the hell up or they will suffer. Ben did not like the latter option – he disdained it greatly – but he leaned towards it desperately. Keller and Brianna would most certainly arrest him and cast him into prison if not. *Whatever it takes, I* will not *go to prison.*

Prison. Sweat pearled his forehead. Ben must've widened his eyes in involuntary terror, because Patty, hands planted on her hips, stalked up to him, head tilted, exclaiming, "You're hiding something from us. I can see it in your face. You've been up to no good, Ben."

"Come with me," he said tartly, walking with an incongruous limp towards the door. "I can't even get a rest. I'll show you. Dominic and you will understand what I mean."

"So, you *do* have Thomas!" Dominic exclaimed.

"Shut up. Come and see."

"You've been lying to—"

"I'm an actor! We're masters at lying. Sometimes, we cannot help it. But you seem to have become detectives overnight, so you win! You win!" Ben held up his hands in defeat.

Right now, he needed all the chances he could get out of this dilemma. But Ben had a voice, he had rights, and above all, he had a following. Surely, he could make his case to prove that Thomas Jones/James Casbolt was the offender and Ben's punishment of him was justified, because Thomas Jones had spewed out the truth very, *very* slowly. *I've gotten trickles of information out of him! I know he knows! Goddamn it, I better not get arrested for this. I refuse. Or I will kill myself.*

Killing himself … How dramatic. Ben chuckled. *Suicide, the stuff of Greek tragedies.*

Brusquely storming outside, Ben strode all the way back to where he parked his truck on the side of the road next to the liquor store and noticed a considerable change of weather. The air felt moist, the sky dark, not just from the evening, but billowing with dark heavy rain clouds. The sky stirred with activity, and Ben heard a distant thunderclap. A furious storm was coming to Arizona.

Rain. It hadn't rained in Phoenix since his father died. A week before his daughter was kidnapped.

A bad omen?

It was then that Ben felt nervous. His chest felt tight again, and his blood pressure was surging. He searched, trying to find some sort of security, some sort of order – why did he search for it so diligently now when …

Patty and Dominic knew what Ben had been doing with Thomas Jones. All that security had been stripped away …

He was unprotected to face the chaos … everywhere, surrounded by it.

Too late.

He had to face this complex disaster. But Ben could not think on the fly of how he could evade the insanity of despair.

Ben was a marine. A stuntman. He *thrived* in chaos. He was Veronica's hero. He rode the storms, he overcame obstacles no matter the stakes, he found purpose in niche places, he found momentum where most people in the world did not. He gave vision to those who were giving up. He had it all figured out in order for others he did not care about to figure it out themselves.

You are too late, Ben.

"I will show this world. I have this all in my hands. In my control. I have *full* control," he whispered to himself as he drove. It had begun to rain; the windscreen wiper was working at moderate speed. Heavy rain. The roads were muddy and wet; he had to reduce speed.

Too late.

Stop, Ben exclaimed to himself – to the voice in his head. He'd go mad. Better to go mad and find his daughter than not.

49

THE EPICENTRE OF LIGHT AND DARKNESS

"'I am Yahweh, and there is no other,
besides me there is no God;
I equip you, though you do not know me,
that people may know, from the rising of the sun
and from the west, that there is none besides me;
I am Yahweh, and there is no other.
I form light and create darkness;
I make peace (completeness, order) and create evil (chaos, malfunction);
I am Yahweh, who does all these things.'"

—From the Scroll of Isaiah, the prophet's disciples, c. 740 – c. 540 BCE. Prophecy of Cyrus the Great (c.580 – c.529 BCE).

A shadow moved from Judd Pounders' vision at the door of his office at Fort Huachuca. Despite the late hour, kept up by dread, he lingered in his office, the tawny lamp light the only source of illumination. For a while now, he had felt the oppressive lingering presence looking over his shoulder, the oppression of a bellicose enemy, challenging his sure resolve.

The dread reminded Judd of his miasma in Haditha Dam. That night when he couldn't sleep and felt no longer in control of his own body.

He was worried about Ben, worried about his men. Bonner's game had gone on for long enough. He'd deliberately ignored aiding him when Judd wanted to send a rescue mission to save Ben – Bonner had no care for the Marine Corps and the men, using them as a means to an end to steal his pretty coffin out of Iraq.

Judd had made the grave mistake to trust the man, but now Judd wouldn't go down without a fight to terminate the Marine Corps' contract with the Alliance.

As if by the wind, the door gradually opened. Across the room, standing wraithlike, silent as a marble pillar, was Alfred Bonner, half submerged in the gloom. Judd found himself tensing, fixated upon the wild caves that held those inhuman eyes, that stern stone face, and that perspicacious air he carried. Judd had known he had been watched from the very start. Once the head-camera footage of Ben's whereabouts leaked, Judd wondered if Bonner had assiduously tried deceiving him.

Judd had to make a start to stand up against the Alliance parasite, even despite his decision to keep the CD for himself. He had snuck into Bonner's office at Fort Huachuca and hid it away.

"You called me," Bonner growled.

"I want to come clean and speak to you personally. Why did you make a deal to collaborate with the Marine Corps?" Judd steeled himself. "From what I have learnt, your side of the deal didn't tell you to steal antiquities and attain the Defence Department CD. It wasn't about fighting for Iraq. Your agenda—"

"You must be indiscreet to play games with me, Judd." Bonner rotated his head slightly; he got so close that Judd could hear and *feel* his strained breath on his skin. *Should I just say it for what it is?* "I do not negotiate with fools," Bonner stated slowly.

"I … just thought that you might've been involved in Joseph's murder and the kidnapping of Veronica."

"No," Alfred Bonner said blandly. "You would be wrong to consider me guilty. But my cooperation rightly discerns that Ben DePaula is a problem. What happened to him was tragic." The indifference of his voice sounded inhumane. "But what if Ben's name was bin Laden? Right? Ben is the son of an antisemitic apologist. Ben has a famous social identity with strong bonds. Bonds make people believe in something larger than themselves. Whether it is the state, or a following, Ben is capable of creating bonds, incentivising others to giving their own life and taking other people's lives.

"This was why I made a deal with you, Judd. Saddam was a common enemy – the Alliance, the Cabal and the Marine Corps came together on this to get rid of this crisis. I have the power to make changes. Understand that our true enemy is the Galactic Tyrant, who dooms us all, not Saddam Hussein. Can we agree on this?"

Judd didn't answer, because in his mind what Bonner said made sense. Only … who was the Galactic Tyrant?

"I used the Marine Corps for the coffin and the CD, yes, but I've never harmed anyone. The end was to prevent chaos, to prevent the Galactic Tyrant's scion, like Ben, from disturbing society. In this way, I was impartial when deciding to work with you, Pounders. Happiness isn't just the most important virtue, though suffering must be reduced. I am impartial. Ben is partial, causing more suffering than he can reason. I strive to maximise good and reduce suffering. Ben's circumstances have nothing to do with me."

Judd nodded, adrenaline stringing within him. "Yes, but why is Ben an—"

"Are you responsible for deciding to sign my contract?"

"Yes."

Bonner jeered, gliding to the side next to Judd. "No matter what you think of my actions in Iraq, we are bound. You can at least agree to keep this meeting between us secret. The CD remains in this installation until I give my word. There are people who could be trying to look for it. So, then. I hope *your* next move would be more … calculating." Slowly slipping away, Bonner's mouth hardly twitched as he spoke. "The Cabal is out there to get you. They don't play games. Keep my CD safe."

Steeling himself, Judd watched Bonner disappear back into the shadows and out the door like a ghost – a ghost of iron and steel.

After Judd's many years of life, showing honour and respect to his peers and superiors had never failed him. But what if too much honour was given to one who misused it to benefit himself at the expense of others and not admitting to it? Judd could see now. Bonner desired to make the deal with him so the Marines could be used as an excuse to cover up the Light Alliance's agenda in Iraq, and Pounders had been foolish enough to be sucked in. And now Ben was on their hit list. He didn't know what Ben and Joseph DePaula believed in to become villains in the eyes of this corporation. What did it take, then, to be marked as such? Even for a mysterious, odd man, dishonour to any human being *was wrong*. But what was honour now when Bonner had no care for ethics? No care for Ben?

The right thing was to respect authority and the one who had it.

But the one who had authority could have problematic authority.

Judd buried his head in his hands, realising the crisis of his situation. There was no Joshua here to help him. No Joshua to relate to and to talk to.

What have I done? Pounders thought. *Alfred Bonner. Must. Go. This needs to end.*

———

It was cold and clear. Clouds scudded in front of the moon; one could not be certain whether it was the clouds or the moon that were moving. Light rain dribbled down tree branches protractedly. The earth had been parched for days.

Reeling in the silk thread, Koyangwuti waited as Ben walked towards her into her den. She perched on top of his mother's house, her eight legs spanned over its sides.

Mothers always cared for their children. Mothers were full of wisdom; they ruled over their children, keeping them within the web. Beneath the lightless and forlorn La Plata Mountains, where the shadows were deepest and darkest, Koyangwuti made her abode. She had disowned her master, Nihitaa', desiring to be mistress of her own lusts. In southwestern cultures, she was an Anaye who survived the vengeance of Nayenezgani, weaving her black webs in the clefts of the mountains. Those webs were what taught the native people to spin thread and create jewellery, the spider's ability to create. They believed her to have woven the four levels of the cosmos into existence. The Navajo especially had a Creation myth of a massive flood that created the Grand Canyon. Koyangwuti rescued a few families by weaving a web to create solid ground to save them from the proud waters of the Great Spirit.

That was what she was doing to Ben now. She sucked up all light and hope that she could find and spun it again in her dark webs of strangling gloom. Koyangwuti reeled him in towards her venomous quivering fangs.

But like all female spiders, when they mated with males, they kept them enmeshed, tangled in their webs, long enough so she could strike back. She did not need Ben to live. He *needed* her.

For her to feast on the male.

Black heart full of lust, she reeled Ben towards her with power.

———

On the subject of her older brother Ben, Patty's opinion was thus:

He was most stubborn, a piece of crap, an imbecile, vindictive, a liar and dishonest. He did not want to admit it, but he was paranoid, and so inwardly focused.

How the hell could Brianna tolerate this man? Patty thought. *My whole life, all I remember was a love-hate relationship between us.*

The house that used to belong to their mother, which Patty remembered well, was derelict. This massive wooden brick house, her home once upon a time, stood imposing over the land.

Ben shone the torch towards it. It was still raining lightly in the dark of the lonely night. Patty and her boyfriend donned raincoats from the toolbox at the back of his truck, but Ben did not wear any coat; he let the rain soak him through.

"Why are you acting like a loser?" Patty found herself saying, her boots plodding through the damp mud. "It's all a tantrum. You cannot control yourself."

"I cannot deal with this crap any longer," Ben growled, turning around, placing hands to his head. "Wasting so much time!" He cast a sympathetic gaze at Patty frowning glumly, water dripping down his face and beard; he did not care to wipe it. "I know … If it was anyone else but you guys … They like who I am, but not as a person …"

"A few do like you," Dominic said.

"Very, *very* few," Patty added. She'd seen Ben's cockiness and vanity as long as she could remember.

"Come on," Ben said, bringing them to the front yard of Mom's house, cacti in the shadows resembling clawed hands, fingers thick and swollen, ripping out of the ground, desperately trying to escape the burning earth and drink the rain ravenously for themselves. Patty had shivered seeing that grove of wild cacti outside her mother's house as a child. She'd always stayed away from that patch of wilderness. It was too scary, and the cacti looked like spectres in the night with bloated tentacles and spikes. It terrified her. Even now, years later, she still had a childlike caution.

"Okay, so you two are agreeable, then," Ben said, reaching the front doorstep. "In that case, you will promise me something. It will be life or death. Whatever you do, if the FBI knocks on your door and asks you about the house and what you are about to see, deny, deny, deny. Got it? *Deny.* It is for our own good. For Veronica and Zoe's good."

Raindrops made sharp sounds on her coat. In the torchlight, Dominic's eyes almost popped out of his head. He did not know whether to address Patty or Ben. "But–But—"

"Deny it." Ben pointed his finger, jabbing Dominic's chest. She could see fear and consternation swelling in her boyfriend's eyes. "Deny, Dom. Deny, Patty. Deny until the day you die."

Patty swallowed hard. She felt an incredible urge to tackle Ben and beat him to the ground, but she restrained her wrath and acquiesced grudgingly.

Turning around, Ben unlocked the front door, letting them in. The house was permeated with malevolence from its age and from its memories. It was a trash site. Everything was upturned and misplaced, unrenovated, decayed and slumping, abandoned the day when Patty was just a young child, when her mother died. The house had died along with her, smelling rotten like her. In the old living room, a single shower from a leakage splattered in a single stream on the ground.

Patty would have wandered off, gazing in wonder at the old house she remembered living in with Ben. Memories from the earliest part of her life jumped out of the shadows. She walked left from the door, forwards into the vast living room, and went down three steps. The room had to be almost eleven feet tall. Patty had loved the large house as a child; it made her feel she was living in a palace. So much room, they could put up a ten-foot Christmas tree every winter. Couches and pillows were old and tattered by racoons. The mouldy carpet that had not been fully taken out smelled awful. A heinous odour of rot infused the house.

Going straight from the living room, divided by a large couch that could become a bed, was the playroom. Memories engulfed Patty, and she froze, standing still in a daze.

The playroom. She faced partitioned sliding doors with glass looking out over the backyard – a posh backyard trimmed and ordered with white paving stones, a massive outdoor table umbrella – now in tatters – and a garden. Off to the side was a fountain with waterspouts shaped like lion heads.

Patty remembered running her toy cars and trucks across the stone ledge of the parapet along the garden, badly scraping it, running the car along the ledge, racing, re-creating scenes from action movies that Ben loved watching. She used to love playing with the cars and trucks even though it had ruined the stone, which now lay shattered. Vines and weeds colonised the sandstone pavement where she had grazed her knees multiple times. They had a trampoline, too, by that large palm tree that still slumped back there, dangling weakly. And there was the cubby house up on the hill with the massive ladder and slide still there, all rusty and overgrown by wilderness. The garden was dead and filled with more weeds and brambles and, worst of all, more bloated armies of cacti.

Patty marvelled at how much time had worn this nostalgic place down – nothing truly lasted forever in this world. She had not realised how rich this house had once been before Mother died. It seemed massive as a child, and now, what she once thought elaborate seemed small.

That's how long I have not been here, Patty thought.

Ben had been the roughest brother – such a thug, such a cheater, such a thief, even cruel at times. He'd bashed her a lot when they played fight games, and it got them in trouble many times. Patty always got in trouble for telling Ben off, and she remembered having tantrums just like him. Patty almost laughed; she smiled as she remembered sobbing, refusing to show she was weak. Ben's overconfidence was innocent back then – he was only a boy, finding his place in the world – but now, Ben had transformed, or he never truly matured. He retained that same brash, childish attitude of the boy who thought selfishly and arrogantly.

Like Cleo – Veronica's mother.

Patty blinked. The sound of prolonged drumming noises of rain continued. Patty felt … comfortable in this darkness. The playroom, once a paradise world of toys and computer game sets, action figures and a TV, was now a cold, empty, sad corner.

She turned right and saw Dominic standing forlornly by her side.

"This was your childhood home?" he said softly, taking a deep breath. Patty nodded stiffly. Dominic always knew how to read her change of body language really well. "It must be sobering to be back again."

Patty swallowed hard. *Ben never changed; he only got worse. The person whom I thought used to strangle me unprovoked in this house now holds a prisoner captive.*

That made her grimace. She strolled gingerly back through the damp living room towards the stairs and the front door, where Ben was waiting underneath the balustrade of the clerestory, his jaws tight, skin grey. Just looking at Ben wearing sad, grey and large loose robes caused her heart to twist. She stood by the stair railings, next to the very spot where the mottled rocking horse, mouth blaring its teeth in exertion, had been. It had scared Patty at night when shadows used to play with its ghastly shape. Like the cacti in the front garden, little Patty had been terrified by it.

Then, at the corner of Patty's eye, striding through the ajar front door, was a woman, her hair soaking wet, wearing unkept clothes like Ben. Patty yelped, and Dominic held onto her.

"You better keep the door locked," the woman said, her voice dripping with hostility. "I think the word is spreading that Thomas Jones has been kidnapped."

"Who the hell are you?" Ben sounded horrified. "How do you know this?"

"I haven't told anyone," the woman retorted. Tall, sinuous and muscular, with light-brown hair, she could have reached Ben's height – half a head taller than Patty – she would have been beautiful. Except that face of hers was used to getting what it wanted. Not petulant, just passionately certain. Grim determination. Around the back of her neck were dark body tattoos, and they were gothic and blotchy – not even nice ones. "My name is Tara. I am an Aes Sidhe." Her beautiful eyes swung to Ben. "You've read James Casbolt's book. It exposes it all."

"I haven't read it," Ben said. "Only heard a summary from the man himself."

Twisting her head, Patty scowled in confusion. This woman was *not right* in the head! "What? What are you talking about? Why are you here?" Patty said to the stranger.

Tara smirked – a one-sided smirk. "I don't have time to deal with asleep people. I'm here to help."

Ben growled under his breath. "You want to free Casbolt. To stop me finding my daughter? She could be trafficked!"

Tara shot Ben a defiant stare, getting into his face. "Don't you dare test me, Ben. Whatever you have done, leave Thomas Jones alone." Tara's voice suggested that she might step on him without even noticing if he got in her way.

"You're an Aes Sidhe," Ben rasped aggressively. "No one but Aes Sidhe could have known about this. You've come to stop me."

"An Aes Sidhe woman will surprise you," Tara snarled slickly.

"What is an Aes Sidhe?" Patty exclaimed in frustration, feeling terribly alienated from Ben and Tara's conflict.

Tara did not even spare a glance at Patty – she gazed, sullen, into Ben's eyes. "Imagine fairies that have been traumatised to the point that they turn into angry X-Men. That's an Aes Sidhe."

"The hell?" Dominic muttered, stroking his hand through his hair, his flashlight cast upon the lunatic stranger. "You're—"

"She's a spy, trying to stop me finding my daughter," Ben said stringently. "You're a spy for the Cabal."

"No," Tara whispered back, serene. "I've got nothing to lose. Once they use mind-control experiments on subjects, once they were done with us, they leave us to break. I have nothing better to do than to help, so thank me if you so wish. Just listen to me. Your life is in danger, Ben. The people who killed your father want to see you buried six feet under for what you are doing to Thomas Jones."

Patty realised something was different about this woman's voice, and she tried to figure out what it was. *I don't like this woman,* she thought. *I don't know, but she has a dangerous vibe. She looks my age, and probably even younger. But the tragedy is that she looks like she cannot trust anybody. What made her into this?*

Heaving out a sigh, Ben met everyone's glances and said, "Upstairs. I'll show you the perpetrator."

The floorboards on the stairs creaked awfully under Patty's feet. Just behind her, she saw Tara digging into her pocket, taking out a cigarette, lighting it, hand covering the flame, and taking a long drag. Her movements were fluid and competent. Smoke wreathed her face, making her appear otherworldly. Patty tried to hold her nose from inhaling the toxic scent.

Upstairs remained just as she remembered – only much smaller and still labyrinthine with arbitrary twisting hallways that served no purpose but to confuse and to make up space for the large ground level of the house. Back when Patty was a child, upstairs and the bedrooms had been off limits and out of bounds when school friends and family came over. Only outside and downstairs were permitted. The rain hushed outside lullingly – an ambient monotone susurration.

Ben led them down the dark-blue winding corridor towards the landing Patty remembered was the upstairs living room. It was barren and empty, with woodwork, tools and construction lamps lying around. The bathroom light was on.

A feeling of dread gripped her. Patty slowed to a halt, crossing her arms for protection. Her heart jackhammered in her chest as she watched Ben creep over tiles and wood towards the small turgid bathroom. Dominic leaned against the wall, his eyes glazed and a hand covering his mouth as he gazed into the bathroom. "Oh my God," he rasped. "Jesus Christ, Ben …"

Heart beating faster for what had struck Dominic, Patty tried to look inside, sweat prickling her armpits. Tara stood next to Patty in the shadows by the hallway entrance near the woodcutting table, face carved out of dark ice. There was a smell like burning plastic. It was the cigarette, Patty realised: it had burned down to the filter. Tara did not seem to have noticed.

Patty stalked to the door – she wanted to see Thomas Jones and what Ben had done to him. Bile forming in her mouth, Patty shoved past Ben … and stopped.

On the ground, trembling weakly, was a young man with a dirty sack covering his head, bound hands tied to the pipes underneath the sink. The strong smell of urine and faeces smothered the tiny bathroom.

The entire house hung in deep silence, and she crept closer, squatting to the quivering Thomas Jones, meticulously removing the bloody sack off his head.

She had not expected the beating to be as bad as what she saw. The face behind the sack was stiff in excruciating pain. It made her heart cramp – her hand came to her chest. The young man's face shone in the faint orange light red as a puffy tomato, completely swollen, inflamed, blistered skin sealing his eyes shut. Blood caked his shirt. His chin and his mouth were covered in dark blood, his jaw looked dislocated, broken even as it hung open, covered in blood. Thomas Jones had been rendered unidentifiable. He smelled of sweat, of piss and of blood.

Hand rubbing her mouth, Patty winced, distressed by this shocking sight. How much pain was this man in because of Ben's beatings? Not even a criminal deserved such a brutal reprimand!

Thomas blindly moved his head, searching for Patty, probing weakly for this sudden appearance of empathy and love. She placed her hand on his thigh, her breathing becoming heavy.

"Please help me," came a small voice.

Tears almost brimmed Patty's eyes. In her own house, this young man had been bashed in the most horrible of ways. Yet even as Thomas whispered for help, Patty felt her mouth forming into a hopeful smile. She had to free this man – kindness was no crime – it precisely helped the weaknesses and the vulnerabilities within others. She had to free this man. He could be guilty, but the rumours of the other man at the vigil a few nights ago had to be the other suspect. Thomas Jones had proven himself innocent at the lie detector test.

Why would Ben do this? Patty thought, numbed from any sympathy towards Ben … Had the military done this to Iraqi prisoners of war? Had it given Ben ideas to treat Thomas like this? The pessimism of his martial grandiosity? Or was this in humanity naturally? Inevitable? That latter made her freeze, staring at nothing. She wet her mouth.

Patty tried to speak – an immense effort to subdue her trembling lips and tight throat. "Can you help us find Veronica and Zoe?" Her voice quivered. Seeing Thomas bruised to death, pity became a higher priority than questioning this man who had already been questioned within an inch of his life. Thomas barely moved. "Have you seen where little Zoe is?" Patty attempted gently. She had to swallow and sniff to keep herself from crying. "Please tell us. Please help us."

Without making a sound or closing his gaping fish mouth, Thomas roved his head slightly, gesturing towards his bound-up hands on the plumbing. He was too weak to speak.

"He's going to tell us," Patty whispered patiently, untying Thomas' bonds. She held his hands, gazing into his battered face. "Please."

"Help ... me," Patty heard. She felt a tear trickle down her nose. "Help me."

"Get the hell in here, Tara," Ben said from the landing. The moment Thomas heard Ben's voice, he lunged, battering Patty's hands off him. Patty yelped in shock, and Thomas scrabbled to his feet, knocking Patty to the floor. Hearing smashing glass, she yelped again, screaming.

"Patty!" Dominic blundered into the bathroom. Ben shoved him aside, Tara following. Patty screamed in panic, writhing into the corner, covering her head.

"The hell are you doing?" Ben barked as a brawl unfolded. Grunts and hisses, scuffing of frenzied feet, attacking, kicking, clawing. Both her brother and Tara tried to restrain the crazy prisoner, grabbing Thomas' shoulders. He tried to escape through the window desperately, punching a hole through it, and as Ben and Tara seized him, he spun around, flinging his arm downwards at Ben. A glint of light reflected off metal or glass in his hand. *Knife!*

"Argh!" her brother roared as the strike swung across him. Patty's heart thundered in her throat. Thomas had swung viciously at Ben's chest, and his face was pale in shock. *He got him!*

Fiercely, Tara clamped Thomas' right hand, smashing it against the wall. Ben cursed, gazing down at his chest, then cannoned into Thomas, attacking him.

There were crashing sounds, body against body, in the cramped bathroom corner. Thomas thrashed like a snake, braying. He knocked Tara in the nose, then went swinging at Ben again.

In his right bloodied hand was a large shard of glass.

Ben caught the arm and rolled the wrist, closing him off. Thomas hissed ferally as Tara bound him in a headlock. Kicks and punches flew sporadically, and clothes were grabbed and torn. Tara and Ben at last pinned Thomas spread out, face pressed on the wall, legs parted, hands raised.

Patty could not watch the terrible, desperate fight. She closed her eyes and whined, her heart a storm inside.

Tara yelled with strain, and Ben roared acerbically, "Gawwwddd damn it!" Panting breaths. "Let it go! *Let it go!*" There were grunts and sighs, and

Patty, slowly emerging from a ball, saw the shard of glass drop from Thomas' hand. Patty panted and realised she had been sobbing. She took a deep breath. How could she be sucked in? He was such a timid man!

"You *untied* him? I told you he's dangerous. You see now? A super soldier is not what they seem!" Ben turned his face to her, a mask of anger, then spun around, bracing and pressing his hands against Thomas' back, holding him up against the wall. "Jesus," Ben panted, growling. "Argh! He's strong."

"This man is desperate to escape," Tara hissed grudgingly. "You've made Thomas into an enemy. You've broken him, Ben!"

"Don't care. Help me tie him back up," Ben grunted, as Dominic pulled Patty off the ground into his embrace.

"Are you hurt?" he whispered.

"No. I'm okay, just … shocked." Patty took deep breaths to slow her tormented heart. She gazed at the massive glass shard on the ground and at Ben, dread upsetting her stomach. "Ben? Ben! You—"

As Tara began to tie Thomas up, Ben spun around. She did not see any bloodstains across his chest, thank God, only a tear of the shirt fabric near his collarbone. He met her gaze, smoothing his knuckled forehead, following her eyes to the glass shard on the ground. He kicked it, knocking it into the wooden wall. "That was close," he said, examining his tear. "I'm all right. But this moron is the one who's going to get stitches if he doesn't stop."

"This is not right!" Dominic exclaimed, clutching Patty as if to protect her from her own brother, his hands cold against her coat. "You're mad!"

Ben, looking scandalised, pointed at Thomas, growling, "You see him lash out? This is why I've kept him captive in this house. It's proof he is a dangerous super soldier."

In the background, Tara clicked her tongue, shaking her head and rasping in scorn. "Ha. Proof."

"Oh," Dominic groaned weakly, shaking his head in distress. "If Keller and Brianna find out …"

"If you keep my promise, all of you, even Tara, we will be spared from jail, and Veronica and Zoe could have a family to come home to."

Dominic went pale. "Oh … What is *wrong* with you? What the fu—"

"It was the only way," Ben cut him off, striding outside onto the landing to meet Dominic face to face. "You know it."

"Man, this ain't right! What if you're wrong? What if he's—"

"What do you mean, I'm wrong? I'm not!"

"What if he's *not it!*" Dominic asserted. "Come on, Ben. This is … Man,

I want my sister back as much as you want your daughter, okay? But, Jesus Christ, *enough!* This is ..." He let go of Patty, and she watched as her boyfriend's eyes were glazed with moisture. "I don't know ..." He was overwhelmed, about to sob.

Patty felt her chest inflate, tight with pain, making her tremble.

"I understand this is detestable," Ben snapped back, taking a step. "But love gets us to do detestable things sometimes. I had to do this, or your sister"—Ben pointed at Dominic invidiously—"*dies.*"

"But this ain't ..." Dominic rasped. Patty watched as her boyfriend wilted before an aggressive man.

"We hurt him until he talks. That's the *only choice,*" Ben whispered, trying to placate Dominic. Patty flared her nostrils, but she couldn't speak. "Thomas is not a person anymore." Ben's voice was low, dense with strictness. "Think of it that way. He stopped being a person when he took Veronica and Zoe. He's a beast. A super soldier who has alters becomes a monster. Casbolt himself told me this before we went to war. Thomas is no longer human, Dom. He tried to cut me open."

Dominic sniffed, tears leaking down his face. Patty could not believe what she was hearing! Would this treatment and torture of a man honour the family Ben claimed he wanted to protect? "He's already hurt too much," Patty rasped. "Ben ..." She approached her brother and felt torn – unable to act to change anything. "You're not saving anybody!"

"Nah, Patty. If the police get him," Ben said, "he'll just clam up. Someone has to make him talk. Someone." He hissed his words out, the blood vessel in his neck tensing.

"Did he say anything?"

"That bastard is playing games with me. He told me something, but he is not specific."

"Are you finished, Ben DePaula?" Tara's peevish voice drew everyone's gaze. She rose from her squat after tying Thomas back down under the sink. The woman's head jerked to her right shoulder three times, grimacing. "What you've done to this man is *horrendous.*"

"No, Tara," Ben said tartly. "The asshole's crossed the line. Don't put him there. Throw him in the shower." Ben, striding in front of the woman, opened the door to the wooden wall, which Patty realised was a makeshift hatch.

Something flashed in Tara's hand – a metallic blade – a kitchen knife! – and she set it against Ben's throat, ready to slice.

Patty flinched and screamed. "Hey! Hey!"

"Don't move a freakin' muscle!" Tara roared.

"Don't!" Patty let out a shaky breath, swinging her head side to side. "Ben," she gasped. "Ben, just … *listen* to her."

Tara remained icy calm – the type of calm that hid seething fury. Sweat pearled her forehead. Tension escaped from Ben's body, but he became indifferent as Tara said, "What you have done was *exactly* what the Cabal men and women did to me. Look at what you've done to Thomas Jones, Ben. Can't you see what you're doing is not getting your daughter back?" Tara held the knife at Ben's throat, trembling from clenching, head twitching again, her eyes fluttering. Every time this girl twitched, Patty almost had a heart attack from the unpredictability of what Tara could do. "Thomas Jones cannot talk. Let him go!"

"But he knows where they are."

"Thomas Jones cannot talk. Let him go!"

"He knows where they are! He told me! In the maze! Patala!"

"Enough of this bull crap!" she spat. Ben was dead as a rock, distraught, but he looked too calm, too focused on Tara and the knife.

"Don't hurt him," Patty rasped. A cool draft eerily seeped into the bathroom through the shattered window. "Please." Patty was crying. Why, after all her extreme criticisms towards her brother, did she suddenly feel for him again? Was this the paradoxical strength of a love-hate relationship between siblings? She cried, primarily from the fear she felt from this bizarre lioness woman. "S–s–stop this."

Tara's eyes were filled with passion. "For all that I know, from all my life – I don't know where to begin – but I know this truth. My father was driven mad with grief when I was a girl kidnapped by the Cabal mind-control programmes. I thought my dad was going to rape me. I don't want that for you, Ben, or Veronica." Grim contention rolled off Tara and Ben. Give a finger to the Aes Sidhe, and she took your whole arm. "You're blind, Ben. You think you can do everything!" Her voice suggested she'd killed men before. Her face became dark, sadistic, sinister. Tara twitched.

A pall of silence followed in the wake of Tara's fatalistic words. Patty felt threatened by what Tara was saying, even though she'd absolutely subdued Ben's cancerous attitude. For such a young woman, Tara *knew* control, and Patty felt threatened by Tara's unbelievable revelation.

"Why does the Cabal do this?" Ben struggled to speak, shifting unevenly on his feet. Patty could see he was nervous. "Why … Why would God let this happen to my Veronica?"

"I saw who the Galactic Tyrant is." Tara contorted her lips and said swiftly, "Your father was a Christian, am I right?" Tara's light eyes glided across to Patty and Dominic.

"Yes, our dad was Christian," Patty said for Ben.

"This is the truth," Tara said, her lips a rictus. Her voice lacked all expression; each word flat and dull, like pebbles being dropped one by one into a deep well. "Why is this happening? The reason your father was killed, the reason why Veronica was taken, the reason why you feel paranoid – it is because the Galactic Tyrant *is God*.

"God is coming to destroy us. All this violence. Humanity is so depraved, and soon the Tyrant will be coming, angry, mad and crazy because his children have been kidnapped and persecuted. The Tyrant is out for revenge. The Tyrant is bloodthirsty, trampling through the blood of the innocent. To prevent this horrific end, secret societies are taking children randomly and turning them into super soldiers, so they can fight the Tyrant and save the universe from this evil. That's the plan. That's why sex trafficking is an elite business. It is to kill God.

"You think he loves your Veronica? You think he loves Zoe? He doesn't. He could have stopped the kidnappers, but he didn't. God is weak. The fact that children can be kidnapped *so easily* proves God's incompetence. He may as well be dead, or he may as well be the Galactic Tyrant. There is no hope in God. All the hope the girls have now is you and you"—Tara pointed to Dom—"but you sit here beating up an innocent man because you think he's it! Like God, you're a *terrible* parent who is bent to smash innocent lives, and you can do whatever you want because you're famous. You *failed* Veronica!"

Tara's eyes were intense, devoid of all innocence. With each word, she seemed out of breath. *Jesus Christ …*

"Oh my God," Dominic's whole body shivered, burying his face. Patty, above all, felt alienated; she had no context for any of this. But she saw Ben's eyes widen, writhing emotion manipulating him. He knew about the Galactic Tyrant.

The room constricted, the cosy pool of light becoming denser with the bathroom and Thomas Jones mangled on the floor.

"Your father's God, your Jesus Christ, is the Galactic Tyrant," Tara continued. "The purpose as to why the secret societies were formed was to wage war against God. When I was kidnapped from my father, raped and tortured, my handler told me, 'Where is God? Is God allowing this to happen? Oh, God will never save you. Satan is the Saviour. Jesus is the Tyrant.'" Tara swallowed, pausing. "You think you're doing justice, Ben?"

Suddenly, Tara hissed, lowering her knife hand, her body going all stiff, eyes blinking wildly, her mouth gaping as she had a momentary fit, leaning against the wooden door, only to collect herself back again, all poised. "Guns. There are people outside." Tara's eyes were spaced out.

Patty froze. Her ears, starved for sound, heard nothing.

Suddenly, the front door downstairs exploded. Patty hollered, jolting, half falling against the wall, tripping over Thomas' mangled feet.

"They're here," Tara intoned morbidly, trotting out of the bathroom. "Hide."

"Who's here?" Dominic called, but Tara had already bound down the landing and through the halls back downstairs.

While the sounds of chaos unfolded below, Patty tried to help Ben, and surprisingly, he didn't resist. He looked dolent, his entire world upside down. Wrapping an arm around him, Dominic aiding her, she turned off the bathroom light, finding a place to hide. Patty knew this place – in the secret walk-in closet in the spare bedroom of their parents, they hid.

They thought they would be safe from the intruders in the silence, when from the bathroom, Thomas howled, his scream tearing out of his mouth, bawling for help.

Voices shouted below, and feet thundered upstairs.

"No!" Ben moaned, tugging against Patty doggedly. His voice was that of a man being tormented. He brayed and wailed like a wild animal. "Nooo! Noooo!"

With all their might, Patty and Dominic pinned Ben down. Ben did not heed any sisterly advice or help – he was the eldest. Tears wet her face, fighting down Ben, roaring until he retched.

Patty was his younger sister. In the end, she couldn't help him.

—

Bounding through the house, seeking the stairs, Tara steadied her heavy breathing, her mind enthralled. She felt giddy that she'd vented all her grievances as a lesson to Ben – that man needed a wakeup call.

Confessions – they were overwhelmingly cathartic and healing. She smiled wildly. Oh yes, she'd seriously had the ability, the impulse, to act like a mother ready to kill her child, ready to cut open Ben's throat, to watch his cold blood pour down her hands. She could have, but better not right now before his family, and now that the FBI were here.

Confessions … For so long, she'd kept silent about the crimes of the satanic oligarchy Cabal and their anti-Christ ideology. The pieces of her shattered chaotic life could be gathered together that way by proclaiming the dark truth.

Words had power, as the experience behind them had power. Words ignored fires of relief. Words could bring tears from hard hearts. She wished Ben would repent.

But in reality, no matter how much Tara honestly confessed, no man could truly appreciate her.

Once she reached the railing, gazing down at the front hallway, trampling over the door were flashings of a police car, casting red and blue light from the windows over a row of five people prowling into the house. Tara, to her amazement, thought, *The Manicheans of Light? Have they come to free Thomas? To find Ben?*

Before she could take action, Tara spun around, slipped her back on the railing, and squatted, waiting for the stalking Manicheans to prowl deeper into the house. The door was still open below, a drizzly gaping angular mouth, compelling her to slip out and escape, cowardly. What good would that do now, after helping the DePaulas? And what about Ian Mastemah, who made his promise?

She couldn't dwell on that now. Slowly, Tara waited for the Manicheans to slip deep into the house, their creeping footfalls no longer in earshot. She stalked stealthily downstairs. Once she reached the door, she whipped her head around, seeing no pursuers.

She skulked outside and saw a police car parked up the street, and three people climbing out of it.

Tara, keeping low, slipped into the scrub, trying to weave through quietly. She twitched, hearing her own breath rushing in her ears. Emerging into a clearing, then into a small ditch leading towards a larger strip of unkept parkland, Tara could see the policemen storm into the building, and even from outside in the shrub, she could hear their raucous commotion. "FBI!" *If Ben and the others had been found, and Thomas too, then good riddance! Justice!*

Before Tara planned her escape route, she caught a glint of blue dim light cast over the wiry tree before her, enough light that she could see her own shadow stretched out before her. Not moonlight. It was cloudy. Faint susurrations rode on the air. Someone was watching her.

Twitching, Tara spun around a tall slanting trunk, and saw an even blue light. Misty smoke swirled between branches, like glowing dried ice, gathering around a manly form, slim and nimble, appearing from behind the trunk. The smoke *seeped* out of the phantom's skin. Clad in a dark grey jacket, the radiant's head was shaven clean, bald like Ben DePaula. He wore a neck warmer, a black veil covering his face from the nose below. His eyes were like blue suns – the pupils shining brightly in the night. In the middle of his forehead was a tattoo – a vertical streak of white and red from the end of the nose tip to his forehead.

Tara's mouth dropped. What was she looking at, and why was strange blue smoke streaming off his body? A hallucination? A ghost or something else?

Hanging from the glowing man's hand, hidden partly behind the flap of his coat, was a crystal sword, short, thin, and double edged.

She pulled out her kitchen knife, taken from The Pageant Queen. It was a great disadvantage against a man with a sword, but unless she could get in close, block him and strike the neck … "Who are you?" Tara hissed.

"Who am I?" the glowing man said. "I'm Bhairava. I've come to take you home."

Bewilderment caught her off guard. Home? Tara had no home.

She took a step, testing the man, then trotted towards him, raising her knife for a feint, to strike him from the outside, to evade the blade. But the phantom man stood serene and indifferent. He'd addressed her, but his eyes were staring into another world.

Stepping into the strike, Tara saw the phantom man dart backwards. Oddly, he didn't lunge with the locomotion of his legs; instead, the smoke around his body screamed, coalescing, sending him flying *backwards* with incredible force. Tara stared as the smoke cleared, and the ghost man stood floating a foot off the forest ground with a great distance between them.

Discouragement filled Tara – she'd very likely fail this mission – her honour was long gone ever since Baghdad, for Barbelo kept her from seeking death when she desperately longed to die and couldn't find it. But if that death came by someone slaying her, she *would* welcome it.

She kept her eye on the phantom man – he was an irksome coward; he didn't swoop in for an offence strike – instead, he zigzagged around in a ribbon of light nimbly through the branches. He looked majestic, light mingling with darkness.

"Come on!" Tara charged, trying to baulk this ghost man, to run the gauntlet – she didn't care if she lost her head. The blue phantom danced backwards, leaping with a twist of his body, landing on a tree branch, perched up there. He was too high to reach, but Tara jumped and swung.

She missed and heard the screeching metallic mist coalesce in her face. The smoke was ice, enveloping her in a billowing cloud of haze. She yelped, running up the tree trunk, clutching a branch as the phantom swooped out of the tree. She ducked and felt the crystal sword cleave empty air. The man twisted in the air, cresting over Tara's swing, not even countering to strike her — he had the perfect chance from Tara's mistake — but he landed on the ground.

He would have killed me by now if he tried, Tara thought, jumping onto the ground. *What is he waiting for?*

Fearful, Tara swung around, slashing. The blue smoke seemed to give the man remarkable agility — he moved as if he were the wind himself. He dodged so incredibly, Tara couldn't land a single strike. In frustrated fear, she jumped for a direct stab, but the man swung to the side, and with his free hand, blocked her arm in an arm bar. Tara kicked back, but the man struck her in the neck.

Blue smoke disgorged out of the man's left hand that had struck her neck. It burned with ice, her clothing turning to frost and drizzle; she heard a thousand whispers. She rocketed into the air as if she'd been hurled by hurricane winds. Tara crashed into the branches of a tree, which stabbed her in sporadic places. She roared out a gasp as she dropped with a tremendous crash, branches breaking and snapping. On landing, a jolting pain burst from her ankle and shoulder. She raised her head, trembling, searching for the knife she'd lost.

Quickly, Tara got up, stunned, gritting her teeth. What happened to her? The phantom smoke had sent her flying dangerously, almost killing her.

She watched as the blue ghost crossed the clearing in rapid strides, raising his sword. He rammed the butt into Tara's face with a backhand move.

Blinding light flashed in Tara's eyes, a counterpoint to the sudden agony that crashed upon her skull. So powerful, it stimulated the spiritual mark in her brain. Everything blurred, her vision fading into darkness.

Pain. So *much* freezing pain.

She roared, agony clamping her shoulders, like someone had shredded her with a hundred needles. She flopped to the ground, rolling in the cold mud, her side making her writhe and rock. Broken rib. Needles pricked all over her body. She had flown right into the cacti. She felt blood leaking from too many stinging scratches where the needles had slashed, peppering her skin. She reeled uncontrollably. The taste of iron filled her mouth. The sting of cactus needles in her body did not compare to the throbbing of her jaw.

Blue light cast over her like a spectral spotlight.

No time for pain. No time for pain. No time for pain. Get up.

She couldn't get up; it was too hard for her body. Her face sunk into the dust, her jaw had shattered, one of her teeth had been bent back, jutting into her tongue.

"There," said a voice that sounded too familiar. "It wasn't too hard to weaken her, was it, Bhairava?"

"Ian?" Her jaw felt numb, stung as she tried to move; it felt unhinged. The phantom had broken it. Blood poured down the side of her face.

The man looking over her, Ian, met the eyes of the glowing phantom man, speaking something that Tara could hardly hear, her stressed breaths tumultuous in her ears, the persistent agony from the cactus needles preventing her from concentrating.

Nevertheless, she recognised what had just happened to her. Tara's eyes bulged. She had been deceived and used!

Again!

Tara sobbed, but even sobbing wasn't relief from her pain.

A bag wrapped over her head, plummeting her into darkness.

50

CRUCIBLE

"Who is this who comes from Edom,
in crimsoned garments from Bozrah,
he who is splendid in his apparel,
marching in the greatness of his strength?
'It is I, speaking in righteousness,
mighty to save.'
'Why is your apparel red,
and your garments like his who treads in the winepress?'
'I have trodden the winepress alone,
and from the peoples no one was with me.'"
—From the Scroll of Isaiah, the prophet's disciples, c. 740 – c. 540 BCE. The apocalypse of the Messiah.

Ben was in tatters as he sat with his back against the wall in the FBI Phoenix Headquarters, hands tucked around his back, his legs spreadeagled before him. An FBI agent stood at his side. An FBI agent who worked for his wife, who worked for the corrupt powers that be.

All his life, he knew, all the people in the world were out to get him. They did not care about others, only about themselves – instinctively, Ben knew that to be true. People hardly cared. And if they didn't care, they had reasons to despise others – what reason was there for Ben to care for them anyway? Everyone selfishly scapegoated other people. He knew from people's eyes and how they would, when it came to the crunch, selfishly preserve themselves and betray others.

Even Ben's closest friends and family scapegoated him. Now he was good as dead.

It's over … Ben felt numb. He did not want to see Casbolt's face *again*. *It's over for me.* The headlines … *It's over.*

Glum with frustration, Ben jerked himself, flinging back his head, only to be slammed back down by a yelping agent. He grunted as his back thumped against the brick wall.

Ben craned his neck, desperately trying to catch sight of his wife. Everyone's features were fuzzy and vague in the atrium. Mingling with the moving bodies of morbid agents in white-and-black uniforms, Brianna dwelt among them, indifferent, arms crossed, her lips puckered in the way she did when she became haughty.

He didn't look at anyone, and no one paid attention to Ben, as they should. Instead, the captives bunched up in a line with him were men in strange hippy clothing – survivors of the Manicheans of Light, his father's murderers. An ambulance also had pulled away from his mother's house, taking Thomas Jones to hospital.

Ben saw Keller Butcher rolling up his sleeves, his long slicked-back hair hanging in strands over his handsome face. He imperiously marched to the other officers, who'd just finished the interrogation of his sister Patricia and Dominic, who were all crestfallen.

"Agent Butcher," one of the officers reported. "These two have passed the lie test – and proven themselves innocent of Ben DePaula's crimes."

Ben quaked. They didn't deny …

"So, it's all a big mistake," Keller said, his lips a rictus. "First things first. We need to find this Tara character and Gladius, the candlelight suspect. According to the description Patricia DePaula and Dominic O'Leary have given us, it's more than enough to go by. Brianna has also to report that she may have found Gladius' address. We will get to him and interrogate him about Tara, too, to see if this *crap* world is smaller than we thought." Keller, vitriolic, pointed at Ben. "But this *man* needs to be arrested. He has been hampering a police investigation, thinking he had the right to harm an innocent citizen to find his daughter."

Two police escorted a man into the room. The man's face struck Ben as familiar. The one man assigned to killing Joseph DePaula, the man Ben had been looking for from the start.

His head was down, but he blasted out a laugh – the laugh of Ian Mastemah was rumbling and wretched.

Brianna appeared at Keller's side, and she stood very close – close enough that it made Ben twitch. She read out from a piece of paper, declaring Ian Mastemah charged for homicide.

Ian chortled, his bloodshot eyes glazed.

Suddenly, Keller rammed into Ian. Brianna aimed her gun at Ian from behind.

"All right, let's get to the point, agent!" Keller spat. "This is so unprofessional! Why did you kill Joseph DePaula? Is the CIA meddling in this dirty game on purpose?"

Ian remained speechless, slumping his head, and not reacting even when he was shaken by the FBI agent. The aquiline man seemed disturbingly at ease, not saying a word. Keller's lips quivered with impatience.

"Don't you bloody waste my time!" Keller growled. "Why did you kill Joseph DePaula?"

A wide villainous smile split Ian's face. "We just want you to know who needs rights. You wouldn't assault an officer of the law, would you?"

"Shut up! I want the truth!"

"You can't handle the truth," Ian whispered wearily. "Is this how you treat Jews? Anyone who's guilty?"

Keller was silent, but he glanced at Ben's wife, staring down at the barrel of her gun. He appeared … worried. Brianna's face remained hard and imperious.

A cackle came out of Ian's throat, rattling with fluid. "Darkness abides in us all. It's just politics, Keller. George Bush, Moshe Katsav, Saddam Hussein. Our only source of salvation is to seek the advantage wherever we can get it. This Realm – existence – is our enemy." He gazed at Brianna. "The Powers of the Void thirst for chaos and disorder, and there is nothing you can do about it."

Ian nudged Brianna's chest – her breast – as Keller hauled Ian by the collar and slammed him down onto the desk, into the wall and into the chair that toppled back with him. Within a second, Ian's smile vanished.

"You know," Keller said coldly, his face pale, his eyes gritty stones. "I really don't like tough talk with pigs like you. Put him in custody."

Three police officers hauled Ian back into the jail ward, handcuffing him. Keller wiped his hands on his pants, gaze swinging from Ben to Brianna. Then, to Ben's horror, Keller's hands touched his wife's shoulders, saying softly, "You okay?"

What in Heaven's name was Keller trying to do? Ben felt that whatever this act of chivalry was, he had no choice but to assume a type of betrayal.

Cleo and James Casbolt had done it before to him, and now *Brianna?*

"No," Ben snarled, breath shaky. "No."

Keller made an angry sigh, glancing at Brianna, who met Ben with a complex stare. "What did you say?" Keller said, scowling.

"What have you done, Brianna?" Ben whispered with rage and hurt. "I did the right thing. Thomas Jones tried to kill me."

Keller rolled his eyes. He raised a hand to his temple, regathering his poise, tucking a strand of hair behind his ear.

"I was only …" Ben lost the ability to speak. The room itself seemed to compress him from the ambivalence that overshadowed it. His sister and her boyfriend had wry body language, looking distant and embarrassed. They, too – his family – had betrayed him.

"No …" He let out a stale breath. "Brianna? What have you—"

Brianna swallowed hard. She looked stressed at what she was about to do, but remained tentative. An exhale of agony seized Ben as he began to quake. "This is the most logical deduction, Ben," she interjected. "You have committed an offence, not just against Thomas Jones, but against me. You know I'm the law here?" She paused, her throat undulating. "Ben, you have been accused, and the allegations are known! So now, I'm going to arrest you. Please, keep calm and—"

"NO!" Ragged breaths battering him, Ben saw the eyes. So many eyes in the heads of people who formed judgements, like thousands of mosquitoes all sucking out his blood, all draining him at once, reducing him, watching him. *Always watching.* He could not escape the freakin' *Truman Show!*

Anger. His own anger felt at everyone. All opinionated. All against him.

"What *the hell are you saying,* yah freakin' bitch? I'm innocent!" Ben laughed. Two officers had to grapple with him, holding him tight, but they underestimated his strength, and with one arm he reeled free, prying them off, pushing Brianna away from trying to get to him with handcuffs. Suddenly, his wife kicked him in the groin; then, wrapping her arm around Ben's neck, she strangled him.

Ben couldn't breathe. His wife was strong, and he floundered in panic.

"For the love of God!" Keller snapped. "Ben, you have crossed the line! Enough!"

Ben refused to back down. He stared the agent down, getting so close that their noses almost touched. "You're not going to stop, are you?" Keller breathed coldly.

"You don't get it," Ben gasped, sweating, struggling, panting. "I am a parent."

"You *knew* what you were doing kidnapping Thomas. You *knew* it would get you into this mess!" With that, Keller threw a punch into Ben's stomach. He gasped, roaring for breath that didn't come. He was suffocating. He doubled over, closing his eyes, hearing Brianna rattling the handcuffs.

"That's for your negligence," Keller spat, massaging his fist. "You *failed* Veronica." Brianna let Ben go from the headlock, holding his wrists.

Another wife. Gone. Just for trying to find his daughter. Hell …

Ben's gnarled hands closed into fists.

Brianna stared at those hands, stared at those fists – weapons she knew could damage her, staring wide-eyed with fear, as if staring at a stranger's hands, skeletal and dead, attached on her husband's arms.

With one hand, Brianna raised her gun slowly at Ben.

"Sit down," Brianna said dully. "Whatever you do, don't—"

Surging with fear, Ben punched Brianna, winding her. She stumbled into the chair, dropping the gun. Keller jumped in, but Brianna was already scrambling on her feet, facing Ben, who attacked ruthlessly. Rage filling his heart, he evaded Keller, shoving him with an elbow strike. A police officer swung a claw at him, cutting his face with his nail. Ben didn't feel it. Wringing his hands and growling, Keller gripped Ben's hands, but he roared, tearing out of Keller's grip, grasping for Brianna, who evaded, darting for her weapon, aiming at Ben.

"What the fu—"

A rough arm smothered Ben, headlocking him.

"Brianna, protocols!" Keller shouted from behind. "Protocols!"

As Ben fought, his vision tunnelled. Only Brianna's stupefied face behind the gun met him. He could tell she was panicking. Muffled, Ben in the middle of a tangle of arms, hands, bodies and shouts, he held off as many agents as possible. He was almost *enjoying* this rough brawl, heart overflowing with fury.

"Brianna!" Keller yelled dangerously. "Drop your weapon! Now! For goodness—"

"Yes, Brianna, drop your weapon!" Ben derided mockingly. "You assaulted your husband! *Assaulted!*"

Sweat pearled her blanched forehead. Panting, she let her hands lower the gun as Ben burst free from his captor. He tucked Brianna's gun arm into the crook of his arm, smashing a right fist into Brianna's gut. The thrill of the fight filled him, the intensity stronger than any coordinated one.

He seized her by the throat, twisting her around, pinning her back against his chest. The arm he disabled, he disarmed, pressing the gun into her jaw. People from all over jumped at him, hollering, begging, pleading for him to let her go.

Screw you. Screw you. Screw you. Screw you.

With a trembling hand, Ben rammed into everyone like a boulder, smashing his way through the crowd into the open, into the night outside, dragging a woman at gunpoint. No one dared come near him, for they feared if they did, a woman of noble rank would die at the hands of a man.

"Hey! *Hey!*" He shouted to the world. "Look! Look at this woman – a fugitive of the law! She tried to arrest her own husband! She's forsaken her daughter! How is this acceptable?" He attempted to add as much insult to injury as possible done unto him, for none of it could be rectified any other way. Ben *seriously* wanted to snap her neck. Oh, he loved how he could feel her fingernails desperately digging into his forearm as he constricted.

"*Let her go!*" Keller screamed, storming out of the station, as he aimed his gun at Ben, his light-brown hair like talons draped over his forehead. Ben grinned at the Mexican stand-off.

"Freeze!" A squad of police flanked Ben, their guns pointed. "Let the woman go!"

Ben set his jaw, his finger hovering above the trigger, slowly walking back into the carpark, where his truck had been towed.

Ben's heart palpitated in his chest. *Man, I'm so stuffed.* But the Actionman often got stuffed in movies. Officers swarmed around him in dark blue, ordering the beleaguered bystanders to stay away. The thrill of action infused Ben then, numbing him, as he plotted a reckless stunt in his mind.

"Let her go!" Keller shouted again, shaking his gun, but Ben didn't budge. He plotted.

"Make me."

"You son of a—"

"*Make me!*"

Brianna drew in a sharp breath, driving her elbow into Ben's side. She grunted, slashing her nails across his arm. Ben gave her a final kick, Brianna's gun still in his hand. He scrambled off, diving beside the nearest car as the guns fired.

"Get him! Don't let him get away!"

Staying low, Ben pelted, swift as the wind. Used to playing robber and cop action films, he easily scaled the fence. *Yeah, might as well go up in flames, then.*

Bullets from misfired guns popped behind. Adrenaline breath raging in his ears, his feet beating against the pavement, he reached his truck, ripped open the door, started the engine with the wired spark and sped off.

The policemen swarmed around him, banging on the bonnet, but he ran them over. Foot like a brick, he slammed the accelerator, zooming right past, causing them to scatter.

Flying over the grass island, he cut through the carpark and sped down onto the highway, slipping into the gap in the stream of traffic, beeping cars in his wake. He gripped the wheel hard. The engine growled. Wind whipped through the window in squalls. Ben thought he had it all easy, when at the next intersection, a police car flew across to cut him off.

Ben cursed, spinning his wheel, lurching to the right on North Seventh Street, which headed out towards the airport to his left. He barely dodged the police car, sideswiping it. As his tyres screamed, he saw flashing flares of red and blue. A second car, turning up right next to him on the wrong side of the road, sped towards him. It caused havoc in the oncoming traffic, and many cars swivelled off the road to make way for the police. Ben laughed, throwing his body to the left as he swung his wheel to the left, knocking off his pursuer.

Punching the gears and kicking the accelerator, his engine blurting, Ben braced against his seat as he wove between cars in front. He swung to the wrong side of the road, overtook, swinging right back into the right lane. The police car did the same, keeping up the chase.

He barrelled past the industrial sites, and before Ben, the highway straddled over the Deer Valley Reservoir, forming a bridge. The only upcoming turn was to the left, turning into a shipping container storage yard.

Time for a technique.

Ben skidded to a stop, pressing the brake but not completely, using his other foot to fluctuate the accelerator at the same time – weaving into the intersection. With a flick of his hands on the wheel, Ben nimbly overtook a car, startling the driver and the police car pursuing. Ben ran over the clear zone at the fork in the road, then threw himself back onto the main road, taking off ahead.

It was too late for the police car to follow and brake. Another car turning in from the driveway out of the shipping container storage skidded over the clear zone. In Ben's rear-view mirror, the speeding police car hit the other car. It flipped into the air, tossing debris with a popping crash, then slammed onto the road, spinning upside down, blocking both intersection and highway.

Actionman! Victorious, Ben took a deep lungful of fresh air.

The smell of burned rubber rushed through Ben's nose as he roared off into the night. He didn't realise that he was chortling nonstop as if he were an excited child. Oh, the smell of burned rubber on the tarmac. He had forgotten how much stunt driving invigorated him!

The FBI were *wrong*. The world was wrong, wronging him ultimately. He would adapt again and go into obscurity. He would find Veronica himself.

"They will know what the world did to a man," Ben muttered randomly, easing down his thundering heart. "They will know what they did wrong. After grooming me, they molest me. Screw this world. Who can be friends with the world? I'll show them. I will find Veronica another way."

And where would he go? Where would he hide and run from the government that wanted to get him? He couldn't pay taxes now; no, he only had his truck – yet if he kept on driving without stopping, at some point, eventually, he was going to need to fill up his tank with gas, but surely his goddamn face would get him caught at any venue. He needed to find Veronica …

Mulling over his stressful predicament, the radio drew Ben's attention from his anxiety. A pastor sounded in the middle of a sermon.

Well, what's fascinating in the First Century all the way through the Middle Ages is that the drug of choice in the religious community was pride. The drug of choice was politics and pride. The idea is that I am superior, and we need a collective centralised authority with rules to rule the world, because we like the dopamine feeling of being over our subjects. So, what I've seen in this Hebrew Roots Movement is a bunch of people, especially young people, coming out of churches with their propositional theologies, which have become mental masturbation – you control an imaginary relationship with God. They are all assiduously seeking for that high, rather than the Most High …

He listened, and listened keenly, and eventually, at the end of the talk, found out the pastor's name: Rob Heller, and the address to his place was Fellowship of the Way, Tucson. Down south from Phoenix.

Ben still felt nothing. No satisfaction of emotion. Only the tautness in the muscles in his forearms, where his veins puffed and congealed, his sweaty hands gripping the leathery steering wheel. The thrumming of the air from the window gushed; its cool blaze eddying around past him in the darkness as his car cut through the highway, the dead world disappearing behind him.

51

SEVERING TIES

"I trod them in my anger
   and trampled them in my wrath;
their juice spattered on my garments,
   and stained all my apparel.
For the day of vengeance was in my heart,
   and my year of my redeemed had come.
I looked, but there was no one to help;
   I was appalled, but there was no one to uphold …
I trampled down the peoples in my anger;
   I made them drunk in my wrath,
and I poured out their lifeblood on the earth."
   —From the Scroll of Isaiah, the prophet's disciples, c. 740 – c. 540 BCE. The apocalypse of the Messiah.

In the early silent morning, as dawn spread forth its rosy fingers across the sky, Judd Pounders strolled underneath the shadow of the Eye of the Army at the entrance to the Fort Huachuca Museum Annex building.

He often entered the museum – the history and what had come before him soothed his mind – for the struggle to free the Marine Corps out of the hands of the Alliance had worn Judd down to bare bones. He felt so alone in this struggle of honour – even though he felt glad that Joshua got out of this state, departed to live in the Pacific Northwest. "Oregon," he had said, on the day of his flight. "To attend university and study, to make the most of life." Judd felt proud of him. In the end, Judd's hope was that none of the veteran marines back living their lives would have to be enmeshed in this mess Ben had fallen into.

Time blended, and frozen in dark flint, the statue looked on ahead. The Apache native scout knelt, guiding in front of the buccaneering navy officer, gruff, with a drooping moustache holding a pair of binoculars in one hand and the other grasping his metal coat. Shaded from the southern sun, tattered here and there with a filthy trickle of bird droppings, he wore a wide-brimmed hat, gazing ahead, following the sacred paths. Trusting, assessing, surveying the unknown land, through the eyes of the Native American. A crescent frown imprinted that whimsical wise face of the Apache, and a rifle leaned on his thigh.

At the corner of Judd's eye, an elderly man appeared in corporal form on the trail towards the museum, walking slowly towards Judd. He had the look of a Native American wise grandfather with a carved faced, diminutive, with long silvery silk hair reaching his shoulders, his face a warm brown map of experience – the Apache statue come alive. He walked with an easy gait, wore a flannel shirt with navy blue, red and purple patterns across it, and baggy trousers. Judd turned to meet the Native American's enigmatic presence.

"Good morning, sir," the man said gently and warmly. "There was a man I suspected you did not see going into that building over there near your office. He has been very curious."

Unsure about what he meant, or whether he was talking about himself, Judd looked over his shoulder.

"I'm …" Judd swallowed, looking at the Native American. It seemed rather odd, for he did not normally meet with Native Americans, and for one to consult him now, in the early hours of dawn, made him more nervous than he had been when he woke up, dreading about what Alfred Bonner would do to him, about what he had told him about the Cabal coming to get him. Judd found himself saying, "Good morning, but … I am not sure what you are talking about. Who are you?"

Don't tell him about the CD.

"My name is Albert Tobadzistsini," the man uttered, taking a step closer, a subtle grin forming on his chiselled face. "Navajo First Nations Chief medicine man." Albert's eyes acutely observed the Eye of the Army statue. "Strange people have been sent looking for something. And I believe it has to do with the CD."

Judd's hand went to his coat pocket, his blood turning to ice. "How did you …?" Judd sighed.

Bonner will kill me.

Judd gawked at the man's face in trepidation, craning his neck around to see if anyone was around listening to this conversation. At that instant, down at the back of the building, was a man, shadowy and ominous, wrapped in a heavy trench cloak, walking past into the back of the building without a glance. Judd's mouth went dry. The scent of hair gel whiffed into his sinuses.

"The Cabal."

Albert shook his head gravely. "I'll tell you; they are unwise."

"Who are the Cabal? Why are they enemies of the Alliance?"

Albert's mouth formed into an austere smirk. "We need to talk, friend. But for now, I'll say this. The Cabal … the way of the Cabal is absolutes. They're exclusive, desiring the residue that remains. The outcasts, the few elites out of the masses. The Alliance, on the other hand, gathers together. It's a hierarchy of inclusivity that reeks of relativism. All of it is foolishness." Albert sighed, exhausted. "I don't fear intimidation. I'm just too old for shenanigans."

"All right, Albert," Judd said dryly. What could an old Navajo Chief do? He had a part to play in this nonsensical game, no doubt. He would know about Ben, Brianna and Bonner's little trip to the Grand Canyon. "I'm going to make sure that man there is questioned."

The reply came with a confident nod.

Judd took a step back, and giving Albert a final sharp glance, he went towards the back of the escape. Power walking with a skip, he slipped through the door, entering the bleak concrete stairwell. He climbed up the steps towards the dim light, feet echoing loudly as he climbed. Then, when the boom of a closing door clapped like thunder down towards the left, Judd doubled back, scaling the stairs. Heart beating in his chest, he reached the second floor below. His hand grasped the knob, but it opened on its own. A force drove him into a wall.

Gasping, he resisted desperately, his legs stagnant, his arms feeble, as the man in black held him firmly. Brown hair, a bleak morbid mask.

Judd grabbed the man's wrists and twisted them. Ramming his shoulder recurringly into the attacker's face, he grunted, stumbling. Grasping the shoulder, Judd went to throw his knee into him—

His head flung back, his breath cut off abruptly, neck constricting in tight pain. Instinctively, he went to pry off the muscular arm wrapped around his neck. Judd slammed into the wall, crushing the attacker. Judd rammed back again, but his neck jerked tighter, constricting his breath.

No thought raced into his head. Judd's vision tunnelled as a second attacker bludgeoned him with punches, tossing him to the side. Pain built upon pain, until he weakly yielded, flopping helplessly.

Let them kill me … Let them.

He jerked to the side with a snort, just as the second attacker sent a recalcitrant hand into his coat pocket, tearing it inside out.

The CD!

By some burst of strength, Judd hissed, smashing his elbow into a third attacker, who held him back. An icy claw grasped Judd's face, making him gasp from the shock. The hand smothered his face, pinning it to the wall, yet it was as hard and cold as metal. If it wanted to, it could have crushed his skull. Robotic fingers dug into his skin.

Judd's eyes widened, jerking aside, overwhelmed as he crumpled to the ground, the cold steel arm letting him go. He glimpsed the attacker wearing a balaclava – face hidden except for his turquoise blue eyes.

The three attackers in black scrambled, their feet scuffing the ground, clapping in an atrocious applause of Judd's luck.

He felt a sting near his eyebrow, nausea afflicting him. Judd found himself exhaling and inhaling precipitously. He vaguely felt the tightness on his neck and the side of his face. It hurt so much that Judd groaned in a heap, trying to find the ground with his hands.

Goddamn it. That was stupid. Why did I follow the bastard?

The CD!

As he panicked, another sonorous door swung open. He snorted uneasily, closing his eyes, leaning against the wall – he felt so old, so weak. Someone lumbered up the stairs, easily.

Judd tried to think, but the Navajo Chief held him up with tender hands. A finger dabbed slightly on the scuff blister on his eyebrow.

"What did they do?" Albert intoned, his tranquil voice an ointment. "Are you okay?"

"They – took it," Judd rasped. "They got the CD." He stared at Albert, filled with dread about what Bonner would do now and wondering what truth this Navajo knew.

"Maybe you should be more careful when making deals with strangers next time, friend," the Chief spoke slowly. "Truth is rising out of the sand. The truth about people, the Alliance and … about Ben."

Now at the mercy of this man, Judd stared at him. *If I have the First Nations people on my side, I have thousands of years of ownership and power. I don't even have half of this mystery sorted, but if Albert is willing … I need to do something. We're done, Bonner! It's over!*

Judd rose to his feet, his midriff and head throbbing with bruises. Albert brought him back up the stairs with a strength that belied his elderly body, leading him to the exit.

—

This time, Judd Pounders was ready to confront Alfred Bonner. For too long, he had controlled the marines. For too long, he had let agents like Ian Mastemah gain access to personal information, leading to the murder of Joseph DePaula and the disappearance of Veronica DePaula. It would be only honourable to respect the ingenuity of Captain Ben to get rid of Alfred Bonner, and above all, save Fort Huachuca from being destroyed.

He will save this Marine Corps – they would be better off without the Alliance cult scapegoating Ben and God Almighty.

Alfred Bonner slowly opened the door into Judd's office. "Earlier this year, I gave you a deal." The scar on his face seemed to twitch slightly as he spoke. His lifeless moribund gaze deep set in his statuesque face analysed the red grazes on Judd's own face. "If you train soldiers for the Shinar Mission, you could establish peace in Iraq while we – the Alliance – fulfil our interests. Do you remember our deal in December 2002?"

"I remember," Judd breathed, rising from his chair. "The only problem is, without Hussein, Iraq is in civil war. So the deal is null and void."

"I see," Bonner growled. "It wasn't all successful, but that is life." His icy eyes met Judd's. "Some interesting phenomena occurred over there that spilt into this predicament."

Judd glared at Bonner, mostly at his irritating stiffness, which did not even look human. "It only exacerbates after every move you make, Alfred. What do you want? The CD and everything associated with it has ruined the life of Ben DePaula."

"I already have what I need." Bonner actually chuckled. "I do not negotiate with punks like you who bluff me."

Judd lowered his gaze to the floor. *He knows!* "Bluff you?"

"You lost the CD. My eyes and ears say it's in the hands of the Thelema." Bonner sneered nonchalantly. "You failed." As Judd took a step back, Bonner made up for it by taking a step forward, ferocious ambition burning from those light eyes and that menacing scar on his face. "You ever thought about what it was like to die in a car crash?" he said coldly. "Even a heart attack is not uncommon for a man your age. Think I'm bluffing?"

Judd's confidence fell apart. *How could he have known so fast?*

"What do you know about Ben?" Judd hissed. "Why do you want him so badly?"

"You saw the head-camera footage. Ben's in allegiance with the Galactic Tyrant. It is seldom for men to survive death, but these are the ones I want. There are many like Ben. We do not know why Captain DePaula had such luck. Is he bonded with a spirit? The Galactic Tyrant seems to be moving his pieces into a strategic formation."

What proof did this moron have that the Galactic Tyrant was the God of the Hebrew Bible? Of Christianity? The Great Spirit of the Navajo? "What were we even here for again, Director? The Shinar Mission?"

A flare of irksomeness fused in Bonner's face, then faded as soon as it came. "You heard about the giant flown out of Afghanistan? Indeed, *you* were on station duty there to cover it up. This is why I made a deal for Mission Shinar, Judd Pounders. The giant and the head-camera footage is precisely *why* I've come to protect the US marines. I am doing the Alliance's will to protect your nation from the Tyrant's forces. I will forge a new future for the twenty-first century, where there is no more child trafficking, no more health care injustice, no more climate, social and political crises. When the Galactic Tyrant comes, the whole world can put down their differences and come together to face a common enemy." Bonner loomed over Judd. "Going against me, you're hampering humanitarian progress. Ben searches for the truth, breaking the law. He wants to know why we are keeping it quiet, for the sake of public safety – that is the simple truth Ben *will never* know. This is why I wanted to protect the CD, because on it … is data about the Nephilim and the Underworld. You failed me, Judd Pounders. You failed to stop Ben and failed to keep important information safe."

He was correct. The truth had been revealed. Judd had totally misunderstood Ben – he wasn't an honourable man. He was a loser who scapegoated an innocent person in order to cathartically unleash his wrath and frustration. Ben had no honour. He was a reckless actor who did things without thinking. He didn't care about anyone except for himself. He didn't even care for his daughter and for his wife. If he did, he would be at home, helping Brianna and Keller investigate, looking for Veronica. But Ben thought, as prideful as he was, that he could do better than them all.

Ben had failed Judd, and Judd felt a fool for trusting this man. He felt betrayed, sickened that he'd been deceived by Ben's glamorous and charming character – a lie.

Yet Judd wondered. Twice dead, and *still* going? Once at Haditha Dam, he had contended with Ben's soldiers, who had set up a vigil for the captain presumed dead. Now Judd almost felt *ashamed* for not giving in to his intuition when he watched the soldiers get on with their duties, still sparing an hour to watch and wait, despite weeks going by. It amazed Judd how he had been proven wrong. Now he found himself in this position, holding on to the same faith as his soldiers.

Father killed. Daughter kidnapped. Hunted by assassins and chased down by police, torturing Thomas Jones; Benjamin continued to fight. Ben was *terrified.* He was outraged at what was happening to him, and the Alliance and the Cabal exploited that reaction. Judd thought he wouldn't do any better if put in the same predicament.

And in that way, the "angelic being" in the head-camera footage did reveal something about Ben that *was* special.

Alfred Bonner wants to scapegoat God and his images. Alfred and the Powers want to substitute God with images in a human for theriomorphic form – an etiolated mechanical Beast, Albert had said.

"Nah," Judd whispered. "You failed *me*. When you knew something, you refused to talk. You made plans and didn't care to check in with us."

"Phoenix prosecutors recommend that you, as Ben's colonel, are to send Ben to military prison. Surely, we can agree on that."

"I can. And I agree. This is a military issue."

"Reports from the police prove my point. I'll be the eyes and ears for the FBI for that matter." Abruptly, Bonner turned his back, gliding towards the door.

"I'm not finished yet!" Judd exclaimed.

The weakness of Alfred Bonner depending desperately on the marines! He had the audacity to admit that Judd had failed, and he still wasn't willing to give up on him? Bonner's stubbornness to Judd made him fume with anger. The ruthless, parasitic man had been working behind closed doors, and after admitting his honesty about breaches of the deal, Judd, in his fear, still agreed to obey Alfred Bonner's authority as if none of that mattered. Judd had to man up and discard any association with Bonner and his Alliance *now*. The Marine Corps didn't need this coercion. Paranoia drove these people in the Light Alliance who thought the end of the world was nigh. And that, *in itself,* as the end to the means, was *dangerous* and *compulsive.*

It's time to end this! "Albert," Judd called to the front office door. It opened and the Navajo Chief stood tall, rivalling Bonner, despite not even coming close to the height of the giant. Walking into the office with an air of confidence, Albert stood next to Judd.

"What are you doing?" Bonner said, shocked.

I've got this, Judd lauded smugly in his head. *And you have lost!*

Standing at Albert's side, Judd exchanged an agreeing glance. The Chief crossed his arms across his chest. He had a stern disappointed countenance, his wrinkles forming a frown.

"This is the part where you kiss my ass goodbye," Judd said to Bonner, grinning.

Bonner lashed out. "You—"

"*You* listen to *me*, you son of a bit—"

Bonner bumped him in the chest with a force that knocked out his breath. "*Don't* you become an adversary to me, Colonel." His blue eyes scorched as burners; they fixed on the Chief within hateful dark caves. "Why have *you* done this to me, Albert? You have no idea what is on that CD. The Powers. The Dragons …"

"My name is Albert Tobadzistsini, and I am a traditional custodian of the land and of the secrets it holds, passing down its knowledge from generation to generation. It is me who you want to talk to." The mature power in the Chief's voice made Judd smirk incessantly.

"If the FBI come down with a case," Judd said, "then Albert here can fluently recite chapter and verse, *everything* on your precious disc, to the public, exposing your worthless agenda! *Arhat!*"

Bonner sniffed in derision. "But those men who took the CD were my enemies. Nobody escapes from the tangle of the Cabal deep state." He stopped pacing. "Nobody," he added.

Albert confronted him. "Remember that, in our tradition, we orally pass down the fire of our stories to the children. The CD was encrypted with the language of the Holy People – *Diyin Diné* – who gave it to their children – the *Diné*. The Navajo. This language was secret. Protected from your evil. Only the holy and the righteous know the sacred language. The Cabal have the disc, but they will never know how to decipher it. The knowledge of culture that I have on the CD has gone beyond you and the Cabal. Beyond what is shaken. It's in the hands of Nihitaa'."

By mentioning the name of the Galactic Tyrant so-called, the intensity in Bonner's face clenched, forehead pearling with sweat. A first.

Beat him, Albert! Show him!

Albert met him just as confidently, which made Alfred Bonner's lewdness puerile. "I promise you," Bonner said. "The Light Alliance and the Native Americans are good friends, good partners, good brothers for growth."

"You seriously think scapegoating God is going to bring about social harmony?" Judd said, crossing his arms, raising his chin. "Don't even try. Because you will make an enemy of the Native Americans. If you lay another hand on my marines, on Ben's family or on the Navajo, I swear to God, I will personally broadcast to the world what your cult is all about." He let those words sink in good. After all, Albert had revealed to Judd, he'd been given the truth on a golden platter. Judd now understood this incredible global conspiracy, this secret society based on fighting paedophiles, was seeking to unite the world by accusing and destroying a particular group of people who worshipped God, convincing everyone to see them as a fifth column.

For the longest time, he saw Bonner struggle vigorously to maintain his poise, and for the first time, Judd had answers about what this moron was all about. "Welcome to the twenty-first century," Judd said. "The era of information. Am I bluffing now?"

Realising he was exposed, Bonner's eyes went wide. Judd struggled to keep himself from chuckling in smug triumph. Bonner spun, storming out of the room, slamming the door shut.

Satisfied and free, Judd sighed, meeting Albert, who nodded appreciatively, his arms crossed over his chest. Suddenly, Albert chuckled. "Mission accomplished," the medicine man said.

Judd gave the medicine man a hug, thanking him with all his heart.

52

APOCALYPSE NOW

Dublin, September 2003

"People slander whatever they do not understand, and the very things they do understand by instinct – as irrational animals do – will destroy them. Woe to them! They have taken the way of Cain; they have rushed for profit into Balaam's error; they have been destroyed in Korah's rebellion.

These people are blemishes at your love feasts, eating with you without the slightest qualm – shepherds who feed only themselves. They are clouds without rain, blown along by the wind; autumn trees, without fruit and uprooted – twice dead. They are wild waves of the sea, foaming up their shame; wandering stars, for whom blackest darkness has been reserved for ever.

Enoch, the seventh from Adam, prophesied about them: 'See, the Lord is coming with thousands upon thousands of his holy ones to judge everyone, and to convict all of them of all the ungodly acts they have committed in their ungodliness, and of all the defiant words ungodly sinners have spoken against him.'"

—From the Epistle of Jude, c. 65 CE.

With duty done and the Marine Corps giving him a silver star and ribbon for Humanitarian honours for saving the Iraqi children and restoring the Baghdad Museum, James Casbolt sat in a bar with his Aes Sidhe friends for a drink. He'd at first been greatly in need of stimuli to distract him. He had proven much – his actions proved he was mirroring his initial intent from the beginning.

He could actually *do it*. He could do good and fight evil without making the same sins of the past. And for the first time in a long time, it made him feel good about himself.

Michael Prince, in his mind, was the one who helped Casbolt. If it wasn't for that alter, he would have failed and sought death before life.

Though his guilt remained, it did not reign.

Last week, Miles Johnson from the online Bases Project interviewed Casbolt at the UFO Conference Panel with famous people and super soldiers like Mat Tod and Duncan MacKinnon of Bear Peninsula of the *Blajini* Aes Sidhe, for the first time, airing Casbolt's testimony to a live audience while also selling his book *Agent Buried Alive* to thousands! Many of the survivors of Mk-Ultra mind-control programmes who faced pure evil were so thankful for his book, some of them wept before him and hugged him for his courage and strength in overcoming the Bleakness and grievous government systems.

And yet, Casbolt still wondered, would this be enough to appeal his crimes to the UN and transgressions of the Antarctic Treaty? Ultimately, his tale – his biography – raised a generation to learn from his miseries and seek to not increase their own and those of others. Casbolt could begin a new chapter in his life – though the Redlion would still be a part of him, he felt more in control of himself.

Casbolt downed his mug of beer, refreshing his confident mind, fond of the din of the raucous bar of shouting men and clinking glasses.

Dublin was such a cosmopolitan city – it blended the traditional with the contemporary. The archaic with the liberal. The future of the Celts – as defined by the Nindingir and the Druids – fused the worlds of the enigmatic, as well as embracing cultural diversity. The Aes Sidhe Casbolt knew were slowly becoming secular. But at the same time, they seemed knee bent on rejecting such multiculturalism in Antarctica.

But Casbolt had to live life – no one knew the day or the hour of the Galactic Tyrant's invasion – so one had plenty of time to eat, drink and be merry. The Aes Sidhe were becoming like the rest of the Irish, Welsh, Scottish and the wider European world.

A bunch of Aes Sidhe as drunk as anyone could be with ale, beer and whiskey got around a circle of onlookers, clearing tables for their dance. The Aes Sidhe were performing the wildest kicking Scottish dance he had ever seen. They tucked their arms straight out under their chins, horizontally to the ground. They stamped their feet, then they leapt high and squatted, and immediately kicked up again, faster and faster, or turning around, some doing backflips. Seven or eight ordinary Dublin citizens watched on with gaping mouths, and some drunks, too, sat nursing bruises and broken bones from trying the dance, all the while cheering and laughing.

"Casbolt, mate," Blake Gates, the Lithuanian Chief of the McMurdo Dry Valleys, said with his lively West Country English accent, spinning his mug of cider in his hands. "So how was Iraq?"

"It was an Indiana Jones adventure, if you ask me," Casbolt said.

Blake chortled. "Really? You know any word of what's going on in Antarctica?"

Kenneth Marrow, a six-foot-tall boxer with dreadlocks and a deep British accent, spat out, cackling. "Eh! An elephant seal bull romped over a group of king penguins. It was *very* bad! They were all caught in rocks, and the bull charged, crushing the bastard birds in his anger. Brutal, man."

That was it. Blake let out a crackling snort, much like an elephant seal.

"Antarctica?" Casbolt responded and saw across the room the girl Meredith walk into the bar. He remembered her, his crush at school. She sat across from him with her older Aes Sidhe brother, Duncan MacKinnon, and his family, mingling with the circus crowd.

"Rumour says it that the old Fomorian Balor is up to no good," Blake said. "Delbaeth the Nindingir has been saying these things lately. And also, they just made some cool new ice core discoveries."

Nothing interesting besides rumours of Balor – and rumours were seldom true – so Max Spiers wouldn't need Casbolt to aid him at this time. "But we are not going to Antarctica, Gates," Casbolt said. "We're in Dublin." He kept Meredith in his peripheral vision – her face was flushed with mirth, laughing, her golden hair so fair, her face so handsome and austere. She had become very beautiful of body in the last few years.

"But what about Max—"

"Unfortunately, boys, we won't be going," Casbolt pressed. "I got in trouble last time I was there, so it is best that I don't go back. Besides, you've got new Iceni to train, Blake. And I ..." He swallowed. "I have a new life ahead of me." He gazed at Meredith; his heart leapt when her pretty blue eyes met his own. *I could have a family,* he thought.

Casbolt was able to pick up a whiff of Blake's cologne as he leaned back, glibly dropping his mug on the table. "James, you're into her, are you? You have plans?"

"Yeah, may as well." Casbolt hid his embarrassment by drinking his beer. How much of his interest in his new calling actually afforded to Max

Spiers' goal to create a new society based on sustainability and scientific research? It was a Nindingir experiment to say the least, to test humanity when the Galactic Tyrant came. With no politics, no religion, no war, no economic exploits, but united to fight climate change, focused on natural biological and geographical science. And some Celtic mysticism for those interested.

Casbolt often felt like half a man these days. An ordinary man named Michael Prince speaking truth and exposing deep underground military bases, the elite child sex trafficking ring, the Galactic Tyranny, as well as asking Meredith on a date, and, above all, his formal duty as Chief Agaid. Casbolt simply could not go back to the South Pole.

"Look, man, I don't know about you," Blake said, "but I'm just saying. Going back to Ant would be for the best. All right, Dublin is *average*. But Ant is an alien planet. I love it. It's an escape from boring civilisation, man!"

"Blake." Casbolt met his friend's eyes, whispering, "I want to have a social connection with other people. I *need* civilisation."

"How was that Puerto Rico guy that you said you met?"

"Julian? Hm, he had issues. *A lot* of them. It's because he has genetically modified Indigo Children chased down by the men in black."

"Men in black, eh?" Kenneth said. "They're still going around?"

"Yeah. To this day, I have no idea where they are. After Julian died at Haditha Dam, I've been trying to catch up with his maid and Canimao, his friend, to see how the Indigo Children are doing. They're struggling."

Julian and his Aes Sidhe daughters! What a perfect way to kill the mood – what a *perfect* subject to speak about at the table during merry drinking at the bar!

Kenneth and Blake likewise frowned, picking at their cups, glancing uneasily at the din of celebration and music in the background. "Erhm," Blake uttered. "I'm sorry to hear about that, man."

"I fear Julian's daughters will disappear," Casbolt said. "Without a trace. It's because they are Rh -Negative blood psychic Indigo Children, no doubt. You would think they would be able to find lost children in this world where governments have such a track record of storing everyone's information with satellite surveillance – it just doesn't make sense anyone could get lost in this world now. I don't know, but it's just strange to me when missing children's cases happen. It's very deliberate, I think, on the deep state's part. They *need* children on a national level in America alone. I could help the investigations, but David Paulides from Missing 411 is already on to all these cases. But… Yeah."

Kenneth followed Casbolt's glance and noticed how it occasionally tracked down Meredith sitting at the table across the room. The Parvus Perception alerted Casbolt.

"You want to talk to her? Go on," Kenneth said.

"Oh … I'm abstemious about it," Casbolt said.

"Come on," Blake said, nudging him. "She is young, slim and gorgeous; you can do it. She has a seat next to her. You're good friends with Meredith's brother. She will respect you."

Casbolt's nerves became like steel, his alter Michael Prince feeling tentative about going over to speak to the young woman.

Might as well say hi and get it over and done with. Confronting his byzantine emotions, Casbolt stood and walked across the dining room. Kenneth and Blake were snickering and whispering about him, but Casbolt ignored them, and took a deep breath, feeling hot and sweaty. He came over to Meredith MacKinnon's table and said, "Hello, Meredith. Hey, Duncan. How's it going?"

"Oh!" Duncan, looking up at him, laughed with mirth. He stood up and shook Casbolt's hand. He spoke with a gruff, bubbly voice, saying, "Everything is good! How's the Chief?"

"Surprisingly good!" Casbolt glanced at Meredith – her slender form, angular features and stunning vibrant blue eyes looking at him, her snow-white, blonde hair gorgeous and long. She smelled remarkably aromatic, and her expression was coy.

Casbolt smiled, beaming on the verge of laughter, and it made Meredith smile – a radiance that brought unimagined joy.

"Chief James," Meredith said perkily, standing up to give him a hug. "Nice to meet you again!"

"It's a pleasure, Meredith. Your brother has told me a lot about you." He spared a glance at her brother. "Some *interesting* things."

Meredith chuckled, her hand to her lips.

Agh, careful not to sound cringing, will you? Michael Prince said.

I am trying, Casbolt thought. *It's a new milestone for me, and I might as well ask her out.*

"So," Meredith said. "Have you and Duncan arranged to meet up in Antarctica at some point?"

"Yes, I will take care of that," Casbolt said, his palms sticky with sweat, his heart beating faster and faster as he stared face to face with this wonderful woman he'd known as a teenager. "You're … all well with your studies?"

"It's all well. I'm doing a trade and hope to become a mechanic. Duncan said I can be very useful and can get a new job in Antarctica."

"Good," Casbolt said. A mechanic woman – the Parvus instincts told him that she was honest, hardy and not afraid to get her hands dirty. She was diligent and had a great appreciation for responsibility. "I … uh … I …" *Am I responsible?*

He saw Meredith incline her head for clarity. Casbolt panicked.

"Uhm …" Casbolt's hand, slippery with perspiration, pulled out the chair. "Why don't we … sit down and have a drink? What do you think, Duncan?"

"Of course, of course," Duncan said, returning to his seat, speaking to his friends who said hi to Casbolt – they all made acquaintance and shook hands in greeting. As the others at the table engrossed themselves in conversation, Casbolt turned to Meredith sitting in front of him, her lovely smile enchanting and otherworldly. *Oh my God, she's beautiful! I can do this! I can find a soulmate! I can have a family! I will never be lonely again!*

Casbolt saw she was good in his eyes and went to take his chance.

"We should … meet up sometime. I would like to get you exclusive access to the Aes Sidhe bases in Antarctica. It's very restricted. Only a thousand people are allowed on the ice continent at any one time. Giving you a VIP ticket, I can show you around."

"Oh, that's sweet of you," Meredith said melodiously, leaning both of her hands on the table, her eyes beaming, smirking as if she were seriously interested in him. Casbolt sat back in his chair stiffly.

Casbolt beamed back at her for five seconds in awkward silence. "Would … next Saturday be a good time for you to book tickets? It's very expensive to go to Ant these days. Max Spiers might discount us. Uhm …" Casbolt became aware of his own voice – he was speaking clearly, but very slowly; he feared if he quickened his speech, he would stutter and make a great fool of himself.

Meredith hummed, hesitantly. "I will have to see what my plans are."

"Oh, then I can come later. Uhm. I'm sure Max and … uhm, Duncan will be willing to offer you a job and … uhm—"

"James," Meredith said, smiling with snow-white teeth. "Sunday is free next week. I'm willing." Then, from out of nowhere, Meredith got out a pen, and clicking it, she scribbled her phone number down on the napkin, handing it over to Casbolt.

His mouth went dry. It took a great deal of unnecessary effort to restrain his hand from shaking. "Oh … uhm …" Casbolt swallowed, heart raging in his chest. *You … got her number? Spartan, you got a* girl's *number! You're in! She wants you!*

And I want her!

"Thanks," Casbolt said. "I will make sure I call you! May I borrow your pen?"

"Sure," she said perkily.

Then, without thinking, Casbolt took his napkin and wrote his number down for Meredith. Her cheeks started to colour now, making her adorable to look upon. "Now you can know when I am calling, so you better call me."

Meredith giggled with joy. "Yes, I will call you." She laughed, making Casbolt laugh with her. Then she stared into his eyes, and Casbolt looked at her too, studying how her freckles dusted her nose, how her eyebrows were slightly darker than her hair and her blithe face. The outside world – the din, the sounds of utensils and glasses clinking – faded, until Meredith was all that Casbolt could see. He would be ready to dedicate himself to her, to share his life with this extraordinary woman.

"Well …" Casbolt said, at a loss for words, lowering his glance.

Meredith bit her lower lip. They looked at each other uncertainly.

"Thank you so much, James. I'm looking forward to this job," Meredith finally said. "Duncan! Guess what? You will be floored by this. James is willing to offer me a job in Antarctica!"

"Is that so?" Duncan exclaimed. "That would be wonderful! So kind of you, Chief!"

Casbolt's heart was thundering ferociously – the adrenaline of battle infusing his body. The thrill was remarkable, blissful and pure. He wanted more of it.

"I … will order some drinks for us if you like?"

"Please," Meredith said happily, waving her elegant hand. "I'll like a lemon lime, please!"

So Casbolt ordered drinks for her and himself, but he couldn't help glancing back at his table of friends, who were trying to encourage and pamper him. Casbolt loved how Blake was raising his fists, screaming in silent victory, Kenneth smiling encouragingly, nodding his head.

Casbolt smiled back, feeling more alive than he had ever remembered in his entire life. *This … I am having the time of my life!*

After getting to know Meredith and her family, the MacKinnons, a bit more after having some drinks, and after saying their goodbyes before heading off, Casbolt went to the toilet as his phone rang. Once he washed his hands and saw who called, he answered it with a smile. "Hello, Max!"

"Hey, James." Max's stern voice sounded choppy from the other side. Max had been in the Pole for four winters straight. It had to be close to the Antarctic record for anyone living there for that long. "Hope you're do--- well."

"Thank you. It is the most excellent night," Casbolt said. "Look, Max, I'll make sure I'll take up some duties again, okay? But I sense something is wrong. Are you okay?"

"I'm fine," Max said. "Beata is doing really well, as is my newborn son Lauchlan."

"Congratulations, Max, my man! I was meaning to talk to you about it. All's well?"

"Yeah, Beata gave birth in the McMu---o Dry Valley base. It was scary and amazing all at once. I cannot wait for you to meet Lauchl—."

Casbolt walked into the male's bathroom waiting area for privacy. "So yeah, what else is going on there down at Ant?"

"The usual," Max Spiers continued. "The last four winters straight, I've been doing research. But … James. I'm go--- honest. I'm in need of your help. You've been evad--- me for too long."

"It's all my fault. I'm ruining you as—"

"James --- your insubordination has been enough already. I'm already at risk for what we did at Fenriskjeften."

"The Aquarians. New Swabia."

"I am trying to unite everyone to ke--- from hostilities. But after what you did to Tulugaak at Fenriskjeften, rumour has it that you are taking advantage of your leave, forfeiting the position of Chief Agaid because you are afraid to take the charges. I took care of your charges as best as I could."

"I'm sorry," Casbolt said. "This is the last thing you want, to be dealing with my issues. You have a baby to look after. That would have been *very* hard."

"Please. I wanted to remind you"—Max lowered his voice tenderly—"that there is no–ing to worry about. You are playing a dangerous game, James, spreading your book around. It will attract more enemies than –ke the masses. Listen --- me. Deprogramming is a phase. You will always be an Aes Sidhe. Your only escape is to Antarctica."

Casbolt swallowed, knowing a large part of what Max said was true. There was a part of him that did not want to go back to Antarctica, but he'd promised Meredith and now Max – who was a father – and he would need someone to fill in for him as Chief. For the problem in 2001 at Fenriskjeften, Max Spiers tried desperately to find loopholes in the Antarctic Treaty for the unofficial occupying of the unclaimed Marie Byrd Land for the super soldier programme to train, conduct genetic research and, surreptitiously, prepare for the Galactic Tyranny.

"Yes … I will come to Antarctica. I'm about to book tickets. But my book …" He sighed. "You never know what things are true these days. I want to do something to help without relapsing and getting triggered, Max. It's bad. It locks you up, and this pain eats you up until you faint."

"Do you ever wonder, James, ab--- a time where people look at the ways we have used, exploited and adapt--- Earth? We want enormous benefits, but of---- we forget that benefits of Earth's gift come --- cost. As we face a more precarious future, a coherent condominium of harmless---, and learning lessons from the past has never been so paramount. Aes Sidhe. The preppers for catastrophe."

"The Alliance is very far from that ideal vision, Max," Casbolt said. "I don't understand what the hell Bonner is thinking sometimes. He's not interested in Antarctica anymore. He's been meddling with everything in the Marine Corps and the Defence Department."

"Casbolt, I'm going to need you to do me a big favour. I'm going to need the Redlion again."

"I am like an animal," James Casbolt said. "I mean, when did people start calling me that, anyway?"

"That's not the ----. Though you are a warrior, deep down, you are good at heart. A head of the pride."

"Max, I'm telling you I'm dangerous. It only takes a small trigger and"— he snapped his fingers—"I've lost myself."

"Deprogramming is a natural phase. It is harder for some than it is for others."

"Okay, I will order the tickets. I will fly down when I can."

"Casbolt, don't hang up!" Max's voice took on a sterner tone. Casbolt froze then. He knew instantly, reading the intention behind the voice, that it carried asperity and anxiety, inferring something bad had happened. "What have you been getting up to in the last few months? What is it between you and Ben DePaula?"

Casbolt's blood went cold. "Ben DePaula? What? I don't understand. Do you mean going to Iraq? Yeah, we butted a few heads, but we resolved our differences. Most of this year, I haven't seen him. I've been getting to know Mere—"

"No, Casbolt. No, this is not acc---ptable! What have you been doing getting yourself into trouble?"

Casbolt stared at himself in the mirror, watching his face blanch, a sense of alarm and fear threading through him. "What? What are you talking about, Max?"

"Man, haven't you seen on the news?" Max said harshly. "Phoenix, Arizona! Ben's family! Thomas Jones looks *exactly* like you! This ---ast year, he's ---used and tortu--- by Ben DePaula and --- proven innocent, ---- ve kidnapped his daughter!"

It took a moment for Casbolt to take in all that information, then he threw back his head and laughed. "Max, come on, that's bogus! No one looks *exactly* like me! What prank are you trying to pull on me now? You know, I may have dissociative identity disorder, but I'm not *that* crazy! Kidnapping children!"

Strange glitching muffing sounds came from the other side of the phone. "I don't know. Just take a look for yourself in the news----. Thomas Jo--- is your exact lookalike."

"*Exact lookalike?*" Casbolt repeated, hardly believing a word. "What is this? You saying Thomas is my clone?"

"Casbolt, I don't know. The Nindingir have been talk--- about it *constantly*."

"Yeah, screw them," Casbolt said, fetching the newspaper on the counter. "It's all another scam about me. A troll discrediting me."

"No … James. He really does look like you."

"Who is this man?" Casbolt said, feeling cramps of worry seethe in his chest.

"Thomas Jones."

If that name was supposed to be important, it did not cause any trigger or any sort of adverse reaction – an unspooling of memories, lightheadedness or a fit. Nothing.

Then Casbolt turned to the page in the *Irish Independent* newspaper with the headline "WANTED, FAMOUS ACTOR AND HOLLYWOOD STUNTMAN BEN DEPAULA ACCUSED OF CIVILIAN ASSAULT AND DOMESTIC VIOLENCE IS STILL MISSING".

Casbolt read the whole article. The journalist was a woman, and, of course, she had extremely scathing remarks and biases about this "toxic white man" and the entire case in general. There was even a ridiculous reward for the person who found Ben DePaula. An *entire saga* had unfolded this year and was still unsolved; it involved Joseph DePaula, Ben DePaula, Veronica

DePaula, Zoe O'Leary, Brianna DePaula, Judd Pounders, possibly Alfred Bonner (though the mainstream media would never talk about the existence of the Light Alliance as fact) and above all, Thomas Jones – who looked *exactly like himself*, and who had been accused of kidnapping Ben's daughter, Veronica. Questions swirled in Casbolt's heart like a storm.

"Cas? Cas! You there?"

Casbolt had forgotten about Max. Presently, he closed his phone, flipping it with trembling hands, exhaling a trembling breath.

Pulling the newspaper closer to his eyes to see the criminal photograph of Thomas Jones, he studied it. He slammed the newspaper down, planting a hand to his forehead. He looked at the image again. His hair stood on end, such as what happened to wolves when faced by danger, and no one in their right mind would describe wolves as pathetic cowards. Not even an Aes Sidhe faced by danger. The Parvus Perception was keen – as much as a wolf – that this resemblance of Thomas Jones *threatened* Casbolt.

He gazed into a mirror image of himself, printed on paper.

Casbolt began to pace incessantly around the bathroom, overwhelmed and confused.

He tried to placate himself. "This is just a *terrible* coincidence."

But why did he feel so disturbed? There was no shortage of resemblances in the world. Twins, for example. Out of the seven billion people on the planet, it was *impossible* that there weren't two people exactly alike.

But … something about this coincidence felt *so, so wrong*. It formed a void in Casbolt's senses. Thomas' image haunted Casbolt's mind, overshadowing it. "What the hell?"

He stared at the image again, long and hard.

Thomas Jones … an alter ego staring out at him. Casbolt went to the mirror, fixed his hair and placed the image next to his reflection for a side-by-side comparison.

The uncanny resemblances struck Casbolt cataleptic. Oh God … They both had the *exact* same eyes, the *exact* same hair – length and colour – though Thomas' hair was more dishevelled and uncombed – the *exact* same facial structure and features – plump, clean shaven and broad, the *exact* same lips, the *exact* same ears, nose …

"I am James Casbolt," he found himself muttering involuntarily. "I am James Casbolt." He looked at Thomas Jones and … doubt and uncertainty settled in.

Impossible! Casbolt leaned back from the mirror, glaring at himself.

"What the hell do you mean, Max?" he said to his reflection. "Clones?"

But Thomas Jones' exact resemblance could confirm that anxiety like an apathy slowly engulfing Casbolt's body. *Oh no. I'll be anxious again!*

Be strong, James Casbolt, it is okay, Michael Prince reassured him.

It was *not* okay. Casbolt folded the newspaper up in his pocket, dashed out of the restaurant to his car and went right home to his family's house to investigate this predicament thoroughly.

Then, for the rest of the night, Casbolt, afflicted with insomnia, stayed up to an unholy hour, searching up Thomas Jones on the internet, sliding down the slippery slope of craving obsession. First, he began to look up images of Thomas Jones. He could not stop scrolling through most of the Google images of random people with the same name, when one photo caught his eyes. He stopped scrolling, enlarging the image. It and others like it were taken outside the FBI headquarters in Phoenix. Images of Thomas Jones, successful schizophrenic. According to Neil the priest …

Casbolt's blood froze. "Neil?"

Neil was his stepfather too! No. Casbolt ogled at the image with amused shock and disbelief. "What the hell is happening?" Casbolt roared.

Then he began reading journalists' articles covering the investigation, from the murder of Joseph, the disappearance of Veronica and the case of Thomas Jones from FBI sources, eyewitness reports and testimonies from news reporters.

After voracious web searching, he felt the ringing in his ears – the same ringing of direct-energy weapons used by Cabal spies. He'd opened so many tabs that his computer started to make a noise – overwhelmed by the number of pages he had opened. It resembled his mind; he couldn't untangle it from the chaos of byzantine emotions that had accumulated since the moment when memory of his temporal life, watching without his knowledge from behind the closed curtain, had been staring at him accusingly. It felt as if someone were in the house. Slowly, unhurriedly, he sat up and listened – to complete silence.

The ringing stopped.

"My life's a waste. Just when I thought …"

Leaving the kitchen bench, Casbolt fell into the sofa, holding the physical and moral collapse of his body, and lay there, head in hands, nervous, stomach churning; he struggled to put his thoughts in order. Not even Michael Prince could do it, for he seemed disabled or asleep.

It was not a coincidence that the Cabal deep state was using direct-energy weapons and witchcraft to stop Casbolt because he was exposing the truth – the Illuminati's mastery over the world, the control of minds, of the justice system, deriding the truth about the other alien races and the Galactic Tyranny. They had to get Casbolt out of the way. To throw him off the freedom train.

Casbolt rubbed his face, feeling groggy with Thomas Jones embedded in his mind. He stared at his hands, letting out a trembling breath. The sense of another presence that had woken him up grew slightly stronger. As he went out, off the sofa, turning on lights in rooms, all he could hear was the pounding of his heart in his chest like a galloping horse. He searched the entire empty house, the corridor, and as he approached the living room, he felt the invisible presence growing denser with each step, as if the atmosphere had been set vibrating.

Casbolt sat on the sofa, scowling. He'd come right back to where he had started again back last year – loneliness and its children: crippling depression and anxiety.

Casbolt stood in the shower, slumping, holding his head in his hands, trying to steady his breathing. The excessive weight of such deep gnarly thoughts, centred on the apocalypse of the existence of an absolute double involved in a heinous crime against Ben DePaula's family, made his head droop, pressing against the tiles. Casbolt's reputation … As Chief … Tulugaak's curse.

What is happening to me? The happiest day of my life – I have a woman's number – and I discover … This?

It was nine o'clock in the morning when Casbolt emerged from the shower and into the light to book tickets to Phoenix, Arizona.

Casbolt's family couldn't help him overcome the anxiety that robbed him of the possibility of trying to live a real life in reality for a change. *I will not let this rest; it's consuming my mind. I have to deal with this first, least my life becomes a misery.* Ultimately, Casbolt felt his personal identity was at great risk. He needed to act before it was too late. *I have to talk with Thomas Jones. I have to go to Phoenix. I have to save Antarctica for another month, Max. I need to find my clone, or else Meredith and everyone I love could be in grave danger.*

And even as Casbolt made the definite decision himself to go to America, the plane trip over the Atlantic without an incursion of Cabalistic enemies was uneventful.

During the entire trip, his alters remained silent – even Michael Prince. While flying, Casbolt enmeshed himself into researching Thomas Jones and the extraordinary events surrounding him further, learning all the knowledge that he could on his laptop. Casbolt felt as if he were in a small boat tossed about in a vast stormy sea, forever longing for that resolve and peace to call to a halt the voracious tumult.

Casbolt didn't want to accept it. He struggled to comprehend this terrible apocalypse. Now he had to respond to it.

53

SONG FOR THE VOID

Mount Hurrum – 8,666 BCE

"Those days were indeed faraway days.
Those nights were indeed faraway nights.
Those years were indeed faraway years.
The storm roared, the lights flashed.
Heaven talked with Earth. Earth talked with Heaven."
—From the Barton Cylinder, Column I, found at Nippur, c. 2350 BCE.

Above Na'amah – the mute and the desolate – the night sky blazed in a web of liquid light in the shape of a twisted ophidian creature, slick and quicksilver, pensive with ecstasy in the skies. The crescent moon was like the horns of an ox. The mountains of the land of Hurrum in the north like the reeds in the field. The standing lith stood placed between the spring and the pyramidal peak of the white mountains touching the stars.

Na'amah danced with her oppressed sisters, gently splashing within the mountain spring, flimsy transparent dresses dripping heavily behind, cleaving to their bare thighs like veiled clouds in the starry milk. Wrinkled, perspiring in the steam of heat suffusing from the warm springs, the women prayed for freedom from their hostile environment. Voracious coats of beady sweat drenched them, drenched her.

Na'amah's body twirled and swirled, stretching her arms above her head as she called to the spirits in the skies. It felt liberating to slither lullingly. Her sisters danced with her before the lith from the local hill country, from the river valleys, from the north to the south, to the east and the west. They all wore different exotic and elaborate headdresses, earrings with gold crescents, red and pink kohl pigment, shell ornaments, ochre for the lips, and were scantily clad in lightweight translucent shawls. Some were almost naked, with transparent white filmy garments revealing the shape of their breasts and curvaceous backs, but Na'amah did not go to those extremes. She dressed herself in a dainty, lightweight white-and-blue dress, tight enough to sculpt her bust and tall, lithe, elegant form. She had much pride in this bodily vessel created by the spirit beings.

The women danced in the stars. The women danced with the rock to attain the divine power.

And yet, Na'amah felt as if she were enduring a waterless drowning. She'd danced before the gods, desiring them, taking in the salacious fertility of the baetylus' power – pressing her memory with a fiery anxiety. The monolith weighed upon her with the intensity of two hands clamping her shoulders from behind that reminded her of her brother, of her father and of her mother.

The women always had it hard. They were always vulnerable. Na'amah recalled the snake ritual during her uncle's funeral in a cave. The master shaman inhaling mushroom fumes, chanting, grabbed a snake and cut off its head before her eyes. She was naked, and no one was ashamed by her nakedness. She watched as that headless snake squirmed to death and was buried at the back of the dark cave with a river at its mouth. The only way to defeat the snake was through seduction by stripping women bare in the snake rituals. Then the shaman would grab her body and begin to coerce her for the exhilarating orgy.

She fought the shaman to his last breath. She'd been exiled because the shaman died when she struck his head against the stones. That snake …

Around the baetylus were clay anthropoid statues, substitutes for each of the living dancing women. They were squatting in three pairs with one superior statue in the centre made out of ancient ivory from a tusk of a woolly mammoth from the Crown of the North. These figurines were nondescript, with no face and a tiny head or no head – not in any way exclusive. But they all had ample bodies with incised features, voluptuous hips and gaping triangular vulvas in various postures. Some were sitting, hands underneath their breasts as though lifting them up to display them. Others were standing up, crossing their arms, and some lying down, thrusting up their buttocks and arching their heads in the air.

The sculptures emanated an air of defeat, an air of failure, of disuse, stirring up dark thoughts.

Na'amah glanced her eyes at Kiskillilla, who was moisturising her skin. As the matriarch of the women's-only cult, her hair was long, curly and black, long enough to cover her nude breasts.

"Luminous beings, we are," Kiskillilla chanted as she stroked her arms, urging the women to refrain. "Not this crude form, are we. Luminous, luminous beings, we are. Not this crude form, are we," she continued, her voice carrying a hypnotic rhythm.

Every maiden here dancing waited for a boon from the outside. From the spirits beyond perceivable reality. After joining Kiskillilla's chanting, the women disbanded in an enthralled frenzy, blending into the congealed shadows of the mountain woods.

Na'amah stood in the water, all alone. Finding a boulder to sit upon, she stared out where the Hurrum hills rose wildly and at valleys with deep snow and wood that had not seen the axe, sloping fascinatingly into incredible darkness. She looked up at the sky – a screen of a watery abyss. The void of what she could not understand fascinated her.

Na'amah had come to know silence well during those months after her mother died, after the shaman's sexual assault, and after her family had given her over to be a slave to another family. And in those times of insipid silence, when she sat, floating in it, she would often come to stare up at the sky.

Nothing about it ever seemed to change, until she learnt to sing to the Seven Sisters by following Kiskillilla and her sky cult. What had given her the most anxiety – trying new unknown things with unknown people, in fear of their ridicule and slander – made her feel deathlike. And all the more, it inclined Na'amah to become a solitary figure.

But she wanted someone who could at least understand her. Somebody … A friend.

From the position on the lonely rock, by the standing natural lith, the figurines sat in separate dimensions before her. Decapitated, the nude statues resembled what she so often felt – what life had been to her. Na'amah lived as if with no head, but still breathed, no one caring that her heart was desolate. She stared at nothing, at the sky and the mountains, for many minutes. They did not seem real, but of something she'd dreamed.

Clouds swung across the heavens as rivers; they moved with flowing bubbles as if stirring up from Dark Earth, the waves churning.

She heaved out a sigh, the mountain's silence incredible. She was not a normal woman. Her orphan brother Tubal-Qayin, whom she still lived with, did not want to talk about their family. And such alienation had caused him to never cease from his obsessive passion of pressure flaking and copper mining, leaving her to her own devices. On that vulnerable, miserable day, Na'amah had run away from home when she had discovered the terrible secret: mother had died from an honour killing, necessary to clear the family name of the demise the shaman had met at Na'amah's hands, whom she killed out of self-defence.

Na'amah often resorted to live in the Hurrum wilderness up high north at the Crown of the Earth during the winter when it was most gorgeous, finding the shine inside that darkness on the mountains. The cool glimmerings when rain rippled down from off the green leaves of trees. An opalescence trickling from off rocks and branches. When Na'amah ventured into the space outside, it made her heart pound. It made her active. But all she had escaped had been her brother's sweltering stone querns and hearth. The engrossed *clack, clack, click, clack, clack, click* of his flint tools irked her meditations. Now he forged with a new magical smooth rock called copper. It was able to be moulded and shaped into tools according to his desire. It had taken over him, concealing him down in the darkness of his crafting trenches under their hut. Within their sweltering clay hut, it felt finite, but outside, the rest of life felt transitory.

Na'amah understood that the world was so vast, to be explored like the nomadic hunter gatherers had done for millennia. To venture out and leave behind her guilt …

Then she sunk underneath the spring, holding her breath.

The water was alive; warm and the colour of silver. It enfolded her, taking her shape. Its sound was soft, as a thin ringing, everything of the external world dulled. The stars of Heaven wobbled as if they were an illusion, then, after a while, Na'amah stilled her body. She held her breath, floating, arms and legs out, her dress gelatinous.

Peaceful silence. Not even the faintest creaking of insects could be heard, nor even the squalls of mountain gale blew. Underwater was silence … and after long enough, Na'amah would think of her failures. Her guilt for causing her mother's tragic death.

If only she could remain underwater forever … Forget …

The water had a glossy motion. Liquid glided over her without shape or form, but it held her with weight and volume. The secret parts of Na'amah, the mute and the desolate, where others should see the surface, missed the more active part of her, in the undertow.

There had to be times for allowing the silence and times for shattering silence. Times of rest and times ceasing rest. Wind blew across the stilled watery surface, rippling it, the moon's light waning behind a sheen of cloud.

Na'amah saw a surreptitious firefly wander in the sea of stars. However, as she ogled, it pulsated with a ringed nimbus. Such pulsating was not singular. Many stars in the sky were joining it in the same wonder.

A deluge of white rain cascaded.

Na'amah floated upwards, kissing her reflection, and breached forth out of the water, sucking in air, ascending.

A whole host of stars plummeted in a flocking formation from the firmament, thundering as they struck the barrier between the sky and the land, popping and riding on funnel clouds. Flaring, sizzling tendrils alight, they penetrated the land, crackling in the manner of lightning, parting through the clouds at remarkable speed. They flashed with green-blue radiance, frilled, veering sporadically, and then smiting the land. The stars scattered as seeds upon the fertile ground.

The ecstasy of the penetration overcame Na'amah – for finding solace had been a constant struggle. Change had come! The spirits had heeded her prayers!

Her heart burning with a clamour of urges and possibilities, Na'amah bounded out of the spring, holding her dress, hunting for the nearest impact crater, rushing through the trees, leaping over mounds, her damp clothes and skin suddenly freezing in the mountainous night.

She broke out of the snarl of plants and saw the long gash of earth smoking and burning with bright chaos fire before her. A dense fading light emanated from the flaming crater. This star had destroyed a part of the lime-plastered stone wall on the outskirts of her summer village, gouging a smearing rut of dark rubble. In her village, on the roofs of the rectangular, tightly packed buildings, families, farmers, hunters, and children ogled at the crash. Slowly, they filed out of the buildings via ladders, over the ruined wall, gathering in shock. Dogs barked madly at the commotion.

Na'amah, above all, feared the standard of being caught in the drift of worthlessness, fearing that being within the silence for too long, she could turn her humanity into something strange. She feared that these villagers would see her and outcast her, dishonouring her for killing their shaman, shaming her family and causing her mother's death. She couldn't stay in the loathsome drift of silence for much longer – she'd found a potential to land.

She must take ... this god for herself. To make her wise.

Na'amah ran towards the crash, into the billowing salty smoke, unable to think, lustful to be the first woman to see the divine being. If the spirit were to see her, examine her to be good in his eyes, she wanted to be the first one that could embody the unimaginable possibility …

Of deity and human becoming one.

"Na'amah!" Tubal-Qayin shouted over the din.

She stepped into the flaming crater, one dainty step at a time, for the stones were hot.

"It's mine," Na'amah intoned.

"Na'amah, you ewe woman! Get back here!" Tubal-Qayin's gruff voice snapped. She forced herself to not turn around, despite how much a part of her wanted to obey and not rebel against him.

Suddenly, a silhouette arose in the midst of the flames, and Na'amah froze, ogling, her heart thumping harder and faster. She looked and saw a goodly man of shadow arise.

A foot appeared, webbed and glossy, like the light skin of a fish. Golden veins could be seen underneath the translucent skin of brawny scaly legs. He was nude, but his body was godlike with strange incredible muscular bulges and shapes. In full moonlight, the tall man looked handsome, with an elusive nimbus around his shape. The spirit man had a silver metallic beard, nicely trimmed with curly dark cords for hair, like a glossy garment passing the shoulders. He had large eyes and a bifurcated nose – catlike. He had a cone-shaped head, and his eyes were livid brilliance – orange as the light of dawn. The golden eyes slanted slightly upwards in the shape of almonds. That aura around his body shimmered with tendrils of light and – Na'amah realised – *lightning*.

Suddenly, the man god raised his mighty arms, and the flames dancing around him responded. The embers *sucked* into him, a great whirlwind surged the flames astir, extinguishing them, drawing them into the god's glowing body, until air, moonlight and smoke were still.

"At last. *Meh* has come," the man said with a sonorous melodious voice. *Meh* – pronounced *may* – from what Na'amah could recall, meant enlightened fertility and order. Ideal optimal function and prosperity.

Thrill sparkled through Na'amah's body. The man spoke like the Lahmu Wild Men did, with vibrations and melodies that were attuned to the rhythm of compassion and long suffering. Na'amah had everything she needed to re-enter the divine Presence of Paradise. The naked man, sensual and delightful to Na'amah's eyes, had no shame. He desired that she was beautiful in his eyes, and it excited her that he could make her wise.

She scrambled forward down into the crater, taking his arms into an embrace. He smelled of the blue menthol fragrance of the salt sea, the snow of a blizzard and the static after a thunderstorm.

The ecstasy of his presence made tears run down her cheeks. Her body melted into the good god – her saviour manifested in the flesh – resting her head against his broad chest, feeling his round warm muscles clenching under his fishy skin. She even managed to hear faint beats of his heart. The divine had come.

Gently, she felt the man twirl her hair, brushing the tears from her cheeks, his gaze feeling as the warm sun upon her. Her entire body tingled, exhilarated by his obsession of her.

"No! What are you doing? Get away from her!"

Na'amah made a weak noise as the god-man held her back in a firm grip. On the edge of the crater, her awful brother Tubal-Qayin, the pressure flaker, hobbled with a limp. He was a lump of a man, with shoulders at different heights, a huge, bulging, misshapen head, bushy eyebrows, and a wild brown beard. His face was red, lumpy and covered with welts, as if he'd been bitten by bees, and then dragged across gravel for many cubits. What a farce, to see a grotesque creature such as her brother approach perfection from the stars!

"Where are your men to rule and subdue you?" the deity said. The rhythmic cadence had a hint of confusion – naïvety or shock? – addressed directly to her. Such a disparaging euphemism in that remark made Na'amah's chest flare with racing passion. He did not even consider Tubal-Qayin. The divine being looked right past him as he would a lump of unturned soil.

"Why do you want my sister?" Tubal-Qayin growled, shaking his fist. "She's a murderess, and you have no dowry to give!"

"We have been watching you, Tubal-Qayin." The spirit sounded bewildered. "Son of a beast who herded many wives, driving them to suicide." He enhanced his voice's volume so all could hear. "You love your works more than your sister. Your women have no emotional security; instead, you all take for yourselves what you want from them." The man raised Na'amah's hands and kissed them, static power coursing through her arms. "Kindness must be."

Na'amah found herself opening her mouth juvenilely. *Kindness must be!*

"No," Tubal-Qayin grumbled, voice caught in his throat, his face burning red. "That's not what I—"

"Why are your women rebelling against your men?" Na'amah's god's questions shamed all men. She tried to stifle a gleeful laugh. "Why do your women long for freedom as much as they do? Why are they so revealing and so vexed?" Her god lowered his dawn gaze towards her, softening his voice, stroking her delicate chin with a single finger, addressing her. "This is my dowry to you fair, lovely tune. Access to El's Presence and eternal knowledge to ransom you from sin!"

"Thank you, Shining One," Na'amah muttered with propriety.

Then, surging with flashing tendrils of lightning running up the god's arm, he extended that shimmering arm towards her brother and all the married men who had gathered around in a circling mob, those *swine men*, who could declare her life with a final undisputed authority. Now she could have full freedom at last! Presently, the god's voice thundered across the valley and mountains. "It was *you* who have cast females away for gain! Vain men, who do you perceive, then, to be wiser? Who do you think you are? Gods? All humanity shall fall under the curse of El unless you repent!"

His voice boomed, silencing the entire land. Many men in the village visibly cowered. Some stepped back from their women, hanging their heads in shame, proving, explicitly, that they had shown themselves to not be men of worth for women.

But Tubal-Qayin gritted his teeth. Thunder protracted along the valley as more beautiful god-men a head taller than the human men collected their women, some timid and some openly accepting the god in front of their spouse's eyes. Salvation of love had power in numbers.

Tubal-Qayin had eyes of abject disbelief, saying, "You're ... You're not going to *steal* our women. Our gods cannot take away our women – how shall this village live? We apologise for our sins, and we repent indeed. But we *need* to control what our women do and what they conceive, for then death will strike either the child or the mother. How can we know who will survive in this cursed world? How can our clans be fruitful and multiply if we do not dominate and depend on our females?"

Tubal-Qayin beheld over twenty shining pure males emerging into the village from the high country and rocky peaks of Mount Hurrum.

"What have you done?" Tubal-Qayin muttered, his eyes widening. "Why are ..." Whipping his head back around to face Na'amah, he roared out of pure fear. "You're in rebellion!"

"Come now," said Na'amah's god, humming to a reassuring cadence not fazed by a mortal's insipidness. "If you let me, I can heal your leg. *If* you want."

At that suggestion, Tubal-Qayin gaped, shoving the god's offering hand away.

Suddenly, a young man in gazelle skins charged from the crowd, wielding a mallet, screaming in a rage. He ran at the bearded god man with skin as pale as the sky. The woman in his arms screamed, and the pale god raised a hand calmly, sending out unseen power.

Something popped in Na'amah's ears. The aggressor crumpled on the ground, clawing at his face, thrashing and screaming, convulsing uncontrollably, eyes turning pink, white, rolling up into his skull. Dark liquid, not blood, but *ink*, seeped and gushed forth from his mouth, nose, ears and tear glands. Slowly, his skin sizzled and darkened as a rotten fruit. The man's chest heaved.

Na'amah watched, mouth open, as the man's entire body shrivelled up, his bones appearing in half relief. Lips puckered, drawing back, the skin deflated, grisly eyeballs sinking into engorged ticks. The man ceased to move, becoming stiff as an old corpse. Finally, he cracked, crumbling into dust.

Na'amah gasped in dread, just as the repulsed onlookers carrying torches descended into a chaotic riot. The god tightened his arm around Na'amah. Tubal-Qayin roared an inhale, hobbling towards the pile of dust, screaming, "No, no, no! My son! My son!"

My brother had a son? At her side, Na'amah's god sighed with a hum of regret. "See? Man cannot resist the sun from rising without burning his eyes. The curse can be prevented by the Great Symbiosis. We meet your needs, and now you meet ours."

To their right, an erudite god with skin as black as the night strode confidently with Kiskillilla in his brawny arm. He looked slim but handsome with a sharp, box-shaped jawline, a pristine shimmering dress and his hair braided in plaits. All the citizens gawked at him with awe.

"Children of men." Black Enlil trumpeted his voice supernaturally, vibrating the ground. "We are the Anunna of the skies. Your crying out has been heard. El has granted you a way to deliverance. Work with us, humans. Manifest the image of El by interacting with the country to bring about new potential and cultural development. The rock in this crater there – the star stone – has what is called crystal ore within it. Work with it as you work the copper and the fruit brought forth from the ground. Though many will strive against you for the star stone, follow us and we shall teach you how to use it to create new spears and blades to vanquish your adversaries, to protect all those you love. Crystal blades have the power to shed blood. Living blood that has the power over life and death."

As if aroused by Enlil's words, Kiskillilla seductively stroked his obsidian bare arm with her manicured fingernails.

Na'amah, looking back down, suddenly became awfully abashed, sick in the stomach. What was she about to commit her existence to? She coyly glanced up at her divine husband for assurance. "What is your name, Shining One?"

The god hummed, electricity crackling down his eyes, arching across his shoulders, out of his ears and down his body. To some conceitful tune, he said, "I am Dyeus Perkwunos. Also called Ishkur. Storm father of the Anunna. No longer will you be called Loveliness, but Na'amayah – Yah's Loveliness. You're a fair and lovely tune, Na'amayah." The storm in his eyes seethed. She sensed the impression that he'd doubted many times if his descent into the world for his love for humanity was good. The god looked vulnerable, limiting himself in the flesh, just for her. He took her hand in a snug grip, and she comprehended how they both sympathised with each other.

Defeated, poor Tubal-Qayin slumped in despair. She watched him fall to his knees, plucking at his hair, whines coming from his mouth.

"How dare you," he trembled, hoarse and broken. Na'amayah hesitated, shocked. That exclamation had been for all: his sister, the women, and the gods. "How dare you women lead the gods themselves astray, whoring to satisfy your wantonness! How *dare you!*"

"No, no, not wantonness," Dyeus rasped in grief.

Then Tubal-Qayin scrambled into Dyeus' crater, flecks of foam gathering at the ends of his mouth. "How dare you kill in *my* land! I thought you were a god, not a coward! Don't let the women beguile you! Leave us!"

"You will realise your dependence on the gods." Na'amayah felt Dyeus' chest inflating, becoming rigid, a pricking sensation rushing down his skin. Chills. Sweat.

"My …" Tubal-Qayin stammered, tears welling up in his eyes, his whole body shuddering as he begged. "No … No, please, must you take my Na'amah away from me? The men will become vagabonds wandering the land. We will have no families to rear and protect us on the face of the ground."

Dyeus ignored the man, turning Na'amayah and himself around so she could only see his body. "For a message I have, and I will tell you. A word, and I will recount to you,

Word of tree and whisper of stone,
Converse of skies with land of deeps with stars.
I understand the lightning which the skies do not know,
The word that people do not know,
And land's masses do not understand.
Eternal life is not far within your reach,

If you hasten to me,
Race, and I will reveal it.
Come in the midst of Hurrum.
Dwell in the holy mountain of Eden."

"I will," Na'amayah intoned.

"First," Dyeus said, with a rhythmic cadence of anticipation and promise, "for the sake of decency, shave your hair on your head. Second, trim your nails, and last, designate time to your mourning rites to honour your lost family who reared you. I'm afraid, by accepting me, you'll see them no more."

And Na'amayah said without hesitation, "I'm willing."

Dyeus nodded. He atoned an elegant tone of pride and enthrallment. "I see you are good to my eyes as a comely fruit tree. I shall take you to be mine, to elevate you from the rule of men, and you shall become a goddess."

At last, Na'amayah's purpose had found her – the cursed ground receiving the rain god. Na'amayah felt her feet leave the ashen ground, levitating, rising in the air, the whole world forgotten, as she drifted with her god, floating upwards into the night ocean of the skies.

END OF

OMEGA PLAN PART II

PART III

SELFLESS LOVE TRANSCENDS OUR TYRANNY

54

REMEDIES

"Keep thy mind in hell, and despair not."
—Saint Silouan the Athonite, 1866 – 1938 CE.

Alfred Bonner, Arhat of the Alliance, awoke with an intolerable stiffness in his muscles. He wouldn't normally get aches. Alfred had a routine in the gym doing an hour of exercise, but today, his muscles felt painful. The life expansion he'd attained from Danu the goddess was according to a rubberband model, stretching his regular lifespan until it snapped abruptly. Now, as the decades wore on and his close relatives perished, the pain of old age would come crashing down upon him unawares.

If his body was deteriorating, his goals to ready society for the Great Reset could be in peril. He needed more time!

Alfred Bonner had a backup plan, of course. And that involved the coffin and harnessing the *ka* of the master of death – Osiris – known to the Sumerians as Bilgamesh (to the Akkadians, Gilgamesh), the seeker of immortality. Life eternal.

Alfred arose, staring at the wall, depicting a frame holding a papyrus copy from the British Museum of the Eighteenth Dynasty *Book of the Dead* of Nakht, depicting the judgement before Osiris, the god of resurrection, and attaining an afterlife.

Alfred sought out the Pearl of Power – *Baidi*, the Autumn Pearl of the

West. Of the white dragon and of Venus, the morning star. He picked up a small leather box on his bedside table and opened it. The dim light emitting from it, the opalescent colours, glowed like a pale dwarf star.

Alfred stared at the Pearl inside, discerning, trying to work his mind before his servants brought the morning test for him to complete. Then his cognition expanded, as if *cleared*. Energised.

He considered not just questions of arithmetic and ethics that could confront him, but also of the inevitable march towards modernity, of the creation of stockholders of the rimland of Asia, to penetrate the heart of the world. Of the Bennu bird's caws of the irredeemable rise of the Eastern powers – if they worked with the West, everyone could prevent the Galactic Tyranny.

Now Alfred could *see* the bigger picture. He could *see* the key to bring the world together was to activate the gates of Agartha. The great empire of Patala.

And yet, Europe – Germany, Alfred Bonner's homeland – was divided, isolated within the European Union and NATO. Like a grand mansion falling into decay, Germany's plastered walls peeled. Vines crept up her body, finding cracks in her ornate rooms, her furniture swathed in spider webs. The once successful West, all burned out from colonial endeavours, looked once more to the East, lusting to learn from them again. The blind Cabal stifled cosmic and cultural progress, hindering humanity's growth.

Patala – the Underworld – will be revealed. Alfred had personally seen the asura and touched their most prized mineral – the voidstone – in 1943, saving the world from Hitler's plan of torment and dominion. That tyrant knew the key to power came from the asura's technology. The Pearl of Power, however, would allow Alfred to attain the same ambition, but with *a redeemed purpose*.

The CD revealed the way into Patala. Restoration was coming, and the Navajo were committing suicide by guarding this truth. The Kandahar giant was an Ullikummi from Patala. It was only the beginning, for according to the Tantric prophecies of Mongolia, the asura from Patala would finally connect humanity to enlightenment.

All these plans were coherent, predicted to come to pass in the Dynamics. Germany could be left out during the Great Reset, going extinct. Alfred Bonner would make sure it *would not*. Patala would save it.

Alfred, enmeshed in the small focal point of the Pearl of Power, longed to restore his homeland again. The Nazi Cabal that had dehumanised humanity with planned caprice had provided so much technological progress to the human race ...

Patala would provide a *remedy*. A kallipolis where Alfred's ways were ingrained into the people, all enemies purged, no need for violence, but use the violence so it can exhaust itself from sectarianism. The goal? AI, Maitreya, sustainability.

The restorative Pearl. So tiny – the size of a marble – and yet, it could grow into the largest mountain.

There was a knock on the door. "Enter," Alfred said, slipping the Pearl into its box as Perseus Euergetes, an Aes Sidhe demigod child of Prometheus, entered. He was young and a skilled fighter, bearing Alfred's breakfast on a tray, muesli in a medium ramekin, poached eggs on toast topped today with mushroom and avocado, feta and pomegranate seeds. Every day, Alfred had a different topping, but his personal delight was mushrooms.

But just as Alfred set the plate down to feast, the broad and tall ginger Jason Morlaix – a poised, austere Manichean – put a hand out, clearing his throat saying, "Arhat? It's time to test the Three Seals."

The test. Alfred looked up, meeting the demigod's orange imperial gaze. Everyone thought he was Alfred's bodyguard, but the truth was more disturbing. Jason would be the one to test the fluency of his speech, the strength of his body and his expressive cognition. If he failed in any of these three seals, then Alfred would be in audit – he would spend the whole day stuck in the base as the Aes Sidhe's prisoner. A foolish man was incapable to operate in the world around him during auditing.

But to pass, then Alfred could master his mouth, his hands and his mind with optimal capacity. He could properly separate things of darkness from the things of light and maintain a pure deposition as an Ascended Master.

As Perseus and Jason stepped back, three druids robed esoterically filed inside Alfred's bedchamber. Alfred sat at his small desk, taking a drink of water – at least Jason allowed him that – and he was presented with a series of speech prompts, exercises, math and philosophical problems.

He didn't feel stupid. Normally, he would immediately recognise the differences. He either felt as a prisoner in his own mind, or he felt so free and in command of everything.

"He is fit for service," one of the druids proclaimed.

If only, Alfred thought. *The Manicheans of Light realise there is no need for religion when the self is made up of bundles of mental and physical states and feelings, and not facts. Their own teachings highlight this fact.*

Jason nodded, then stepped back, allowing Alfred to complete his morning meal. Life could be interesting when cleared of setbacks, where each morning often determined different levels of intelligence. Most of the time,

Alfred was between the two extremes.

After finishing his meal, Alfred said to Jason, "Let me see the Survival Dynamics." There was an innate deterministic drive in Alfred, an eagerness to get as much done as possible in the days he had left of his rubberband life. If he'd been a regular person, he could be verging on his late nineties, edging on one hundred. He still looked in his late thirties.

The Alliance recognised Alfred Bonner to be part divine.

Jason stepped aside, allowing Alfred's mistress Deirdre – a Nindingir – to approach, holding a thick leather-bound volume, setting it before him on the desk. She brought the Masonic hard copy – the same Dynamics had also been digitised. The woman wore a Celtic aqua-green robe loose over her bare bosom and had a red-and-white *tilak* on her forehead, between her eyes. She was an elder member of the Bodhisattvas, an Initiate of the Third Initiation, and in her late twenties. Much, much younger than Alfred Bonner, she was determined, impressive, sublime and learned in Agarthan lore, believing in what Alfred had been called to do.

Alfred rested his fingers upon the book and felt a moment of … reverence? That couldn't be right – no doubt, he hardly revered anything except his wife.

He opened this holy – set-apart – book, marked by a reed. Inside were scribbles – frenzied, bombastic and majestic, that made no sense to the uninitiated. It was a mess, but genius.

He recognised his own writing. The wavy, straggled lines he wrote on the edge of the massive page, the way he would write when running out of room. That being said, most of it came from another hand during the hours of ecstatic lucid obsession.

"You look concerned, Alfred," Deirdre said.

"I was just exposed in front of the Marine Corps. They've terminated the contract and will revolt against us," Alfred said. "We must get ready for them. The hour grows late, and smoke is arising from the bowels of Dark Earth. The spirit of Osiris is moving. The Pearl of Power of the West was in the Grand Canyon, under my nose, in the hands of the Navajo. I should have seen it sooner. Judd Pounders has slowed me down, but Osiris has shown me in a dream that we can use this time to counter Pantokrator."

"Time?" Deirdre's voice trembled. "How much time do you think we have?" she asked, her eyes searching Alfred's face for answers.

Alfred evaded the question of time. He needed more time to think about it. "Osiris is regaining much of his strength. He cannot take physical form, but his name and his spirit has not lost its potency. The Pearl of Power and his coffin is the bane that will defeat the Galactic Tyrant. The Lord of the Dead concealed in Patala – the Underworld – sees all … This is why around the time of the paladin incursion at Haditha Dam, the words of the dying spoke of the day of destruction as they departed into the Underworld."

"What do you mean?"

Alfred gave a subtle wry smirk. "It's the mouth of Maitreya, Osiris, Gilgamesh, Marduk. They are one. They blaspheme the Most High. Very soon, Osiris will summon an army great enough to launch an assault on the old fool. It's more than just an enterprise to save children from paedophiles and traffickers. We breed the super soldiers to deter the foolish Tyrant. We are building Maitreya's army. We can change history."

Consternation shrouded Deirdre's countenance.

"Always worrying … Once all the Pearls are in our hands, then God is dead. So the servants of Maitreya will find the Pearls … and kill the ones who carry them."

"Pearls?" Deirdre said. "You said there was only one. The Navajo—"

"Gilgamesh is revealing this to me slowly. There are four more Pearls. The Navajo were protecting the Pearl of the West. They have allied with Ben. Why did they have to do that?" Alfred growled. He really *hated* being outsmarted by the elders. Alfred *always* achieved his ambitions. "They knew all about the war, the conflict between the Sky Beings, the Aeons, shapeshifting creatures of the Dragon and their scramble for power over the nations. It's beginning. We must unite the gods… against Yaldabaoth."

There was a knock on the door, and Alfred Bonner closed the Dynamics, saying, "Come in."

He expected Perseus had come to take his dishes, but striding into his chamber was a man Alfred remembered. Cloaked in white, bald, shaven, wearing a *tilak* with azure eyes, tall and sinuously built, Michael Oppenheim – the Initiate Bhairava – entered his room.

I am still his master and superior. But Bhairava had come a long way since the 1930s and 40s. His dead eyes … were godly.

Alfred shot up to his feet. "What are you doing here?"

"Arhat, we need to talk," the Initiate said.

Alfred, taking a deep breath, eyed serene Deirdre warily. He took a step forward. Bhairava – he was officially on the FBI records of most wanted – followed his Jewish friends of the Manicheans of Light to murder Joseph DePaula.

"Have you found Veronica and Zoe yet?" Deirdre asked.

"My Aes Sidhe have been sent hunting a child sex trafficking ring down in Columbia," Bhairava reported dryly. "The Nahash sex offenders are operating in a tight network. They like keeping their teeth and nails clean. They don't trust strangers. But my team have been luring them in. The paedophiles you have already captured here in Dulce, Arhat, recognise the pictures of Veronica and Zoe. They said their friend sold them to the Nahash rebels in Columbia. In no time, we will find the girls." Bhairava whispered his words coldly, eyes dead, swaying like a cobra. "But Arhat. That is not why I am here."

Alfred raised his chin.

"I have brought *your* daughter back, Arhat. The Cabal abandoned her."

Alfred stared. *This man is not sane,* he thought. *This man would become the most dangerous weapon in all the world.*

But his daughter ...? Alfred had a daughter who was kidnapped, taken into a world of suffering, riddled with disease, oppressed by lawless tyranny and gratuitous violence without any hope that life would be any different. The chaos of his loss had brought about a great sadness in Alfred's life, malfunctioning him, but he moved on because he convinced himself that the girl had died.

But if what Bhairava said was true ...

Alfred buried his face in his hands and trembled.

There was something special about Reyhan. When he first met her, he knew she was genuine. Smart. Magical. Reyhan faced many obstacles in her life and education due to her ethnicity, but when she emigrated to America to go to university, she said to Alfred that nothing would bring her down. She said that with a quizzical light in her eyes and a smug smirk. Reyhan succeeded, got her doctorate and became associate professor of archaeology and anthropology at Harvard. She had been involved in the excavations and studies on the burials in Taklamakan and Xinjiang's Tarim Basin and the mummies of Ürümchi in Yanghai along the now-dry Peacock River. There, the famous women with auburn hair wearing red woollen fur cloaks and feathers placed in their bonnets were buried in boat-shaped structures covered in cowhides. These mummies of Ürümchi genetically and culturally resembled the Bronze Age Celts who established their biggest settlements in France and the British Isles.

Reyhan proved these ancient Uyghur mummies were Celts. The Uyghur were Aes Sidhe.

But Reyhan, despite living her dream, wanted nothing more than to have her own family. Alfred knew, from the start, she was going to be an incredible mother. No matter how difficult it was, Alfred trusted her, that she would never give up. She had two children. A girl … and a boy.

Loving parents would do the best they could for their children. But nothing could prepare Alfred for what happened to his daughter.

Alfred closed his eyes and suddenly slumped, leaning on the bedside table, knocking the fork to the floor. His muscles were stiff, they were so sore.

"Where is she?" Alfred demanded.

"Your daughter helped Ben DePaula." Bhairava swayed back and forth, not conscious of his motions. The shock numbed Alfred. "I … I had to disable her because she was a Carnute—"

"Carnute?" Alfred roared. "What did you do to her?"

"Forgive me! She's still alive. I'm … I'm afraid the Cabal have already broken her." The unstable man who had once been Michael Oppenheim slipped away, covering his baleful face with a neck warmer. He'd been given the same life extension as Alfred and became a very effective servant capable of leading his own team of super soldiers. He'd succeeded in finding Alfred's daughter without even trying. Envy raged in Alfred towards his friend. He would never fail. It was unthinkable. *Bhairava works for me! I found her! At last!*

"Go," Alfred said to his mistress. "I need to see if my daughter is okay." His mistress went, and Alfred ran to find his long-lost daughter.

—

Waking up from a hispid coma, Tara was blinded by neon lights, sterile and banal. Her entire head felt light, she could barely feel her jaw, and the broken rib in her side was swollen, that claustrophobia of the undisturbed bruises irritating under her skin.

She was lying flat on a gurney inside a clinic. She roved her eyes, and immediately became aware of her jaws and face enclosed inside tough, malleable plaster.

I've broken my jaw. Someone put me under anaesthetic and tried to heal me.

Something reeked of fish oil – a pungent, rancid oxidised odour filled Tara's nostrils. She couldn't tell where the fishy smell was coming from – it cleaved to the walls, ubiquitous, permeating without source.

But out of the corner of her left eye, she saw an elaborate object – a massive box, egg-yolk yellow on a flat rectangular benchtop set against the wall. The box was decorated with recesses forming cut-out panelled niches emblazoned with patterns. For some reason, Tara attributed that strange smell to this enigmatic box.

Tara lay waiting in insipid silence for a while until the clinic's glass door slid open. Striding inside was the New Age cult leader of the left-wing secret society, Alfred Bonner – the man Barbelo had told her explicitly to evade. She had failed, but she no longer cared.

Alfred slid into the clinic like a billowing fog, hands folded behind his back, wearing his regal white-and-navy-blue suit, striped with buttons with glittering cuffs.

"The recovery is going smoothly," Alfred Bonner said, calm and tender. "The surgeons and doctors did their job well. I paid for you to have the most optimal procedure. You're feeling better?"

Tara wet her lips, feeling Bonner's gaze, fermenting invidious tremors through her body. Why did he sound so kind? He paced around her gurney, past her bare feet – she was stripped to her underwear, covered in a white gown.

No. No, don't panic. He's not going to … Panic choked Tara. *Stay calm, Marcell! Stay calm, okay!*

It was difficult. Her mind began to disassociate as it naturally did, recoiling backwards like the eyes of a slimy snail, retreating into the recesses of her shell – fragile and cramped.

Bound in bed … half naked … a man staring at her.

Tara involuntarily accelerated her breathing. She tried to rise from the gurney, but her vision immediately swam, and she sighed, dizzily collapsing on her back.

The skin between Alfred Bonner's eyes creased. "Don't move. The surgical anaesthetic needs to wear off." He held out an icy pole. "Please suck on this. It's to regain your fluids."

Tara hesitated, then held the frozen hydrolyte in her hands. She instantly felt powerless. She clenched her fists, her nails digging into her palms. The faces of the other young women and children flashed in her mind, their desperate eyes pleading for salvation from the torment they endured. Most of them didn't survive the cruel experiments, succumbing to the merciless grip of the Bleakness.

"No," she muttered, refusing to stick it in her mouth and suck on it. She should heed medical advice, but her mind was filthy, and she wasn't in the mood. For too long … "You're going to do the same to me?" Tara rasped, her voice quivering, her jaw and tendons in her neck, a little section to the right, throbbed as she formed words out of cold fear. Her body was already clammy.

Alfred looked at her, his face unreadable. "I don't understand. But I know what you have been through. You must loathe me right now for failing you."

Irk made Tara tense. She exhaled a distraught sigh, and when she tried to breathe in again, she struggled. "W–why do you want me? I don't know you. I'm … I'm your enemy."

"You don't remember who I am."

Tara stared, her mouth going dry. *What? What does he mean?*

There was a commotion echoing outside the clinic room, and through the glass door, Tara saw a procession of trollies, pushed by hairy hominids with bulbous heads, Neanderthal in appearance.

Sasquatch. They were huge and unsettling to the eye. Hominids walking on two feet, pushing trollies holding crates that held capsules of boxes and packages.

"How did you fail me?" Tara asked.

Alfred sighed in grief. "I have no time to waste." Alfred glanced at the Sasquatch pushing the trollies. "The majority of the world's population is unable to meet their most basic needs," Alfred said. "They are poor in the absolute sense; their lives are utterly hopeless. No food, shelter, education, sanitation, health. They are trafficked, raped and forced to do heinous crimes for their masters." At that, Tara's heart leapt, because she knew Bonner was talking about her. A wretch, a thing with no free will, subject to inequality. "This is the normal situation of our world, even though we might not see it here in the West. This is why the Alliance trades for Mycomantic fungi and Augmenters from Patala – the Underworld."

"What?" Tara said, shocked.

"Fungi and sonic frequencies and, ultimately, the voidstones, are the future. This is an answer to our crisis. Humanity needs more renewable resources. This is what I am doing for your own good. We need to save as many lives as possible.

"We need a Reset."

Tara felt the mark on her forehead burn. All this insidious innovation… What made Alfred Bonner so different from the Cabal?

"This Patalan technology can help humans militarise space," Bonner said. "We must plan for the worst, in case our planet is destroyed. It is all for the Kallipolis."

Tara frowned. "What are you?"

"A forerunner, Tara," Bonner went on, leaning forwards. "Our world exists at the expense of many. That is just the reality. Our morality has evolved over time; we cannot go back to the old way, we can only be uncertain. But fungi and Augmenters will help us to create a balance in the world. They are tools for sustainability. It is for the sake of future generations. We must humble ourselves and accept that there are not enough resources to go around for all of us. Not enough food, not enough love, not enough money. People are dying. If it is in our power to prevent hunger, disease and death from happening, without sacrificing anything of moral significance, then we must – we *ought* – to do it."

"You didn't answer my question. How did you fail me?" Tara questioned.

Alfred swallowed hard. "When paedophiles took you away from me, Tara, I sacrificed much of my wealth and donated much of my savings to child-trafficking-relief organisations. It is wrong for me to gain for myself, unless it has beneficial consequences for the world. I deprived myself. I did everything to stop this evil, because I ought …" Alfred Bonner took a deep breath, and the exhale was shaky. He closed his eyes for a long time.

"What do you mean?" Tara said. "Who are you, really?"

"Tara … You are … my daughter," Alfred said succinctly, opening his azure eyes. They were brimming with moisture. "And you've finally come home …" His voice was strangled and sorrowful, hanging in the air like a shroud caught in the wind. As he spoke, Alfred Bonner was clearly fighting to keep himself together. "You were taken from your family when you were only little. All my efforts have at last paid off."

Tara would have twitched, but her bandages and bruises on her body felt stiff. She didn't believe a single word from Bonner's mouth … though a part of her wanted to have her parents come to save her. "Prove it." She smiled smugly. "Do you have evidence?"

Bonner dismissed her for a few minutes and returned to the clinic, holding a birth certificate in his hands. It was written in Chinese, but since Tara had grown up in western China, she had a vague sense of how to read the characters. She couldn't believe what she was reading; it was so shocking, she thought she misread.

Alfred Bonner read out a translated version. He was her father, and her mother, Reyhan, was Uyghur.

"No. You're insane," Tara exclaimed.

"I met your mother at Ürümqi when I was a teenager," Bonner recounted. "After you were trafficked by the fashion photo shooters with other children, we did all we could to find you. You have been raped by men, abused due to your nationality. Your disappearance turned me into a monster, Tara. I killed men trying to find who had taken you, but it was worth it. It *was worth it* because *I am* your father. You may have heard and believed terrible things about me for what I've done. All this: this base, the Alliance, is partly here due to your disappearance. The love for a child causes one to commit unthinkable things. Love is stronger than ethics, but the fruits of my labour have not been in vain."

Tara felt as if her chest were filling with concrete. She felt heavy, chilled through, formless. She couldn't remember breathing.

Memories struck her viciously, destroying her connections to reality, to love, to wholeness. A fist smashed her face, blood blinding her as she reeled, men stalking her, seizing her with sharp fingernails and foul breath, brief bursts of warehouses and ships. She screamed without a voice as she was thrown into a room, the door slamming shut.

Her father had failed her. Those men who trafficked her, who told her that Shaitan was a saviour while she was being raped, those men who drugged and browbeat her, were all the same. They said that her father hated her, and she was here because of his failure. Some said that Allah hated her for her nationality, and that Shaitan cared, because he too was neglected by the angels. Those same men sexually abused her, dehumanising her, stripping away her dignity, displaying her exotic beauty to traffickers to sell her. All that loathing and terror and insipid drugged mind rushed back into her existence. With the procedures of being tortured and sexually abused so many times, she couldn't tell which man had done what to her. She gave up remembering them, finding safety in the darkness of her heart.

Men and God were to blame. *They were* the virus, the plague that needed to be eradicated. It was *stupid revolting* Christianity and Islam that said women were evil, who caused sin in the world, and men were just innocent victims. Women had to know their place, and it was the men's mission to humble them. Just like promiscuous Eve.

It was the lie Tara knew she believed when she took up the gun.

Your father hates you. With repetition, eventually, the mind became desensitised.

If Jesus Christ the man was God, then why didn't he go to Hell?

Sheer powerlessness. Sheer desolation.

Tara let out a scream. She let out another scream – a groaning cry of desperation – arching her head. She felt sobs erupting out of her mouth and dropped the hydrolyte and the certificate. "No," she hissed in deranged repetition. "No, no, no, no, no."

Alfred took a step towards her.

"Get away from me!" She almost slipped off the gurney's rail from recoil and pain. She let out a weak groan.

"It's for your own good that you are here. The world hates people like you, Tara. You became a monster. But I still love you. I will protect you. You *are* my daughter."

Everyone hated her, a Uyghur, almost a school shooter. "NO!"

"Yes. Tara—"

"NO!"

"YES!"

"NO!"

Alfred gritted his teeth, his face scrunched in frustration. He touched her arm, and Tara roared a gasp. He retracted as if he had touched a poisonous snake. "So … you really do believe that I … abused you?" His voice was hard as ice, and his eyes filled with tears.

Tara let out a series of wild screams. She could smell his body. "No, no, no, no, no, no, no, no, no, no." She felt like a pathetic child again. She quivered so hard, her broken bones burning, and the gums around her broken teeth began to bleed. Her mind felt as if it were rushing through a funnel of fire, endlessly.

"Come back to me, Tara," Alfred begged. "Please!"

She was a poor, frightened, weak adolescent again, and there was no escape, no help. He towered over her, beating her. There was no stopping it. She cried, and he liked it. She hated him, *despised* him.

"Whatever you are thinking, they are lies! You are strong, Tara!"

Marcell was helpless, innocent.

"You're Aes Sidhe."

Aes Sidhe could fight back. They were as the saints of old – they refused to give up, even when encountering unbearable sins. They had incredible hope when they suffered. In the face of persecution, bound at the stake ready to be lit with flames, or facing the lions, they were rejoicing. Even in death, the saints fought the good fight. They stood up straight, shouldered the weights, forsook their sins and found the will to continue living.

"Fight, Tara."

She couldn't fight. If she did, she would be punished more. What was the point of living that way, knowing there were women like her who were successful and never had to suffer like she did? Young girls who got degrees and made a living for themselves. Not for Tara. She got Hell.

She wanted to rest, to sleep now. But when she woke up again …

The pain would return.

Bonner threw back his head and arms, roaring in frustration. "For goodness' sake! Tara, listen to me!" He gripped the gurney rail hard. "Your impression of me is false! It's a Cabal lie!"

"Get out!" she shrieked, her sore gums bleeding. "Get out! Take me away! I don't want to see you again! GET OUT!"

Bonner stared with shock and apprehension. And at last, a single tear trickled down his cheek. He sniffed, lips parted in bewilderment. He clamped his mouth shut and turned around, stepped to the clinic door that slid open, giving her the silent treatment. But he did not walk through; he took a deep breath, his back facing her, and said with a grinding, disappointed voice, "My daughter is strong."

And he left the clinic. The room with the strange ornate box felt poisoned, gnarled and thick. It didn't go well with the blood oozing in her mouth.

Only then did Tara break. She sobbed like a child. Working her jaws made them hurt, and the painkillers wore off. The procedures Bonner had done to her meant nothing. She wanted to curl up in a ball, but in this disjointed purgatory, defensiveness gave in, and exhaustion overtook her. She was nothing but a broken weeping husk. She tensed until she thought her blood vessels would burst. She gnashed her teeth, feeling the ones that had been broken. There was no regrowing them. Her beauty and her body were marred forever. She cried over that, as well.

Wretch, wretch, wretched Tara. You know who you are, and now you're more of a wretch than before. Why don't you just ... end it. You have no hope. There is no God to save you. Just die.

But requesting assisted suicide made her feel shameful.

A few minutes later, walking into the clinic, ducking its massive head, was a bearlike Sasquatch with a pudgy nose and onyx eyes. Tara developed the impression that it had heard her weeping – for the chaos creature had a sad, drooping countenance. With one placid, gentle hand, the giant soothed her, and Tara was fond of it. It heaved a sigh, a wind through caverns. It rumbled in samurai chatter, a bumblebee the size of a mastiff.

The creature had taken pity on her and started to push her gurney out of the clinic, leading her away. Tara lay on her back, still, mildly calm, but in terrible physical pain.

This is treason, she thought in dismay. *Treason. Alfred* is not *my father.*

Why? Why did men do this? Why did they lust after girls and women? Why did they scam? Why did Alfred abandon her to traffickers?

The Dulce base was silent when the Bigfoot unstrapped her, walking her into a sterile, square apartment complex.

Tara fumbled inside the apartment block with a window viewing a large industrial warehouse. She tucked her chin into her chest.

This is what you get … for living.

Tara found the bed and groaned in pain. She wanted to yell out all her agony, but her jaw was throbbing, so she wept even more. Sniffing and sobbing, she lay there on her bed, blood and tears wetting the sheets.

55

DUTY AND DESIRE

"And I saw an angel descending from heaven, holding the key of the abyss and a great chain in his hand. And he seized the dragon—the ancient serpent, who is the devil and Satan—and bound him for a thousand years, and threw him into the abyss, and shut it and sealed it above him, in order that he could not deceive the nations again until the thousand years are completed. After these things it is necessary for him to be released for a short time."
—From the Scroll of Revelation, John the Apostle, 95 – 96 CE.

"**A**s we discussed earlier about the Ptolemies, I spoke about hard and soft power."

Joshua sat in the theatre enthralled, listening to the last lecture of the semester with the brilliant archaeology and ancient history professor, Andrew Connor. He had a melodious voice and an admirable sense of humour.

"Hard power is the exercise of coercion and military might to subjugate subjects. It is not pleasant and so not often employed by the Hellenistic successor states, but for example, if you're dealing with a deviant family member taking over Cyrene or Cyprus, causing a bit of a muck … Welp … You're a Basileus and your power is in peril, you have no choice. You ticked someone off and someone ticks you off, you gotta crush them with hard power!

"On the other hand, with soft power, you can create social appeal. I mean, killing people outright is … ugh, well. Confronting. Soft power is effective when you make higher education more expensive to keep most of the population in manual labour jobs. Most are indifferent to soft power when subliminal messaging is used to inform the unconscious. Like the Ptolemies, you construct libraries and places of learning to create a milieu of scholarship, for knowledge nourishes power. So basically, this ideology is *Pax Romana.* Or rather … *Pax Aegyptius."* Andrew Connor chuckled. "Yeah … Latin … So, uhmm. You make everyone think you are pro-culture and give them their freedom. Syncretise their native culture with your own, and then the people will willingly come under your rule. I know it's pretty generalised, but this is *basically* what soft power is.

"But if you were like the Ptolemies and the Attalids sponsoring the humanities, you were on a mission to smuggle books and boycott papyrus productions so you could become the greatest library in the world. I mean, this is basically inebriation at the state's expense. The Ptolemies initially did a good job of strengthening the bonds between the ruler and the masses. Not very different from today, huh. I wonder …

"History is a cycle. It repeats itself. And in this cycle, there is progress towards significant events. And these events are what give time momentum to push forward."

———

Inspired by Andrew Connor's lecture, Joshua remembered the Alliance. Two hours later, he sat in the quiet Hatfield Library studying about Osiris and why the Alliance used the Marine Corps to uncover his tomb that they thought was in Uruk. This thought had been living in Joshua's mind since spring, but only now did he have the spare time to investigate the situation.

What is clearly evident in the Abydos royal cemetery is the ideology of kingship, as symbolised by the mortuary cult, Joshua read from *The Oxford History of Ancient Egypt* by Ian Shaw[1], talking about the emergence of the ideology of Egyptian kingship and how the unified state came about from the perspective of the changes in mortuary material culture. The controversial finds at Uruk – still unpublished – had been given by word of mouth from Marcus Theis to Joshua. From his testimony, the coffin Alfred Bonner found there *seemed* to be from the latter part of the Early Dynastic at the end of the Uruk Period (c. 3200 – 2700 BCE), containing niched palace facade features that reflected Pre and Early Dynastic (c. 3050 – 2686 BCE) Egyptian mortuary structures. If true, this coffin could be one of the earliest pieces of evidence of a two-

1   1: Bard, Kathryn A. 2002. *The Oxford History of Ancient Egypt.* ed Ian Shaw, 70.

way exchange of Egyptian and Mesopotamian culture. As of yet, the official consensus was a one-way transmission of Sumerian architecture into Egypt. Marcus' story suggested that evidence for a two-way exchange exists, but Alfred Bonner, with his soft power, covered it up.

But Joshua was determined that there had to be hints and answers about such connections hidden in the research. He read on.

The king was accorded with the most elaborate burial, which was symbolic of his role as a mediator between the powers of the netherworld and his deceased subjects, and the belief in an earthy and cosmic order would have provided a certain amount of social cohesion for the Early Dynastic state.

Joshua flicked to the back of the volume to the index, searching for Osiris and kingship, finding an interesting entry[2].

The ideology of kingship not only encompassed the world of the living but also gives the king a critical function beyond the grave: the living king is the embodiment of Horus and rules the living; the deceased king is Osiris, king of the dead, but, at the same time, since Osiris in this context was assimilated with Ra, the king expected to participate in the cycle of cosmic action. In order to propel the king into his life beyond the grave and maintain him there, an elaborate programme of ritual was devised, the most spectacular surviving illustrations of which are the pyramids of the Old and Middle Kingdoms and the New Kingdom tombs in the Valley of the Kings and their attendant cult temples.

Joshua set aside Ian Shaw's volume, then picked through the books at his desk. His studies for his last assignments and essays were done in time for the reading period, and now he had some time on his hands to continue his research into the topic that most interested him.

On the other side of Joshua's desk, Pawani's book rustled as she turned the page. Joshua glanced at her. She was in his class, completing the same ancient history essay, reading and taking notes on her computer. For one semester, Joshua had only gotten to meet her while studying – she attended one of his classes – and for that reason, they'd become comfortable, simple friends.

Pawani was not an extravert type. She always set a high standard for herself. She was young, perhaps twenty, holding herself with a stately poise, tall and slender with deep, thick onyx hair, part of it rolled up in a bun. The rest tumbled down behind her neck in small, tight twisted curls reaching her shoulders. It seemed that her favourite colour outfit was a dark violet; she wore a blouse, trousers and a dark-purple woolly jumper – an immaculate blend of formality and the casual. Statuesque with a full bust, Pawani was

2   : Lloyd, Alan B. 2002. *The Oxford History of Ancient Egypt,* ed Ian Shaw, 378.

intelligent and pretty.

Focus. Joshua glanced at his notebook and wrote: *The divine ordination made the Egyptian king a god on earth. This meant kinship between the gods and the king was reciprocal, and the political and divine were inextricably linked with the reigning pharaoh as the literal image of Horus, and in death – eternity – Osiris.*

And this is why the Alliance has the image of the Bennu bird/phoenix as their symbol. They are invoking the god Osiris and the metaphysical power of the pharaohs.

But why the pharaohs? Joshua almost chuckled out loud, but stifled it, glancing at Pawani's concentrated elegance.

Gilgamesh was *not* Osiris – but they *did* become the judges of the dead …

That's interesting. The only similarities between the two were their power to judge the dead … but not the living. Sliding a slim book out from under the stack: Assyriologist Thorkild Jacobsen's *The Treasures of Darkness: A History of Mesopotamian Religion*, Joshua turned to the excerpts from chapter seven.

Further evidence of Gilgamesh's prominence as a power in the netherworld comes in a composition of about 2100 BC dealing with the death of the first king of the Third Dynasty of Ur, Ur-Nammu. Gilgamesh appears as a judge in the Realm of the Dead. He occurs in that role much later, in magical texts of the first millennium, where he is appealed to for judgment against wayward ghosts and other evils.[3]

Joshua tapped the page, thinking. He wrote down a note saying: *Gilgamesh in the Ur-Nammu story is a judge of the underworld, like Osiris. This is also confirmed by Andrew George (2003, 128 – 129)[4]. The story discusses Bilgamesh (with the superscript divine derivative* dingir *before his name) as a chthonic judge of the underworld with the gods Dumuzi and Ningishzida, as well as with Nergal, Bidu and Etana. Compare to Osiris depictions in the* Book of the Dead.

Joshua glanced at Pawani, admiring her presence, and continued writing.

An Early Dynastic Egyptian royal tomb in Early Dynastic Uruk was nonsense. The new article published by Susan Sherratt in *Archaeology and Myth* revealed the need for objective archaeological eyes to reconstruct evidence without the aid of texts such as the Bible, the *Gilgamesh Epic* and Homer's *Iliad*.

<u>*Evidence of*</u> *offerings for the deified Gilgamesh appears in the mid-third*

3   : Jacobsen, Thorkild. 1978. *The Treasures of Darkness: A History of Mesopotamian Religion*. Yale University, 211.

4   : George, Andrew. 2003. *Babylonian Gilgamesh Epic Introduction, Critical Edition and Cuneiform Texta – Volume 1*, Oxford.

millennium (George 2003, 122-127), Joshua wrote down, synthesising his notes. *The epic Sumerian stories would have been sung during wrestling competitions and pit rituals during the New Year's festivals to venerate great ancestors. Osiris' story too was celebrated at the sacred city of Abydos – the necropolis of the Early Dynastic kings, the place of Osiris' tomb and the Gateway into the Daut (Underworld) – as the festival on the Stela of Ikhernofret records (Gunnels 2003.)[5]*

Alfred Bonner's subjectivity was crazy. He was an impish opportunist who tried to look for something unlikely. Like the tombs of Alexander the Great and King Arthur, it was erroneously impossible to uncover the tomb of Gilgamesh. Yet, a tomb *had* been found in Uruk, legendary enough to attract Alfred Bonner to smuggle it. It wasn't so different from the majestic mausoleum of Qin Shi Huang, the god-emperor of China, with his breathtaking terracotta armies. Remarkable evidence for remarkable truths.

Joshua revisited a section from Andrew George's new translation and critical edition of the Babylonian Gilgamesh Epic and referenced it. *George asks, "Could … the Epic of twelve tablets … be put to ritual use, sung or recited, for example, at funerals and in memorial cults? Was it perhaps performed at the funerals of the kings?" (George 2003, 54). It could be part of a large-scale purification ritual. This might suggest that these figures (Osiris and Gilgamesh) had the same ontological function. The only thing they have in common was their relationship with the dead, immortality and their divinity after death, casting out evil ghosts, and their role as a judge.*

Yet, this is all frivolous speculation. The evidence is not strong enough to make a solid case that Osiris and Gilgamesh are the same god.

"But *why* is the Alliance so interested in them both?" Joshua said frustratingly. *I need to get an extensive study on death and burial in Sumer,* he thought.

"Hmmm?" Pawani asked.

"Oh. Sorry," Joshua smiled. "I was thinking out loud."

"What are you studying?" Pawani asked. She had a calm recognisable Indian accent. She seemed to know English very well, and Joshua could not tell if it was her second language.

Joshua glanced up at the young Indian woman – she was leaning forward from across the desk, hands folded over her book. "Death and myths in Egypt and Mesopotamia," Joshua said.

A modest smirk appeared on her face. "That's wonderful. You're studying

5 : Gunnels, Naomi L. 2003. "The Ikrenofret Stela as Theatre: A Cross-cultural Comparison" In *Studia Antiqua 2, no. 2,* 3 – 16.

for an assignment?"

"No, I'm having a break because I submitted all my assessments. I'm researching for my own interests now," Joshua said, trying to make himself appear that he was at least dedicated to his studies – all his course fees paid for from Pounders' pocket couldn't go to waste. He had to make the most of his time here at university.

"Ah," Pawani said softly, tilting her head. "That's cool."

"What are you studying? The assignment?"

"I got an extension on it," she said. "I'm doing trade contact with Seleucid cities and India. I really like this question, because you can talk about Hellenisation and such, but then you can talk about Ai Khanoum with its cultural bricolage. I like this cultural entanglement idea because it's … underrated."

"Yeah. The Seleucids are not well known. They had parchment that degrades in moist alluvium. Egypt's deserts preserve tombs and loads of papyrus. Most of the evidence survives in Egypt. Except for the clay tablets. Clay tablets in temple archives are imperishable."

"Yeah. The Seleucids were the most powerful of all the Hellenistic successor states to become an empire. Antiochus the Great. Elephants. Family court politics. Awesome!" Pawani smiled, leaning her chin on her hand. She was just *wonderful.*

"Ha, you're right."

"Hmm. That's why I chose that Seleucid essay, because it connected things for me. When I was young, I studied the Mauryan Empire and Indus Valley cultures out of general interest. And the Seleucids were the first to make contact with King Chandragupta of the Mauryan Empire for five hundred war elephants, opening the Silk Roads to the West."

Joshua's mouth formed an intrigued O. "Woah, yeah, I remember. Since that's your passion, I hope your work goes well. Better than me, at least."

Pawani giggled – a deep chuckle, impressed by his humility. Pawani, just by her appearance, her presence, meant she was mature beyond her years. For a girl like her – she was incredibly smart. She was doing a double degree in anthropology and biology, while also doing an elective on Hellenistic archaeology and ancient history.

"I already handed in my essay," Joshua sighed.

"You're punctual. How did it go? Which essay did you do?"

"Oh, the one about Ptolemy's policies as a satrap. You know. Soft power. The priesthood." The only issue was Joshua had no level of enthusiasm compared to the enthusiasm Pawani had for her assignment, and it made him feel a lack of achievement and distraught that he had to mention it.

"Great question," Pawani said.

"Yeah, I guess … You grew up learning about Indian cultures?" Joshua said. He wanted to give Pawani a chance to talk, desiring to learn more about her. "I know nothing about them. Where did you start studying it? I mean, you've travelled to India a lot, I assume."

"Yes," Pawani said. "My family is from there." She swallowed, and suddenly her serious sternness became extremely awkward. Her eyes roved around. "It began when I went to school in New Delhi. But yes, my father, who was an archaeologist, exposed me to the Indus cities. I assessed the fieldwork at Rakhigarhi on weekends. On holidays, I would help him."

"And how old were you?"

"It was my first job. I was in middle school, so about sixteen. Yeah, but even before that, I've been fascinated by religion, not just from my own culture, but in the Mediterranean as well."

Joshua twirled his ballpoint pen in his hand, smirking. "Wonderful. You know, I used to help at dig sites, but when I did it, I kind of … let's just say … I tried to be an Indiana Jones wannabe. I got in *big* trouble. I even went to prison." Joshua's face burned. How could he be so honest about such a shameful past? Pawani would think he was unstable! Yet … he could afford to gamble his honesty with a privileged, pretty girl like this. He blushed furiously. "Yeah. I screwed up."

Pawani laughed – a short melodious chime of amusement. Her smile radiated wonder. "You're such a *bad boy*."

Joshua blushed harder. "Well … Look. I don't like talking about it. It's in the past. I learnt my lesson. I hated myself back then."

Pawani nodded eagerly, suddenly sympathetic.

Joshua lowered his glance in humiliation, fiddling with the page of his notebook. He felt foolish for willingly making himself feel self-conscious in front of this girl. Her brown eyes glanced at him. Pawani had *no idea* where he had come from or what anguish he'd gone through.

Joshua had been observing Pawani lately – they were studying the same archaeology unit together – a course that most normal people would think was interesting, yet completely irrelevant to life and what was in demand in the market. Ideally, it was cheaper to do commerce, business, design and science than arts, history and theology. Why would a normal person want to waste their money studying something so niche and different from everyone else?

That was why Joshua admired Pawani. Not only did it remind him that he wasn't alone, but just like Joshua, they were different and the same.

"So, uhm …" Joshua intoned. He wanted to make this conversation about Pawani – he didn't like to think about where he came from. "You have any plans for the future after you graduate?"

Pawani leaned forward on the table. "Well …" A one-sided smirk appeared on her face, and she shook her head. "I want to do masters and become an academic. As for my thesis in primatology, I want to go along with it, but … Josh, unfortunately, I haven't been getting a lot of traction lately."

"Okay. Why is that?"

Pawani huffed out a sigh, her chin in the V of her fingers. "I don't know. I think, in part, it's because of factors that I cannot change – I am a migrant Indian from a large, fairly average, middle-class family. I'm at this point now where I could only gain money from scholarships and part-time jobs on campus."

"That's rough," Joshua said. "So I assume you don't get enough savings for travelling, then?"

Pawani shrugged. She determinedly gazed at her screen – at her research. There was a longing in her brown eyes. "I wish there was something I could do. But better not focus on that now." She smiled. "I'd rather work on my essays and pracs, then worry about all that other stuff later."

"I agree with that. You know, I could help," Joshua said. "I could fund you. I have a well-paying job. And since I worked in the military, one of the colonels became my legal guardian when I left the Middle East. He's given me a tonne of money. It wouldn't hurt me if I transfer some cash into your account. I suppose it's the best I could do."

Pawani looked stunned – her mouth hanging open, and she gazed at Joshua in the eyes. "You're serious?" her voice sounded passively surprised.

"Yeah. Now that I've spit it out, I guess. Serious."

A part of Joshua felt pained he had to do this, but the Spirit within him felt accomplished by his generosity.

Suddenly, Pawani's hand, reaching across the table, held Joshua's hand. His heart swelled, and he sweated.

For what seemed like the longest time, Pawani studied him intently, and then smiled. "That is *so kind* of you, but also extremely stupid."

"What?" Joshua slurred.

"You don't just give money away to strangers, silly."

"But you're not a stranger—" His face was burning now, but he couldn't hide now from her, he couldn't even *think* straight!

"I don't want to become a liability," Pawani whispered, leaning towards him. She still held his hand. "But … If you're willing … That would mean my life. Thank you." She tilted her head and grinned fondly at him.

Joshua felt his mouth go dry. His insides started to melt, and all the world vanished except for Pawani and her face. It made him tingle, to the point he feared he might not have full control of the strange physiological reactions occurring in his body.

He cleared his throat and gazed at his sweaty hands, letting go of hers. All of a sudden, she had this ambitious glint in her eyes – but it quickly vanished. "Josh, I appreciate your kindness."

"Ah, it's nothing."

That had not been entirely honest – but Joshua did feel it was something – he felt pleased with himself. As an image of Christ – a priest – he'd bore God's name and aimed to give to others and to cultivate a virtuous character above all.

"Can I ask you a question now before I forget?" Pawani said. "Do you … Well, you are also studying theology. I'm curious. Not interrogating you or anything, but do you believe in God?"

Joshua paused, shocked. The opportunity of witness had come. "Well, well. What a pickup line, girl!"

She laughed, throwing back her head.

"Let me ask you first, I think. Do you believe in God?"

"No."

Joshua felt a part of him go cold with disappointment, but he listened, intrigued.

"I'm an atheist," she said boldly, "but religion always intrigued me, and I've thought a lot about it and concluded that there is no higher power. My upbringing was Hindu. As I grew up, I became very critical of Hinduism's caste system. If the gods are real and are good, I don't understand why they approve of that." Joshua felt disappointment – apologetic pushback arguments formed in his mind, but he forever held his peace. "The supernatural seems very much like the things of fiction and imagination, not reality. And God is the greatest invention of fiction. So yeah. I believe in truth, reason and integrity. But I'm happy to be wrong and change my belief according to the evidence."

Joshua's hand covered his mouth, and he thought, *Fascinating! She desires to seek the truth and is not afraid to change her mind? I have never met an atheist who thinks like this!* Suddenly, Pawani's love of truth, reason and integrity became very relatable, despite her atheism.

"Now, do *you* believe in God?" Pawani said.

"Oh! Pawani, you're putting me on the spot!"

She chuckled. "It's okay. I will not judge you. You don't have to answer if you don't feel comfortable."

"Yeah, Pawani … I'm a theist." Pawani nodded acceptingly. "I believe in Christianity because its universal moral truths can be found in all religions and … and I found purpose in Christianity. I grew up as an atheist – a nihilist, in fact. I was in a very dark place in my life. Atheism for me is depressing. It made me into a scam, a horrible person who was jealous and succeeding at the expense of others. In prison, I had a religious experience. It was *so powerful* that, when I served in Iraq, I refused to use a gun and became a medic. I was *very stubborn* about it. A bit too stubborn, I think."

Pawani's eyes were wide with wonder. "That's … wonderful. Well, look, that's your truth, and you have no doubts. Albert Einstein said that all empirical knowledge comes from experience. And your experiences are *powerful*." She was nodding, enthralled, her brown eyes locked on his.

"Yes," he said abruptly. "I feel like saying being Christian in a secular world is not conventional. But our world is culturally relative, so … it should be normal to believe in God, but apparently … not anymore."

"But as long as you are brave about it, wise, and you're a kind person, it's okay to believe, I think."

Then, out of the corner of his eye, Joshua saw a tall man walking sturdily towards him. An erudite man with jet black skin, hair just as black, with purple eyes, wearing a slick suit and tie.

"Nefer?" Joshua squealed, almost having a heart attack. He jumped to his feet, startling Pawani. "*What are you doing here?*"

"Greetings," the angelic scholar and seer said in human form, shameless and bold, a sly smile splitting his onyx face.

"Y–You shouldn't be here!" Joshua exclaimed. "How did you—?

"I couldn't help it. I found out that I can blend in, and I find your library is *very* immersive."

"Ohh. Couldn't you … Couldn't you *just wait?*" Joshua wheezed, rubbing his face with both hands, humiliated.

"What is waiting?" Nefer boasted. "Your concept of waiting is very inaccurate. I don't wait. I simply am. You might as well say a tree is waiting."

"What are you doing? You're not ready to—"

"What are you talking about? Of course I am ready, silly."

Joshua's mind was racing, with terrible wrath projected towards this spiritual being. He felt himself flushing as he saw Pawani slowly sliding on her chair away from the spiritual being in the flesh – to her, it was a queer African man with pitch-black ebony skin. But Nefer didn't care; he was smiling boldly, eyeing the young woman with a lofty gaze, his purple eyes probing pensively.

"By the way, nice to meet you, Joshua's girlfriend," the scholar said, smiling, holding out his hand to Pawani. She gladly shook it. "Your name?"

"Pawani …"

"Ah, Pawani," the angel proclaimed loudly. "I'm Nefer. Joshua's spiritual father."

"You're … a priest?"

"No. I'm an agent of order, an astrophysicist and a philosopher of prescience, assisting the cosmos in divinatory guidance to the concealed—"

"Shhh," Joshua sounded. Pawani was grinning with perplexed delight at the candid angel's peculiar professions.

"Sorry." Nefer lowered his voice. "I'm full of joy now that I can interact. But this is a library. And libraries hate noise. But you mentioned God." He looked at Pawani. "I'm *fond* of God talk." Nefer chuckled.

Pawani was completely silent. She looked shocked and set back.

"Oh, Nefer," Joshua groaned, his hands rubbing his face. "Why? You ruined everything. This is why you're not ready to socialise."

"I'm perplexed that you don't trust me after all I have done for you." The scholar sounded disheartened. "And no, nothing is ruined. In fact, you two are blessed."

Joshua wilted, overwhelmed. He felt himself blushing terribly, so much he felt as if the hair on his head were turning red. He saw Pawani frowning deeply. "Nice to … talk to you, Josh," she said very slowly. "It's getting late, and I've got to go." She gave him an awkward smile, hastily packing her books and laptop away into her bag. "See ya!" She waved, smiling wonderfully at him, and departed.

"Nefer," Joshua said, clenching his fists. "What are you doing?"

"Ben needs you, Joshua."

"What?"

Nefer's voice became stern. "Ben is suffering grievous thraldom. He's alone. Staying here is great, but now is the time to act as you were meant to act. When your studies are over for the semester, return to Arizona."

"What?"

"Your friend is homeless."

"Ben is not my friend!"

Nefer ignored him. "No one loves him, no one prays for him, and no one has the capability to understand him at this time. Only you can do this. You call yourself a theologian? Then get out of the library and get into the field!"

Joshua sighed, slumping. "So this is why you came. To get into my face when I was talking to a girl. Such *bad* timing."

"Oh, but my timing is always perfect."

"You better give me a good reason to leave after reading period," Joshua growled. "I made myself clear. I will *never* go back to that … layman virgin city again!"

"I have a good reason."

"Yeah, what is it?"

"Josh, it is to participate in the Kingdom of God! What better reason is there? And boy, did I ever say that you're a whiner? I had to put up with your whining when Pounders enlisted you in the marines, and now you whine when I enlist you to serve the Kingdom of God? You're *not* going to Phoenix, buddy. Return to Tucson. That's where Ben is right now."

Joshua had been humbled again, frustrated and persuaded by being humiliated. If an angel had come with a mission on his lips, then he could not hesitate, no matter what he felt.

"When are we leaving?" Joshua said.

"Next week. I've ordered you tickets for a nine thirty flight to Tucson on Sunday. A strange portent is coming."

56

THE SIGNS OF THE TIMES

"I saw thrones on which were seated those who had been given authority to judge. And I saw the souls of those who had been beheaded because of their testimony of Jesus and because of the word of God. I also saw those who had not worshiped the Beast or its image and had not received its mark on their foreheads or their hands. They came to life and reigned with Christ a thousand years. (The rest of the dead did not come to life until the thousand years were ended.) This is the first resurrection. Blessed and holy are those who share in the first resurrection. The second death has no power over them, but they will be priests of God and of Christ and will reign with him for a thousand years."
—From the Scroll of Revelation, John the Apostle, 95 – 96 CE.

Lugging butter chicken curry and basmati rice in a foil plastic packet inside a bag, Joshua walked between bronze trees with orange and yellow deciduous leaves, confident that Nefer knew where Ben was.

But what made Joshua even more worried was that Nefer had given him visions of different possible futures. They were conditional prognostications, based on the behaviour of the people, and were not fated to happen regardless of what one did. Blessings and curses – good outcomes and bad outcomes of the prophecy – were contingent on the people's actions. God was shaping Ben like a potter shaped clay. At any moment, the potter could change the shape of the clay to make a new vessel.

Joshua realised that his visions depended on the acts of the people, and the future was left open and malleable, to help give the people a chance to prevent the prophetic disaster and delay it.

If Nefer didn't force him, Joshua, in his free will, would have abandoned

Ben in his needy state. Ben then would live long enough to become a villain. This was the great disaster fated to come upon Ben if he did not repent.

But this could change. In the best possible world, Joshua could avert disaster. In it, he was helping Ben, guiding him to repentance, showing him grace and compassion. And then Ben became one of the greatest saints in history. *Ridiculous! The Actionman, a saint?*

So Joshua chose to come to Tucson, hoping that the latter, more positive vision, could actualise.

Prophecy appeared at face value, like chance, but Nefer was far from a fortune teller. As a diviner and astrophysicist, he revealed a schematic administrative calendar for Joshua to help Ben, who was having visions of the past. Joshua was naturally sceptical if he should trust the visions, but Nefer had become confident in Ben. *The calendar is to bless Ben only,* Nefer insisted. *Do not use the calendar for anything else but for Ben, says Yahweh.*

The spiritual scholar expounded about a celestial alignment and Ben's gift of visions of ancient history – a rare convergence between the past and the present. But what was interesting, the past was revealed as *fixed and true,* whereas Joshua's visions for the future *seldom* came true. They were often cancelled. Indeed, Andrew Connor in the "Judaism During the Time of Jesus" Unit once said that in the ancient Greco-Jewish world, there was barely a concept of linear time in a *kronos* sense – the abstract flow of time separate from events, divided into days and years. But Hebrew cultures emphasised time in a *kairos* sense – moments in time that herald great, sudden change. Something would not be at the right *kairos* time unless it was within the conditions appropriate for it to occur.

This was why the Kingdom of God was here and the end was here. In a *kairos* sense, it was the next thing on God's soteriological "to-do list". It didn't matter how long it took. Two thousand years in a *kronos* sense felt long, but in a *kairos* sense, it was the next thing here. *But for that to happen,* Joshua thought, *the world has to repent first.* And if Joshua could help Ben repent…

Joshua knew his visions that came true had the best outcomes, important for *kairos* time. And in that case, Joshua would come down to find Ben where he was at and tell him this revelation.

Joshua found the dirt road, gravel crunching loudly under his shoes. The sun's warmth through the trees and the orange leaves was thick and hot. He found Ben's truck parked in a campsite in the middle of nowhere. Joshua froze behind a tree, thinking, *Does Ben even know I am coming? This could be a gnarly confrontation! Nefer, why did you have me do this?* Joshua stood behind the tree, procrastinating, filled with trepidation. Vulnerability was foolishness when dealing with a man that was as problematic as Ben.

Toxic, abusive and a vindictive person, Ben had all the wealth and the fame of Hollywood. The FBI were chasing Ben. He ought to be paranoid and aggressive at this point.

Joshua longed for the university setting. The opportunities. Longed for scholarship, longed for researching ancient cultures, archaeology, religion and languages. *I've had enough traumatising experiences this year already! Give me a break, God! Why don't you send another Christian and not me?*

But that was exactly the same excuse Moses gave to God. And God got angry for the first time in the Hebrew Bible because of it.

"Ben. Hey, it's Joshua. The Bookworm. Ben, if you're there, just know I'm trying to help you. I have no intention of disclosing your location. I promise. Here, I have some food for you in this bag. I also have some advice about your visions."

He heard a sleeping bag rustle. "Show yourself, Josh," Ben said, voice deep and croaky. "How did you find me?"

Joshua turned from behind the tree trunk and walked into Ben's campsite. "An angel told me," he said honestly. Ben didn't react. "Look, it's a long story, but I decided to come and help you."

"Fair enough. Anyone associated with me will ruin their track record. Are you afraid of me?"

"Yes," Joshua said, lifting his chin.

Ben chuckled. "Brave man. You're being silly. I would never hurt you, Joshua."

"But I'm being honest. I have to come clean."

"Joshua … Seriously, I want to see you. I want to talk to someone face to face for a change."

It was as if something had died inside Ben, slowly infecting him from the inside, spilling out occasionally in emotionless silence. The summer had been brutal on him. His skin was tanned, and he slumped, looking underweight. He'd let his mottled bushy beard grow long and fuzzy, obstructing his sunburnt face. His bald head was covered by a wide-brimmed hat. Ben wore a singlet and biker pants, and he reeked of sweat and body odour. It was depressing seeing a model failing to look after himself.

"So, how are you, Ben?" Joshua said, as Ben offered him a seat on a weather-worn wooden bench. "You're going through a liminal time. Must be tough."

Ben sighed deeply. "It's pretty crap if you ask me. Gets cold at night. I have nightmares. I worry every day, making no progress. But … the DePaulas are tough oxen."

"I'm sure the DePaulas are," Joshua said, placing the bag of butter chicken and rice on the table.

Ben glanced at the bag, fingering it. "Thank you. You made it?"

"No. I went to a restaurant that a friend of mine recommended to me. This is her favourite food."

"She?"

Joshua shifted his feet. "She's an undergraduate from Willamette University, and we study archaeology together."

"Sounds hard," Ben said dully, pressing his lips together. After months of not getting caught by police, living in the woods, Ben had changed, developing a restrictive nature. His eyes told Joshua that. They were full of mistrust and disbelief. "My father used to study the same thing. He believed in angels. I think one ruined my life … So, a girl, you were saying?"

Joshua swallowed hard. "Well, she is not building a fiefdom like your father did. She is scientific, loves scholarship and is very lovely."

"Good. Someone not poisoned by conspiracy Kool-Aid for a change," Ben said. "And she's single? What does she look like? What's her hair colour?"

Joshua gawked with unease. *Why is he asking me this?* Ben was a womaniser – he had been deprived of women for months, so he couldn't help asking about a young cute girl. It made Joshua feel shameful about his masculinity. *Oh, this is terrible. I'm wasting my time here!* "What? Why?"

Ben shrugged. "I want to know what my friend Josh has been up to." He grinned. "Virgin."

"Ah!" Joshua blushed. "That's just an expression. It's a nicer way than calling you an uneducated layman, but … Pawani and I are not dating."

"Pawani? Is she Mexican? Canadian?"

"Indian. She's nice."

"Is she tall? Skinny or corpulent?"

Joshua sighed protractedly. "Tall. Healthy. Loves good academia. Okay, can we stop? Don't be getting ideas. She is definitely *not* your type."

"Hahaha!" Ben threw back his head, guffawing. Joshua frowned. He felt envy creep into his heart at how Ben could become so light-hearted during his ordeal when Joshua didn't. *No! You're privileged, Josh! You're blessed! You need nothing of Ben!* "But Josh, *you are* her type! You're like what – in your early to mid-twenties? You should go for her. You're not a virgin – you're a lady's man!"

A pesky grin crept over Ben's face.

"Man, Ben, you just … don't get it."

"I do?"

"You know the effort it took for me to come here was very painful? I had to leave as soon as the semester was done. It's very embarrassing. I think Pawani will hate me because I am associated with you."

Ben sighed. "I'm sorry, bro … I'm cursed …"

Cooling down his anger, Joshua took in his surroundings. He inhaled the variety of pungent natural smells from plants and tree bark. *Now … why are you here, Joshua?* Anxiety and fear paralysed him. His mouth quivered. "Yeah … Uh … Ben, I have something important to tell you."

He's going to think me insane when I tell him about religion, the visions and the moedim. Ben's light-heartedness vanished. He remained stone hard with tension, a dangerous expression on his face. Swallowing, Joshua met those narrowing eyes looming over him, mad with grief.

Tell him. Speak the truth in love.

"You have visions of ancient times, am I right?" Joshua said.

He beheld the transformation on Ben's countenance: confusion, then shock, fear and anger, morphing and unsettled.

"Look, I can give you advice on it," Joshua said. "God has communicated what you need to do in the light of the Kingdom of God through dreams and the positions of the stars and planets." Joshua felt dismayed – it was *not* an ideal way to introduce Ben to the zodiac calendar, because he would probably think that Joshua used astrology to divine the future.

But Ben did the unexpected. He made an impish expression, saying curtly, "Nostradamus. Nice."

"Nice?" Joshua started, the tension dissolving. "I'm *not* a Nostradamus. I'm giving you advice *for the present* so you can change *in the present* in the light of God's future life. I cannot divine the future like an oracle. It's impossible."

"I don't know if that's a good thing or a bad thing," Ben said.

Was he willing to suspend his disbelief? "Oh, I have something to give to you." Joshua reached into his pocket and handed Ben a slip of paper with the dates Nefer had given to Joshua. For a while, Ben studied it closely.

"What is all this?"

"Well, Ben, those are the seven holidays of God in the Pentateuch – the first five books of the Bible," Joshua said. "They are called *moedim*. They are like … literally, it means a time for an appointment or meeting with God. A holy convocation."

"How did they calculate it?" Ben said.

Joshua grinned. "In Genesis, the sun, moon and stars are to be for signs and for sacred feasts and for days and years. The celestial bodies regulate the lives of humans by ruling space just as humans regulate and rule over the Earth. The whole point of these *moedim* is to celebrate God's creative and redemptive work in time and space. To rule in him. Understanding these *moedim* is understanding the very mind of God."

Ben's eyebrows rose. "But these *moedim* are *Jewish* holidays! Why are they so important for me? I thought Easter and Christmas were the important days."

"For us, they are. But Christmas is a man-made holiday to honour Jesus' birth. Easter is a distortion of Passover – the original *moedim* of God that it was based on. The *moedim* contain wisdom, revealing secrets hidden since the world began."

Frowning, Ben leaned towards Joshua. He reeked, yet Joshua held out the small chart and used his finger to point out details. "All the feast days fall during the equinoxes, three in the first month and three in the seventh month. So ultimately, the calendar operates to maximise fruitfulness and surplus. The idea is anticipating a world that lives off Eden land. In the modern West, everything we use to calculate time is so removed from nature and how humans have been calculating time since the beginning, we miss the stellar tune of God's calendar."

"All right, I'm following. How can you actually organise this?" Ben said softly. He didn't sound interested, and Joshua felt a wave of doubt flow through him, and a dismayed thought flashed by in his head saying, *This is worthless.*

I've already started. I will finish educating him.

"There are three main divisions of this calendar," Joshua continued. "The days of the week are determined by the moon's phases, divided into four quarters. The months are determined by the star constellations and the year by the sun."

"But why are there seven of them? What does this mean?" Woebegone, Ben's forehead accordioned as he swallowing hard. "What *moedim* was it when I had my visions? The last vision I had was in late March. Which *moedim* would that be?"

"Pentecost, most likely."

"How do you know?" Ben said.

"Well, in Israelite culture, the year was divided by the twelve constellations. The zodiac – the Greek word for the Circle of Animals – and in Hebrew, the Mazzaroth. They are determined by the sun travelling – the Earth orbiting –

through each of the twelve chambers of the sky. Twelve constellations equal twelve months. This helps anchor and fix the calendar, so it doesn't intercalate or change every year where you have to add a thirteenth month and an eighth day of the week all the time. These days all go from sunset to sunset the next day. This is because the Hebrew calendar is inclusive, and includes the night as part of a single day."

Nefer, in the span of a week, had showed Joshua so much about the Israelite calendar given to Moses and his elders, forgotten completely to history. It was amazing. The truth had come to Joshua as a gift he had never asked for.

Ultimately, the big difference between the calendar of the Israelites and the Babylonian Jewish lunar calendar was the intercalated thirteenth month. As any accurate modern calendar revealed, a thirteenth month didn't exist. The moon phases didn't add up to three hundred and sixty-five days, making the intercalated alignment between the solar and lunar calendars ad hoc, uncertain and inconsistent.

Joshua was told by Nefer that Ben's apocalypses would happen just when the conditions were right, on the sacred space of time on a day of a *moedim*.

Yahweh does not work on our schedule. He works on his own schedule, Nefer had said. *We are at the culminative point in history where the Word of God is going to conquer the nations. He invites us to participate in an authentic and embodied Kingdom where all humans who accept the Word can belong and have fulfilling lives. Ben's visions are to prepare him for this. But he is lost and living in the Flesh. You need to help him. Don't worry, we have time. The end will not come until all that needs to be accomplished is done. When this Kingdom is accomplished, then it will move God to act to send his Messiah. All the most important events of God's plan have come to pass. The next and last big things to happen, during the appropriate season, is the Kingdom and the Second Coming. The time is indeed near. But it depends on the world. Depends on Ben. They need to repent first before the Second Coming can happen.*

"So, to answer your question, Ben," Joshua said. "The reason why you had a vision was because that day in March was Pentecost or Shavuot in Hebrew. God's appointed time."

"And … what am I appointed to do, exactly?" Ben remarked, shifting uncomfortably on his seat, forehead creased.

"Prepare for the Kingdom of God. You need to repent. There is a big sign coming. A blood moon will rise on the fall equinox this year. The Powers of the heavens and the Powers on the Earth will be punished, and they will be locked in prison. Both the sun and moon will be dismayed, because God Almighty will reign in Zion and Jerusalem with great glory. Cosmic and social upheaval is coming. It is God punishing the fallen gods who deny Christ's crucifixion and resurrection – the act that reconciles them with God. Earthquakes, eclipses and blood moons. They mean the annihilation of rebellious power, not the end of the physical world."

"That's … something." Ben gazed up from the *moedim* schedule. "What month of the Hebrew calendar are we in now? I've lost track of time, and I want to be ready for my next vision."

"Leo. But Virgo is coming soon. And in Virgo, there are three very important *moedim*."

Ben sighed, dismayed. "Okay. So, I have three visions coming, and there's a stellar alignment on the fall equinox this year. This sounds apocalyptic."

"It *is* apocalyptic," Joshua said. "A lot of people lose hope, and they scoff because God is being slack. For they deliberately overlook this fact, that the Earth existed long ago, and it has been through many extinctions of fire and flooding, yet life has evolved to survive. God is not slow to fulfil his promise as some count slowness, but is patient towards you, not wishing that any should perish, but that all should reach repentance."

"What does this entail for us?" The skin on Ben's face appeared to blanch. He seemed in awe and in reverence to Joshua now, seeing him for what he was – an Envisager.

"I came here to offer you hope, to show you a path of repentance. It's crucial to turn away from your sins and embrace change. I was compelled to come from the Pacific Northwest to assist you, Captain, not to flaunt my righteousness or knowledge. Repentance is essential, because without it, you perpetuate destruction."

"What is repentance?" Ben whispered.

"Turning a one eighty from your pride and turning back towards God," Joshua said. "God seeks to abolish death, and by embracing Jesus, you can find salvation before it's too late." Joshua paused, taking a deep breath. He had to be blunt, taking this Gospel risk. For it was better to take a gospel risk and fail than fail to take the gospel risk.

Joshua noticed Ben's mouth was parted in shock. "I thank you, by the way, for forcing me into the Iraq war," Joshua said. "It was a momentous event that changed me to who I am now. One thing I learnt from the experience in war was to submit to my fate. Troubled times are coming. So what's the point of trying to change momentous events beyond your control when you, more often than not, allow personal events to control *you?* Repent, brother."

Ben studied Joshua, reflecting on those words. "This is heavy. Thanks for telling me this. I really appreciate that you can do this for me, soldier." Then Ben muttered, "I promise to keep this conversation between us."

God's cool breeze blanketed the camp site, and Joshua nodded curtly. "I will tell no soul."

"Joshua?" Ben said softly. "I hate myself for what I have done. I *want* to repent."

"I understand," Joshua nodded. "When I was in prison, I hated existence. Jesus was my only hope."

"I alienated you. Will you forgive me?"

Joshua was being exposed. He clenched and said, "I do."

"Thank you ... I have one more question before you leave, brother." Ben's eyes scowled in concern. "What are the First Fruits?"

"First Fruits?" Joshua said, tapping his cheek in thought. "That's one of the *moedim* that falls on Easter Sunday. It's a type of offering the Israelites would give in the Tabernacle. It has to do with the tithe from the best of the flock or their produce they gleaned for the harvest, so that they give ten per cent of their produce to the Levite teachers."

"No, *who* are the First Fruits?" Ben clarified. "It's not a *moedim*. It is a *group of people*. I know it."

Joshua paused, stunned. "I have no idea what you mean."

Ben gave Joshua a complex frown. "That's all right, I just thought ... I heard a voice telling me in the visions to 'Gather them, the First Fruits'. It's a riddle – I have no idea what it means, too, but I *feel* like I should know what it means." Ben smiled whimsically. "It *must* be symbolic."

"I don't know, Ben. You need to go to a Hebrew Bible expert."

"I know a man who is an expert," Ben said, nodding, his eyes looking off into the wilderness pine trees, gazing off faraway. "His name is Rob Heller – a pastor my father learnt from. I came to Tucson just because his ministry is set up here. I feel ... I *feel* he could offer me some answers. But I've been reluctant to go as you could imagine." Ben swayed, as if he wanted to take off walking, but restrained himself. "I will find the ministry for you. I had been thinking about going for a while, but I couldn't be bothered. Now ... Now you had the audacity to approach me and speak to me, and now you've encouraged me that I have to go. Now."

"Ben," Joshua uttered. "If you think about going, just remember that I am praying for you to repent."

When men now looked at Ben these days, what they saw scandalised them. Not Joshua. Ben was broken, just like he was, and needed healing.

"I hope I do, Josh."

"May God bless you and keep you, and may God grant us the wisdom to act in time."

57

THE WAY OF THE SERVANTS

"And when the thousand years are completed, Satan will be released from his prison. He will go out to deceive the nations that are at the four corners of the Earth, Gog and Magog, to assemble them for battle, of whom the number of them is like the sand of the sea. They marched across the breadth of the Earth and surrounded the fortified camp of the saints and the beloved city, and fire came down from heaven and consumed them. And the devil, who deceived the world, was thrown into the lake of burning sulphur, where the beast and the false prophet had been thrown. They will be tormented day and night for ever and ever."
—From the Scroll of Revelation, John the Apostle, 95 – 96 CE.

After a long hike with a small hobble through the woods into the urban sprawl, wearing a neck warmer veiling his face from nose downwards, and a hat covering his bald head, Ben found his destination.

But uncertainty and trepidation almost made him collapse. What he was about to do would put himself at great risk. He'd already passed the point of no return.

Turn around from my sins? Stop doing what I am doing? Is looking for my daughter a sin? It can't be!

God's the Galactic Tyrant! Joshua is deceived.

As he walked, depression draped itself around Ben's shoulders like some invisible but almost tangible shroud, and the weight of its presence dulled his eyes, stooping his shoulders. Even his efforts to shake it off were exhausting, as if his arms were sewn into its bleak folds of melancholy. Lately, as he ate, worked and dreamed in this garment of heaviness, he endured a murky despondency that sucked the colour out of everything.

He also had dreams of Veronica being taken. They made Ben bolt upright in his car, sweat dripping from his tortured body, while waves of nausea and guilt rolled over him like a cataclysmic flood.

Why am I getting these visions? Ben wondered as he hiked. *Why? How is it that I am getting them after all the crap that happened to me? Either I am going insane because of the stress, or God is telling me something. If I don't get to the bottom of this…* Ben wasn't given a promise that finding out who the First Fruits were would solve his problems, but he had a feeling that, if he tried, it might reveal something about Veronica.

That meant, ultimately, he had to trust God. Whatever he was. *God is the Galactic Tyrant. But … who else is right?*

The sun scorched the land as Ben crossed the road onto the pavement before the brick building. Once Ben hobbled towards the threshold, he was perspiring, and his heart roared like a drum in his chest. He raised a hand to his forehead. That hand quivered. Never had he felt so self-conscious and skittish entering a building in his life. He knew the ravenous frustration of justice for his misfortune. From the paladin whisking him halfway across the world, to Joseph's death, Veronica's disappearance and Brianna's treason, to the inconvenience of homelessness. All of it was burning him up like a log in a fireplace.

Paranoia. Dominic had accused Ben of that. Accusing him when Thomas Jones had been bashed in his mother's house. Ben's body quivered, his hand balling into a fist. He wore the same horrible ragged grey clothes the Navajo had given him during the healing ceremony. He had not seen a shower for days. If anything, his smell would draw attention. He was not ready to return to society.

I can turn back now and … And remain hanging? Find Veronica? Who do I gather?

His heart raced. He hissed a curse. *Why am I here?*

Repent.

Gather them … The First Fruits …

Adjusting his neck warmer over his face, Ben steeled himself, proceeding deeper into the building's foyer, down a carpeted corridor, its walls estranging. *Remain calm,* Ben thought. *Remain hidden. Use a fake name. Make up a story. Improvise. You're homeless and want company. You're good at this.*

There was a service going on; he could hear music playing in the background and a voice singing with a passionate choir.

"By the breath of your nose, the waters heaped up;
They stood like a dam of a stream.
The deeps congealed in the heart of the sea.
The enemy said, 'I will pursue! I will overtake!
I will plunder! I will fill my hunger!
I will draw my sword! My hand shall possess them!'
You blew your Spirit;
the sea covered them; they sank like a stone in the mighty waters.

Who is like you among the gods, Yahovah?
Who is like you, majestic in holiness,
Fearsome with praises, who works wonders?
You stretched out your right hand;
The Underworld will swallow them."

Ben peered into the auditorium and took a seat at the back so that none would notice him. There were a good number of people spread out before him, and on the stage was a choir, led by a brown-haired woman, a young man playing a guitar and an elderly man tapping bongos. The stage was decorated with banners of glamorous fabrics of the colours blue, red, purple and white. At the centre of the draping were two main banners, one of a black-and-white leopard pattern. Hebrew letters were woven onto the one on the top register with a picture of a cluster of purple grapes next to an ox. The other banner contained a standing lion. Ben shuddered, hugging himself, trying not to think about his father and his cults. *Crap! I'm so desperate! I've come to church for answers, for goodness' sake! Crap!*

But Ben was doing this for Joshua and for answers about his visions.

The woman continued to sing – fierce and dulcet.

"You led with your loyal love people you have redeemed.
You guided with your strength towards your holy pasture.
The peoples heard. They will tremble.
Anguish seized those in Philistia.
At that time, the chiefs of Edom were dismayed.
Shaking seized the members of Moab.
All the inhabitants of Caanan melted.
Terror and dread will fall upon them.
By the greatness of your arm, they will be as still as a stone,

Until your people, Yahvoah, passed through.
Until the people you acquired passed through.
You are bringing them in and planting them on the mountain of
your inheritance,
the Sanctuary, Adonai, established by your hands.
Yahovah will reign forever and ever."

The lead guitar player ended with an elegant climb of high-stringed notes and set the instrument upright. The woman singer ceased her melody, and the auditorium erupted in a round of applause. The singer smiled, curtsying, and joined the choir filing off the stage.

"Wow, praise the Lord," came a voice from the loudspeakers. "You could really feel the power in that ancient hymn." Ben matched that voice to a tall, lean man in his late thirties, with a small mic attached to his shirt, walking across the vacating stage, grabbing a pulpit and placing it on the left-hand side of the stage. He had a narrow face, with glasses over his eyes, short black hair, large ears, and a short, squared beard. It had to be Rob Heller himself. Placing a face to the charismatic voice Ben had so often heard on the radio was a delight.

Setting up the pulpit, Rob Heller waited for everyone to return and began his teaching. "Our reading today is from Revelation 3:19-22. It is the risen Christ's heavy message to the Church in Laodicea – the church who had failed to attain holiness. Yeshua tells Saint John to write to the seven churches in Turkey to repent in the face of Roman and cosmic opposition of God's rule. He promises those who conquer will be rewarded with a gift in the new creation."

God is the Galactic Tyrant, Ben thought morbidly. *The Omega Plan. The Alliance. They have scapegoated God ... and then they are handed over to the violence they created. This is the wrath of God. Or at least ... according to my father. No one is getting any gifts. No one. Only Hell.*

"So, if you like, follow along in your Bibles in Revelation 3:19-22." Rob opened his copy of the Bible resting on the pulpit, flicking to the end of the book, and began to read. Ben crossed his arms as the sound of rustling pages hissed and crackled around him. "'As many as *I love,* I *reprove* and *discipline,*'" Rob read dramatically. "'Be zealous, therefore, and repent! Behold, I stand at the door and knock! If anyone *hears* my voice and *opens* the door, indeed I will come in to him and dine with him, and he with me. The one who *conquers,* I will grant him to *sit down with me on my throne,* as I also have conquered and have sat down with my Father on his throne. The one who has an ear, let him hear what the Spirit says to the churches.'"

Ben took a deep breath. He thought of Joshua's haunting, prophetic words. *Repentance is essential, because without it, you perpetuate destruction.* A gradual burn of worry, of not finding answers to his visions, the futility of his journey here and looking for Veronica, seethed his stomach and tightened his chest.

"Jesus is at the door of our hearts," Rob preached. "He is waiting to unveil it. To open it. But only we have locked the door. If we open the door, a transformed life culminates when we sit down at God's table. This is a very personal, intimate and hospitable image of salvation. Meal-sharing in fellowship conveys the news of God's invitation to all to participate in the peace of his rule."

Ben felt a sudden shock of stress strike him like a tonne of bricks. *No!* Ben thought with grievous offence. *Come on! What are you saying? Can you sleep at night, knowing one of your kids doesn't sleep in her bed?*

"In other words, this anticipates a world that will be healed. God *never* destroys. God is life, love and light. The one on the throne says, 'Behold, I will make all things new,' and that includes consuming hostile, violent enemies of God. Pharaoh and his chariots will sink into the lake of fire, and God's people will pass over it in the second resurrection. God is just and loving, no matter what suffering or trial we face in this life. This is the hope *we must have*, or else we will not make it into the Kingdom of Heaven. Make up your mind. If you are not going to be hot for the Lord, if you are not going to be serious about following Christ, then you may as well never even try following Christ. Because every time you hear the command of God, and you don't obey it, you are piling up condemnation for yourselves on the day of judgement. You're cold.

"So strive to enter into the narrow door *now*. The door *will not* be open forever. Be boiling hot before it is too late. Jesus is knocking.

"But to those who *do* obey and those who *do* open, they will conquer! They will sit on the throne with God! What does that mean? Well, the word conquer comes from the Greek word *nike*. It is a military term."

Ben rolled his eyes, smirking grimly, his heart black with discontent. *Yeah, wait until you lose your family. What then? Will God grant you victory? God's the Galactic Tyrant, brother! He's coming to bring Hell on Earth because of our violence.* Ben normally did this. When he got bored listening to Rob on the radio, he found himself enmeshed in a bad habit, criticising and commentating, making fun of the man.

Rob preached on. "Why would someone describe a persecuted minority group in the Roman Empire as conquering? They aren't winning, they're being killed unjustly, they're *losing* the battle. This isn't conquering. How disorientating. When the Lord of life returns, all those ideas and systems we take for granted will be *shaken* violently." Rob made a shaking motion with his fists. He used gestures appropriately. His diction was clear and engaging. "This is what is going to be revealed! It is the truth that our world is upside down! This is the apocalypse! This is the death and resurrection of our Lord! Yeshua, done in by the powers of his society, scapegoated by the murderous mendacity of the way people live their lives. But you know what happened? Yes, Yeshua rose from the dead."

What's wrong with God? Why did God send me away from Iraq across the world? What happened to the baby? Why did God give it to me? Why did he kill my father? Why did God take my daughter? Why did God bring chaos into my life, have me torture an innocent man and turn my wife against me? Why did God make me homeless? I've been killed …

"Death, the inevitable last enemy of all, has been conquered." Rob paused and turned to his notes to get back on track. "It brings me back again to this beautiful verse. Verse nine. 'As many as I love, I reprove and discipline.'" Rob's eyes met Ben's for a brief moment. "Tribulation is coming first to the Church before it comes to the world. Get ready, brothers and sisters. Death is coming, suffering is coming. But it is not the end! All of it has been questioned! In fact, corrupt political powers that use the fear of Death to stomp on us have been shaken! They have fallen! And as we hear Yeshua's voice and obey, what is revealed is that God's love is stronger than Death! More powerful than all those systems based on the fear of Death!"

Ben suddenly became self-conscious, and he sweated.

Gather them. The First Fruits. Repent. A knocking on the door of his soul.

"We conquer by loving and being loyal to God and our fellow humans. The calling of the ancient Israelites at Horeb was the same calling Yeshua gave to his disciples. The same calling the Holy Spirit gives to the Church today."

Ben shifted in his seat. He shivered. Vertigo afflicted his vision. He didn't think everyone around him listening so peacefully could be so … unpleasant.

"All humans have sinned," Rob proclaimed. "The saint, in their strength, protects the vulnerable. Strength does not make one capable of rule with victory and power; it makes one capable of service. This *is* victory and this *is* rule. You will sit with God on his throne by giving up your life."

All this upside-down language of conquering, glorious victories and sitting on divine thrones by dying and acting in impossible Puritan righteousness … Ben felt condemned in a sea of holiness. He didn't deserve to be here. *Man … I'm crap!*

"As great as this may seem, the promises are *not* a reward. We do not reclaim eternal bliss in Heaven, to sit on thrones like gods. We cannot live our old lives anymore. We need to live our lives according to the Holy Spirit. We need to wake up from our complacency. The Epic of Eden unveils that humans need a divine-human representative to die and suffer and rise from the dead after three days to proclaim peace and repentance to all the world."

Ben was really thinking of leaving, and then he thought, *I need to get answers from my visions! It could be what is holding me back from finding Veronica.*

He thought it rude to just leave; he thought it would draw attention to himself. There, two men and women stood up at the end of the next row beside him. If he got up to leave, they would surely turn and notice him.

"The Christian Church is Adam and Israel. We are the microcosm of the whole world. Everyone is included in the Covenant. But we either obey the commandments or choose death. But for two thousand years, Christianity – the Catholic, Orthodox, Oriental and Protestant – cut themselves from their Hebrew roots, claiming infallible church authority, colonising nations, and deceiving. We have become our own gods – dictating a position on the throne ourselves."

How much will Rob know? Will he mock me? My visions … Something is happening to me. I need to see if the visions are real.

"But God *still hopes* for humans," Rob said. "As we start to hope in God, he's *already hoping* for us. He never gives up hope in the human race. Tribulation is coming upon the whole world because of what Christians have done to the world. This is inevitable. We have a great responsibility as priests." Rob took a deep breath, nodding at the audience. "Be zealous and repent!"

—

When the service was over, Ben sat doing nothing, indifferent and voyeuristic, watching the faces of this strange church community passing by, paying him no heed – but Ben studied their faces.

He liked studying human beings. Back in a time when he was an actor, he had taken this for granted, but now he enjoyed the expressions on people. He could see that a considerable number of the church women wore head coverings. There were a lot of black people. Couples had large families – the largest was a troop of seven young boys; the women looked medieval in their dresses, and the father's beard was bushy and long.

Appearances told Ben much about a person. It was why he had to go to great lengths to cover up his own. He was very good at knowing people he did not know. *Blows being famous.*

It was then that Rob Heller noticed him with neckwear covering up his face and a wide-brimmed hat covering his bald head.

"What is your name, brother?" Rob Heller said, approaching Ben, despite his smell, to sit next to him.

"My name is Jacob," Ben said.

"Let me guess, if I may?" Rob said, his expression soft. "Are you homeless?"

A lump formed in Ben's throat. He nodded briskly. Now that he had got himself into this, he had to adapt. Improvise and act. "Yes … And I don't like talking about it," he snapped grumpily. Ben stood up, scowling. "Do what I say and not what I do? I came to the wrong place." Ben turned to leave.

"No, no, Jacob. We do things differently here," Rob said, holding out his arms. "Tell me, brother, what's your story? I will not judge you, Jacob. I just want to know so I can show you some sympathy. The world has been giving you a hard time. But not here. Mark my words, in this church, you're allowed to do whatever you want. Trust me."

Starting, Ben thought that he could capitalise on this opportunity to ask this Bible scholar a question about the First Fruits and his visions, and yet, he feared Rob, too, was like Joseph.

Ben sat back down and said, "I became homeless because my daughter went missing. People in power tried to take control over my life. I got charged and lost everything. What the government did to me was a crime against humanity, but the things I did, I realise, were just as much crimes. I used to be a fun guy, and now I recognise that what I thought was right was wrong."

Rob nodded, accepting. "It appears, Jacob, the government are not even smart enough to be as evil as you're giving them credit for. They're blind, just like you." Rob smiled pointedly. "And yet, you had the audacity to stumble into a church! Well done! Adonai's spirit is guiding you!"

Ben grumbled. "I have *a lot* of questions."

"Yes! Go on. I'm listening."

Ben smiled. He wanted to get to the point, but he wanted – at the same time – to learn about what Rob believed, to discern if he was a cult leader or a genuine theologian. "Do you believe in miracles?"

Ben noticed the stimulation in Rob's hazel eyes. "Miracles? I see them every day. The rising sun. The breath in my nostrils. My wife."

"No, I mean ..." Ben sighed. "The supernatural."

Rob paused. "Yes. I mean, I don't see them, but I don't deny they *can* happen."

"I came here because I had dreams. I ... I'm afraid," Ben uttered with a trembling voice at his bare honesty. "God is speaking, and no one's listening."

"Dreams can be interpreted in different ways," Rob said.

Joseph was going to interpret my vision, until he died.

"Rob? Have you heard about the First Fruits?"

"First Fruits ..." Rob wondered with a fascinated whisper. "That's interesting ..." He paused. "Was this in one of your dreams?"

"Yeah," Ben said, his body relaxing. He *wanted* to trust this man. *But don't get sucked in, don't get fully on board! He could be hypocritical and venal!* "Yeah, it was in a vision. I ... was told precisely to gather them. The First Fruits."

"Gather *them?*"

"Any ideas who the 'them' could be?"

Rob tucked his lips together. "Well ... First Fruits can refer to the first offspring of the womb belonging to God," Rob explained. "This includes children and animals, who are set aside to be sacrificed."

"Wait, so God wants child sacrifice?" Ben's eyes bulged.

Rob chuckled affectionately. "No! You need to read the passages in context to understand them better. We already know in God's instructions that he hates child sacrifice with a passion."

"Who wouldn't?" Ben said dejectedly.

"First Fruits is a time of year around Passover in which the first produce of the new year was eaten. The firstborn sons are to be redeemed with a subsidiary animal sacrifice, a financial gift to the Tabernacle or Temple of God, or through service as a Levite priest. The point is that everything belongs to God, and in return, God blesses the harvest or your livestock. In a world with high infant mortality, being blessed with many children is a valid concern. Does that make sense?"

Nodding, Ben felt guilt, anguish and despair seethe his stomach with nausea, and he felt like vomiting. *This was the most worthless explanation! I have no idea what any of this crap means! Are the visions real, or am I just going mad?* "What you said earlier about victory was confusing," Ben said slowly. "If we die selflessly, then we are victorious. But how if we are dead and the powerful continue to be powerful? We're just that. Dead. Sounds like self-deception to me. Not a good selling point."

"Oh boy, you just asked me if I believe in miracles, and now you're telling me that you don't?" Rob said. "You know, Christ is called the *First Fruits* of those who have resurrected from the dead? He's the true victorious one."

Ben's heart jumped in his chest. *Jesus was one of the First Fruits?* "Wait! Did you say that Jesus is a First Fruits?"

Rob nodded. "Yes. He's the First Fruits of those who have resurrected."

"How? Does that mean Christians are the Frist Fruits?"

"Yes, they are, Jacob," Rob said, a gentle hand on his shoulder. It sent warmth through Ben's weary body. "The First Fruits means that Jesus' resurrection guarantees the rest of the harvest will come. That is, those saints who submit to Christ, participating in Christ, will resurrect as Christ resurrected into new bodies. For in Adam all die, so in Christ all will be made alive. The saints are God's servants, and they offer their lives to him like a sacrifice. The First Fruits are the victorious army of Jesus because they conquer by the blood of the lamb and because of the word of their testimony, they didn't love their lives unto death."

There. Ben leaned back in awe. He had found his answer after all this time. The First Fruits ... they were the triumphant saints. The Church! Ben's heart was thundering at his victory.

Gather them. Gather the Church.

Which Church?

Rob went on. "The First Fruits are enjoying the spiritual resurrection, awaiting the final second resurrection, which will be transphysical[6]. All those who repent from their sins to act as heralds of life everlasting are experiencing the first resurrection. This means the resurrection has already begun with our acceptance of what Jesus has accomplished for us. The resurrection is a culmination of a life of sanctification. The perishable must clothe itself with the imperishable, and the mortal with immortality. You become Christian, and your resurrection is guaranteed. That is why the Bible uses language that you're glorified now."

Ben nodded, genuinely enthralled. Though what much of Rob was saying sounded incredibly lovely, he could barely comprehend these sophisticated concepts.

"You know, Jacob, Messiah is the first to be resurrected, but we are already receiving the First Fruits of the Spirit. The final transformation when the reign of God is fully realised is in the future. We are already conquerors, ruling this

6   6: Coined by Bible scholar NT Wright, *Surprised by Hope*, 2008, 44

world, living in the already and not yet."

"You're a reformist?" Ben said.

Rob paused for having been interrupted and shook his head. "I am neither Reformist nor Roman Catholic nor Eastern Orthodox. Religion is the Whore of Babylon."

Ben flinched. The what, now? "Then … what are you? Jewish?"

Rob laughed. "I don't like endorsing myself, but yes, I am." He stroked his short beard. "Let's just say I'm not your traditional Jewish rabbi. I'm a Messianic Jew with a background in theology. I believe that Jesus Christ – or Yeshua Hamashiach in Hebrew – is the Anointed One Who Will Save – predicted in the TaNaK – the Old Testament."

Ben nodded. Could a Jewish heritage make Rob Heller any better in terms of truth? "I respect that. It makes sense because Jesus was Jewish."

"Most people don't think Jesus was Jewish," Rob chuckled.

"Funny." It occurred to Ben that his unusual visions and Joshua's prophetic powers were linked to the Hebrew God of the Bible. Yahweh and Adonai, these people called him. On a par with this, Ben had noticed ever since he had his very vivid King David vision on the plane trip to Haditha Dam and the paladin, God had been calling Ben out, warning him. To repent.

You will find the Truth.

"So, what is your background, Jacob?"

Ben told Rob half-truths rather than fabrications. "Complicated. Before my father came out of the closet calling himself a born-again Christian, my family only had a vague notion of religion. Faith seemed unnecessary. I wasn't raised explicitly religious. I was baptised by the Catholic Church, but except for Christmas and Easter, twice a year at best, I did not attend services. It was more of a cultural thing to go to church than being pious. I never prayed. Biblical stories were nothing to me but … stories. I couldn't stand the dullness of the Catholic mass and going through the dry motions. I just wanted to play and make noise. The sacramental bread became a tasteless reward for good behaviour."

Rob smiled warmly in the theatre room devoid of activity. Just him and Ben. "Okay. Okay. How would you like it if I gave you a small job here, Jacob?" Rob said.

Ben looked at him and worried that by accepting the job offer, he would get sucked into another world of nonsense and …

"A job?" Ben chuckled. "This is so out of the blue! Why?"

Rob's smile was contagious, radiating with enthusiasm. "Oh, I know God is speaking to you! It's *so* powerful! You, an average Joe, called to gather the saints as one body! This is *so* profound! I need to tell everyone about this noble calling! You're *so* interesting. I want to learn more from you, Jacob. I'm offering you a job because it's only right to offer homeless people opportunities. It's what we do here at Fellowship of the Way. We care for the unfortunate, providing shelters and food for them. But God spoke something *incredible* to you, and …" The pastor lowered his glance and swallowed. His smile faded. "Sorry. I need to slow down." He met Ben's eyes. His smile returned. "For too long, I have been too quick to get everything done without even thinking that God has already done it ahead of time."

"Why are you smiling?" Ben asked briskly.

"Jacob, you are probably the most sensible person I've met. This is why I want to hire you."

Sensible?

"You're wrong. I would never call myself that sensible. Normally, religious people see it is easier to attack a person's virtue and credibility they deem lesser than accept advice on being wrong." Ben slumped, feeling dismayed. *God, I thought Dad was like that! I hated him. But Rob … Man, he's so generous. So kind.*

"See, Jacob?" Rob beamed, sitting up straight. "You have potential within you to understand other people like me."

"I guess when I put it into practice. It really isn't that hard."

"Yeah, we've been in Diaspora, suffering pogroms for a long time, waiting for God to do something to redeem us," Rob said. "People are shocked when they find out I'm Jewish and I believe in Jesus. They accuse me of being anti-Semitic. I haven't spoken to my Jewish family in decades since I got baptised. You see, it is not easy being a Jewish Christian. I have many enemies. I've always found myself getting into people's business, and some lash out and call me names. And because of that, I often get very impatient, so I get it, man. I get it. Homelessness, without a place to plant oneself, has been the experience of my people for over *two thousand years*. I've had the death threats. The death fears. All of it. Jacob, we're in the same boat."

"Yeah … Thanks for sharing. Anyway, it's been a pleasure talking to you." Ben shook Rob's hand.

"Ah, please, brother. Don't go," Rob said. "I need to show you something. I think I might have the perfect job for you."

Rob took Ben to a small AV studio set up at the back of the theatre at the top of the stairwell where lighting, computer monitors and cameras were arranged.

"We're planning to make a DVD series soon, but it seems God's given us more than we originally asked for. I'm looking for someone who is good with AV, editing, producing and filming, working with sound, cameras, lighting."

"Perfect," Ben replied, grinning. "I used to do theatre. AV should be easy. I can get right to work, then."

"Now?"

Ben shrugged. "I need a job. Just like you said."

———

Two weeks later, Ben meandered into the church's dining room to find a seat, feeling as if he was under a divine curse. He found a seat, feeling cool.

Ben still didn't trust Rob completely, but he suspected that the virtuous Jewish man, offering Ben a perfect opportunity to earn money and to learn about the Church for his visions, would be the key that will help him find Veronica.

It wasn't logical, Ben realised, but he'd become desperate lately, and had no options.

It was not long after he started out as a cameraman filming Rob Heller's sermons that more people asked Ben why he was wearing a mask and a hat. And Ben would often reply, "Because I used to do cycling, and I got in an accident and marred my face. Don't ask." The great accident was Joseph's death and Veronica's kidnapping. It did not save his face, and at least people left him alone.

How long will it take until they know? Ben shivered in his seat.

"Jacob? Jacob, are you all right?"

Ben gasped, startled by Archie looming over him, a plate of lunch in hand. Ben blushed furiously, letting his gaze slide. "I feel shameful of what we have become, Archie," Jacob said. "We're equals."

"I know, man." A light seemed to pass through Archie's eyes. He was Mexican, with tanned skin, diminutive, with long tresses tied up in a ponytail. This man was where Ben was about to be – a drug addict in search of counselling. The church tried helping him overcome addiction, but he still compromised; he still drank too much or smoked a little bit of weed. Somebody, one time, even abused him for having long hair and said that he should be given over to Satan. *That is what our lives have become,* Ben thought. *Given over to the Devil. The filthy underside of the holy church. I'm not a saint.*

"Ah. Yes, brother. Jesus bears our mistakes. You're not alone, Jacob."

Ben already had his meal – in private. It was for free since he was an employee at the church. He had eaten a Black Angus burger with the lot, with non-dairy spicy sauce with sweet potatoes. There was no bacon or shellfish here – the meat and dairy kitchens were kosher – but the sweet potatoes here were better than the ones at Barachina, San Juan, Puerto Rico, or in the bars in Arizona.

Ben did not know if he could return to Phoenix again in his life – or if he could, would he?

Keller Butcher would surely find him. Brianna … Veronica …

"What's bothering you, Jacob?" Archie asked, munching on Ben's sweet potatoes. "You're quiet today."

Ben sighed. "My past haunts me," he said, adjusting his neck warmer on his nose. Many times, he often thought that other people were worried that Rob had hired an Islamic jihadi on the AV team. "I've done things that would make you want to kill yourself."

"Far out. You're guilty? A criminal?"

"Don't talk about it."

"Fair enough. Us broken men don't talk about our pasts."

"I'm crazy, Archie."

"It doesn't matter if you're crazy or not. Crazy men are the good types. You're not a killing-people-in-their-sleep type of crazy, but we follow crazies all the time. They are called pastors and presidents. Jesus was crazy too, apparently. So … what was I saying? Yeah! You want to join me tonight? I'm having a party at my house."

Ben's heart leapt with ecstasy. "A party? For what?"

"Ah, just for the sake of it. Should be rad. It's good for mental health to have a bit of fun."

"Yeah, I'll go …" Ben bit his tongue.

Now, he needed to find a way to mask his identity …

—

Later that night, Ben went to the house party wearing a random smiling-man mask from the dollar store. It drew uneasy eyes, but Ben preferred to be hidden rather than exposed, in order to evade the police.

He raised his mask only a little to eat. People judged him, and his friends looked at him funnily. Ben didn't care. All he cared about was how foul and broken the world was, and whether he had earned enough money to pay for his car fuel to continue his quest for Veronica. He didn't want to think about how she could still be alive after …

He pinched his fingers around the cigarette slipping between his exposed lips. Ecstatic relief filled his body. He inhaled the sedating smoke and exhaled a thin plume. Everything faded: loud music reduced to a dreamy backwater, the raucous laughter, clinking drinks, all of it. Ben released a protracted sigh, leaning back on his chair, and, resting his feet on the tabletop, he embraced all the euphoria, drowning out the suffering.

Ben did not even mind when Archie accidently elbowed him. Archie spoke with Samuel, returning with drinks to Ben and his friend's table.

"Nah, I'm good," JJ said. He had only reached twenty years old. Some hours before – Ben didn't care how long – he had been smearing his face with a plate of strawberries coated in liquid chocolate. "Have you asked Jacob about a drink? Why doesn't he take off the mask?"

"Nah. We don't talk about Jacob and what he's been through," Archie said. "He said he was a cyclist, and he had a terrible accident, so he wears a mask all the time. He stays up serving with the AV crew and vanishes after his shift. I dunno … He's a creepy type. Doesn't talk much."

"Shhh. You think he is listening?" Samuel said impishly.

"Doubt it. The guy could fall asleep practically anywhere."

"You wanna play blackjack?" Samuel remarked, slamming something onto the table. "Let's gamble."

"All right, I'll take the bet, but not for money," Archie said. "When I win, you take a shot."

"No!" Samuel bellowed.

"Okay. Then I want your cap."

JJ laughed. "Samuel goes *crazy* when he is drunk!"

"Yeah," Archie said. "That's why I want your cap."

"It's just a cap," Samuel grumbled. "You can buy one just like it from Walmart."

"Nah. Nah," JJ said in an obnoxiously jovial voice. "What's the point if you're not even an Ultimate Frisbee fan?"

"Ah come on, Samuel!" Archie prodded. "Samuel!"

"What?" he yelled in mock anger.

"I'm going to do you a favour. Win and burn the thing."

JJ bellowed, guffawing. Everyone picked on little Samuel. He was from Hong Kong, had spiky hair and glasses.

Ben opened his eyes slowly. The light from the DJ ring cast a navy-bluish hue with dark red shadows. In the throbbing music and the hum of indistinct murmurings, there was a lingering warble. Ben thought for a moment it was part of the remix, yet it persisted in harsh abbreviations, railing on louder and louder.

"You are my girlfriend, so start acting like one!"

"A girlfriend cares about what her partner takes!"

Ben slowly sat up and slipped his mask down to cover his mouth. He saw a man, almost bald in his late thirties, clearly drunk, prowling around his high-maintenance girlfriend near the kitchen.

"You promised you were not going to take GHB anymore!" the girl yelled at the top of her lungs.

"Hey, Olly! Stop pissing her off!" Archie barked, marching from his seat.

"Who *the hell is* that?" JJ exclaimed.

Ben blinked his bleary eyes, feeling partly annoyed and pitiful for Olly as the music slowed to a stop.

"Kiera, you slut!" Olly spat, pacing, the words slurring and growling. "You don't understand me!"

"What are you—"

"SHUT UP!" Olly's voice descended into madness, with a gargling croak as he bellowed in his girlfriend's face, making bystanders snicker at him. "You're a conniving control *freak!*"

"Oh really?"

"Yeah! Controlling my life in what I can or cannot take!"

"I don't want to get into this!" Kiera crossed her arms, turning her back. Olly crabbed around her, stomping, snorting with a clogged nose. By the looks of it, if someone didn't do anything, someone was going to get hurt.

"How? How?" Olly screamed.

"We're done!"

Kiera shoved Olly away, thrusting out her chest, prying open her bra, uncovering her breasts. Most people in the room gasped. Ben didn't recoil in shock like everyone else did. Whistles and uneasy laughs came from Archie and Samuel, and even complementing advances came from a few other guys nearby.

Ben sat there, numb. Next to him, poor JJ blushed furiously, hiding his face in his hands. *Oh man, what have I got myself into?*

Olly lost it. Flinging his fists, he charged at Kiera, whacking her in the side. She yelped, falling into her circle of friends, who caught her. Growling like a maniac, Olly kicked over the chocolate fountain, sending a deluge of brown across the entire room, then flung glasses off the table.

"All right! All right, you animals, that's enough!" Archie snapped, storming to subdue the chaos.

Huffing, Olly flipped a table with food and snacks in the small backyard at the patio door. He barrelled right into Archie. With sporadic hits, Olly smothered Archie, slamming him against the wall. Olly tugged at Archie's long hair, dragging him down onto the ground, wrapping him in a dangerous headlock. Gagging and squirming, legs drumming, Archie gritted his teeth.

A woman screamed. "Oh! Help him! Somebody *do* something!"

Why don't you do something? a neutral voice said. Ben strode towards the brawl, confidence in his chest. *Look at them. Nobody cares. Nobody. I've done nothing but sleep, all bored for five hours. I need to do something.*

Ben stalked roughly into the blue light. The men aroused by Kiera swarmed him, immediately blocking his path, but he bumped right through. Morons, they should've gotten a life when they still could. They didn't have a family that died or have children who were kidnapped. They were pimps because they wanted to be, and it sickened Ben. *If you do what is right, you will be victorious,* he thought. *You will sit on God's throne.*

"Please, let him go, Olly," Ben said compassionately.

Olly let Archie collapse to the floor, exhaling a gigantic breath. Olly looked down at his victim and then back at Ben with dazed confusion. This man was *incredibly* drunk. He retched, loudly, and Ben snarled, getting a whiff of his vile breath.

He didn't vomit, luckily.

Ben could feel the leering men behind him, the people watching him. *Let them watch.*

"There you go," Ben coaxed. "It wasn't so hard."

In Olly's eyes, overflowing with dense anger, Ben saw himself.

"Olly should *really* get a life because he can't live like this," a moron said. "Poor Kiera."

Olly curled his lips, snorting, nostrils flaring like billowing exhausts.

"Hey, now, Olly! Hey! Easy, who—"

Ben barely dodged a hurling hook of mindless power.

"Git off me! Git away from her!"

"What? Wai—"

"Git lost!"

Ben blocked with his forearms. He stepped back into a nimble fighting stance. Smacking flesh sounded in his ears as he deflected attacks effortlessly.

Ben bumped into a wall. Forestalling Olly's hook, Ben ducked and felt … nothing. Ben straightened as another fist came for him, and he moved aside slightly. His reflexes had a rapid heightened awareness unlike any time Ben could remember when in a fight.

Ben blocked and evaded each attack. He narrowly evaded another punch, and it pounded the wall, creating a hole. Ohing, Ben, bounding around Olly, taunted him. The drunk swung in a blur. Ben *moved* in a blur, away from each rapid jab. Olly missed. The impossibility of it, the absurdity of it, made Olly madder and madder.

Ben felt like Neo in *The Matrix*. Untouchable. Sporadic jabs missed him by an itch each time.

Reaching the zenith of his anger, Olly clawed Ben's smiling-man mask, damaging it.

Ben gripped Olly's arm and twisted it into a figure four, bending it backwards. Olly growled a deep guttural yowl. Ben threw him into a headlock. He could have judo flipped the guy off the ground and landed him on his skull, though what good would it do to kill the guy outright?

Saliva dribbled over Ben's forearm. "Man! Take a chill pill!" Ben shook Olly. "Go to sleep, go to sleep, go to sleep, go to sleep."

"No!" Olly heaved, flicking his head back, kicking multiple times into Ben's thigh, knocking him, almost smashing into a table.

"Work with me, Olly!"

"DAH!"

"Work with me!"

"DAH-DAH-DAH-DAH!"

"Fine!"

Ben punched Olly's face, knocking him out completely. "There!" Ben dusted his hands. "Easy." He adjusted his broken mask, sweeping his gaze at all the onlookers. Some cheered, some clapped, and others turned, leaving the party.

"I guess the party's over, Archie!" Ben called.

"Thanks for giving me a hand back there, amigo!"

Ben lugged Olly along like a bad dog on a chained leash, and nonchalantly, he replied, "No problemo."

"Who is this guy?" Susurrations filled the house. Ben's heart palpitated. He'd almost been exposed. *Time to go.*

———

Thirty minutes later, Olly had awoken, letting out a series of gut-wrenching wails into the night.

He flopped half dead over his pot belly poking under his shirt against the brick wall near the front stairs leading to the front yard of Archie's flat. Ben sat by his side patiently, seeing nothing else better to do; he reluctantly disciplined himself, not feeling in the mood to take another drag. He held out the packet of cigarettes, and after a few attempts, he finally crumpled the packet, discarding it.

God, Ben thought. *This is going to become an addiction ... Like Olly. Nobody cares for him. Like nobody cares for me.* As he waited for Archie to finish cleaning the destruction – and there was a lot – Ben babysat Olly in the meantime.

The sound of clicking high heels echoed down the laneway, and Ben slowly stood up, glad that his tedious wait was at an end. Archie arrived escorting a young woman trying to hide behind a tissue. She had straightened hair, a short tight dress tasselled from being ripped, her handbag dangling lousily by her side. Ben caught a whiff of her perfume. Kiera, distraught, twisted an ankle and crashed into Archie.

"Oh! You okay?" Archie said.

Kiera got up tenuously, hissing in thanks with sharp breaths. Ben winced. He recalled one time someone from the modelling industry told him that high heels were invented for the purpose of changing women's bodies and lower back. It made them look "sexier". It was prostitution, and Ben had endorsed it, taken part in it. He always found it odd how women could wear such things, knowing how bad it was for the thighs and lower back.

Rob talked about the saints – of stories and ideals of pious, virtuous people. Why couldn't anyone be simple like that? Why did people have to always rely on dreams and self-centred passions like fashion, sex and drugs? It got them nowhere.

Why did Ben have passions? He was a father and had a daughter that needed him. He couldn't repent from being a father.

When Ben turned around, he was surprised to see Olly awake. His eyes were open, looking at the horizon, unblinking, expression pale pink and still. Like a lion suffering from heatstroke, looking at nothing. His nose was snotty, his shirt ripped, trousers baggy. He wore no shoes.

Ben looked through his mask at Olly, thinking, *I could have become like you, man. You have nothing. You are absolute trash.*

"I want my stuff back." Olly slurred. "Where is it?"

Ben turned around, grimacing, leaning on the railing. "I don't know," he said. "Sorry, but you can get your stuff back tomorrow. It's too late. Gotta go home."

Starting to make his way down the stairs, he procrastinated. Kiera's car took off into the distance, and that could only mean one thing: Olly was taking a ride home with Ben. The only problem was, Ben didn't have a real home. Cold anxiety spread through his body. *Goddamn it. Crap. I don't even have any stuff. How on earth …*

Ben caught movement at the periphery of his vision. Olly, with a ghastly gasp, flew towards Ben.

Olly collided into Ben with pulverising force. He fell, bracing the rail, Olly tumbling over his shoulders, flipping him down the stairs. In a messy scramble, Ben ducked, slipping down a step, holding on the rail. He landed on his knee, grazing it.

Olly however, dived headfirst towards the concrete, sprawling in a heap. Ben exhaled, clutching the trembling railing with bruised hands.

"See?" Ben chuckled, wiping his calloused hands. "See, you moron. *You knew* that was going to happen. You can't win."

Slowly, Olly raised his head in response. He was okay, fortunately.

58

DISCIPLINARIAN

"But Christ has indeed been raised from the dead, the first fruits of those who have fallen asleep. For since death came through a man, the resurrection of the dead comes also through a man. For as in Adam all die, so in Christ all will be made alive. But each in turn: Christ, the first fruits; then, when he comes, those who belong to him. Then the end will come, when he hands over the kingdom of God the Father after he has destroyed all dominions, authorities and powers. For he must reign until he has put all his enemies under his feet. The last enemy to be destroyed is death. When he has done this, then the Son himself will be made subject to him who put everything under him, so that God may be all in all."
—From the Epistle of First (Second) Corinthians, Paul, 53–54 CE.

When Ben allowed Olly to share his secret camp site, it was one of the greatest mistakes he'd ever made. When he thought he could embark on a quest to hunt for his daughter, spontaneous misfortunes halted him once more.

"Wait until I tell everybody! There is no more hiding, Ben DePaula," Olly mocked from the bench behind, cackling smugly. "I can't believe it! It is actually Ben DePaula! In my camp! Oh, you poor fella! The higher they are, the harder they fall! Hahaha!"

Ben scowled deeply. Of course, Ben had driven home, leaving Olly at Archie's house. But it was when Ben thought his upheavals were at an end, Olly had found his way to the ministry and creepily followed after Ben to base camp after his shifts. Having someone live in his secret camp meant one thing; they would see his face, they would know his identity, and they would invade his privacy. "You tell anyone who I am," Ben snarled. "I will look for you, I will find you and I will *kill you.*"

"Ooohh," Olly derided, the man who Ben nearly strangled when he first strolled into his camp. And like the pungent stink of alcohol poisoning the air, he wouldn't go away. "Freakin' Ben, you are a coward!" Bending over, a whooping cough wracked out of Olly. He looked seventy years old when he should have been thirty; his skin hoary, with a bald head, grotesque face, a hunched back and a pot belly. *Like Cleo.* "Gah! You going to bash me like you did with Thomas Jones, huh?"

"You finally starting to realise that your addiction is a problem?" Ben said condescendingly. "Look at the chaos it has caused in your life."

"Yeah, can't help it."

"You're not sleeping in my car, though! That's the rules!"

The poor man had colonised half of the base camp and wanted to take over Ben's car too. Overflowing with half-empty alcohol and liquor bottles and plants, the piles of strewn garbage on Olly's side of the camp made Ben sick in the stomach. "You bastard," Olly slurred. "You shouldn't really become like me. It's not my fault I am like this, but my friends forced me to do it."

"It's *your* fault you are here! Leave! At this rate, we are never going to get our lives back! You hear me?"

Archie had said that Olly's parents had taken out a restraining order against their son, meaning Olly could either stay at Ben's camp or at Archie's flat. "Listen, Ben. I have to tell you something. Something important."

Ben sighed, burying his face in his hand, arching his head in frustration.

"Imagine there is no Heaven, but only Hell. Imagine you seek to understand the Hell we are in. You may call me a dreamer, but I wanna let you know there are more people like me. Begging for money. Begging for food and shelter. Watch out, in case you become like me. Understand. Deception is the prison that we live in. Deceptions we tell ourselves of success and of dreams. Deceptions within deceptions within deceptions. They are transient. A drunk is one way out and death the other … This is the deception we live in, Ben." Olly took a drink.

Ben stood stunned. *Imagine there is no Heaven, but only Hell. Deception is the prison that we live in. Deceptions we tell ourselves of success and of dreams. A drunk is one way out and death the other.* Those words haunted Ben, entrenching into his being. Drink … Death. So easy. He'd already started to get into a routine of smoking and drinking way more than he would have done … It was beginning …

Ben was becoming like Cleo and Olly …

Veronica. I'm so sorry. I will not give up on you! Frustration dulled his eyes, and he wanted to cry so badly, but his cheeks were dry. *My family! My reputation!*

Those dark thoughts assaulted him so often now, mainly out of effort to conceal his own pitiful feebleness, vexation in the place reason should be. But when Ben got alone – always when he got alone – the torture became physiologically *unbearable*. His stomach and chest physically hurt from the pain.

"Olly … You are upset because I cannot do anything about you. Just … What do you want me to do? It's not like you have a job at the ministry! It's not like you are helping *me!* This is not doing any of us good, fighting over space and where to sleep and eat! I have to find my daughter!"

Olly rolled his eyes, dreamy and inattentive, hand fumbling for another drink. "Here."

Ben crossed his arms pessimistically, shaking his head.

"Aw, then kill yourself," Olly rasped. "There can only be one on this hill. You want to look after me? Kill your bloody self."

Kill yourself.

No! Veronica!

Ben took a few steps away from his car and then stopped, wondering if he should get away from this moron and go to the counselling area in Fellowship of the Way so he could stop this.

But if he left Olly be, the bastard would steal his car and do whatever the hell he wanted in it.

Later that night, Ben resolved to sleep in his car, and became vaguely aware of Olly trying to find a way inside. He asked a few times if he could borrow some money, but Ben growled in rebuke.

Then Olly snapped and attacked Ben, grabbing him through the window, and Ben raised an empty bottle of yellow whisky and bashed it across Olly's thigh. The man squealed as the shards sliced him, letting out a retched roar, wheeling himself around on the ground in the dirt. "All right. All right," Ben spat. "Go! *Go!* Here, take my money! Take it! There!" Ben threw cash at the worm. "Go! Limp on that leg! Good job! Yeah. Good. Limp. If you come back with a drink, then I'm not letting you in the car."

Olly took the money and walked out of the camp. It was then that Ben had his own fit of rage. He thumped the dashboard of his car with his hand, roaring in an outburst of frustration at himself having wasted half his money on this drug addict! He wanted to cry, to sob.

Olly returned that night with more clinking bottles.

Forty minutes. It only took *forty* minutes, and he couldn't help himself.

"Ya bum! Ya stupid bum! Open the door!" Olly creaked, kicking the car door. "Open it! Please, I'm sorry! I cannot help myself! I can't! Please let me in! *Let me in!*"

Ben waited. He could do this *all night* if he had to. The desert nights were cold. Mercilessly cold.

Fear and woe inflicted him, his car like a moribund tomb, as he rolled about within it, punching his bed. Throughout the night, he sweated uncomfortably, despite the ice cold outside. He tried praying for forgiveness too.

Brianna. Pounders. Veronica. Ian. Olly. The Alliance. Keller. Brianna. Pounders. Brianna. Olly. Veronica. Ian. The Alliance. Keller. Brianna. Pounders. Veronica. Ian. Olly. The Alliance. Keller. Joseph.

Ben's thoughts went around and around as he sat frozen. Each thought hurt, punching him in the stomach as they passed through his brain.

From the things he read in the Bible about Jesus coming quickly like a thief in the night, burning all this evil suddenly, became refreshingly appealing. Addictive.

"You've crushed me." Moaning, Ben slammed the side door of the car in an outburst of anger that pulsed through his veins.

Silence. So, God wanted to play it that way, then?

Pastor Rob Heller would be his only hope.

—

Covering half his face with his neck warmer and hat – ridiculous at night – Ben stumbled into the Fellowship of the Way, relishing the heated rooms and halls. He would die to live in a house again.

He found Rob Heller in the counselling room, sitting at a round table in the middle of a debate with a man in a suit whom he didn't recognise. A man who appeared to have had too many sweets, with a corpulent body and a plump face that scowled, his brow and stringy hair slick with sweat.

"You cannot keep *all* the Torah!" the corpulent man said. "You're not living in ancient times! You're saying you will stone your children! Are you going to isolate women from church when they're on their period? And what about sacrifices?"

"No," Rob said. "I—"

"You cannot follow the Law! The Law is morphing into new forms all the time. The scribe could supplement a text – even change it! The laws by Jesus' time were Talmud and Mishna – the lying pen of the scribes!"

"You interrupted me, sir. Will you let me speak?"

"Yes, sorry."

"Torah is customary law with justice principles set by precedent to guide you to live a life that you ought. It is *not* a law code, but *wisdom principles*. The Torah is very hypothetical, didactic and cannot be prescribed to all people and situations. The Torah is not an ideal system. It is God accommodating the wicked Israelite culture and helping them take small steps forwards towards the ideal ethics. Torah was a gift to Israel for where they were at. Compared to other ancient cultures, it was democratic and just, but it was not perfect. Slavery was part of daily life; you couldn't get rid of it, but you could regulate it. So of course, Torah is a means to an end. But its *principles* are still worth embodying today."

"But I am not obligated to follow the Torah because I am not under it!"

Ben left the room, pacing, waiting for the hopeless theological debate to end.

"Hey, Rob," Ben said, after the debate was over. "Rob, I want to tell you something. It's urgent."

Dismissing his friend, Rob took a drink and met Ben, saying, "Jacob, my man! Good evening! I tell you, one key takeaway from that is, may our eagerness to understand scripture never become the means by which we avoid the more important task of faithful obedience."

"Okay, nice, but can I ask for advice?" Ben said insistently. "I can't handle Olly anymore. I want a solution *now*."

"Now?"

"Yes! I'm sick of him!"

Rob nodded. Suddenly, a wide jocose smile manifested onto his face. "He's been a grievous curse to you, hasn't he?"

Ben stared. "A what?"

"The greatest curse is the blessing that you know you are missing out on. The curse is getting what you want. What that means is you need to change your wants."

Ben felt a tremor of uncertainty in his chest and throat. This was the antithesis of what David had said. *Being a man was desiring what one cannot get.*

"Is there hope?" Ben rasped.

"Something needs to be removed," Rob said. "If God wants you to gather the Church, there are three things you need to get right. One: Establish harmony and relationships with individuals. Two: Clean out the sin in your personal life, and three: obey God's Word. This is *faithing*. You need to surrender to the source of life."

Ben raised an eyebrow. "Faithing? Is that a word? You made it up!"

"Yes," Rob said. "Ten seconds ago."

Ben led the pastor through the park with his flashlight. Now, he could afford to disclose its location to Rob, mainly because he trusted the man to be a genuinely good and virtuous soul. If he found out who Ben truly was, he would very likely not slander and spread the rumour around. And yet, Ben still feared Olly might expose his true name – that reckless asshole didn't know how to control his tongue!

"Do I have to do anything? To help?" Ben asked, his heart palpitating in his chest.

"Just watch and learn," Rob said with a spice to his voice, heavy and stern. "You can't learn how to fish unless you watch someone fish."

"I suppose that makes sense," Ben said, wondering what Rob might do.

"All right," Rob said, crossing his arms, speaking authoritatively into the dark camp. "The doors of utterance have been opened! Come out, Oliver!"

A startled rustling noise drew both Ben and Rob to Olly, who had woken with a start from his sleeping bag. He made a slurred grunt, craning his neck around the clothesline to see who had come. "Huh? Oh, you mother—" Olly cut off once he laid eyes on Rob. He straightened up, making a posture to look resplendent with mock professionalism as he flattened his rag. He tucked an empty bottle into the folds of the sleeping bag. "Ben, what are you doing?"

"Ben?" Rob said, startled.

Ben's blood went cold. "Who's Ben? My name is Jacob!"

Confusion set in Olly's face, and instead of belching out the truth, Olly's shoulders shook as he guffawed.

Pursing his lips, Rob picked up an empty bottle, his forehead scowling deeply. "There is a dark void inside you," Rob said forthrightly, tossing the bottle, taking a step forward.

Olly ceased laughing.

"And somehow you wish you could fill it. You try to find purpose, drinks, girlfriends, masturbation and drugs so you can have the impression of belonging. You've done all you can. But you've been led astray."

Olly nodded, a ghoul in the night. "What … What do you want?" Olly said with a raspy voice, raising his head stubbornly. He made a long groan as he twitched, a hand stroking a flask. "No one wants me. Trust me. I'm bad."

"Very bad?"

Olly nodded vigorously, sniffing snot up his nose, which he wiped with his sleeve. "Oh yeah. Very, very."

"Well, that's good. That's very good. I want to show you someone who cares for the bad because he's very fond of you." Ben's heart leapt. "I can tell you about somebody who can save everybody," Rob pressed, taking another step.

Olly's face seemed to blanch.

"Look at me, Olly," Rob said. "I have friends who are bums too. They want to know how to *feel* again."

"Why are you …?"

"I will keep on annoying you until you talk. You wish you had someone who could guide you out of this."

"Who is this?"

Careful, Rob, Ben thought. *You think that you can bring this man to Christ – this fish will turn into a shark!*

"What do you *see in me?* What did Ben tell you that interests you so much?"

Rob remained unperturbed. Meek, yet poised; he did not seem to notice – Ben hoped – that Olly had slipped again by using his real name. "Every hair on your head is numbered," Rob said.

Tipping back his head in fear, Olly's eyes widened.

Rob chuckled. "Seriously. Every hair on your head is numbered. There is one that I know that gave me a purpose in life."

"Haha! You're getting me to believe in a higher power! Loser!"

"I will show you. The One."

"The One?"

"God. In his people. Jesus Christ."

Olly laughed in disbelief, a mad sadistic laughter that echoed through the dark woods. "I was taking you seriously there for a second, but *Jesus?* For all I know, that's a swear word!"

"Come and see," Rob said.

"Oh, a church is … I don't belong in a church. Don't worry about me."

"I'm serious."

"Screw church. Leave me in Hell, and if Jesus is God, then he should go to Hell to save me! But he doesn't."

"You can't say that," Rob said, lowering his gaze.

"I can say whatever I want, Pastor! I'm just telling it as it is! Can't I do that?"

"Yes. And to answer your question. Yes. Jesus *did* go to Hell." Rob smirked.

Olly stared, dumbfounded.

He did? Ben thought, surprised.

"Just … come and see," Rob said, raising his hand to stop Olly. "That's all I want from you. Come to our Trumpet service. It's all about the second coming of Christ. I promise you will not feel alienated. There are people in the church who are suffering just like you. Come and see."

Olly shook his head, jowls sagging, saying, "I—"

"What? You will be late for work? Late for your girlfriend?"

Olly's neck went stiff, his nostrils flaring. Ben sweated.

"Your whole life," Rob said fearlessly, face to face with the wrathful Olly. "You wanted to live with purpose. You wanted to be a good person, so people don't deny you. But you were led astray by drugs, and now you cannot help it. I will have you meet the Spirit of God, the merciful, kind and patient ruler of the universe. There will be surprises. You will not forget it." Rob became stern, austere, his voice enigmatic. "And if you do, I will refund your misery. But give poor Jacob space. Got it?"

"But … But …"

"I don't mess around. The Spirit of God is no drug that has ever been or will be." Rob took Olly's hand and said once more, "Just come and see. Just this once."

———

Ben ate his dinner in private, then returned to the church when it was safe to watch Olly embroiled in communion with the ex-addicts.

"By the love of … You gotta be … No!" Archie growled over the din of people in the dining room, celebrating a special function. "No, that cannot be Olly, Jacob!"

Ben gestured with a whimsical expression hidden behind his neck warmer. "See for yourself."

"You're kiddin'!" Archie narrowed his eyes. "What happened to him?"

Ben shrugged. "Don't ask me, bro." He glanced at the clock and saw that it was already nine thirty. "He's not going to stop talking, is he, Archie?"

"Nope. He's getting drunk by the company!"

They chuckled together, watching the religious communion and worship around them.

I cannot do this alone, Ben found himself thinking. *Unite the Church.*

War is coming. The Nephilim. The fight to find Veronica. The tightness and the heaviness gripped his whole body. *Don't get laid back. It's a battle.*

But who will figure it out first that I am Ben DePaula? Ben thought in a panic. All these reflections about exposure brought him full circle back to his great shame for his public identity. Rob had been the closest to come to grips with the truth, but Olly … only he knew.

I need to stop Olly. I need to … I need to take him, lock him up—

A blast. A cawing trumpet droned throughout the room. Jumping, Ben's heart punched his chest as the crowd cheered like a gushing wave of the sea, clapping like a downpour. More pealing trumpets blared in an eerie, droning melody. Looking around desperately to find the source of the clamour, Ben saw three men in Jewish shawls blowing large, corkscrewed ram horns. Olly and his friend howled and clapped in frenzied revel. "Blow again!" Olly shouted. "Blow it! Blow the trumpet! Blow the trumpet! Yeah!"

"Jacob? You're pale."

"What?" Ben hissed harsher than he intended. "Archie?" Panic choked him. "Was … there supposed to be a holiday today? Can you remember?"

"Bro, it's the Trumpet feast tonight," came the jubilant reply. With studious eyes on the raucous din, Ben's skull throbbed with a migraine. He had been slack when it came to referring to Joshua's *moedim* schedule.

And that meant the vision could come upon him unawares. Since biblical days always started at sunset in the evening, it meant any time now.

"Jacob? Are you okay?"

Ben shot up on his feet and powerwalked away, looking for the green exit sign, cringing at his rudeness. Weaving through the crowd, not bothering to excuse them, head down, fear and shame urged him on.

"Jacob!" Archie. He was following him! *Get away!*

He couldn't bear anyone seeing him. Bilious colours settled in his vision, buzzing like the sounds of a thunderstorm. The entire escape from the main hall was mind distorting. Once he reached the foyer, Ben blundered, grabbing one of the chairs, fumbling feebly. His world swam faster and faster, becoming increasingly dizzy. The signs of an oncoming vision. A deep sleep. He looked this way and that, making sure no one had followed him.

"Not now! Please," Ben growled in protest, pressing a palm into his temple. He got up, walking towards the exit – that green beacon of hope.

Toilets? Occupied. Ben thought the kiosk would be safer, on the couches.

No one was there, blessedly.

It began as Ben flopped onto the couch.

59

CURSED FLOOD

"Woe to those who call evil good
and good evil,
who put darkness for light
and light for darkness,
who put bitter for sweet
and sweet for bitter!
Woe to those who are wise in their own eyes,
and shrewd in their own sight!"
—From the Scroll of Isaiah, the prophet's disciples, c. 740 – c. 540 BCE.

He blinked. He stood pressed against massive stones, on a heist to save his cousins, the children of Dammaranza – from the shaman families of Du-Ku who smuggled them.

Ben was Sava-Qayin of Nagaland, hiding between two cross-shaped stone pillars about ten cubits tall. He stood in a dim oval enclosure reinforced by dry, coarsely built stone walls interconnected by stone benches. Two larger pillars held the reed timber roof over the enclosure, which sunlight passed through.

Sava-Qayin walked out from between the pillars rising from a shallow pedestal and studied them. These strange cross-shaped pillars were blocks that only the giants would have been able to put in place. Sava-Qayin killed many of those brutes. Nephilim – the Lahmu – were violent, depraved animals, so it struck Sava-Qayin as strange that they could build holy structures. But he knew from all his years of slaughtering them to extinction to save his race that iniquity existed within all ordinary humans, not just the Lahmu Nephilim.

I'm in someone else's body! Ben thought. *What the hell?*

Stay focused, the voice of Sava-Qayin thought to his internal self. *I need to be ready to kill the shaman before Sheva-Qayin's ambush.*

For some reason, Ben felt his own self pushed to the side. A foreign mind took control of his body. To it, *Ben* was the foreign mind.

It was cool in here; the sun's scorching heat had blighted the face of the land, cursing the ground. Rain hadn't come to the highlands in years. The lack had strangled and oppressed all life, turning humans against one another. None was with a whole family – everyone had lost something. Everyone suffered.

Sava-Qayin prowled, looking this way and that. The enclosure was dead silent and still. A wide range of wild animal reliefs of several ducks, foxes, snakes, gazelle, vultures, spiders, scorpions and a headless human were incised on the megalithic pillars holding up the enclosure. Above them was a carved pattern of basket-shaped motifs and ovals with mirroring semicircles and vertical lines. Were they telling a story? Did the stones have apotropaic aspects? The two larger central pillars had carvings of long arms wearing belts. One of them held a fox in the crook of its right elbow on the flat relief. A highly symbolic world of the ancients.

Sava-Qayin crept towards the entrance, pressing against the wall, prowling stealthily into the corridor of stone.

Sounds of domesticated animals – the braying of sheep, barking of dogs and honking of geese – and the smell of dung proliferated the air. *What are the sex traffickers using these sanctuaries for now? A grazing pen?*

Disgusting. Child-lovers profaned holy stone.

And yet, was not Sava-Qayin and the Naga raid about to profane this stone?

Killing was endemic. How could anything be sacred now? These thirty curvilinear sanctuaries on top of the mountain of Du-Ku were primeval. No one knew what the enclosures were built for. The sequential construction and their intensive use maintained cosmic power for generations. They were relics of an ancient past, serving as a pilgrimage destination and for filthy barter to be made to the powerful shamans.

Ben was enthralled by this stream of consciousness. So much foreign and unusual rich information. *If I can trust these visions …*

Writhing emotions made Sava-Qayin gasp for breath. He stopped in the middle of the causeway corridor in the shadows. Was he having a miasma again? This was reality, and every day people lied and stole resources and children from clans. During a crisis, identity became more important. Conflict was more interesting, but abuse made life for men like Sava-Qayin.

This wasn't a vision, but a bleak reality he had to endure.

There is a time for everything. Now, it's a time to kill and a time to save my cousins.

The child-loving shamans were ravenous; they exploited, using the exploited to trade across the land, for famine struck the land of Eden grievously. The ground, unyielding, became feeble, and rain was scarce. The extreme summer drought in combination with extreme winters led many to desperation, deception, raiding parties, cannibalism, and above all, preserving seed.

The young were sought after by the elders. The older women couldn't get pregnant. The men were no longer fertile. In the face of extinction, young girls were sought after so elders could reproduce their lineage, and even boys were kidnapped by shaman women who wished to harness the power of their semen to impregnate themselves. In times of drought and cold winters, children vanished as the tree leaves did in season. And in times of crisis, the desire to love grew fierce.

Sava-Qayin ran and ran after the sex trafficker that snatched his child. He just saw him, behind the tree, tossing his six-year-old daughter over his shoulder. He ran after the monster, roaring, spear in his hand, throwing it, missing, running and hunting for hours.

My daughter ... Throbbing anguish and wrath swelled in harmony within Ben and Sava-Qayin.

He stalked into another enclosure with cross-shaped pillars. His cousins were not there.

He touched his dark dusty clothing – a black tunic sewn up with two small bones with a tattered, knotted, netlike rag over his shoulders, clipped to his clothing by four thin animal bones. Around his neck, he wore amber beads with agate and jasper. His beard was long, black and bushy, and in each of his hands were two gazelle horns. Along his left forearm, he wore a wooden vambrace with feathers and small bones and horns attached to it. His face felt dry, like plaster. Black face paint covered his visage.

Suddenly, there was movement. Sava-Qayin raised his gazelle horns. Coming into the enclosure from the entrance was a shaman dressed as a vulture.

Sava-Qayin struck.

Horn slashing his throat, Sava-Qayin lay the shaman to rest, blood dripping on the burned lime and smooth white clay floor.

Kill the sex traffickers. Leave no survivors. Save our children taken from us. Those had been the orders of his brother, Sheva-Qayin.

Sava-Qayin subdued Ben – Ben could only stay back and watch, like a prisoner in chains.

Sava-Qayin had hardened himself since he was conscripted as a boy to face the Nephilim who had murdered the matriarch of his village. He had failed his Naga masters so many times and fought up the ranks tirelessly. All his past was blurry, monotonous. He mustn't compromise now.

Prowling the way the shaman had come, Sava-Qayin crept towards the short corridor towards the next enclosure. These corridors were open to the air. Under the sweltering sun above, he could hear mirthful voices behind the wall and smell wonderful perfumes and spices.

The inner concentric wall of the enclosure proper had wooden rafters and a slanted reed roof covering the top, making climbing over the inner wall impossible. Once Sava-Qayin climbed this outer wall, he would need to prowl around the enclosure to find the entrance. By then, he hoped the Hunters of Nagaland would come in time.

Sava-Qayin found two crude handholds in depressions in the lime-plastered rocks, and pushed himself up, feet gripping into place. He slowly climbed the wall, mounted the top, and eased himself down the other side.

He could smell smoke from a fire, roasting meat, alcohol and beer.

Heart racing, Sava-Qayin went around the enclosure and saw domesticated animals penned inside the structure. He wove between them. Each of Sava-Qayin's steps made the goats, sheep and deer skittish; it felt as if each step should've made bloodied footprints.

Pressing his back against the rough wall, Sava-Qayin slid out of the outside enclosure along the inner wall that stretched out as a narrow entrance, out into the open. This gathering was occurring outside, just before the entrance into this sanctuary.

Hunkering down, Sava-Qayin hid behind a chair with an old man reclining on it.

Lamec. The Nephilim child sex trafficker.

Women and young children were on errands preparing for the feast, carrying baskets and flowers. And there were his cousins and bleak children gathering at the occasion. The faces of his cousins and the trafficked children were filled with sadness. He twitched, a killer's reflex, ready to save the innocent.

A woman stood next to a life-sized statue of a red, white and black wild boar, horned, blaring its tusks and teeth. She was a tall woman, likely trafficked, beautiful, with brown curly hair tumbling to her lower back with tanned skin. Her dress was snow and pure with a long hem. Her hair was woven with flowers and a white veil covered her face. Her smile shone as bright as the sun, and she smelled of pollen and spices.

Before her was the patriarchal shaman, gazing upon his love, carrying a docile white lamb in his hands. Wearing a well-cut brown fleece of a shepherd, with flowers in his hair, the sex trafficker's face was all planes and angles, his eyes icy blue and his hair was blond.

As the sunset cast an orange hue across the land, Sava-Qayin closed his eyes. He could hear the dead already screaming. They grated against his soul, wearing it as a grinding stone, reduced to nothing.

Foolish children of perverts! It is your fault that I must kill you!

A loud startling whoop warbled as movement broke forth from the distant hilltop. A pack of warriors in black-and-grey furs of skinned Nephilim, carrying obsidian spears and some carrying shields made from tiger skins, charged towards the ceremony. The attack had begun.

Sava-Qayin watched as the wave of black-and-grey-veiled warriors descended, crying like gibbons, brandishing their obsidian weapons. The sex traffickers spun around, stunned.

Sava-Qayin struck. He sprung on his feet from behind the chair, slamming the horn deep into Lamec's body. The child-lover retched, dying with a grating sound. He ripped the horn out, spraying blood.

The children screamed. Dropping the lamb, a roar ripped out of the shaman – a bellow vibrating with a thousand discordant rhythms. Adult women and men traffickers tried to restrain Sava-Qayin, but he cannoned into the shaman, howling. All around him, Naga closed in, besieging the child sex traffickers, slaying them.

Sava-Qayin charged at the shaman, his horn raised. *My daughter!* He locked eyes with the ferocious child-lover, forehead pressed against his forehead. Sava-Qayin, at this moment, got a good look into the shaman's icy blue eyes. They wrestled viciously, pushed and shoved, twisting and restraining arms.

All around, people died and screamed. The children were spared, and they huddled together in fear, watching the chaos timidly.

The sex traffickers fought back the Hunters of Nagaland. They beat against the tiger shields. The spears slashed the reprobates. Naga cut off hands. They slashed off noses, and men who were skewered vomited blood. Flint knives whistled into the air from the hands of Tideimi' Lavar – the Sons of Rock – repeatedly stabbing the child-traffickers' necks. Blood spurted from them, dark jets gushing from mouths in mighty floods of red until the whole ground was covered in puddles of blood. The lamb wallowed in that life blood of crying humans.

Out of the bloodbath, the children were rounded up by the Maidens of the Spear – the Varatti'quwinal. The trafficked children were stunned, and many were crying, hugging each other. Then the Naga parted, making way for Sava-Qayin's brother.

Sheva-Qayin, the head-hunter, was a middle-aged man with black-grey hair, with a hawkish face that reminded Ben of Ian Mastemah, under the shadow of a boar-tusk helm. On his back, he wore the jawbone of a colossal beast, a family heirloom of a stone replica of an extinct sabre-toothed creature, made into a deadly weapon. Clean-shaven, wearing an ornate necklace of jasper, amber and agate, he trod the blood-spattered ground, hands behind his back, eyes cast down at the slaughtered child sex traffickers, nodding.

Sava-Qayin grunted, pugnaciously shoving the shaman against the wall fiercely. The shaman attempted to dig his thumb into Sava-Qayin's eye, but he pressed the horn into the shaman's neck, pressing slowly. He howled, struggling violently.

"STOP!" the bride screamed. Gathering around her were Sava-Qayin's female cousins, youthful girls with head coverings gleaming with shells and gems, hands to their cheeks, eyes wide with shock. Their brothers stood with them, knees knocking, some running to defend their adopted parents, only to be tackled by two or three Nagas, holding them in place and carrying them away.

Sava-Qayin took a deep breath as the bride ambled towards him, hands raised. Behind her white veil, only her mouth could be seen on her opaque complexion, open with despair. He could not see her eyes or any facial features. Just a whimpering, sobbing mouth.

The lamb of the shaman writhed on the ground at her feet, squealing, struggling to get up from a puddle of blood. Sava-Qayin looked down – it was a newborn – when the shaman dropped it, it broke its leg.

The bride made a noise – a weak, small mutter. She looked into Sava-Qayin's eyes, and he saw her …

Veronica.

Numbness cleaved to Sava-Qayin. He refused to feel pain now. He pressed the horn harder against the shaman's neck.

No … This revenge … is not right! Ben thought.

The bride roared out a gasp, collapsing on her knees at Sava-Qayin's feet. She tugged at his garment, blabbering and groaning. "Spare him! Please, *please*, have mercy! Spare him! Spare him! What did he do wrong? Please!"

Sava-Qayin looked and saw his abducted daughter – the beautiful bride. She was only young, barely sixteen years old.

Sava-Qayin looked into the wicked shaman's eyes, resembling Alfred Bonnor. They were filled with wrath and fear. In days when Sava-Qayin had been an apprentice to his herbalist mother, before she was slaughtered – she told him that wounds that were beyond healing had to be cut off – broken fingers or a limb ill repairable must be amputated. It hurt. But it saved lives.

Kill to save lives.

Thunder rumbled in the sky as the sun rode down in violet clouds erupting with crimson flames in the sky.

"What are you doing, Komana? This man isn't your husband. He kidnapped you! Finish this, Sava!" Sheva-Qayin's command was fierce, and Sava-Qayin nodded.

His daughter shrieked in woe. She got up and attacked her father, Sava-Qayin. Nagas lunged, ripping at her dress, pulling her back, ripping at her hair as she struggled and groaned. She brayed, bellowed and howled like an animal, spit flying out of her mouth.

Sava-Qayin closed his eyes, attaining the void.

His horn rammed through the shaman's stomach. Sava-Qayin hugged the enemy, gripping him as he twisted the horn, shoving it deep.

What have I done? Ben thought in shock. *This is not me! It's a nightmare! I cannot ... I cannot control myself ... I cannot make choices ... When will this vision end?*

It didn't. Gripping the shaman's blond hair, Sava-Qayin tore out the horn. Blood splattered everywhere, raining over the ground.

Chills beset Sava-Qayin. His hands were covered in dark red blood. His vision almost doubled. His stomach seethed.

Sava-Qayin tried to keep himself from smiling. His daughter's suffering ... He'd never heard her sob like this before.

The sobbing reproached him for ruining her existence on the land.

Oh my God! Veronica! Veronica, I've ruined you!

Silence! Sava-Qayin's fierce consciousness fought back. He shuddered. The madness. It was getting worse.

Veronica ...

The air descended with a shameful low moan as dusk came down. The sun sank like a decapitated head, descending into the Underworld. Shadows spread, the soaked ground became dark, set as obsidian glass, reflecting the faces and the images of the bloodied Nagas, the dead and the survivors. All was dark water, all but the low moaning, infuriated by the sobs of the wretched bride.

Sava-Qayin watched the Nagas rounding up the kidnapped children. They had spent months planning to rescue these children from the shamans. Fifty-four boys and girls aged eleven to eighteen. This wasn't a wedding, but an *orgy*, and Sava-Qayin's daughter had been about to engage in it.

None of the rescued children smiled, nor laughed at their freedom. They huddled in silent, bleak doubt. The only sound of freedom now was the mourning cries of Komana.

So much suffering and death. It was as if it were endemic to existence.

Was there hope for humanity? They abused those they loved. What good was it to fight, what good was it to win, what good was it to live, if there was no difference between family or enemy? What was victory? What was harmony? But vanity. What did the deaths of Sava-Qayin's loved ones mean? Nothing. The whole world was a pustule, sickening red, oozing, infested with corruption.

This is a lie, Ben thought, but he was too stunned by what he had been forced to do. *I know what this is …*

Majestic thunder roared in the heavens, like a parent seeing their children killing each other, bellowing out in pain, wanting the suffering to stop. The rumblings of the land tremors, the beating of El's chest, his own detested heart, aching and throbbing.

Then it began to spit. Weeping tears fell to the ground from the eyes of the gathering storm clouds.

… the Flood…

Thunder cracked with an ear-splitting pulse. Some of the girls began to sob. The air temperature plummeted, and Sava-Qayin shivered.

"When I was just a little boy," Sheva-Qayin said to Komana – Sava-Qayin's daughter. His head constantly nodded as he spoke. "My parents told me of the stories when the Anunna gods descended to the land. They gave us agriculture and bureaucracy. They took our girls, giving birth to the Nephilim. Half human. Half gods. Those girls became evil goddesses. Their offspring of chaos waged war against humanity – years upon years, desolation after desolation. The Sages who made callings and bonds with spirits failed to protect us. They betrayed us, so ordinary men fought to protect their lives by themselves. When the Nephilim kidnapped you all who stand here today, they married you.

"This is why I dedicated my life to find victims. My great-grandfather began training women survivors, rescuing them. We gave them sustenance. We gave the women back their freedom, and now, they fight for freedom. If the Naga don't save the children, the whole world will be consumed by Tiham."

Crimson blotching her tainted white garments, Komana sobbed.

Why? Ben faltered. He'd done the same with Thomas Jones. Ben had the same attitude. Taking matters into his own hands. Guilt shredded his soul.

"All this," Sheva-Qayin continued, walking towards Komana, looming over her, "in the end, is about seed." He dug his hands in his seed sack, grabbing a handful. "Today would be the day when your corrupt Nephilim seed is cut off the face of the ground!"

Sava-Qayin watched as his brother slowly opened his hand, pouring the seeds over the corpse of the shaman. The corpse of Alfred Bonnor.

As Sheva-Qayin ambled off, Sava-Qayin saw Komana stand up. She walked up to Sava-Qayin. She flicked back her veil. Her face was just as Sava-Qayin had remembered – his daughter was mature now, handsome, gorgeous and austere, olive skinned, and her blue eyes pink and glazed.

And Ben recognised her. The woman resembled a mature Veronica, but she had the face of a grim stranger whom he had seen but never met.

Thunder shook the ground. Everyone looked skyward. At the darking sky.

As soon as Sava-Qayin looked up, Komana grabbed his wrist, tugging it. Komana clenched her jaw, trying to pull the horn towards her clenching body. Her breath became intense, and her eyes were fearless, determined. She was trembling with tension, pulling the point closer to her stomach.

Sava-Qayin closed his eyes.

He couldn't let his daughter kill herself. He'd just saved her life. Sava-Qayin strained against her taut grip and let his hands go limp, dropping his weapons.

Thunder pealed through the air furiously, a snapping clap that jolted the bones. Komana gawked at the sky and Sava-Qayin as well. The children cried out in fear.

Black clouds tore apart. The windows of the sky ripped open. Thunder pounded like the drum of El's heartbeat, vibrating the very stone. Over the mountain of Du-Ku coming from the north-west was a thick storm wall, mighty in strength on the land. The darkness was dense, for the sun was gone, and the deluge formed out of wind, stones, dust and water came closer.

The Nagas broke protocol and began to take shelter in the curvilinear enclosures. Sheets of rain rushed on them wrathfully, drenching them.

Komana gave her father Sava-Qayin an odious look. Her jaws were hardened, and her eyes flinty in the blackness, lightning flashes flickering her ghostly outline. She hated her father. She had actually been attached to the perverted shaman he killed. The cries of distressed children rang, ghastly, all around them in the wind. *Veronica … Brianna … Cleo …*

Ben was sobbing.

A popping snap quaked the earth, and the cross-shaped stone pillars that held the enclosures trembled.

The ground was already inundated, with muddy water reaching his ankles. So sudden this rain had come. A miracle.

The storm wall rumbled closer, cutting off all life. An angry sheet of white lightning syringed out of the thunderhead, like a spear of war, spasming with cosmic fire.

The screaming. The children, his cousins, and the Nagas in the chaotic darkness, turned against each other for space on the narrow enclosure terrace. They knew it was over.

Then the head-hunter, Sheva-Qayin, rose up against Sava-Qayin. *What?* Ben moved with Sava-Qayin, grabbed the sabre-tooth weapon and elbowed his brother, grabbing his arm and shoulder, sweeping his legs from under him. He splashed into a massive puddle. Sava-Qayin violently wrenched the jawbone out of his brother's grip and hammered it down. The tooth embedded itself deep into Sheva-Qayin's throat.

Why did he turn against me? Why?

Freezing water stabbed his skin like ice spears, freezing him from the skin inward. A loud, savage scream cut through the warring rain and thunder. The winds screaming with Komana.

The storm wall hit.

The wind and water nearly knocked Sava-Qayin out.

He stumbled backwards, rolling along the ground through the mud. It was deep enough now that it cut currents into the ground, pulling him down into a small cataract. He fell, splashing down a small hill.

Furiously, he tried to get a firm purchase. Muddy water was in his eyes. He fought the current and katabatic winds, scrabbling for the enclosure.

Lightning flashed in fitful bursts. The gales bellowed like a screaming eagle. It made him feel he was blinking his eyes quickly, light and darkness alternating.

His daughter was gone. She was dead.

He lunged forward for the stone wall, but wind, water and debris were warriors striking him and the land. His screams were a mistake; the coldness coursed down his throat and into his chest. One gush lashed him viciously, then slammed him down, dragging him along the rock wall. The rock shred his skin. Sava-Qayin couldn't think. Large branches and stones torn by powerful gusts crashed into the structure.

The enclosure was quickly filling up with watery backfill. He picked at a rough-feeling section of the outer walls, trying to pull himself up. Handholds were slick and wet, and he cut his fingers many times. The water reached his thighs. The mortar depression gave him a grip, and he held on tight. One step and the current reaching his hips would take him down to damnation. But Sava-Qayin held on for his life. He bore the storm, his eyes pressed shut.

He shivered in the darkness. Silt and thick sediment made the wooden rafter groan. The roof in the adjacent enclosure caved in, shattering from the accumulating weight of the mud, killing everyone inside.

Only Sava-Qayin survived. Barely holding on, his feet slowly slipping.

What is this? Ben bellowed in outrage. *They all died! Why are you showing me this?*

The nightmare didn't end. Towers of water shot into the air, and the fountains of the Great Deep, very mighty, split the land apart. The violent mighty water that rained down struck the land, forming an incredible wave.

Sava-Qayin stared at the chaos of uncreation. His final battle would begin. The battle for life.

Ben screamed internally.

The wall of water attacked him, the cold of a thousand spears stabbing all over his body. He slammed into the wall, scraping against it from the force of the current. His clothes and flesh tore, and he felt a blow to the neck. Thrashing, Sava-Qayin swirled in the darkness, the lightning his only light.

I'm going to die.

An ember burst alive within Sava-Qayin. Ben *refused* to die. He would fight as the Actionman would for his family, for his loved ones.

Sava-Qayin felt himself hit another enclosure wall, rubbing against something hard and soft.

A wood beam.

He hugged it with both arms. With legs and arms, Sava-Qayin strained, reaching, clawing. His head came above water, and he roared a gasp of sweet air. The cold was astounding, making him yelp, his jaws clattering. The tempest had gained a steady flow, but the flood assaulted the land.

Sava-Qayin smiled in awe at the cosmic storm. It had no mercy. It washed away all evil.

At last. Justice.

Sava-Qayin felt the wood slip, and he sank into the deep. Anxiety ruled him for a moment, and he bellowed. The waves churned in a maelstrom of chaos.

The Nephilim – the hairy Wild Men – when he used to kill them, he'd notice that they were attuned to rhythms when they fought, when they died. Rhythms of pure song.

As he floundered, Sava-Qayin was attuned to *something*. A war rhythm clashing between victory and loss. Confidence and angry zealous tones merging together.

He slammed into a wall again and held on belligerently. He hit his head again. He bled. His bones had broken.

He fainted and sank.

Then the storm ceased, and there was a dim cold light piercing the darkness.

Ben was himself again. He gasped, hyperventilating. *Was it over?* Fog steamed up from the ground, shrouding a tall, radiant figure in opalescent plate. The armour was interlocking, a helm covering the lithe warrior.

The paladin?

A deep, booming voice came into his head. GATHER THEM. REPENT.

Ben was blinded by sunlight. He was squatting over bags of seeds, inspecting them in his hands, smelling them to see if they were spoiled or not. He spat them out of his mouth.

He looked at his clothing, felt his skin and realised he was Sava-Qayin once again. Ben dreaded he would be stuck in this cycle of the nightmare forever. *Am I dead? Will I ever wake?*

Waves from the ocean coast rumbled and hissed as they crashed, and the sweet smell of salt and sand filled his nose.

Sheva-Qayin, next to him, crested a small mound of sand into a wide dip behind dead palms. Around him were the female Naga warriors, all veiled, obsidian spears ready. Some leaned on their shields – human sized, made from the skin of tigers.

Sheva-Qayin stared into the pit. In the pit was a man, rolling wearily. His naked body was crudely covered in loose grey wraps of shoddy, rough-spun fibres. In his hand was a wine skin. He spat something out of his mouth, eyeing Sheva-Qayin deliriously.

The man who had awoken was southeast Asian. His skin was tanned and caked in sand, and his eyes were slanted with an epicanthic fold. He looked middle-aged, but the creases along his face were roadmaps of hardship. His hands clutching the wineskin looked calloused, the hands of a craftsman. They quivered. The man blushed in shame.

The drunk man got to his feet. Sheva-Qayin turned to Sava-Qayin, asking him to smell him and search for weapons.

The man smelled like sweat, alcohol and seaweed. He found a horn and a small wooden elephant in his garments and tossed it to the ground.

The man let out a vexed grunt. "Bastards," he slurred. "He can't stand the sight of blood! Give it! Give it to me!"

Ben stared at the small toy – an intricately crafted elephant – turning it in his hands. The wooden carving's details were amazing – the folds of the skin, the trunk, the body proportions, to the hairs on the tail. *At least I have full control now,* Ben thought. *Who is this drunk man?*

"I can't do it anymore," the man said, staring at his sloshing wineskin. "Waste." The man shook his head, sniffing, stifling what may have been a chuckle.

Ben stared into the man's eyes. *I cannot take this elephant from him. It's his.* Ben gave the elephant back, and he snatched it from his hand.

"Are you behind this?" Sheva-Qayin said, adjusting his boar-tusk helm. "Are you loyal to Lamec?"

"What?"

"Are you involved in the child sex trafficking cult?"

The man's eyes widened slightly, mouth hanging open. "I had a father named Lamec," he said. He didn't sound fully stoned. "He was a good man. He's dead."

Sheva-Qayin nodded, saying in a low voice, "Lamec is a common name."

The man swayed, swerving his head, chest heaving with a sigh. "I don't care what anyone thinks of my family. The Day of Reckoning is at hand."

Sheva-Qayin's head jolted at that. "Ah, that makes sense now. This world is consuming itself. A Day of Reckoning will come. Yes. Which family do you come from?"

The man stared, dumbfounded.

"You speak of the Reckoning. There was a Sage long ago named Methuselah who spoke of such things. Methuselah, son of Hanok, son of Yared." Sheva-Qayin grimaced. "The one who descended. The Sages. Seven orders of them betrayed us like the Nephilim."

The man chuckled. "Is any one of us honourable as the Sages?"

Sheva-Qayin nodded, eyes weighting the balance of this man's integrity. "I don't like men preaching the traditions of the Sages."

"I'm sorry," the man said, nodding unconsciously. "My lineage, my mother's kin, are pragmatic."

Sheva-Qayin smirked, lowering his gaze, nodding. Chill air hovered over the sea; Ben tasted sharp salt on his lips. The sea surface of membranous green-blue shimmered, undulating and swelling. Crashing against the seashore, small swells kicking up, rising then never forming but nothingness kept at bay. Chaos water swirling with bubbles and seaweed and turbid sand gathered, then collapsed, battering the dry land like the sound of battle, and receding, new waves replacing them. Endlessly folding back over, repeating itself, occurring in tumultuous eternity under the summer climate. Ben still vividly felt the memory of the horrible deluge and the cold hard pounding rain all over his body. The roars of the sea were many voices, transforming endlessly.

"Your children and your cousins have been kidnapped, despising the Creator for not exercising judgement. Justice is the Creator's alone," the man said.

"I don't despise the Creator. What do you want to gain—"

"What do I gain? Ha! I have gained wild and waste!" the woebegone man exclaimed. "I did not want this – I wanted to be a bridgeman. But … the famine happened …" The man sighed protractedly. When he spoke, he was on the verge of tears. "I got what I needed, not what I *thought* I wanted. My mother's kin believe that justice only belongs to U-Blei, and we are to accept our cursed lot."

"Unbelievable," Sheva-Qayin grumbled condescendingly. "Your family is a disease, condemning innocent successful women and children because you are *jealous*. And then you whine. Is that fair?" The man closed his eyes. "No. You stole my seeds because you think the world is going to deluge. The famine has only gotten worse, and the days increase with heat."

The man went taut, nostrils flaring. He nodded. "I'm sorry. I wasn't clear. My family bear the sins of the Sages who wanted justice, yet were thirsty for revenge. But we cannot do anything about what is happening now. Yes. I stole your seeds. I'm sorry for my theft. But understand, my family is starving."

"Everyone is starving."

"U-Blei, forgive me, but no one is innocent. We are to drown with mud in our lungs, and now … That is justice. But mercy …" The man swallowed, sniffing. "Is holding back what we deserve. The door of mercy has been nailed open for millennia. My family have found that door."

Sheva-Qayin placed a hand on the man's shoulder, speaking into his ear. "Spare me your drivel. A god that destroys people for the sins of their parents … is not a god of justice. And if he spares you—"

The man smiled. "I was not spared because of justice. But because of *grace*."

"Grace?" Sheva-Qayin leaned into the man's ear and rasped, "The world needs justice. What is grace?"

"Justice is giving what we deserve," the man rasped back, squinting. "If mercy is holding back what we deserve, then grace"—tears ran down the man's face—"is giving what we *don't* deserve."

"Why?"

"I'm not worthy to receive this gift. But what I do know is that Grace found me. Grace worked *in* me, *through* me, making peace with all." He raised his wineskin, shaking the contents inside, then threw it away, discarding it into the palm brush. The man twitched his nose. A squall of wind tousled his hair. He stared at the waters and the white coast longingly. "I don't think I will ever be purely clean. I try. But U-Blei's *khesed* and grace holds up the cosmos from chaotic Tiham." Something was fatalistic about the Asian man's tone. A sure conclusion at the zenith of his intense life unsettled Ben – his eyes, his face, his clothing – but his words … they were captivating and confident. Almost … almost as if they were the truth of experience and meaning that Ben *needed* to witness. "*Khesed* is about relationship and service. This is what the Khesed Bond was when the calling to return to the Garden was made between the Seven Sages and the gods. When it became about killing Nephilim for revenge, they lost sight, and great was the Sages' fall. They broke the calling, and the Garden of Eden was eradicated. They made the Khesed Bond about glory rather than love. Relationships are *never* about power, and one way to avoid the will to power is to choose to limit oneself—to show *khesed*. Let us remember the recreance of the Seven Sages."

Sheva-Qayin listened, but his eyes were not looking the man in the eyes. He was still nodding, still stone faced. "But if you're undeserving, then what's the point? You cut down the forest, only for it to regrow again from a corrupt seed. It's hopeless."

The man slumped his head. He remained silent, the winds and waves the only sound. Then he reared his head back up, and Ben thought he saw colour in his light brown eyes, and his voice had a power to it. He spoke forthrightly. "My only hope is that one will come from my seed. The one from my loins. He who began the good work within me will continue and succeed. He …" The man took a breath. "He is Grace itself. The seed of Khavva, who will crush the head of the snake, while the snake bites his heel. In restoring all things, innocent with *khesed* and grace, he will suffer because of *love*." Then the man closed his eyes, tears running down his bronze face. Presently, he sighed, hand reaching into his pocket. Ben saw that he was playing with the elephant toy in his hands. "I'm at peace in the presence of my enemies." He lifted his chin and prayed curtly, "Thank you, U-Blei."

Then Sheva-Qayin said, "I hope your family finds U-Blei. Because I have a family I need to find." He leaned forward and said, "Justice is in *my* hands."

The holy man didn't scoff, he didn't yell in petulance, because now Ben knew what he and the Nagas were about to do. They were terrorists, about to launch an attack on an orgy of paedophiles and trafficked kids.

The holy man's skin seemed to gleam, radiant in the sunlight. He took a deep breath, gazing at the azure sky, renewed. "My friend. I discern you're wilder than the beasts. The animals will have hope, but not men." Patting his hand on Sheva-Qayin's shoulder, the Asian man climbed up the sand dune, the Nagas parting a way for him, their eyes the only part of them visible under their black veils. They were pacific, subdued, wondering about this holy man.

"Wait, friend," Ben called, his mouth dry. "What's your name?"

The waves thundered loudly, and the wind tossed and turned tempests of sand.

The holy man, reaching a thick grove of palm trees a good distance away, turned around.

"My name ... is Noah," he called back.

———

Ben gasped, fumbling awake on the couch between two pillows. He sat there, breathing in and out, thinking.

The vision ... it was real, another world, making the present reality seem more dreamlike by comparison. It was God speaking to him like a prophet, traumatising him with terrible realities. *Noah ... The Flood. Gather them. Repent.*

"AHH! Ben's alive," a voice said. Ben whipped his head around and saw Olly on the other side of the couch, sipping his cup of tea. "Feeling all right there, Ben? Haha! Thought we lost ya! Hahaha!"

"What happened?" Ben meant it as a demand, but it sounded like a groaning plea.

"Oh, you mean when everyone saw your face?"

Ben grabbed his hat, scrunching it up, feeling his neck warmer at his neck. "Oh no …" Ben leapt to his feet, his chest hurting with shock. "That's it. Farewell, Olly … It's nice knowing you." Ben hobbled towards the exit as fast as he could. "Got to go."

"What? Ben, who are you hiding from?"

Ben froze. Was that question genuine or rhetorical? Ben opened the back door and ran outside.

"There is only mendacity," Olly called from behind. "You're screwed, Ben!"

Grace worked in *me*, through *me*.

Ben thought of those words Noah had said to Sheva-Qayin. *God, give me grace! I need it now.*

He jogged the rest of the way to his camp until his hip hurt. He didn't want Rob's church to call the FBI.

Hastily, unruffling the old sleeping bag, Ben immediately preferred to be in the car, and yet a part of himself couldn't neglect Olly's suffering. In the end, Olly had won the base camp. The man was free. He could start a new life, and Ben had done nothing but dehumanise him.

Wretch.

"What am I?" Ben croaked like the insects that clicked around him. "Why have you given me these visions?"

Sava-Qayin was a father, but he'd also been a serial killer. Sava-Qayin, so deluded by revenge and resentment. *No, I will not become that depraved!*

But what if Veronica *had* been kidnapped, raped and married her rapist without even remembering?

"It was just a dream." Ben's eyes were used to the dark. He could see the faint outline of the treetops – an inky black in the foreground of the sky. And they swirled in the chaotic current of the mighty waters.

"But it was so real. You need to help me, God. Aren't you a god of justice and righteousness? Or are you a liar? Is that where love gets ya? Turning me into a monster? Is this what the dream meant? Oh! I know! You want me to let Veronica go! Why can't I love her? Huh? Why can't I care for those I love? You want me to be dead? It's *my life* and not yours!"

That life he loved was the battle to conquer the horrible, inevitable sentiments of inadequacy. He had to prove himself to remain standard in the eyes of those who saw their idol; to break through that wall of meagreness, discovering that he was some kind of special human – something *more*, something *meaningful*. And from that glory, Ben knew, he would reach a stage, eventually, when he would think of himself as mediocre and a failure.

Again and again, Ben's drive as an actor, stuntman, marine and a father boiled down to this incessant fear of being mediocre. It spurred him on, distorting him into Sava-Qayin – a beast. Fear made Ben into a beast.

When he agreed to serve in Operation Iraqi Freedom. When he fell from that burning building and destroyed his hip. When he found the baby and his father died. When his daughter went missing. All of it. When everything could have been different, it had been all taken away.

Ben stood face to face with mediocrity. He felt inactive, clogged inside a web of failure – and he *hated* it. He *loathed* it. "God! Help me *understand* what is happening to me! Please! If I am to face Keller in the worst-case scenario, help me do it! If you are real, *answer me!* Give me answers! No more riddles in dreams!"

Thin silence.

Ben sighed and hid his face. Could he confess all his sins and beg for mercy in court without getting arrested? Or could he go to a priest? An endangered species of mankind. Why would Ben ever want to go to one for help?

But he couldn't be bothered doing all that. He was exhausted. He knew it was his depression and anxiety that was wearing him down.

"Argh! I don't know what to do!" Ben cried. "Wasn't killing my father and taking Veronica enough? Do you have to toy with me, too? With visions?" In a blind rage, Ben threw his hat into the dark. He grabbed Olly's bottle on the ground and smashed it. "God! God! I hate you!"

Ben had nowhere to go.

But the Navajo. The Pueblo. The Apache. They thought very differently from everyone. They were all about kinship and love. They were not of this world and would accept Ben, despite what he had become.

They could unlock the mystery of my visions!

He would find Albert's Navajo. But the Navajo also gave Ben what he wanted to his great detriment: they translated the CD, they healed his hip and saved his life, just for him to continue to suffer again.

But Keller could be coming now if Ben didn't act quickly. He saw how Keller had treated Ian Mastemah. Because of that, Ben had reacted out of fear, as a depraved human being. A frightened beast on the run.

Ben started his car engine. In this darkness, he felt lost again in the maze of the forest.

"The righteous and the wicked both perish."

The moon's head peeked from behind the horizon, hesitant at first, as if making sure it could stealthily pursue the sun. It was a clear night, and the stars shivered high above. The scar of the galaxy spanned in a swath of multiple-coloured stars. Late-night sounds whispered and hooted, but the sound of his tyres on the gravel scared away the nocturnal creatures. It seemed so still, so calm, when the world appeared to fall to the wrath of an angry god.

Ben's eyes were heavy. He knew it was vexation and the dislocation of being homeless. He could no longer trust anyone except for Joshua and the Navajo. Not even Rob – that hypocrite. Keller hunting him stole much of his lean strength he'd cultivated while a marine and a stuntman. He felt tired all the time, even when having a regular meal and having a good night's sleep in the car. He could never feel … energised again, full of action, as he once was.

As Ben began to drive, leaving the camp that had been his home, a creeping panic began to penetrate his consciousness. But the inner compulsion to go back to Phoenix was irresistible. And there lay the vortex of his pain and fear.

"I'm done, God," Ben whispered. "I can't do this anymore."

Three months from now, he wouldn't have cared that he'd done nothing at all – he would have felt trapped that he didn't take matters into his own hands. He'd been there, done that and knew how he had failed taking justice into his own hands.

The visions were right. But were they true? As true as video-camera footage?

And yet, he still felt it *right* to rise up against evil.

"The righteous and the wicked *both* perish."

60

MAZES OF SHADOWS

"And I saw a great white throne and the one who was seated on it, from the presence of whom Earth and Heaven fled, and a place was not found for them. And I saw the dead—the great and the small—standing before the throne, and books were opened. And another book was opened, which is life. The dead were judged according to what they had done as recorded in the books. And the sea gave up the dead who were in it, and Death and Hades gave up the dead who were in them, and each person was judged according to what they had done. Then Death and Hades were thrown into the lake of fire. The lake of fire is the second death. Anyone whose name was not found written in the book of life was thrown into the lake of fire."

—From the Scroll of Revelation, John the Apostle, 95 – 96 CE.

*T*he night Neil had been arrested, Thomas Jones disappeared. The next day afterwards, Ben disappeared. No surveillance watch was kept on them because we did not have the time to watch innocent people.

That had been the official FBI report that came in this morning in the paper. Keller sat in the dark room of the Phoenix FBI department, rewatching his video-recorded interrogations with Neil Jones, and then with Thomas Jones. Sprawled on his chair, stressed, frustrated, starving for new information, Keller held his head, watching the video in a daze. Almost three months, and he *still* hadn't solved this case. If Thomas had not been entirely involved, the new suspect from the vigil who attacked him would be another chance he couldn't miss.

"Tell me about your van? What do you do in your van?"

"I drive in it."

"What music do you listen to?"

"Radio."

"Did you drive in your van alone? Do you have any friends that come along?"

"I–I … Is Neil coming?"

"Do you have any friends that come along in your van?"

"No."

"Do you know or have any friends that are from the Manicheans of Light?"

Thomas paused, staring with wide eyes at Keller in shock. "I … I don't know."

Keller fast-forwarded the video, eyes locked on the screen, his mind fried from boredom.

"Take a look at these. Have you seen these girls?"

"No."

"Have you seen this man? This man was the girl's grandfather who was killed a few days before she was abducted. You know this man? Did you participate in his killing?"

"No."

"Did you participate in any way in the abduction of these girls? Did you premeditate—"

"No. No."

"Keller," Brianna said from across the computer room, her aromatic perfume announcing her coming. "You've got a call."

Fingering his forehead, Keller sighed, closing his eyes, and realised how exhausted and weary he had become. He couldn't give up, not now, despite having come back to square one.

I need to be patient, so this can be over and done with!

"All right," he grumbled.

"Keller. It's from a woman who owns a children's clothes store. She said when she saw the sketch of the man who attacked us at the vigil on the news, she recognised him. She said to me that he comes often to her store to buy children's clothes and sewing kits."

Confused at why a grown man would want to buy children's clothes unless he had children of his own or he was a paedophile, Keller jumped out of his chair, eager to get to the bottom of this gnarly case.

"Does the woman know the suspect's name?" Keller asked, striding with Brianna through the hall.

"Gladius Huyard. I have his address. North Central Heights."

"At last, progress," Keller sighed, jogging in front of Brianna.

———

When the call arrived that Gladius Huyard's residence had been found, Brianna DePaula, on one hand, felt a bestial sense of relief, and on the other, emptiness.

She'd been staying at Keller's place for the last few months, feeling so tired and so drained, she asked the FBI for leave from the investigation. She had no friends to see – they departed because of Ben, or were mourning Ben's side of the family, or scolding her for trying to arrest him.

It also didn't help when her stepdaughter was still missing. Three months had passed, and she was convinced Veronica was dead.

There was still no evidence for the Manicheans being the perpetrators of the kidnapping. Ian Mastemah had denied he took Veronica, but the lie detector test suggested he *knew* who took Veronica, only he refused to tell the FBI the truth. With close ties to the Marine Corps and members of Mossad – covert Israeli intelligence for counterterrorism – Ian Mastemah was a right-wing revisionist Zionist who curried favour with the American corporation of Alfred Bonner's Alliance – long supporters for the Jewish state. But Ian did say that Gladius Huyard was a child-loving creep who needed to be found.

Keller parked right outside Gladius Huyard's house – a single-storey flat, white, plain and dilapidated.

Brianna followed Keller, stalking towards the front door, and knocked.

The door opened immediately, revealing a man – tall and slender – with a boyish dark-red haircut, a moustache and blue eyes. "Hi." He smiled.

"Hi," Keller greeted back, just as friendly.

Brianna showed Gladius her FBI identification. "Good morning," she said.

A strong, rancid odour reeked from inside his house.

After a strained, anticipatory silence, Keller said, "Why did you run away from me back in May? You remember us, don't you?"

Gladius's smile shrank. "I've never seen you two before. Sure you have the right house?"

"Have you been doing some clothes shopping at the mall lately?" Keller inquired civilly.

"Yeah," Gladius nodded, clearing his throat. He maintained that factitious smile – it belied all his innocence. "Why is it a crime to shop there, Officer? I can't afford to buy suits from George's." He sniffed an amused chuckle.

Brianna sneered as Keller chuckled with Gladius, playing along with him. Already, Brianna's gut feeling told her this man screamed guilty. His blue eyes, swinging to her, were deep and wide, filled with secrets. His smile died when he glanced at her, sweat appearing on his face.

"Yeah, I know," Keller said, beaming. "You bought children's clothes. Why's that?"

Gladius' smile lost its intended effect. "Did I?"

"Are you a father?" Keller said, frowning.

"No." Dread riddled his frail voice. Heart pounding, Brianna's hand involuntarily crept to her gun as she saw Gladius' face blanch, eyes wide with consternation. He went taut, swallowing. "I … I'm n–not … a—"

Keller lunged. Gladius flinched, pushing the door shut, but Keller threw the door back open. He slammed it so hard it knocked Gladius backwards, the door rebounding against the wall. Grasping him from the back of the head, Keller drove Gladius' face into the wall, then threw him to the ground.

"Get him!" Keller exclaimed, squatting on top of the man, knees crushing his thighs, hand grasping the collar of his shirt.

But Brianna saw the robotic arm before Keller could. As he went to bar his arm, Gladius' arm slipped out of Keller's grasp. "What the fu—?"

"Keller!" Brianna ripped out her gun.

Gladius growled, his metal arm striking Keller's chest before he threw Keller off like a rag doll, and, spinning around, got to his feet. He kicked upwards, winding Keller, then threw him into the wall with his metal arm.

Brianna aimed and fired. Gladius gasped, grasping his right thigh from the wound. Capitalising, Keller pushed and kicked Gladius to the floor. He stomped on his robotic arm, and with both hands, pinned it. He tried extending the bionic elbow towards himself.

Brianna slid to his aid, piling on top of Gladius. His nose disgorged dark blood, crimson staining the carpet. Cheek on the ground, Gladius' lapis eyes were glazed and wild. She took his flesh arm, latching it into the ring of the handcuff.

"Quick," Keller managed through gritting teeth. The robotic arm had to be very strong. It made Keller's muscular arms tremble. Even as Brianna clasped the handcuff over it, she feared Gladius could snap free.

Brianna hammered her gun into the back of Gladius' head. She grunted, watching the wretch go flaccid.

Panting and out of breath, Keller met Brianna's eyes – they were vitriolic and intense. He hauled Gladius up, locking both hands into the cuffs, gasping. "I'll take care of him," he gasped.

Brianna searched the house thoroughly for anything to do with her daughter and Zoe O'Leary, the hope that they were still alive instilled in her heart.

As she stalked through the living room, she looked at the wall – grey as flint stone, patchy and unpainted. It struck her as odd, though on closer inspection, she realised that the walls had a series of labyrinthine markings spread across them. They were everywhere; drawings in marker and grey lead pencil, outlines of mazes, infinitesimal details of sophisticated passageways. Brianna felt a biliousness settle in her stomach.

She approached the living room, the walls also stony in appearance, covered in more bizarre drawings. Here, she noticed unpleasant symbols on the walls – swastikas, whirlpools – like snowflakes. There were others – unknown symmetrical glyphs and symbols patterned in vertical columns like calligraphy.

There was a fetid musky powdery stench prickling her nose. If kidnapped children were on the premises, Brianna knew she'd finally found the place.

Her stomach and bowels seethed with adrenaline. She peered into the sink of the kitchen, the powdery smell molesting her nose. What she saw in the basin almost heaved her stomach, making her mouth salivate.

She did not even know what it was. The basins had something that looked like a … a pile of human foetuses. They were grisly lumps of flesh, pink and raw, mashed tiny human features, elongated heads, spindly arms, slimy ambilocal cords, all soaked in blood. Flies and maggots feasted in the basin of blood and foetal remains.

Brianna immediately spun around, exhaling, letting out a small whimper as she inhaled again, overwhelmed with bewildered repugnance. Her heart was thundering in her chest so hard she trembled.

Brianna slipped into all the rooms she'd came across, opening doors and closets. They were empty of people.

Yet, one door was locked. Brianna kicked it down, gun raised.

Three black chests were on the floor. The glyphs on the walls were thicker here, in permanent marker, involving concentric circles of passageways and elaborate entangled labyrinths.

Putting her gun away, Brianna's body vibrated with outrage as she came towards the chests. They were locked with padlocks. "Veronica?" she said with a muffled voice and cursed. The chests were small, but they couldn't be locked in here! "Veronica? Zoe?"

She needed a crowbar immediately. In haste, she dashed back into the main room, and outside, where Keller had shoved Gladius into the back seat of their car.

"There are three bound chests in the house," Brianna said in frustration. "I'm going to open them." She reached the car boot, scrabbling for tools.

"You found what?" Keller exclaimed in shock.

"Follow me," Brianna said, slamming the boot, carrying two crowbars, running back into the house. Once she showed Keller the chests, he determinedly grabbed his crowbar, breaking the first lock, swearing under his breath. Brianna smashed the other locks, opening the chests one by one.

Brianna found clothes inside. Velvets, cotton and polyester, stashed and packed. They were women's clothes – from lingerie to dresses.

Brianna swung her head to Keller, picking out a lace. And Brianna's heart swelled – she saw a small white shoe of a little girl in the chest. One that Veronica would have worn.

Oh no.

Hastily, Keller pried open the next box and found … human teeth. Hundreds of them. Some rotten yellow, some from juveniles.

Brianna had to pause – she almost threw up. Her vision blurred. She took deep breaths.

When they came to the last chest, Keller doggedly flung it open, gritting his teeth with strain. Brianna watched him heave a gasp, jolting up on his feet. Brianna suddenly saw giant black cockroaches, or crickets – massive bugs with wings, pincers and claws with ugly faces – leaping out of the chest and flying across the room.

She yelped in fright, covering her head from the swarm of giant flying bugs dashing against the walls. Massive slender scorpions, clambering out of the chests, flew into the walls, smearing it with their ichor. Some scattered on the ground in fright, into corners and out the door.

Brianna screamed as the bugs flew past her, and once their swarm ceased, she peeked into the last chest and saw something else inside. A book with a leather cover, covered with clipped fingernails and toenails. Keller courageously grabbed the book, brushing away the revolting nail clippings. He leapt backwards from anything else that might jump out. He eyed the bugs croaking and buzzing warily. He handed the book over to Brianna. It felt cold in her hands and waterlogged, and on the front cover was a serpentine rippled fractal glyph resembling the face of a crustacean creature with horns and appendages stemming out of it.

She wanted to vomit now. Incredible pain surged through her stomach and chest. A retinue of resurfacing images of all that she had seen washed through her mind, confronting her, gripping her into a paralysis. A basin of dead human foetuses, Veronica's shoe, human teeth, giant black bugs, fingernail and toenail clippings.

Inelegantly, Brianna excused herself, retreating outside to empty her stomach.

———

The discovery of Gladius' fractal symbols, aborted human foetuses, human teeth and girls' clothes were serendipitous. Ian was right. Gladius was the suspect all long. He'd killed the girls.

The final proof was revealed when Keller gave Patricia, Dominic and his parents the recovered girls' clothes from the chest. Once they saw the white shoe, Dominic's parents broke down into tears.

It was over. Brianna's stepdaughter had perished along with Zoe. And Ben … an outlaw still on the run. Keller felt numb. He'd wasted time – he'd *wasted bloody time* hunting Ben for three months. Guilt afflicted him, and he didn't want to talk.

Gladius had been there at the candlelight vigil. He'd been there in Brianna's neighbourhood. He knew the area. Ian was right. *How was that moron right?*

And now, Keller had this uncanny feeling that there was more to uncover, that the case was not as simple as he thought. He couldn't stop hoping.

I let this happen, Keller thought morbidly, gazing bleakly for a long time at the image of the shoe.

"Being hopeful is my only flaw," Keller said to Brianna when she tried to preclude him from interrogating Gladius, asking if he was okay. "I need a body. I will not stop until I find their bodies so we can bury them."

He reported back to the FBI headquarters. The head officer had Gladius handcuffed in solitary confinement in a highly monitored room. The man had been obstinate, begging that someone could bring him a pencil and paper to draw on. So hysterical had Gladius been about the paper and pencil, the head officer complied, giving him sheets. The strange thing was – and ultimately the thing that vexed Keller as he watched the video feeds – Gladius drew those same round mazes and snowflakes that resembled a styled face of an insect or crustacean with horns. He drew these two symbols repetitively and vertically, from the bottom left-hand corner of the page to the top right-hand corner. Even with his hands cuffed and his robotic hand, he worked vigorously on his art. An infuriating phenomenon.

What do these signs mean? Keller thought.

Keller found himself locked inside the monitor room, stroking his chin, staring at the extraordinary Gladius at his desk through the window.

Studies on the diary found in the chest contained very similar images that remotely resembled geometric visual patterns, such as dots, zigzagging lines, as well as grid patterns. It had been uncreatively dubbed, "Gladius Script". The diary contained catalogues of the alien script with abnormal characters of some language. These undeciphered letters were of a calligraphic and radial form, artistic expressions typically having a bilateral symmetry. Whether or not they had been composed to resemble distinct phonemes, their spruced twists to represent breathing, consonants and vowels – or no vowels – Keller did not know, as he was not a linguist. But as a detective, however, he could see there were patterns in those pictographs. There were clear word forms, suffixes, prefixes and sentences. Most interestingly, they began from the *bottom* left corner, then read *upwards*.

Other pages had single glyphs, but these were more elaborate works of art than the letters of Gladius' writing system. These were the most diverse shapes of elaborate lotus flowers and horned crustaceans with spidery crab legs. They were crisp, intricate synecdoche shapes from pentagons to decagons, some more elaborate than others. Spirals issuing out of the centre in symmetrical form, mirroring each branch as it spread outwards, mazes within mazes. *This man is a mad artist,* Keller thought, flicking through the pages of the diary.

His eyes fell on Gladius again, consumed by his art.

What was he achieving by drawing all these? The symbols look like a map. But of what?

"How long has this Gladius Huyard been working like this?" Keller mused aloud to Brianna.

"Three hours, about," she replied.

A map … A map to lead me to the girls. "We aren't getting anywhere without questioning him," Keller said.

"But you should—"

"I'm talking to him!"

"Keller!"

"Get out of my way!"

Keller had enough of this crap. This man raped and kidnapped the girls. Keller would accuse this man – this freak, this killer! Gladius' puny appearance, his moustache on his baby face and his stupid symbols were starting to do Keller's head in.

Keller swiped the key card. Opening the door, he stalked towards the slumped paedophile.

"All right, are you done now?" Keller rumbled, hands on his hips. "Tell me what you're drawing. What is it? A map?" He pointed to the half-finished oblate maze. Gladius didn't respond. "Looks like a freakin' puzzle. Tell me what you're drawing." Feeble grunts came from the man – his bloodied nose was bandaged, and his flesh and robotic hands looked cramped drawing the elaborate labyrinth. Even the passageways and their shape all mirrored one another on each of the four sides.

Keller didn't let the skill dazzle him. Wrath and anger burned away all sensory awareness until all that remained was an urge to break something. *I have to solve this case!*

"Tell me what you're drawing!" Keller shouted.

Gladius sniffed, hand levitating off the page.

Keller grasped Gladius by the shoulder, throwing his back against the chair upright, getting in his face.

"I can't!" Gladius bellowed, face contorted in agony, eyes wringing out tears.

"Yes, you can!" Keller roared, shaking Gladius, who sobbed from the rough jerks. "You can! You *freakin'* can!" He drove Gladius' face into the desk. "Yes, you can!"

Gladius opened his mouth as if to scream. He was silent. Keller twisted the man out of his chair, lifting him up by the neck, strangling him, yelling, "Don't waste my time!"

Gladius whimpered.

"Yes, you can! Yes, you can! Tell me! Tell me!"

Brianna and two officers poured inside. *Bastards!* They grappled Keller's shoulders, pulling him away from molesting Gladius. "You can tell me! You can!" The two officers scrambled to keep Keller away with their bodies.

Then he felt someone grabbing his gun in his back pocket.

"Oh crap!" Keller hissed. "Gun! Gun!" Brianna and the officers spun around, pulling out their weapons.

Gladius' face contorted, grinding his teeth, holding Keller's pistol in his cuffed hands.

"Gladius, don't!" Keller shouted desperately, hands outstretched. "Put the gun down!"

Gladius nodded, muttering something under his breath. He raised his metal hand in an "okay" gesture, his face pale with humiliation and torment, smeared with blotches of blood.

"Gladius! Gladius, *put the gun down now!*" Keller yelled, his voice trembling with regret. "Put it down! Gladius!"

Gladius raised the gun under his chin.

"Put the gun down!" Keller's heart thundered in his ears. His last chance was slipping away. "Gladius! *No!*"

Standing up straight, Gladius screwed his eyes shut, inserting the gun barrel into his mouth.

"No, no, no! No, no, no!"

There was a pop, a wet splatter, and a gush of red. The glass observatory cracked amid a massive red explosion of blood and brains. Gladius crumpled to the floor.

"Crap!" Keller was shaking. He stared at his last chance – the suspect, the criminal, the answer – leaning dead on the wall.

No ... I need ... No! "Call emergency," Keller said, holding his head. Brianna and the officers, who took a few seconds to recover from their shock, enflamed Keller's indignation. "Call the freakin' emergency!" he shouted, making them scatter. He knew the emergency would do nothing. The suicide was fatal.

Keller thought coercive action could knock the truth out of Gladius. It hadn't.

Keller paced, berating himself for his misbehaviour, hand clasping his mouth. He buried his face in his hands, rubbing his temples. The smell of blood – rancid and metallic – suffused the room.

The blood of the man who had trespassed against him, against Ben, against Brianna, a trafficker of girls, who killed himself.

The blood that scorned Keller.

———

Keller sat in the waiting room in front of the FBI head officer's study, bored and morbid, the squeaking screeching of the gurney wheels that held up Gladius' corpse towed away behind him.

Why the hell would he call the paramedics when the man was good as dead? Did he think they could revive him back from the dead so he could stress himself out and wring this man again for answers? And the strange thing was, Keller actually *yearned* for that – for stress and anger. It was his vocation – his life. To obsess over the clues and what they could mean, to solve the complex case, gaining data, rather than feel the triumph solving them. He was supposed to be the person who contributed to this world by protecting loved ones from evil.

Anything but this sitting … and waiting.

He twitched. He'd failed … He felt fire burning in his mind, the dark fire of being deprived of what gave him purpose in life. Without it, life was hell.

He'd *failed!*

The sorrowful head officer appeared from his office, carrying in his hand a page containing the picture of the paedophile's fractal glyph, showing it to Keller.

He felt lost in that maze of lines. He had to find a way out.

"He explained this before he ate the bullet, Keller?"

Grasping the page, Keller glared at the image. *No … No, he didn't. It was because of me. I lost the case when I could have …*

Gladius sticking his own gun into his mouth, firing the trigger, his head lurching, his neck shattering from recoil. Blood smeared the windows, smearing Keller's mind. The scene replayed over and over again. Keller's bloody shame was as painful as death.

He creased the page in his hand. What did it mean? A fractal …

"You know," the head officer said. "You may have lost this one. All right? It happens. You did all you could."

No, bastard! Am I not a professional?

The significant swastika … Keller felt entangled by it; it haunted his mind. He closed his eyes, hands covering his ears, and still he could see the oblate warrens and infinite caves sprawling away at random, thrashing with frustration.

And Keller sank … It was *wrong* – he *can't* be sinking; he *can't* get lost. He *helped* the lost cope. He couldn't … lose himself.

"Look, you want fulfillment," the head officer mumbled. "You need to find a girl. Brianna would be nice. She's divorced her husband. You need to comfort her. You need a social life. Start a family, have some kids."

Keller trembled.

"Let the case go."

———

Brianna sat dejected in her office cubical, finishing typing up her report on Gladius and his shocking suicide. An inconclusive case, data yielding negative results, and her daughter dead or gone. Brianna felt like an empty shell. She drowned herself in a second glass of strong wine at her desk today.

Then Keller appeared, ambling around the corner.

"Keller," she said, sitting up.

His face was carved from stone. He looked very cold, skin pale grey. In his hand, dangling from his fingers, was a sheet of paper.

"Keller?"

She watched him approach his desk. Then he lurched, banging his hands on the table viciously, swinging them across his desk, destroying everything. His lamp shattered, papers and folders flew into the air, the mouse and the mouse pad, pencils, stapler and utensils crashed off his desk and onto the floor. Collapsing into his chair, he held his head in grim defeat.

Brianna gasped, hand gripping her mouth. She'd never seen Keller so distraught before. Perhaps he held it all in, never showed it, never belied it at all to her, but now he couldn't, the visage of absolute stoicism broken. A first.

There had been a long moment of stunned, still silence. Then Keller lunged for the keyboard, and with both hands he smashed it twice against the desk, then flung it into the air, tossing it away, burying his head in his hands. The broken keys bounced sporadically, like clicking beads.

Brianna took two steps back, glancing behind her at the silent FBI agents, all rising from their office desks, rubbernecking at Keller.

Slowly, Brianna approached Keller, the tendons in his neck bulging, his shoulders rising up and down as he heaved out laboured breaths.

"Hey," she said with a soft, strangled sound. "Hey."

She was close enough to see the man's face flush a deep red. His forehead creased into a deep scowl, and he turned away, hiding his face from her. "Leave me," he rasped.

Brianna swallowed a lump in her throat. "Don't take this personally."

Keller managed to turn to her. His wry grey eyes were red-rimmed, and she shivered. "The girls are dead." Those hard words sounded torn from his chest. "I promised you I would find them … I'm sorry." Presently, he raised his head, resting his chin on his hand, looking away from her. He was doing everything in his strength to not cry in front of her. He'd placed an expectation before himself and believed he was strong enough to exceed it. Pain for Keller's grief made tears well up in Brianna's eyes.

"Keller," Brianna placed a hand on his shoulder. "Talk to me. It's okay. You did everything you could."

He sniffed. "No."

"What do—"

He gently brushed her hand aside, letting out a protracted sigh. "You would … You would think that you could stare down at the face of pure evil and defeat it." He shook his head. "All the discipline you've built up from years, all the effort you have done to make yourself into a measured agent … it was all for nothing." He swallowed, closing his eyes in exhaustion. "The evil is absolute. You can't fight it."

"Keller," Brianna whispered. "You realise you were speaking to yourself in the second person?"

Keller shrugged, his eyes glued on the photographs of the mummified man in Neil's basement.

"Do you know what that means, Keller?" she said.

"It is because …" he muttered, "I want to detach myself from failure."

"It's because *you are* a strong person," Brianna pressed. Keller gazed at her. "You think that you could handle the chaos all by yourself because you are serving others. And it's terrifying. All alone. But you are *not alone* …"

Pursing his lips, Keller gave an ever-so-subtle nod. "Thank you," he said, but his eyes were fixed on the floor, strewn with the photographs. Brianna, following his gaze, watched him inhaling through his nose, picking up one of the images. "Wait …"

"What is it?" Brianna inquired, studying the page. A close-up image of the mummified man in Neil's basement wore a significant symmetrical silver geometric diamond-shaped pendant on his chest with a small upside-down five-pointed star in the middle.

Leaning over, Keller reached for a crumpled piece of paper – a drawing of the exact same symmetrical diamond. Both the pendant and the drawing were similar.

Brianna wet her mouth, watching Keller gawk at the two images side by side, his face returning to the stoniness she was used to. "They're the same," she whispered.

"Not exactly, but close." Resolved, Keller sat up straight, determination revitalising him. "Gladius and Little Ladykiller are connected. You remember Gladius' walls? It's a map to the girls. It's …"

"Keller," Brianna said, hand rising to her forehead, feeling overwhelmed. "Keller, you … It's *not* a map, it's art. Gladius and Little Ladykiller are wannabes. The glyphs have been studied by linguists, and their conclusions were that Gladius had been drugged with methadone and LSD that made him hallucinate, creating this fractal script. It's all psychological."

Keller threw up his hands and shook his head, petulance attempting to overcome him. "What are you saying, Bri? What are you saying? You saying this guy is a fake? How did Gladius Huyard get those clothes? How did – How did the parents *positively ID* those clothes? How did *you* ID Veronica's shoe?"

Brianna scowled deeply. "That I can't reconcile."

"What do you mean, you *can't reconcile*?"

"You … Keller, you think *everything* is so simple! But everything is complicated, Keller. This case … is bewildering."

Keller threw back his head, laughing.

"Come on, Keller. You think you can solve this case alone. You're sticking to your guns, but it's going to fail again. I'm telling you; Gladius *is not it*. He got access to Veronica and Zoe's clothes because … Oh! Oh, the candlelight vigil! Gladius was in our neighbourhood, and the window to Veronica's room was open!"

"Open?" Keller asked, hope in his eyes.

"Yes, I remember! Come on," she said with urgency. "I want to show you something."

———

Brianna arrived at her house with Keller, under the looming dominance of North Mountain. Together, they rounded the house to the backyard, which led out into the wilderness of the national park, looking for clues.

Jumping the gate, Keller squatted before the bushes growing under the corner of the house below Veronica's window on the second floor. Brianna had remembered the window being open during the candlelight vigil. She'd gone inside to close it just now to prove it.

"This window was wide open," Brianna said.

Fixated on the bushes, Keller picked from out of the grass with a pair of tweezers a white shoe. The second to complete the pair. He shook his head, chuckling. "Ha. Of course, Bri. You've got a damn load of optimism, and I admire it." He shot up to his feet, looking not the slightest bit abashed at being wrong.

Brianna stared as Keller chuckled and slipped the little girl's shoe into a Ziploc bag as if it were the answer to all his crises. And with that, Keller walked around the backyard, saying, "This is crazy."

"I know it is," Brianna said, smiling, crossing her arms. "What it proves is that Gladius was not guilty, but a victim himself. He's trying to divert us from who really did this. I think we need to look corporally. The Alliance secret society, I think, might be behind the murder and the kidnap."

"Did the Alliance have Gladius break into your house? You forgot to lock the door."

"I always lock the door."

"Then how did he—"

"The windows. You could theoretically open them from the outside if you had tools to unscrew the locks. Gladius' robotic arm, his metal fingers."

Keller smiled. "Gladius must *love* clothing."

"Yes, he does. He had Amish clothes in his chests. And his haircut resembled the fringe of Amish men. He was Mennonite, who are a little bit more progressive and lenient than their strict Amish neighbours. But still pretty conservative. Reveals that he was once part of the Amish community and somehow got shunned."

"I wonder why," Keller said. "Having a robotic forearm doesn't seem very conservative to me. Everything post Industrial Revolution is heretical for that lot."

"True. But that's beside the point," Brianna said, feeling good about herself that she'd found more data. Helping Keller back up from his anguish and exhaustion made her proud. *Told you, Keller. You are never alone.* "We need to figure now why he got those clothes."

"And," Keller added, "we need to bring Neil into this. We need to ask him about the pendant, the symmetrical glyphs and about the Alliance. See if he knows anything."

61

ADULTS AND CHILDREN

"For you were at one time darkness, but now you are light in Yahweh. Walk as children of light, for the fruit of the light is in all goodness and justice and truth discerning what it is that pleases Yahweh, and don't share together in the fruitless deeds of darkness, but rather reprove them. For what is done in hiding by them is shameful even to mention, but everything that is reproved by the light is made visible, for everything that is made visible is light."

—From the Epistle to the Ephesians, Paul, Tim Mackie's Literal-literary Translation, c. 60 – 62 CE.

Joshua Tanrıöver arrived at his old flat in downtown Tucson; he saw that in his mailbox, a letter had arrived. As he read who it was from, he froze in shock.

The letter had come from Istanbul – its postcode was his old postcode – meaning it was from someone important. Someone from home, back in the Middle East where Joshua had grown up.

His bowels turning into concrete, he contemplated what the letter might say – it was an envelope into the past. The death. The person Joshua had once been. The fraudster. A scam.

At ease, Joshua, he thought, slowing his heart rate, stopping his knees from shivering. *Take a deep breath. It's not you anymore. You've changed. You're an undergrad. You're a scholar.*

Once inside, he opened the letter and saw it was from his father, Hitesh Tanrıöver, written in English.

It was about the disaster at Damascus in 2001. After Joshua was taken by

Judd Pounders, Salafi jihadis had gotten hold of the plundered artefacts from Jabal Qasioun. They were incensed by mosque vandalism. In retribution, the extremists went to undermine the people involved in the scam dig by going to Joshua's hired Lebanese Druze retainers. They were tortured. This may have been caused by Syrian animosity towards Lebanon, which was brimming with sectarianism and civil war.

Hitesh was furious when he found out about the Palestinian crew Joshua hired. Any Palestinian dispersed in the Middle East was considered a potential fifth column – supposedly proving the so-called rumour that Joshua – a US ally – had been dabbling with the Palestinian Liberation Organisation!

Christ! Salafi jihadis are out to get me!

As a result of his defiance, a Salafi squad was sent into Joshua's childhood home in Adana with a search warrant of the premises. The search aimed to uncover incriminating evidence for connections to the archaeological fieldwork that had been conducted at Jabal Qasioun. In anger, Hitesh, earlier, contacted the Palestinian workers who had uncovered the strange artefact from the *Magharat al-Ju* (the Cave of Hunger) and decided he should covertly bury the material remains at his oldest son Tristan's basement, rather than donate it to the museum, in case information leaked and the jihadis assassinated him. Hitesh, as well, tried to garner the support of the Shabiha militia, but his inquiry failed for some reason.

As Joshua read and reread the letter, a fist tightened around his throat. He struggled to read, his eyes blurring as guilt gripped him. "The consequences of sin … God, have mercy on me. Blood of Jesus wash me."

Due to the intensifying economic crisis in Syria, and the Qamishli riots caused by Assyrian Kurds in retaliation to Saddam Hussein and Ba'athist activists, Hitesh's second family house in Damascus was becoming increasingly destitute. Hitesh's nephew – Joshua's cousin Can – went to smuggle the artefact from *Magharat al-Ju* from the basement of Tristan's house in Adana. Can was kidnapped on the way, taken to jail and tortured in an electric chair.

Hitesh lost much sleep for his family's safety, but he knew he had to see his nephew. With his brother, he made the dangerous trip to Damascus and bribed the prison guards out of desperation, who allowed him to enter the prison occasionally to visit Can. Hitesh and his brother then began to smuggle in painkillers to help alleviate the traumatic physical effects of the shocks and torture. To do all this illegally, they stayed undercover, forcing them to sell more or less everything they owned, restoring them to sleeping under nothing but an oak in a public park. The letter read explicitly that if

Hitesh and his brother had not visited Can, he would have been "sold off to human traffickers".

In the end, by a miracle, Can was put on parole, where Hitesh quickly took his nuclear family – except for Tristan – to Istanbul. Once in Istanbul, he wrote the letter, and then quickly departed on a ship to Heraklion, Crete, to make a new life there. Joshua wanted so badly to write back, explaining how sorry he was for them, to apologise.

I need to find my family again, Joshua thought, aspiring to book some tickets ahead of time for next summer. He had the money now given by Pounders and from the work he'd been doing for his scholarship at Willamette University. *Perhaps while I am there, I could pass by the Minoan palace of Knossos and the Saint Titus Basilica in Gortyn. That would be fun.*

All the drama had been for a single ancient artefact unearthed by his supervisor Makam Arabaeen. Why? Oh, Joshua was, in part, glad Arabaeen had died at the hands of the jinn's fire sword guarding the Cave of Blood. Better that than being hunted down and tortured by Salafis.

"Shalom salutations, my brother Joshua. How are you faring today?" the voice of Nefer sounded as he bled red light in the air like dye in water. He appeared cone-shaped, glowing like a gelatinous deep-sea jellyfish.

Joshua blinked in shock. "Nefer. I'm officially on a jihadi's hit list!"

"Oh yeah," the spirit said blithely. "That. Don't fear. Saints are blessed, though more often distressed, but never let hope rest, because you have God."

Joshua flinched. "Nefer, I'm *not* a saint. I cannot do miracles. And when I die, I don't think anyone would want to take a piece of my hair, turn me into Father Christmas, or curate me like a museum artefact."

To Joshua's astonished surprise, Nefer guffawed. His form became a pulsating crimson glob of spasming, strobing lights, combed cilia flickering, giving off a light display of gleaming rainbow colours. "Oh, Joshua, you bumpkin! I didn't mean that!"

"I'm being honest. When I think of a saint, I think of a cult of manicured morgues."

"You really?"

"Yeah. The veneration of saints often involves the veneration of martyrs and decayed body parts imbued with the saint's miraculous power. It *clearly* goes back to ancient Greek hero worship and veneration. In ancient Greece, a hero refers to a person who has died and become a supernatural being. A hero is 'heroic' on account of the enormity of their crimes rather than their morality."

Nefer sighed, saying begrudgingly, "All right, all right. Lecture on …"

"Being heroic or saintly is not a *moral* term, but rather a *cultic* term. And these cults came up because of the archaic Greek and Homeric collective memory about the lost age of heroes, symbolised by the Mycenean Bronze Age ruins conspicuous in the Greek landscape. These Late Bronze Age people were corresponding with the bards and scholars of the Hittites, who were in correspondence with the epic traditions of Mesopotamia, who celebrated the divine acts of Sargon the Great, Narma Sin of Akkad and, ultimately, Gilgamesh. Gilgamesh, the first god-king! Alfred Bonner's idol! It comes full circle! And even worse. The Greek *merops* comes from the Semitic Ugarit word *rapa'um*, which is similar to the Hebrew Rephaim! Rephaim *gigantes*! The Kandahar giant was called a Rephaim by the Nephilim researchers!

"In conclusion: the cult of saint worship is the cult of Nephilim worship and idolising rulers."

Nefer laughed. "Joshua … You're a numbskull. Everything you said right there was absolute nonsense. I thought you were smarter than this."

"Oh, come on. I was being deliberately sarcastic to get across the point that the cult of saints is idolatry!"

"Yes. It is idolatry. But you missed the point of what I am trying to say. Saints are those feeble and filthy who will be made into immortal gods and goddesses, dazzling with radiance and much joy, patriating in the divine nature. The process to reach this is long and painful, but no. You are not worshipped." Nefer paused. "Hopefully."

Nodding, Joshua looked at the letter in his hands and thought about the finds he made at Damacus and then the Alliance's finds at Uruk. He looked up and noticed two books on his shelf: Georges Roux's *Ancient Iraq* and *The First Fossil Hunters: Palaeontology in Greek and Roman Times* by Adrienne Mayor. Together, they combined two ideals – the war of Iraq, and the mystery of the Nephilim – the Kandahar giant who had been the catalyst that brought Joshua into the war in the first place. To Haditha Dam.

"Iraq …" Joshua whispered. "You claimed that the place of Haditha Dam was haunted by demons."

"Oh yes, indeed," Nefer said. "Extremely unpleasant."

"The Iraq war, I think, tells us that Babylon is rising."

Babylon the Great, as the Revelation of John recorded – the land between the rivers, the genesis of imagination – was a symbol of evil. Babylon the Great, Mother of Harlots and of Earth's abomination. In Revelation, it was Rome. The social, cultural and political powers were not restricted to one locus. But never had a city been like Babylon, so revered and so demonised in God's word for oppressing God's people. For two thousand years, the real, physical metropolis lay buried, while another ghostly city of vice lived on.

The Alliance was part of this evil power. They, and their superstitious Alfred Bonner, wanted to find the coffin of Gilgamesh – a Nephilim god-king. Like Nimrod, he was the first hero and the seed of Babylon's evil.

What did Bonner aim to do with the coffin anyway? It made Joshua wonder what other artefacts the Alliance had smuggled from the tomb in Uruk.

And I stood upon the sand of the sea, the words of Revelation 13 echoed to Joshua – words that he had memorised.

And saw a beast rise up out of the sea, having seven heads and ten horns, and upon his horns ten crowns, and upon his heads the name of blasphemy. And the beast which I saw was like unto a leopard, and his feet were as the feet of a bear, and his mouth as the mouth of a lion: and the dragon gave him his power, and his seat, and great authority. And I saw one of his heads as it were wounded to death; and his deadly wound was healed: and all the world wondered after the beast. And they worshipped the dragon, which gave power unto the beast: and they worshipped the beast, saying, Who is like unto the beast? Who is able to make war with him?

"What did you tell me the night before we went to war?" Joshua asked Nefer, as he paced around his library. "You told me something about the Beast not being a human being, but an amalgamation of multiple gods from Babylon, Persia, Greece and Rome."

"I did?" Nefer intoned, his form paling into a white transparent congealed brain, shimmering with orange cilia.

"It's okay if you don't recall."

"No. All I can remember from that discourse is that there is a cosmic pattern that shows itself in understanding the Scroll of Revelation's symbols, which can be beneficial to us in any time period, even if we acknowledge that they refer to a first-century context and that they will happen in the future."

"I agree, but no, it was about Alfred Bonner, Nefer."

"Bonner is one of the horns of the Beast. It is a war against two politics: the politics of imperial power and the politics of the New Jerusalem. The Beast is not one system, but animalistic humanity without God. All political powers are the horns. But I think that being a beast and a Nephilim are simultaneous. A condition of being of pervasive savagery, violence and madness. It's not genetic. Being a beast is being a savage Nephilim. Get it, brother?"

"Yeah, I think. Just it is so contrary to everything I heard. Our views today are *so alien* from those of the ancient world."

"What is six, six, six, Joshua?"

Joshua started. "The Devil's number. You're testing me."

"Wrong!" Nefer chuckled as if he'd been setting Joshua up. "It's *your* number – the number of humankind. Six, six, six. Low-functioning dragons of disorder, harming everything. See the truth? The world is mixed with disorder and order. We are in need of remedy from this universal pollution."

Joshua sighed. "I know. Jesus' atonement is the only remedy to this condition of disorder. You're enjoying this, aren't you? Enjoying having intellectual superiority over me when I know that the eschaton is coming. We have to work together. I don't have time for debate."

"Yes," the angel said. "I was not mocking you for being a deleterious creature. You're a co-ruler in Christ, and the Beast is wrathful of it."

"Yes. Alfred Bonner is not the Beast but a *horn* of the Beast," Joshua said slowly. "The threat is much bigger than we thought. A human ruler in allegiance to a chaos creature made of many gods. All right, then." An epiphany struck Joshua. "Nefer! What I learnt at university this year is that Alfred Bonner found a coffin that was part of a larger mortuary tradition aimed at the cult of Gilgamesh – the judge of the Underworld. Like Osiris, he is a god-king – a Nephilim hybrid."

"The offspring of Fallen Anunna," Nefer confirmed, moving in tune with the currents of an unseen ocean that surrounded Joshua's world. "The giants. Though Gilgamesh himself was once a human who bonded with Anunna and became a god."

"They are coming back," Joshua shivered. "The Fallen Angels and the Nephilim. That's why Bonner had to intervene after the Kandahar giant attacked Ben's marines. He wants to do something about the Nephilim coming back. I suppose the coffin and the Kandahar giant are connected … But this is the reason for Ben's visions. It makes sense now. God is warning him to prepare the world for the Nephilim's return. Bonner is going to bring them back."

He had a plethora of questions stemming out of research, but he couldn't address them all now.

"Babylon …" Joshua said, fiddling with his father's letter. "Fallen Angels. It must be connected to the Apkallu. The Seven Sages."

Nefer formed into a flowing worm of gelatinous orbs. "The Sages *are not* children of the Anunna. You are mixing the Book of Enoch with the Scriptures again."

Joshua sighed. The Book of Enoch. Joshua regrettably went through a phase of impishly trusting First Enoch as a true prehistoric text. Not anymore. He'd since revised his beliefs. It came when he discovered that the popular RH Charles translation omitted verses from earlier Ge'ez manuscripts that outrageously associate the Sage Enoch with the Son of Man – a title given exclusively to Jesus Christ. He marvelled at how Ethiopian Christians could take this Antichristian book at face value. Nefer had a *very good* reason to scoff at these blasphemies.

"The Fallen Nephilim are the children of the Anunna gods who taught humankind evil," Nefer said. "They *needed* to use humans, causing a boundary violation between the two Realms. From this hubris came the Seven Sages, emanating from the Seven Spirits of Yahweh's power and discernment on the Earth."

"But the Seven Sages *are* the wicked Nephilim, Nefer. The studies show."

"But *not* in history. The Mesopotamian myths *are not* your data-based history. They are theological histories. The truth is in the significance of the account as it applies to the present. Originally, the Apkallu Sages were the children of Adam via Seth, human beings turned into Holy Ones because they made a zealous call to return to God and to undo the sin of Adam and Eve and the Dragon. In the end, they became like Cain and the Nephilim by killing Nephilim. There is a lot of hidden history here. Do not your scholars confirm parallels to the Sumerian Kings' List and the *Bīt mēseri* incantation with Genesis 5? The Sages are the patriarchs from the line of Seth."

Joshua slumped. "You obviously know what truly happened then because … you're an eyewitness."

"Indeed, I am. I admire your curiosity, Joshua, but I want to warn you to not be led astray by focusing so much on Nephilim. All mysteries belong to God, and all revelation belongs to us – his children. Once you focus on something that is vaguely talked about in the Word – like extra-biblical texts – it is easy to miss the point."

"Extra-biblical sources are useful, not bad," Joshua stressed, irked.

"I agree, but you cannot treat them as the *medium* of God's Word. Especially when studying the lies of the Nephilim and Fallen Angels," Nefer said stringently. "Many are led astray with *preposterous* ideas. I don't want that for you. The Genesis scroll will *never* yield its secrets to those who will not cease trying to look for them. The purpose of the truth is to *procure liberty, restoration and love* in the lives of broken people. The whole point of Genesis 1 to 11 is about trusting in God's good creation and seeking his Presence and respecting the boundaries he made. And to not be foolish Cain, Lamech, the Fallen Ones and Nimrod, who transgressed those boundaries by defining good and evil for themselves. You understand?"

Joshua groaned, gazing at his own collection of books.

"The darkness will be exposed, but not by you," Nefer whispered. "One day. Ben's on the run again. Oh, his pain. He needs healing right now. Father is always working through love for the betterment of his children. That's what good parents do, sacrificing for the sake of others. Father's timing is always perfect. The darkness will be judged."

I promised myself that I will not get involved in the shenanigans with Ben, Joshua thought, shuddering. "Nefer, what are you up to? Why did you get me to come back to find Ben? Why did you create this calendar and get me to break my promise to leave the Pacific Northwest?"

Suddenly, it became apparent that Nefer could be lying. A possibility. A *strong* possibility.

Paul says that unclean spirits masquerade as angels of light.

Doubt blackened Joshua's heart. He felt a sudden sensation of shock in his stomach that came with this realisation – a realisation that it could be true. Once he hadn't given it much attention; now it made him feel a fool for not acting upon it right away. He considered Pawani – she'd seen Nefer in his human form. Then Joshua wondered about Saint Paul's statement about how women must wear head coverings because of the angels. Angels seemed sexually attracted to women with long hair … Nefer never manifested himself before another human, so why manifest before a pretty young woman unawares, and it *sickened* Joshua as he considered the Genesis 6 drama of women mating with angels. "You *never* show yourself. Why did you come to me in person before Pawani?" Joshua intoned. "An angel is invisible. They never show themselves like that."

"Brother. Though I know what you mean when you call me an angel, when will you learn that I am *not* an angel? I am a scholar and a seer! There are many of us: priests, healers, singers, warriors and cherubs. Angel means *messenger* in Greek, remember? Some spirits feel offended by being called angels!"

He's evading the questions. Joshua's blood went cold.

"I know, but why did you *appear* before Pawani in human form? You're not supposed to do that, to entice women … You didn't do it around the soldiers – the men. But, ah, I see, she was a woman! That's why you appeared to Pawani, all jubilant and witty. You thought her beautiful in your eyes."

"Nonsense!" The seer scholar sounded offended. "I came to deliver your calling! I merely felt … ambitious."

"Before a woman?"

Nefer deepened to a congealed Sierpinski gasket – shattered glass shards in the bilateral shape of a scarlet gelatinous form. "YOU DARE USE MORALISM AGAINST ME?" His voice cracked like thunder, and the lights in the room darkened. His form grew larger.

"Yes. I am," Joshua remarked astringently, despite his fear. "You know that God *hates* angels messing with humans after the Nephilim disaster. You're in rebellion!"

To his astonishment, Joshua saw Nefer's thunderous form shrink – his comb jelly form almost fading away instantly. The lights in the room illuminated brighter. "No … I'm here to *help you*. To establish the Khesed Bond."

"That's *exactly* what the Fallen Angels wanted," Joshua said sceptically. He was afraid, mostly, that he had been deceived for three years occupying an unclean spirit. Spirits were curious beings – like children, but with incredible power. Angels could fall and not be redeemed like humans – it made them jealous when humans could be redeemed. Nefer was not indifferent to vice.

Test the spirits … Guilt crippled Joshua.

"Joshua Tanrıöver! I'm *not* trying to deceive you!" Compassion and confidence returned to the god's voice once more. "I'm trying to help you. Don't be led astray."

"I'm not led astray! I just …" He sighed, as guilt for breaking his friendship with the divine sickened him. "I just need reassurance. Why did the Fallen Angels get judged?" Joshua asked gently. "Tell me, if you're not one."

"The Fallen Angels were blinded by pride. They estranged themselves in the Underworld. They despised the will of Yahweh."

Joshua felt calmer. "And what happened when a human accepts an angelic rebellion?"

"The Mark of the Beast. It marks your mind, Joshua. I *despise* the Fallen, for they grieve me greatly, as the darkness of Shaitan the Dragon – the first rebel – dooms them all. My mission is to follow Christ and *redeem* what was done by them! Come on, Joshua! Have faith! Master your integrity, for you've sinned against me!"

Joshua's heart smote him, and he fell to his knees and held his hands in prayer.

Nefer's attitude reminded him of the words of GH Charleston. An old soul, unlike a young heart, couldn't survive while bound to monotony and turgid routine. Joshua had come to realise over the last year that work could grow morbid. *Our passions have grown dim*, Joshua realised. *We deteriorate in faith the older we get. Only God is constantly young because he is consistent. And I … I used to think everything was a game. I used to hate adults with passion. God is the great adult I thought I could scam! Instead, God pulled the rug from under me!*

He fingered his father's letter – he'd been grasping it this entire time. He thought of his parents, now without a son. "Nefer? You forgive me?"

"Yes, of course I do, bumpkin."

"Why does Jesus say that if you don't become like children, you shall never enter the Kingdom of God?"

"Why are you asking for the answer?" the spirit said. "You know what it is. If you rediscover innocence, humility, wondering at simple, small things, the capacity for fun and open-ended trust is becoming a child. Being young is submitting to God. Being young is submitting fully to God because he is the foundation of your existence. You trust the God of Truth, not because it will give you benefits, security and success. But because it is for the delight of God. The Devil hates this childlike innocence and wants to break it because he's a coward. Now, Joshua, you desire Truth. You have faith because you are willing to sacrifice for the truth, not living in lies. It's by your *childlike character* that you can *conquer* malevolence, because you *were that* before. Now you know its weakness. It entails you have mature wisdom. Being childlike is not that you lack mature wisdom, it means that you have more of it."

"Yes … Amen. I just really miss my father, my mother and my family," Joshua said. "Their lives have been destroyed because of my archaeological interloping. I'm reflecting about how I used to think – that all adults were fools, and that I was a responsible adult – when really, I was actually acting like a *stupid child*." Joshua felt tears brimming the edges of his eyes. "Until God saved me." Then Joshua simply confessed, cathartically. "I cannot question adult authority arrogantly. I'm a child. I need to trust. But … Oh Nefer, I just questioned you! God is not a man that he will lie, but he is consistent with his good purpose for creation. You are here to redeem the darkness of the rebellious gods.

"But Nefer, listen to me. I just fear … the university will discover my track record and my criminal charges and deny me from graduating. I am ashamed. I know that sounds ridiculous, and it probably is. But my greatest fear is others I want to work with will see my sin and disqualify me from studying. I hate fearing this! I hate it! It's a burden! No one gets it, not even Pawani, except for you and except for Christ. The anxiety is consuming me, dulling my love for academics, and I long for the time when I can just love studying for the sake of learning again. But I'm supposed to be a saint. Yeah, I'm not a saint. I'm … a derelict coward. Father, help me not be ashamed … for what I have done."

Rotating slowly, cilia fluttering, Nefer drifted closer compassionately. "My lovely brother. It was *all your fault* that the Islamists have you on their hit list, not God's. It is *your fault* that guilt never goes away, not God's. It is *all your fault* that you lost all your money, got sent to war and lost all your friends. It's not Pounders' fault. You know why it is your fault? Because *you* decided to become a con. *You* deceived to isolate yourself. *You* decided to go to war. Only *you* are responsible for what you have done."

"Yes. That is absolutely true. Saints are sinners. Broken sinners."

"When the world sees you afflicted, responding with hope, they're going to want to know. They're going to ask, 'How do you do it? How can you remain full of hope when your life is devastated?' …" Nefer pulsated blue light, ejecting a small spray of twinkling dust out of his orbed ring of orange clouds. A nimbus of glory.

"I need a ready answer," Joshua said. A mature child … That was it. This was who Joshua was. The culmination of it all. The truth among all things, simple and yet difficult to see at first hand, abundantly undervalued. Joshua let tears fall down his face, and he humbled himself. "I don't deserve forgiveness."

"It is my delight to forgive you, regardless. When you trust in Yahweh, you will not be put to shame. He will even lift the shame of our disappointment and childlessness. The eyes of the Lord are searching the Earth to and fro, seeking hearts that are completely his, who on his behalf can show themselves strong. You, as part of the Holy Ones, have inherited pure glory that was promised to the ancients. Blessed opportunities are coming."

"All creation groans as in childbirth, in this state of delayed order and rampant sin, waiting to be set free with those who have the First Fruits of the Spirit. The youth of this world … They *need* to hear this. They *need* to repent." Joshua looked up at the spirit. "Revival is coming."

"Indeed, yes. This is the whole purpose of tribulation, Joshua," Nefer said. "I came to you to be your spiritual father so you can endure when tribulation comes. I am *not* deceiving. I'm preparing you for tribulation. Tribulation is not just to test the righteous and to punish the wicked. Because out of persecution comes … revival. It is completing God's mission to proclaim the Gospel, preparing Earth for the conquest of Heaven."

Suddenly, Joshua heard his phone ring. He reached for it and answered. "Hello?"

"Josh, this is Pawani." Though the youthful woman remained tranquil, she sounded a tad bit timorous. "How are you?"

"All right," he said. He gave Nefer a mock aggressive expression, pointing at the phone. "You?"

"I'm good, I'm good. I hope everything is going well for you down there in Tucson. Oh, did you hear about the news? They found Zoe O'Leary. She's dying. At John C Lincoln Medical Centre."

"What?" Joshua said, shocked. "Zoe?"

"Yeah. That's strange. I rang to just see if you're okay and when you might be coming back to the Pacific Northwest."

Joshua felt chills. In his act of kindness, he'd just attracted a young girl … *She … loves me?*

"Uhm. I will definitely be back by October, Pawani," Joshua said. "I promise. And thanks for telling me about Zoe. I'm not one who watches much TV, regrettably." He chuckled.

"Oh, that's fine. I wish you all the best. Bye."

"Bye." Joshua cringed as Pawani hung up, and he rubbed his face, love and worry raging inside of him. "Nefer! What just happened?"

"Noble brother," Nefer remarked as Joshua quickly gathered his bag and car keys. "There is a chance for you to serve! Judd Pounders would like to see you again; your father misses you."

"I will go and see him. He probably knows about what happened with Zoe." Joshua smiled, departing out the front door.

"And know this!" his scholar called out in a loud voice. "There are more enemies on the road than on the battlefield! So drive safely, for Christ's sake!"

"I will." Joshua sighed, closing the door.

62

BEGINNING OF SORROWS

"Truly, I say to you, unless you turn and become like children, you will never enter the Kingdom of Heaven. Whoever humbles himself like this child is the greatest in the Kingdom of Heaven.

Whoever receives one such child in my name receives me, but whoever causes one of these little ones who believe in me to stumble, it would be better for him to have a great millstone fastened around his neck and to be drowned in the depth of the sea ...

See that you do not despise one of these little ones. For I tell you that, in Heaven, their angels always see the face of my Father, who is in Heaven. For the Son of Human came to save the lost."

—From the Gospel of Matthew, c. 80 – 90 CE

The scent of disinfectants lingered in the air as Brianna DePaula, and Keller Butcher beside her, marched vitriolically into the John C Lincoln Medical Centre operation theatre.

Young Zoe, with her eyes fastened shut, lay as still as death on the bed, wearing a medical gown, fluids attached to her right arm. Surrounding her were her older brother Dominic and his partner Patricia; Morgan, the younger brother; and the middle-aged parents, Noel and Tracy O'Leary. They gave them distraught glances.

"How did she get here?" Keller demanded sharply.

The group of nurses ogled at him. One of them, a plump black lady, held her arms out for Keller to sit down. "Sir, please—"

Skin smacked against skin as Keller backhanded her advance, pulling out his ID. Brianna followed suit. "We're from the Federal Bureau of Investigation.

I've been assigned Zoe's case. I am asking you a question. How did she arrive here? Who brought her? Was it paramedics? FBI?"

The nurse blinked nervously, her gaze unfocused, stammering, saying, "Sorry, sir, but I'm afraid I don't know. Zoe was found in this condition when I arrived on shift. Please be patient and sit here while we consult Dr Grono. He has a heavy schedule. We apologise for the inconvenience."

Keller stamped his foot in a rage. "Has anyone been able to wake her up?"

"No," Noel – Zoe's father – said bitterly. "She'd been found like this when the emergency centre called us."

Soon, everyone was escorted out of the theatre so that the nurses and doctors could perform procedures to try to alleviate Zoe's critical condition. Woebegone, Brianna turned and sat down in Patricia's offered seat, her legs almost shaking. After waiting impatiently, listening to the subtle hum of medical machines and feeling the chilliness of the hospital, a semi-corpulent man with thick glasses in a stark white cloak strode out of the theatre, clutching a writing pad in his hands.

"Mr and Mrs O'Leary. All right," he said with a clipped voice, peering through his spectacles. "I promise the procedure won't take much longer. We're just trying to dispel all the excess substances that have been used to drug her, but what we found is that her oxygen levels have plummeted, which is rupturing her metabolic functions. We are baffled at how she could have lost so much liquid and proteins from her body without any signs of transfusion. And I'm also very sorry; I tried, but I couldn't find out who brought Zoe into the hospital. Authorities never recovered Veronica's body."

"So, she just … appeared?" Keller's neck muscles clenched. "It wasn't paramedics? FBI? Anyone?"

Brianna saw Tracy was struggling – staring at nothing, her balled fists blanched, stiff on her lap.

Brianna saw a jolted movement from Noel; he rocked to his feet, scowling. "This is ridiculous! You're saying she was drugged, and you cannot determine if it caused her oxygen levels to fail?"

"Pardon me, Mr O'Leary. Your daughter is severely dehydrated. And when I mean dehydrated, I mean it's really bad. We are giving her transfusions now."

Zoe O'Leary's mother, Tracy, grasped Noel's pants. "No, no, no, no, no, no. Please do something!"

Sweat pearled Dr Grono's brow. An incongruous grimace appeared on his remorseful face as he let out a deep sigh. He looked very heavy with distress. "I … I detest saying this, but … I'm not confident that Zoe will ever wake up again. I'm *so* sorry."

Brianna's hand covered her mouth as Dom's eyes went wide, and Patricia pressed her lips until they were bloodless. Keller snarled under his breath in sharp frustration. As for Tracy, she arched her head back, eyes shut, hands groping the sides of her head so hard as she let go to stagger and stumble into her chair. Noel tried to sit her down. She rocked back and forth – undergoing excruciating agony that seemed to bring to terms Brianna's own numbed grief of being a failure of a mother.

"No …" Tracy's whining became more hysterical, so frenzied with despair as she kept on blabbering. "No! Don't take my baby from me! Please! No! No! My little Zo Zo! No … please, do something! My daughter … Please!" She began to swear and curse everyone so maliciously that Brianna shuddered. Noel tried to speak over her to silence her tantrum.

Dr Grono didn't need to speak – his departure alone made it final. Zoe was beyond saving.

Little Zo Zo was dead.

Tracy violently rocked back and forth, elegiac groans ripping out of her mouth. Despite Noel's comfort, the woman was absolutely inconsolable – she broke down wailing, sniffing and weeping, hands trying to break things, tear at things, cleaving to her husband. Brianna unclenched her jaw – she'd been clenching it the entire time, feeling hollow inside. If Zoe was dead … Veronica was …

Brianna wasn't a mother. She wasn't an FBI agent. She didn't know what responsibility was. She was a *poor* choice for being a mother.

Brianna found herself departing the hospital, struggling to breathe, jogging towards her car. Keller followed her, looking intense as always.

"Do you think this could mean anything?" Keller said, opening the car door for her. Brianna swung inside. "Zoe's body had been completely drained of water. And why Zoe? How did she escape? I'm confident someone from the Alliance saved her. She came from Dulce Base. Neil's stories about abductions of children in Tucson and Phoenix sound to me that there is a connective tissue to this investigation we have overlooked. It is Alfred Bonner. His abuse of you at the Navajo reservation and his desire for the CD make him a suspect in my eyes."

Brianna froze. Keller could be so cold sometimes! She did remember the ordeal at the Grand Canyon. Alfred Bonner, a terrifying man, held her hostage just so he could get the CD. And if that man knew so much about the murder of Joseph and the kidnapping of the girls, he and Ian Mastemah must have been in on the diabolical crime.

"You believe all that?" Brianna rasped.

"It's plausible," Keller said. "I need to try to verify it. It's better than deciphering Gladius' glyphs."

Brianna sighed. "All the answers we could ever have are gone."

"That's why we must try Dulce. I was called up by Judd Pounders, who had just terminated his contract with the Alliance leader. He's willing to exterminate the society for their crimes, and he requested FBI aid. Going to Dulce … This could be our last chance to solve this case, Brianna. And just because Veronica hasn't been found, it is not a base indicator that she is dead. But until I see a body, I *refuse* to believe Veronica is dead." Keller met her eyes. "Do you trust me? Dulce will be our last run."

Brianna stared at the man. *But what if we don't find Veronica?* No, she could still be alive in a gloomy underground military base at Mount Turnbull. Brianna *hoped* Keller was right. "I … Of course …"

Keller noticed Brianna's hesitation, softening his glance. "How do you feel about all this?"

Brianna held her breath. Was Keller now doing the same to her – making himself vulnerable out of respect, after he'd honestly revealed his deepest thoughts and secrets to her?

But despite Keller being an honourable and advanced agent, she still remembered how violently he treated Gladius – and how he'd destroyed his office, berating himself for being a failure, not being strong enough to save her daughter. If only Ben had reacted in a similar way. She would have had pity on him.

"How do I feel?" Brianna restated Keller's question. "About …"

"Everything, Bri. The investigation."

What did Brianna feel, knowing that logic demanded her daughter was dead like Zoe? A part of her was glad that the unbearable tension of the last few months was finally over, a part of her sorrowful for the O'Learys. She was partly relieved that Keller was not torturing himself with guilt and doubt anymore. A part of her relieved for the Marine Corps and the FBI to team up and raze Dulce Base to the ground. A part of her was fearful that Ben was still alive, a part of her yearning for revenge for what he did to her, humiliating her, making her regret marrying a pessimistic misogynistic actor. A part of her screamed without sound. Why should this happen to her now, after all the other things that she'd suffered already? *My daughter …*

Brianna couldn't handle the uncertainty any longer … She gazed up out the window of her car into the brown darkness of passing shadows, cast incoherently by lights, disembodied in the night. She saw beyond the bitter moment into a window of alluring and peace, a long procession of years where there would be no man to compel her and impose their will on her. Acts no less a crime.

I trusted Ben more than anyone else, Brianna thought. *Just like I trusted my father, who beat me and betrayed me, Ben beat me and betrayed me. I trusted those two men more than I trusted Keller, and now that trust was in vain.*

"I feel … desperate," Brianna said simply. "I feel betrayed. I want this to be over. Now. The investigation has destroyed my family!" Yet Keller – he'd always been there for her. He'd always looked out for her, he'd fight for her, and he worried about her when he didn't have to. Ben didn't. When this was over, Brianna needed to plan her future. *I … want you, Keller.*

She locked the car doors.

Keller's expression turned wary – he seemed to read what that implied. Locked inside her car, at night, intimate, just the two of them. He swallowed hard. "Brianna, it's not proper. Benjamin—"

"Benjamin!" Brianna snapped. "Why must everyone focus on him? Why must everyone talk about him, write about him? He's not here, Keller!"

"I want to find him," Keller said, lowering his glance. "I want to … arrest him so I can be sure that you are safe from him. I want your permission, so I don't feel guilty."

"Of course! Don't ask my permission! But what about *the wife*? What about the woman in the relationship? Had anyone considered *me*, all that I have gone through? All I get is fake pampering from other women who have *no* idea! You see what it did to Cleo? It made her go insane, being with Ben. And now people look at me and they get uncomfortable – they are *shameful*, for what Cleo did, for what Ben did! They're disgusted that I even *thought* of marrying him! My girlfriends at the FBI have refused to talk to me! Everyone has left my life and … I don't understand why this is happening! It was like *I* was the one who harmed him! 'Oh, how dare you touch the Actionman!' 'She deserved all this!' Does anyone care about my Veronica too because she's a young woman? Oh no! The daughter I genuinely love is gone, and now everyone focuses on my failure as a mother! I used to *hate* Veronica's mother because of that. Cleo didn't care, but I cared. I *freakin'* cared! I wanted to become a mother and demote myself to a part-time FBI agent to raise her. I cared all along, when nobody cared, Keller! And Ben … He's a traitor! I can't trust a man anymore."

Keller grimaced. "I'm sorry."

But Brianna wasn't done yet. The agony was still cleaving to her chest, ready to vomit out. She raised a hand to her bosom, her voice rasping. "We're friends, Keller. Even before I adopted Veronica, we've known each other since grad school. You still know me as me, not as an agent, a mother or a partner of a star, but as Brianna." Tears burned her eyes, swelling until Keller's shocked expression blurred. Rarely had she been so sincere with anyone, not even with Ben. Her throat writhed with sobs.

She stared at Keller, and dazed, Keller stared at her. Then, pulling her into a tight embrace, Keller kissed her.

Brianna's eyes widened, pressing her mouth onto his. She melted into him, her tears running freely down her burning cheek, wetting his own, leaving them both damp with moisture.

It lasted long. Too long. *Wonderfully* long. Her mind screamed at her, coerced to watch something horrible. But a part of her had wanted this for years – years of inhaling Ben's toxicity, and how fond she'd become of Keller's strength, support and guidance. When she was hurled out of Ben's life, she rolled into Keller's. Without him, she would never have become what she wanted to become.

A detective investigator. An FBI officer. Protecting people from evil. Keller had made her vocation possible. She made his vocation possible in turn.

The taste of him – the smell of him, the warmth of him snuggled against her – was *too* sweet, washing away all the guilt. And for a moment, she couldn't remember the worry over her daughter, the sadness over Zoe's death, her insufferable shame.

She could only think of him. Wonderful, smart, selfless, every second of Keller's life dedicated to service – so strong and determined – both of them would serve each other. She clung to him, something she could hold on to as the chaotic world raged around her.

Eventually, he broke the kiss. She looked up at him, dazed. Guilt flooded Keller's scarlet face. He gently tried to push her away, but Brianna clung to him, hugging him tight.

"Brianna," he whispered.

She hummed in comfort. Keller sighed, letting her hold him.

"Sorry. I should have—"

"Your consent is granted," Brianna cooed.

She felt the rock hardness in Keller's chest soften. He was relaxed, complete and whole. "Everything is all right, Brianna," Keller said, hugging her. "I'm here."

Brianna raised her head. "Wow. You … Wow."

Keller actually smirked sheepishly, blushing. Another first. Keller never showed emotional affection. "Don't be getting ideas already. I'm not romantic."

"I understand poker face," she smirked, snickering. "I've been through it. It will be *exciting*."

"Yeah … I have something to tell you."

"What?"

"I found Ben," Keller said. "Reports came in, and I forgot to tell you when we heard about Zoe. I am going to arrest that bastard. A Christian ministry in Tucson reported him having a mental meltdown in their building. He was part of the homeless shelter there, and they were so blind and so kind that they actually gave him a job!"

Brianna gasped. "What in the world is wrong with these born-again Christians? Don't they have any idea?"

"They're gullible. Ben was living with them for two weeks, wearing a mask, lying about his identity. No doubt he's panicking about being found out."

Brianna couldn't believe what she was hearing. She stared and yelled, "What the hell?"

"Brianna, I—"

"Keller, we need to do our jobs and get him!"

"Brianna, Ben's just another man now."

"Yes. Another man …" She heaved out a frustrated sigh. She found it difficult to get intelligible words out, intoxicated by Keller's kiss. Why did she feel so flustered about that? Why did Keller have to leave that piece of news now after … after what he just did?

Oh God, Ben is not *my husband anymore! I'm free at last!*

"I need you, Keller," Brianna said. "More than ever. I've known it for years, though I feared it would destroy you with guilt, so I kept my love for you a secret. But I couldn't, not with how Ben treated me. I'm terrified, Keller. Ben's still on the run, and I need you. When I saw you lose all hope at your desk, it …" Brianna gasped, feeling tears brimming her eyes. What would people think of their union? Would they slander or congratulate them? More likely the former.

"You want to stay at my place while I arrest him for you?"

Brianna nodded gratefully. Now she could have respite, and she felt excited about it. Keller's house … She leaned back in her seat, closing her eyes, at rest.

"If you hoped to soothe my worries for the day," Keller said, shifting in his seat, "then this didn't help."

Brianna opened her eyes, folding her arms. She could still feel where Keller had hugged around the back – a tender touch reserved for an intimate family member. "We're family. It's what we do."

"I need to get ready to hunt Ben down."

"You always want to do things *now*, you roadrunner." Brianna smiled. "Don't forget this night—"

"Brianna." He gently cut her off, smiling. "I will not."

"It was *you* that started it. That kiss was *yours*."

"*I* started it?" Keller stammered, face contorting from amusement, elation, worry and guilt at the same time. "You *seduced* me."

"Aww!" She rubbed his shoulder fondly. "When should a hard, no-nonsense agent ever feel seduced?"

"Come on, Bri," Keller said curtly, his cheeks stained red, gazing out the windscreen.

"I never seduced you. I was just being honest."

"I know," Keller said, smiling. "That was the seductive part. I guess I did it to you too when I had my breakdown. I was *so seducing* in my anguish, wasn't I?" He turned on the engine. "You know, it's a *wonderful* thing to have someone you trust at your side." He eyed her longingly. "Thank you."

63

DISHONOUR

"And afterward,
    I will pour out my Spirit on all flesh,
your sons and daughters will prophesy,
    your old men will dream dreams,
your young men will see visions.
    And even on the male slaves and on the female slaves,
I will pour out my Spirit in those days."
    —From the Scroll of Joel, late 5th Century BCE.

Ben stood cold and soaked, neck warmer veiling his face. Rain fell gently in sheets, the stiff wind spraying across the bed of dried brown leaves and granite tombs of his father and the new addition behind him in the children's cemetery across the road.

The burial of Zoe O'Leary. Buried by her family. The fact that Ben was unable to bury Veronica's body magnified his failure as a father.

"You coward," Ben growled. "Why?"

Water dripped down his face and into his scruffy beard. His feet were cold, his socks and shoes soaked through. He *hated* having a long beard, the way the whiskers pricked his mouth, its long tufts getting caught in his jacket zip. But it conveniently hid his identity, shadowing his face.

A day after the incident at the church, Ben's anxiety subsided in arbitrary intervals; the worst of the darkness pushed aside. Yet, still, after running back to Arizona from Fellowship of the Way, he felt that his prayers were an abomination, going into silence.

He closed his eyes at Joseph's grave.

He'd promised himself to go back to the Grand Canyon to find the Navajo again. But he instead came to the cemetery. In that, he failed for reasons that were nothing more than cowardly laziness. All motivation had been drained from Ben.

Why be moral? Why torment himself with the Navajo – so pure and so human – the objects of his envy? Being moral was hard. Being bad was easy. Why should he follow any moral theory if he was already finished?

Before, Ben had cried out to God for help so many times and only received tremendous silence. Surely, God heard people's prayers, but did he hear their screams? Veronica's screams?

What a vindictive tyrant, ready to destroy my soul! Ben thought. *What kind of man am I? Why did I do what I did? I'm evil. The Navajo brings me the pain of envy. There is no end to guilt. No matter where I go. A man knows how bad he is until he tries very hard to do good and fails. So why try? No one cares about me anyway.*

To be a man is to desire what one cannot take.

Anti-iconic as Joseph's will had said, Ben stared at the tombstone and the ground interring the father he could've known. Etched on the polished granite with gold letters were his father's name and a verse of scripture. John 14:1-3. There had been a gravestone prepared just for Ben, an identical slab to this one, when he arrived at Joseph's house after the paladin man transported Ben back to Arizona from Haditha Dam. That felt like a lifetime ago.

It was ready for Ben.

Only a matter of time …

Ben *refused* to see Zoe's grave. It was too painful. He'd come at this strategic time just after the funeral to evade the eyes and ears of Keller and Brianna.

Ben wanted the darkness to go away, but it had lingered within him for so long, he wondered if this was truly who he was. A frustrated, depressed man, crippled with guilt, caring nothing about his family, or even for his marines.

No, *God* was condemning Ben. God was the Galactic Tyrant who created suffering and evil, and that was final! The crazy Aes Sidhe were right in that regard.

It was not a question of the fact that Ben's father wanted to love him. But maybe, Ben thought, his father did not know *how* to love him. Ben remembered how his mother treated his dad, leaving the house with Lisa. Ben's mother decried that father struggled to love. Ben reading half the Old Testament at Fellowship of the Way ministries had *repulsed* him. Father God, too, was everything but love.

The Galactic Tyrant was ultimately insecure. He burned sinners, demanded child sacrifice, was a megalomanic who stripped women naked to be raped, and ethnically cleansed Palestinian nations. Terrible male Jewish authors. Talking snakes, consented genocide, maledictions for slavery, not working on Saturday!

God didn't care. An arbitrary narcissist who deprived people of making choices.

To be a man is to desire what one cannot take.

Why did the Navajo heal me? For me to keep on living in this sin-cursed world? They're servants of the Tyrant. That's why.

Nothing is simple, Ben. You must know that. The words of his father returned to him. *The Law of Triumph. That is the timeless principle. They said suffering is coming upon the Earth. Suffering is soul-building theodicy …*

What was Ben doing here, enmeshed in the past? Putting himself in danger, and yet, here he was. At the Phoenix cemetery in a worse situation than where he had begun. He felt nothing if Keller arrested him or not. There was a type of fearlessness in being apathetic. Power and freedom of not having to care.

Deception is the prison that we live in. A drunk is one way out and death the other.

It was better to not resist. He'd been doomed from the start anyway. Better to not wake up again, because if he did, he had to face the constant dread again. Everyone was his enemy – they could never know that Ben had died, grinded by dread ever since he found the child in the rubbish.

Ben must've broken road rules when he reached his North Mountain house. All was a blur. He took with him the gun he stole from Brianna and unlocked the door of his house. He entered the living room, vastly spaced, with an open view of the backyard and a grand ensuite.

It was derelict. Untidy, reeking of fish, with no one home to maintain it.

Your goodbye to me is perfect when you leave me and never look back. Joseph. *To focus on living your life and helping the lives around you is what I want for you. It's an unpleasant thing to miss someone still here.*

Having a house was a fortune of success for any person, and it would've been easy for Ben's parents. They worked, succeeded, had lives, but they divorced when their firstborn Lisa suffered schizophrenia. Mother had hated Ben and Patty since their birth – Ben felt the hate. She left with Lisa when she discovered that Joseph converted to his Hebrew Roots cult, making him go crazy, and in the end, they all died. And Ben thought he could do better than his pathetic parents by raising his own family.

He ended up the worst off.

It made him sick. Sorrowful of soul, weary with his life, hanging in suspense, fearful of the night, uncertain of his fate.

A drunk is one way out … and death the other.

Ben stood in the silence, welcoming the smothering sensation. He went to cross the room.

He didn't make it.

He sagged down to a squat, his back against the back of the couch, his hand digging into his bald scalp. Ben gasped, hyperventilating. He convulsed, his skin rippling, bones grinding from the exertion.

With an irritated jolt, Ben gritted his teeth, flicking his head back violently. He ripped off his shirt. Wheezing, he tossed the clothing and huddled, all alone.

Desperately, he reached out for Brianna's gun on the floor. He wrapped his hand around it, then froze. He could almost see a black chasm opening up in the floor behind the gun he was staring at, a darkness sucking any last vestiges of hope from his heart. Killing himself would be one way to strike back at God – the Galactic Tyrant – if God even existed.

Ben closed his eyes. He turned the gun towards himself. He opened his mouth.

No. Stop, Ben. STOP THIS!

The doorbell rang. Ben opened his eyes. For a while, he simply sat there in the dark, staring at Brianna's gun. He ignored the ringing until it became insistent. Ben swallowed, gasping as if he just realised what he had nearly done.

Brianna or Keller was here.

Ben had to prepare himself for the worst. He *had* to accept this. No more running. But he … he was too weak to even kill himself. He refused anyone to see him like this. He *refused* to die. Rob, who encouraged him to keep living with renewed benefits, instilled hope in him that Ben needed his daughter in order to be human.

Ben put his shirt back on and opened the door. Judd Pounders waited in the dark clear night, his expression troubled in the dim front light that coalesced around him. Beside him was a handsome, young and poised Keller, face determined and emotionless. Taking a step towards the door, handcuffs clinking in his hands, Ben slumped. *Damnation of Hell.*

Pounders barred Keller's way with his arm. "I want to talk to him as a soldier first, Agent Butcher."

Keller nodded, and Ben gripped the door frame so hard he thought he would make an impression in it.

"What do you think the soldiers would think when they see you in the deplorable state of your misconduct, Captain?"

That last word flayed Ben, fuelling hatred in his heart. When did Pounders become so … harsh?

"Ashamed," Ben breathed. "Abandoned."

Pounders nodded. He fished something out of his bag, pulling out a certificate. Ben incredulously saw that it said, "DD-214". His blood went cold. It could only be a bad paper, but he wasn't even in military service to be qualified for a penalty. *No … No, I was never officially admitted a completion of military service.* "I trusted in you, Ben. What example would that be for younger marines who look up to a failure?"

Ben's eyes went wide. "I know. *All* men are failures. We desire what we cannot take." His voice quavered on the verge of tears.

"Take it," Pounders said, holding the DD-214 like a weapon. "Take it!"

Ben snatched the paper, not looking at it. Obviously, the negative determinations would have been broadcast to all the world – the news would've informed Pounders about everything Ben did – from torturing Thomas, to threatening his wife in public, hiding from the FBI in a church, lying about his identity and money laundering. *My wake of destruction has been uncovered,* Ben thought. *Now I'll carry all this sin.*

"It's unacceptable," Pounders whispered sharply. "I have the right to legally forfeit all your honours and your weapons from service in the Marine Corps." His lips became a taut line. "You're having Duck Dinner."

Ben swallowed hard. Duck Dinner – the worst form of legal military punishment – for treason, misconduct, desertion and assault. They all meant dishonourable discharge, where all benefits were forfeited, regardless of any past honourable service. Then Ben would need to undergo a tedious process – those given Duck Dinner would face around one hundred and twenty days in custody in a military prison before being brought before the tribunal at the martial court. If his lawyer failed, Ben would be in prison for a very long time. For decades.

This was the equivalent of slavery. In military prison, morals were loose, and death sentences permissible for the worst of crimes committed. Ben would never return to civilian life. He was sure. This was the end.

Gather the Church? No.

The heavy toil of his sentence weighed on him numbly, twisting his heart to dust. *No …* A surge of anger erupted in Ben, but his melancholy was already too pervasive, and Pounders' authority unquestionable. A bully drill sergeant. And at that moment of shadow, Ben felt small, as puny as a private.

"So, you're *not* negligent," Pounders whispered. "You moron."

"Go ahead," Ben growled, feeling tears trickle down his face. "Take it all! I've got *nothing* to lose, Pounders! Go ahead! Discharge me! I was only trying to *save* my daughter and *avenge* my father! I don't need people like you to dictate—"

"Stop!" Pounders snapped, foam forming at the ends of his mouth. "You *think* you can get away with murder? You can't! Not on my watch! Not according to the law! You're leaving with dishonour!"

Ben chuckled. He knew all these punishments were just.

"You're going to military court." He grasped Ben's arm, dragging him out of his house. Keller stood like a languid imperial Roman statue – all his doing, all his manipulations – scapegoating Ben.

The first station of Ben's torment began. Ben was a ruin, nevertheless obliged to make an appearance to his men out of consideration. On his front lawn, he saw all his men – the marines, except for Julian – he'd died at Haditha Dam. Derek Fish stood stiffly with crossed arms, his brow furrowed, staring at the lawn. Jason Laycock looked incredulous and shocked, Marcus Theis grounded his jaw, Mark Randal shadowy with embarrassment and Johnny Best slumped, gazing incompetently. Joshua was in absentia.

It only seemed like yesterday he had led most of these men in Desert Storm and in Afghanistan. Yet now they no longer knew what authority they were under. *I'm sorry, guys.* Ben couldn't speak. His throat constricted.

"Take a hard look at your men," Pounders whispered. "This will be the last time you will see them."

And suddenly, from out of nowhere, Marcus Theis stalked up to Ben, spat at him, and then punched Ben in the gut.

He gasped, doubling over, the pain blinding. His hip strained, recalling previous trauma.

Waves of shame and anguish drowned Ben. He really wished he had pulled the trigger faster, that he'd been more fearless to end his life before this … *insufferable* shame.

Johnny Best looked up, sympathy in his eyes, his mouth parted in shock. Ben could feel in the air some of the marines wanted to talk, but they restrained themselves.

I hate what I've become. Ben groaned, his heart feeling as dry as basalt. He didn't look the men in the eyes.

"We're doing this for the sake of the Marine Corps' reputation and for justice, Captain," Pounders sounded from behind Ben, pulling him upright.

"Why are you calling me captain?" Ben said passionately. "I wasn't even in service …"

"It *does not matter* if you were discharged or not. What you did is *worth* dishonour. You went missing during the war, you went out and committed crimes. Technically, you *were not* discharged from service. You were still under my jurisdiction."

Ben could see his men out of the corners of his eyes, watching, concerned and punctilious like he'd been. He eyed Keller – so indignant and cold. Evil. He was possibly thinking about Brianna and Thomas Jones. Ben felt so sick he wanted to vomit, then die.

"We all have to confront what we do not like, eventually," Pounders said as Keller followed him like a shadow.

"Why did you have to bring them all?" Ben rasped. "*Why?*"

"The Marine Corps is going to shut down the Dulce base," Pounders said, lips drawn in a tight line. "The Marine Corps has been manipulated by the Alliance for too long in its misuse and breach of our agreements and procedures during the war in Iraq. We're going to destroy their main headquarters at the end of this week. And you, Ben, will have no part in it."

A mission to kill Bonner?

"In other words," Keller said, "the Marine Corps and the FBI have collaborated to finish this investigation once and for all. To avenge your father and save your daughter."

"What do you mean?" Ben quivered.

Keller's face was unreadable, but he took a step, studying Ben closely. "The Alliance are known for taking young people in this country. Neil Jones says the secret society wants to do this in order to prepare for the end of the world. This breach of civil rights must be dealt with, and it starts now."

Without a word, Keller stepped around Ben, clasping his hands together in metal handcuffs.

Ben gazed at his men. They turned their backs on him one by one.

Ben felt something writhing in his chest. Perhaps it was better off that way, not like before, as Ben had shown to them that he broke every outstanding moral and word he had taught them daily. Perhaps they saw him as a shadow, a scapegoat who had been cursed, where prosperity and order should be.

But Ben, above all, had experienced death inside himself. The cosmic black hole, a fire, purposely made by himself, was suddenly growing. The flames of Hell were unceasing.

"Where is my wife?" Ben's voice was hoarse as Keller put him in the back of the police car. An awful question – Ben didn't want to see her, didn't want to talk to her – his misery was already too much.

"Your wife?" Keller snarled, one hand on the steering wheel. "You don't have a wife." He pulled out of the driveway, sending Ben to his next station – the Phoenix military detention centre.

64

THE IMPOSTER

"I will show wonders in the skies and the land,
blood and fire and columns of smoke.
The sun will be changed to darkness, and the moon to blood,
before the coming of the great and dreadful day of Yahweh.
And everyone who calls
on the name of Yahweh will be rescued;
because on Mount Zion and in Jerusalem there will be deliverance ..."
—From the Scroll of Joel, late 5th Century BCE.

James Casbolt arrived at the house of Thomas Jones in Youngtown, Phoenix, sitting in his rental car, procrastinating with his alters.

He had come, once and for all, to meet Thomas Jones. He waited for him.

Coincidences like this don't happen, Michael Prince stated. *Two voices, like two people, might be similar, but not absolutely identical, so perhaps it's your imagination.*

Casbolt sniffed in derision, replying, "I find that very hard to believe, Michael Prince. How can I get to the bottom of this if I don't know if *you're* my imagination? Are you my identical double?"

No. I am you. Could it be black magic? Michael speculated.

"Michael, whatever this means, we need to monitor Thomas Jones if he comes. He will not leave my sight. I must know if he's friend or foe."

The thought of having another alter – unbeknownst to him – made him feel sick with existential dread. A formless deep self, something ... free from him.

A few minutes of waiting passed, when, from the rear-view mirror, Casbolt glimpsed a young man his age, looking just like himself, walking a dog, ambling down the street just behind him. It made his heart rupture, and he started to sweat. Casbolt beheld the terrifying revelation of the existence of a man who, to judge by his body and by his general appearance, was his very image. Yet there was something off about this Thomas Jones. His posture, the way he held himself, was a posture that had never known combat or valour. Casbolt hoped that to be the case so he could claim a stark difference between them and thus be done with this futile distraction.

It was now or never for Casbolt, and wanting to end this madness, he emerged from the car, obstructing Thomas' path. Standing tall, he stood there, not intending to move aside. Upon noticing him, Thomas shuffled, yelping, trying to move to the other side, but Casbolt deliberately rescinded him. Thomas whimpered, moving to the side, but Casbolt blocked his path.

"Woah! I told you! Look at me, friend," Casbolt said with an unyielding voice, crossing his arms. "You look *exactly* like me!"

Thomas met Casbolt's eyes – his own eyes. Pure ambivalent bewilderment appeared on his face, and he knew then who Casbolt was. The realisation. The Parvus. Thomas studied James Casbolt, and in him he saw himself, externally projected. An enemy interloper.

Fear sweat began to rise from Casbolt's skin in the humid air. He had lost all awareness of relative time. Here, Casbolt could render out details one could never see onscreen. Unbelievable details that confirmed his darkest of nightmares – that he was no longer himself anymore.

Head hanging as if trying to abscond behind an invisible wall, Thomas stepped backward. Two steps.

Casbolt proceeded forwards.

Thomas took another long step back, eyes evading.

"I'm not here to hurt you, Thomas."

They stared … again, Casbolt and fearful Thomas, ogling, gazing, gawking, and scrutinising their features. From hair, to face, nose, eyes, skin, lips, to neck and body – mostly the face – seeking for one iota of a difference that would nullify their terror. There was nothing.

Thomas was blushing, and he didn't seem to know if he should stare at this stranger examining him with probing eyes or turn away. His hand blanched, gripping the dog's lead.

Casbolt wet his mouth – parched and dry. "Show me your hands."

"Why?" Thomas rasped coyly, eyes sliding to the pavement. "Wha …

What are you?"

"Please. Come on. Show me your hands," Casbolt prodded, gently this time. Thomas didn't respond, stupefied. Casbolt led the way, splaying his two hands out before Thomas, palms facing the ground. It was an effort to keep them from quivering.

If Thomas was Casbolt – a programmed Aes Sidhe, a killing machine – he seldom displayed any signs of it. In fact, Thomas embodied the exact opposite – he looked a menial helot. In that way, Casbolt could trust he wouldn't assault him, but perhaps he was thinking the same thing towards Casbolt as well – it was only right he lay down his guard if they were going to talk.

Casbolt perceived something with the Parvus Perception – from the trembling lips, reddening cheeks, and dread in Thomas' unstable eyes. He read paranoid humiliation. *I have to run. Run. Run.*

And yet, acquiescing, Thomas held out his hands. Fingertips to fingertips, Casbolt saw uncanny subtle resemblances – the shape of the hands, the texture of the veins and tendons, pores, the pigmentation, and even the nails were clipped.

Casbolt turned his hands over, palms facing him, and Thomas did the same. The lines of the skin didn't betray signs of difference. A single brown dot on Casbolt's left wrist was there on Thomas' left wrist.

He is literally *me* ... Casbolt's stomach began to churn.

"I ..." Thomas' lower jaw shuddered. "I ..."

"Are we twins?" Casbolt asked. "Clones?"

Thomas stared at him with wide blue eyes.

"Do you have ... do you have a birthmark on your chest?" Casbolt said. That question terrified him, mainly because he had a feeling that Thomas would have one. The one distinguishing exclusive marker caused by chance could only belong to James Casbolt and his body. Presently, Casbolt unzipped his jacket, lifted his shirt and pointed to the small darker blemish on his left side. It was faint; the Nindingir genetics allowed for diversity and perfection, but it did not prevent the deficiencies that occurred in the birth canal of his mother. "This one?"

Thomas Jones simply ogled, mouth dangling.

Casbolt felt his stomach turning into water, yet he managed to smile faintly. "You do know, don't you?"

Thomas slowly took a step back, countenance traumatised.

Casbolt took a step forward. "Did you train in Antarctica?"

Thomas started to circle Casbolt. "Wha ... What do you ...?"

"Hey," Casbolt said, fixed on his image and likeness. "I want to talk—"

"Go away!" Thomas shouted, darting down the footpath, tugging his dog, running into his house, slamming the door shut.

Casbolt did not follow, for who wouldn't run off when suddenly met with a double? Casbolt knew he would've. God, he probably would have, by reflex, broken their nose, tripped them, and run away. He probably would have thought them a spy or … *Is Thomas Jones a Cabal spy? A huge ruse?* There was no evidence to verify that, but there *had* to be an explanation for this!

Thomas, I could tell, Michael put in from the Parvus input, *thinks he's going insane. After Ben tortured him in the shower … He might call the police.*

"An exact replica of myself," Casbolt whispered. "You know what this means?"

"What *does* it mean?" Michael Prince uttered.

"It means that Thomas Jones is Aes Sidhe. If he has my *exact* genetic imprint, then he's got Aes Sidhe DNA. Nindingir bread. Rh Negative blood. Psychic abilities, very likely."

"Oh … that's not right. Why would the Nindingir create a clone of you and not tell you?"

Casbolt zipped up his jacket, idly rubbing his birthmark. "I've not been told many things, Michael. The occult keeps truth and answers hidden, and I had to discover the truth myself. It wouldn't be surprising that the Nindingir and the druids cloned me."

"But … cloning technology is not even advanced yet!"

"I know. This is what terrifies me. What else could this be?"

"You know what we are going to do?"

"We shall speak to our mother," Casbolt said, opening the door to his car. A part of him really wanted to get out of this neighbourhood – he'd recorded the address on a piece of paper in his pocket in case he came back.

To gain definite answers, he would have to ask the person who gave birth to him, the genesis of his genetics, Kate Casbolt. He was never told many things about his birth – his mother would get a glazed look in her eyes, not able to recall the events clearly. He wouldn't be surprised if she had twins, but … what if she hadn't?

"Meredith and Max will be worried," Michael said. "Time must be used wisely. Go with this."

—

Later that evening, Casbolt returned to his rented apartment and phoned his mother. Gazing out his window, he watched the curry sky slowly darken and the twisted power lines innocuous below him like a net spread out to entangle him. The saguaro cactus garden grew like hulking stakes in the stony ground with needled spines.

"Hello? Who is this?" said a British voice over the phone.

"Mum? It's me, James," Casbolt said. "I'm okay. I'm in America right now."

"In Americ—" Kate caught herself. "Of course you are. Why did you leave so suddenly?"

Casbolt bit his lips. His mother's voice had a sweetness to it, a honeyed tone that invoked all the lovable childhood nostalgia – the very few fond childhood moments. "I know. I know, but can I ask you a question?"

"What is it?"

Casbolt procrastinated, struggling with how he could word his problem concisely, so it made sense to someone who couldn't understand. He found himself sighing, holding his head, perplexed. "Mum, I've been trying to track down a man. A man who looks *exactly* like me. And I don't mean some lookalike. I mean, an *exact* clone. And today, I met him face to face. His name is Thomas Jones – and he … he has my eyes, my face!" Casbolt chuckled to himself. "I know I sound crazy, Mum, but … it's stressing me out! I cannot help myself; I've been obsessed. I cannot get this out of my mind. So, I'm wondering, Mum, did you ever have twins, and no one told me?" Silence. "Has there been a secret you've been keeping?" Silence. "Mum, do I have a twin brother? I *need* to know!"

"Son." Kate's voice sounded husky behind the phone.

Casbolt wondered, *He's Aes Sidhe. Aes Sidhe have anxiety issues. His guardians must be sex traffickers.* How could Casbolt have coped in such an individual world, where all he could ever want was in his hands – his family, his new life? All of this weighed down on Casbolt with pangs of loneliness, worry and depression that worsened his condition.

"I … What are you talking about?" Kate said.

"I have a clone, and I'm losing the plot."

"A clone? How many times have you met him?"

"Once."

"Once?"

"I need validation that I'm not going insane."

"Nobody is the same person," Kate said, voice cold. "Even genetic traits run out of their expression of trait diversity. There must be *some* difference."

"There isn't," Casbolt said.

"He cannot be *exactly* the same." Kate sounded confident. She knew his condition and knew Casbolt was unstable. She often judged him for it. "Psychologically, you are different. Your characters are different. Different places and circumstances are what form your differences. If I told you that you had a twin you never knew about until now, even then he would have slight differences from you."

"Did you have a twin son?" Casbolt muttered, gradually easing his weary body into a chair.

"I don't know. I only donated my eggs to the Nindingir, and then they injected one back into my womb, fertilised by unknown sperm."

"Whose sperm was it? Who is my father?"

"Oh James, if only I knew. The Nindingir genetic programmes are stingy. They never said. They fertilised my egg with random sperm in their secret dark caves in Antarctica. But James, you and Thomas Jones *are not* clones!"

Who is my father? Frustrated, Casbolt rubbed his temples. "We are."

"Did you take your clothes off in front of him?"

"No."

"Okay, then. The last thing you need after all you've been through is to meet strange men."

"Did I have a twin?"

"No," Kate said. "No, I never had a twin boy."

Numbness clouded Casbolt's mind. "Then ... Who?"

"I'm going to pretend I never heard a word of what you just said." Kate sounded forthright and final.

Casbolt closed his eyes, and he slumped even further, hands covering his face. Vexation seethed within him, so many emotions squirming like a thousand worms in his body. "Please! I'm going mad! I just wanted some help!"

"If you want my help, stop this, and fly home! Meredith wants to go on a date with you! Don't ignore her!" Those straightforward incentives made a part of him want to obey them. "I don't want to hear any more about this! You are my *only* son! I am your *only* mother!"

Casbolt stared out the window at the sky, desolate with deformed clouds in a sultry red, forming haunted shapes. He thought he had died, for a great numbness overcame him. But it was only a trough of a wave of pain that slammed him a second later. He honestly didn't know what to do with himself – he felt like a mangled thing, an unfortunate puppy that had run into a fan.

"Don't do this to yourself," Kate snapped. "You have a nice house in

Dublin, and a girl. And to be frank here, you need to quit your conspiracy theory addictions and UFO cults!"

She is not yet deprogrammed, a part of Casbolt said. *She's still asleep. Do not trust your instincts. Question everything.*

Casbolt recalled something Max Spiers had said to him once – the same thing, but different. About responsibility. About change.

"I know this sounds ridiculous," Casbolt snapped. Oh, anger made him twitch; anger and hopelessness didn't mix. He stamped some of it down, but he was already out of his chair, pacing. "What was this? Some sort of spell from the Cabal?"

"James! You're overthinking!"

"Tell me! When the Nindingir performed controlled breeding, when they gave your egg to their IVF programme, did they make a mistake? Huh?"

Kate let out a protracted sigh. "Not that I know of."

"Well, see? That's the only explanation for this!"

Kate laughed.

"The Nindingir bloody cloned my embryo in the cave! It's all staged! It's a test! They set this all up for me, because Thomas Jones is their mistake." And yet, Nindingir were the epitome of perfection. They *never* made mistakes. The idea of a Nindingir – virgin nun scientists, disciplined, commanding vast knowledge, having perfect decorum – making mistakes seemed *outrageous*. Or… they didn't make a mistake. Rather, the cloning could've been premeditated, a prophetic plot to curse Casbolt as punishment for killing the Aquarians. *Outrageous!*

"James," Kate said. "Even if the Nindingir and the druids brought me ten men identical to you, all dressed the same, and you were stuck in the middle of them, I would point straight to my son. Maternal instinct never fails. There's nothing in the world that can overcome maternal instinct."

"I know," Casbolt groaned. "I just wish you were here to see for yourself."

"You need to take a deep breath. Think about Meredith and go home! I'm telling you, James, for your own good. All these truth rabbit holes you're getting yourself into *are not* going to end well!"

Casbolt nodded, grimacing. Outside, the sky was dark purple, and the stars were flickering in pinpricks. Arizona had an arid beauty to it – raw and wild. So different to England and Antarctica. "I understand."

"Hm. Of course you do. I will see you soon. Bye."

As soon as Casbolt hung up the phone, loneliness, like a heavy, clogging grey web, suffocated him. Casbolt couldn't simply let this go or brush it aside.

He had to explain to himself why he could interact with an exact biological entity that *was* him and *not* him at the same time!

Casbolt retreated into the bathroom – and Michael Prince took control.

"Could you live with a family – a wife and a child – with the knowledge of our other's existence?" Michael asked as he slowly ambled towards the mirror. "We need to go back, do we? Antarctica. Dating Meredith." He rubbed his temples. "Thomas wouldn't want us. But what if this is a clue? Thomas was suffering from the Bleakness. He's us, but acts like a child."

A child or not, Thomas Jones, according to the news reports, had a stepfather named Neil, reminding Casbolt of his Neil, who was a drug abuser, who scandalised him with pornography, and he'd also kept snakes and scorpions as pets. He'd used one of the harmless snakes one time when performing a Cleopatra VII ritual orgy on him for Hiram Abiff.

Who was Hiram Abiff? Casbolt groaned, letting out an exhale of such a random thought. It was all too much. The Bleakness …

"Am I really a mistake?" Casbolt rasped. "Are the DID and the trauma-based mind control finally taking their toll? How am I supposed to be a strong leader – a Chief of the Iceni – to fight the Galactic Tyrant, if I cannot even … If I cannot even …"

We're a mistake, a voice poisoned his soul.

A shiver of fear ran down his spine. Casbolt stared at nothing – he couldn't put into words what he felt – the incredible failure and insecurity. He watched as a single tear trickled down his cheek. He wiped it away with a curt motion, snarling at his pathetic self in the reflection. He clawed at his face.

He lingered in the bathroom for a long time. Time did not matter when his very existence, his dignity, could be in jeopardy.

Suddenly, he tore off his shirt, touching the birthmark on his chest.

"I have a whole reputation – a whole life – ahead of me," Casbolt sobbed. "I have a new hope – to change, to become a better man, and it's all slipping away from me!" He slammed the sink basin, roaring in frustration.

"Fight it!" Redlion growled. "Enough, Snowchick! My family is mine! Meredith is mine!"

"I am James Casbolt!" He thumped the mirror with his palm, staring at his wobbling reflection vitriolically. "I am James Casbolt!"

"Cas," Michael Prince said.

"What are you doing to me?" Casbolt moaned. "Whatever you are doing to me … Stop."

"I'm not doing anything to you," Redlion growled.

"Whatever you are doing to me," Casbolt muttered with a small voice, staring deep into his own blue eyes. "Stop it."

"It's not me," Michael said.

Redlion cackled.

"Then what is it?"

"I don't know."

Casbolt punched the mirror, his hand stinging. Cracks webbed out across the panel. "You're *supposed* to know!" he bellowed in a burning fit of rage.

Suddenly, he paced, taking a deep breath, regaining composure.

"The best solution, the simplest, would be to end the relationship," Casbolt said. "I need to keep my family safe. I need to listen to the voice of Laocoon, the priest of Troy. To harken unto his warnings, for the city would be destroyed if the horse made out of the wood of Achaean ships enters through the gates. Pious Laocoon is always right. He desperately fought the giant serpents off his sons. How many Troys have fallen when they failed to hear Laocoon?"

"There is no wooden horse outside your walls, Casbolt," Michael countered. "You have to end this pathetic crisis now, and quickly, to get back to Meredith. You're *totally* convinced that the Cabal have cast an evil spell on you. Who will remember you as a competent father, a glamorous intrepid Aes Sidhe? When Cu Chulainn swooned, it caused Laeg, his charioteer, and Eithne, his mistress, to go to great efforts to find a cure. They struck a deal with Li Ban of Lough Neagh to restore the warrior's health. Eithne and Laeg were loyal to the end. They saw a problem and sacrificed much time to solve it. Where would *kleos* – glory – be then, if you do nothing about this Cabal curse? Find a cure for this, or it will continue to poison you. Don't bet that Eithne and Laeg will save you. Rise up, Spartan. Take your shield and come back with your shield, or on it!"

Curtailed and insubordinate, two people lay before James Casbolt's eyes – Michael Prince and Thomas Jones – each with different fruits. And, resolving in himself, he went for an amalgamation of both.

Both seemed right in his own eyes.

"To get what we both want, we need to get Thomas Jones. But something is going to happen if you don't get into the car," he mumbled, unified in one purpose, in a trance. "Thomas Jones still lives. The UN will surely mistake him for me. The UN will see his crimes and accuse me of it. I will never be vindicated for what I have done. Never, because of this *freakin' moron, Thomas!* It's a Cabal curse. It will get worse if I ignore it. Thomas Jones will take Meredith on a romantic getaway. She will not know the difference. And when I come back home, he's going to take all my things …

"What am I talking about? No, I need tactics to think this through. Battle tactics. If Thomas Jones still lives, I *have to kill him*. To live … I *need to kill* … kill him … slit the throat, pour out the blood, cut the limbs, trample him, cast him away!"

Redlion, Michael Prince and James Casbolt's concessions had a contradictory agreement – not Casbolt's dependence on Michael Prince, but Michael Prince's dependence on James Casbolt, and the Redlion optimizing that. Their mammalian urges merged then, until he saw distinction no longer, nor knew whose will influenced the other. They were of symbiotic self-preservation.

Thomas Jones – his implacable enemy – *had* to go.

———

James Casbolt knocked on Thomas Jones' door persistently later that night, hoping that he was alone. Michael Prince was in control to restrain Casbolt from going out of hand with insomnia.

As soon as the door opened, Michael Prince barged inside, bumping into Thomas Jones – a ferocious imposter wreaking havoc in the lives of Ben and Casbolt. The room of the apartment was as plain and bland as his own – even the space and arrangement were almost identical, but something was wrong about the place. The shelves, the bench, the wall painting, everything seemed *darker*.

Michael Prince shivered. *Oh, this is witchery.*

"What are you doing here?" Thomas gasped, almost choking on his own words.

Michael Prince preferred not to look at his double. He paced, exploring the house. "What is this place? Is it where you live?"

"Get out," Thomas said stubbornly. "Go away!"

"No. No, I want to talk to you personally," Michael said, turning around. "I'm here to protect James Casbolt. So, you're going to answer my questions. Answer correctly, build my trust, and you can go free."

The twin twitched. "Get out. Or … I will call the police."

The Parvus suggested that Thomas Jones wouldn't call the police at all – he was too terrified to even do that. Michael chuckled, shoulders trembling. "Oh, go ahead! What will you tell them?" Michael smiled smugly. "What will you say to them, man? What?"

Thomas wilted – his face going dark.

"There are some things I want to tell you, man to man."

"Why did you come looking for me?" Thomas asked, voice distressed. His blue eyes were unreadable. "Why do you look like me?"

"That's what I want to know," Michael Prince said slowly. "You broke James Casbolt. Are you a Cabal hex?"

Sweat pearled Thomas' forehead. "Casbolt *is me*."

"We *all* are." Michael Prince smiled. "So, tell me? If you are James Casbolt, and I am James Casbolt, do you have a girlfriend?"

Thomas Jones went pale, his chest inflating. "I don't know what you are talking about."

Parvus Perception told Michael Prince that Thomas was lying. *Kill him! Kill him! Kill him! I will …*

Redlion's knuckles went white. *Summon the Spear. Kill –*

SHUT UP! Casbolt roared back.

Kill …

Michael Prince fought for control once more. He felt exhausted. He'd been staring at nothing for a few seconds. "Man, just answer my question."

"You're crazy," Thomas yelped, swaying off balance, hand fiddling with his jumper.

Michael Prince took a step back, raising one hand to calm him down. "All right." There was something about that remark – that he was crazy – which had an objective cogency to it. If he was James Casbolt and the Redlion was frothing to kill Thomas – to end this futility, it would all be so easy – so passionately insane to call himself unstable. "I'm crazy. You bring my loved ones into this, man …"

Thomas looked up at Michael Prince fearfully. His lips moved, but no sound came out.

Michael stared at his clenched fists. "Tell me!" he bellowed, beating his chest. "Am I crazy? Talk to me! *Am I crazy?* Do you know a woman named Meredith?"

Suddenly, at that name, Thomas' face lit up.

Eyes bulging, Michael Prince let out an exhale. "You … know."

Stalker …

"What do you know about Meredith MacKinnon?"

Michael cannoned into Thomas, pushing him into the wall. The sheer confused terror on Thomas' confounded face and body slithering down the wall said that he knew. He didn't restrain Michael Prince from giving in to his wrath. James Casbolt, at the back of the mind, trembled in woe.

"I swear to God, if you bring Meredith into this," Redlion hissed, Michael Prince clashing, trying to restrain the indignation.

Strangle him! Michael Prince's hand clasped around Thomas' throat. *Crush him! Do it!* He held out his other hand, ready to summon his Curruid Spear.

A tremendous force assaulted him. Thomas pounded Michael Prince's arms away, flying at him with wild attacks. Michael Prince staggered, but Thomas mewled like a dinosaur. Thomas pushed Michael, then crashed into a shelf, hands scrabbling for a bottle of vodka. He threw it, striking Michael Prince's head.

65

THE TURQUOISE ROOM

"'Awake, Sleeper!
  Rise from among the dead ones!
And the Messiah will shine on you!'
  Therefore, watch carefully how y'all walk, not as unwise, but as wise, redeeming the
time, for the days are evil. Because of this, don't be foolish, but discern what is the will of
Yahweh."
  —From the Epistle to the Ephesians, Paul, Tim Mackie's Literal-literary
Translation, c. 60 – 62 CE.

James Casbolt awoke slowly, head throbbing with a terrible concussion, his skin sticky. The ground vibrated lullingly, as if he was in a moving vehicle.

His nose twitched – his Parvus Perception alerting him that something was *very* wrong, due to the heavy, sweaty, sour smell of alcohol around him.

Don't rest, Michael Prince said. *You're in danger.*

Casbolt's eyes flew open and saw a dark covering above his head. He stretched out his hands, feeling the hard wooden walls on both sides of him. He tried to extend his legs and felt his bare feet strike against more wood.

Darkness enclosed him; the heat was so oppressive that sweat covered him. Buried alive.

He was taken to Wiltshire. To Danu. The purple girl.

Thomas attacked us! He's the enemy!

Casbolt tried to yell, but his throat closed with petrified horror in a strangled gulp. Heart blundering in his chest, he refused to accept that there was nothing he could do to save himself, so he raised his arms, beating the shadow looming above his head.

His fists hit soft canvas. His panic only partly subsided. He had a lapse on how he ended up here.

Casbolt tried retracing his steps, painful step by painful step.

He'd come to the badlands to hunt his clone Thomas Jones. From there, things became a blur. Michael Prince took full control out of compassion for Casbolt.

We were attacked! Casbolt thought. *Thomas Jones attacked us!*

Clumsily, Casbolt rolled to his side, trying to poke the sheet above him. He pushed it harder, as if trying to break through. He found that the canvas, the farther he pushed, went taut, as if it was clipped to something.

The ground shook, trembling as if the loud vehicle had hit a bump in the road. The ground of the dirt road, indicating …

I'm in a truck! Someone's kidnapping me! Away from people to save me.

Very unlikely, Thomas' van had been confiscated by authorities due to his illegal driver's licence. The only obvious answer was that Thomas sold him off to his superiors.

Relief, shame and horror warred in Casbolt's mind, thoughts tumbling over one another.

As this last despairing thought invaded Casbolt, Michael Prince reassured him.

We just have to wait until these people take you out. Then you can find a way to sneak away when they're not looking.

Suddenly, the swaying of the vehicle ceased. The sounds of slammed doors and feet crunched against the ground. There were low, mumbling voices. Deep voices.

Casbolt played dead. He sweated profusely, dripping with it from the stuffy heat, as the canvas unclipped. He felt the entities gazing at him, their breathing heavy and grotesque. Seconds felt like minutes, and a robust hand hauled Casbolt out of the box, grabbing and pulling his sweaty shoulders, arms, his bottom and his legs. About three or four pairs of hands were carrying him outside. It was night, for it was cold. Casbolt with the Parvus could pick up the crunch of footsteps, the crickets chirping and occasional cars passing by on the road.

I'm being carried by men, Casbolt thought. He strained his ears to hear and his nose to smell. Was that hair gel?

The men grunted, feet scraping the ground as they hauled him to a dark area and laid his body down on smooth paved stone, back propped up against the wall.

"You have the key, Fire Bringer?" a man's voice said.

"No need. Circe's already home with some guests." Casbolt could tell that this second man was the superior – a dry, deep grumbling voice – he was full of malice and conceit.

The doorbell rang and opened.

"Ah, Fire Bringer. It's you again." A woman with a strange accent sounded miffed. "Who the hell is that?"

"James Casbolt. The Aes Sidhe Chief from Antarctica."

"Does it look like I don't know? Did we ask for a delivery? We wanted the Puerto Rican girls! Not a barbaric berserker!"

Casbolt's heart leapt. *What girls did they want? Puerto Rican?*

"I think you did. We have them."

"This all must be a great mistake."

"Wait!"

Silence.

"It would be unwise to rescind asura and a Skin Walker."

"I'm not aware of what agenda you have or what your masters have. They told you to seek me, didn't they?"

"Yes, Kadlu."

"Crap. How the hell did you get your hands on James Casbolt?"

"Don't ask for details. It's a focal point."

Tension and anxiety riddled the air. The woman possibly thought about *geas* and the revenge of the Aes Sidhe coming to rescue their Chief. Casbolt knew because he had done it before. The Aquarians, Temarunda, and saving Heather Baglio and Blake Gates from Tulugaak's hands. But what concerned Casbolt the most was the mention of the girls from Puerto Rico.

Julian's daughters?

You've been kidnapped by the men in black, he thought with the Parvus Perception. *Thomas sold you off to them.*

"Very well." The woman sighed. "This is what happens when there is a lack of communication. Might as well bring him in now. See what the Devi can do with him."

Someone punched him in the stomach, and Casbolt grunted, flicking his eyes open.

His captors loomed over him, reaching seven feet tall. Three of them. They wore dark suits, fedora hats and sunglasses. The leader wore a cape and was of a darker complexion than the others. Now the hair gel smell made sense – these vampires had emotionless faces, for they were the men in black. Cabal agents.

Casbolt growled, trying to stand up, but biliousness set in, and he stumbled to the side, into one of the men in black's arms.

"Why did you lie to me, Camazotz?" Kadlu said stridently.

"The concussion had worn off, sister," the pale, almost blue-skinned giant said. He wore a wide-brimmed hat, polarised glasses and was tall and broad, his face like Alfred Bonner – rectangular and mean. On his hand that grasped Casbolt was a watch in the shape of a Batman bat. Next to him was a giant a head taller than everyone. Under his cape, he wore a leather jacket, an allusion that made Casbolt think of the Terminator.

Why the hell do they wear sunglasses at night? Curiosity got the better of him, and reaching out his hand, he pulled one of the man's glasses off.

The third man in black, with grey polychrome marbled skin, hissed, his large, slanted cat eyes squinting from the light inside the house. "What are you doing?" He shoved Casbolt roughly, picking up his glasses from the ground.

The second man, with the Batman watch – Camazotz – punched Casbolt, weakening him. "He's a fool, Fire Bringer. Not thinking straight," he said dryly, hauling Casbolt up. "Bind him, Khonsu."

The polychrome grey-skinned man Casbolt had humiliated growled, pulling out a string from his pocket, and began to bind Casbolt's hands behind his back. He resisted, but the men in black held him down.

"Enough fighting on the doorstep, boys!" Kadlu snapped. "Come on! You lot are worse than men." The miffed woman was Native American, tall and willowy, wearing an orange tightly fitting dress that sparkled in the electric light from inside the hotel. She had dark eyeliner, her hands on her hips and smelled of pleasant perfume.

Casbolt gazed at his surroundings. He was in some courtyard, on the porch of some elaborate house or resort. A pathway went around a well-cultivated Scottsdale garden with fountains watering them, and the walls were palace-like, orange-pink with ceramic decorations. The premises were as large as a manor, with thick adobe walls finished with white stucco – hacienda-style architecture.

"Where am I?" Casbolt asked, holding his head. "Where's Thomas Jones? Tell me!"

The woman chuckled. "Chief Agaid, this is La Posada Hotel," she said in a languid hauteur. "Follow me." When Kadlu walked, she swayed; her high heels made clanking sounds on the stone. "Hang your hats on the hanger.

Circe the Devi will deal with you."

The men in black did so, removing their hats, hanging them on the hanger by the entrance on the orange walls. None of them removed their polarised glasses.

The leader turned to the other two, scowling at them. "Not one ounce of dignity in you two," he grumbled. "I foreknew you would be incompetent for this task. I should have been wise enough to pick from the others. When we get to the Crater, I can be rid of you imps."

The Crater? Alarmed, Casbolt stared at his giant captors – the man with the glasses Casbolt had removed. Camazotz's mouth was in a rictus. Two vampiric teeth were prominent.

The men in black hauled and pushed Casbolt to walk inside, holding his arms at his back. The hotel was warm, welcoming and curated with displays and antiques like a museum gallery. With arched doorways made of stone, shady porches, and massive, coffee-coloured domed roofs hanging with small, black, iron chandeliers, lighting up the room in gold, brown and bronze. A dark paved stone floor stretched out before him. On the walls were Navajo-styled fabric cloth of navy blue with yellow, white, and red patterns. Casbolt was led by Kadlu and the men in black towards a three-way junction at the end of the hall. Before them was a glass doorway leading outside and two rooms to the right and the left.

Voices groaned down the hall to the left, and Kadlu led the men in black that way. The room was separated into two parts. The ceiling was made of elaborate undulating patterns – aqua turquoise with diamond mosaics. Chandeliers and feathery webbed dreamcatchers hung on the ceiling, lighting up the restaurant with numerous tables and chairs, converged into one large table for the feast. More Navajo-patterned fabrics covered the walls, and to the left were three colourful stained-glass windows of saints. At the far corner of the turquoise restaurant was an empty hearth, with two sofas and two wooden chairs, standing lamps and a decorative statue of a mischievous spirit on a pedestal that reminded Casbolt of a Polynesian tiki.

It confused Casbolt as to why the Cabal would select such a lavish hotel for his thraldom.

Classy men and women sat on the table drinking and guffawing. At the head of the table was a woman with a low neckline exposing considerable cleavage. But her eyes were hawklike – she took notice of everything. They unnerved him, for those eyes seemed all-knowing, Parvus aware, like his own. Pure amber irises glittered like two solar jewels in her austere and beautiful face. She wore black lipstick, eyeliner thick with kohl, and her hair a tawny light brown, long tresses winding around her swan neck and over her left shoulder. She was Mediterranean, and her corset and dress were opulently embroiled in gold-white to a pale brown. It showed off her body well with the tones of her skin. On her hands were beige leather gloves. She was poised and in control.

But the woman's eyes were strikingly disconcerting. They were radiantly wonderful in the lamplight.

That's Circe, Casbolt thought. *An enchantress of dark magic. Beauty queen. Sex worker. What a romantic name to take for oneself. It must be her epithet.*

The people feasting were a mixed lot, who included matronly women and shabby-looking businessmen. Their light eyes stared at Casbolt with vitriolic annoyance – as if they all recognised him. Some, already enjoying their wine, gave him a gaze, and, laughing, they mocked Casbolt with a slur of awful words. They wore smart casual clothes, from suits to shirts with distinctive styles.

Upon Kadlu and the three men in black's approach, the golden-eyed woman arrayed sumptuously stood up, stretching out her arms to silence the din. "Grace honours me with your presence, Prometheus Pyrkaios – son of Iapetus."

The tallest of the men in black bowed his head. Something about his looks reminded Casbolt of Alfred Bonner – sharp angular features and that strange pink tentacle scar that ran down his neck, under his collar and possibly across his chest.

Casbolt frowned as considerations entered his mind. *No. Prometheus is one of the Titans of mythology. It has to be a nickname.*

Yet, the men in black's cloaks hung inert, and they walked with a viper grace. Inhuman, but not exactly divine. *What is this gathering for? This might be a special occasion, a festival the Cabal celebrates.*

"The Aes Sidhe has come to our feast unexpectedly," Kadlu intoned contemptuously, eyes sliding across the guests. "Sit," she said to Casbolt, her imperative sure and sharp, pointing to a lone chair next to the hearth, away from the feasting table but close enough to Circe that Casbolt could smell her and speak to her. "He will not be served, for he is cursed with *geas* for his massacre."

Massacre? The Parvus Perception confirmed: Carnutes. *The Horned Ones. The Aes Sidhe that I killed and ran out of Antarctica, working for the Cabal.* It would explain these people's light hair and their light eyes and their disdain towards Casbolt.

As Casbolt was thrust into the chair roughly, the murmur of conversation began, and the soft music resumed.

"I've been here longer than most of you," the giant Prometheus said, taking a seat with his two servants near the head of the table. "Like the rest of you, I figured we could get by on what we got."

One of the men at the table, wearing a holiday Hawaiian shirt, with pointy, upturned black eyebrows, bellowed out a drunken laugh. "Parties, hotels and chickens! Anywhere we go, you can guarantee there will be chickens for sale, and there are plenty of young ones to go around."

"Michael Aquino," Circe sighed. "Now is not the time to be horny! We need to be ready and at the Crater by three twenty-two a.m. The alignment is a revitalisation. A renewal."

"Indeed," Prometheus rumbled. "I foresee that it is our only hope to maintain our power in our assigned homelands. When people migrate, they bring us on their back with them."

"The Tyrant's demarcation of our hegemonic landscape is compromised and crap," came a scrappy voice from an unruly woman, wearing a backwards trucker's cap, lean jeans and a striped pink, black and white shirt some rock star would wear. Half of her long hair hung over her right shoulder and the other half of her head was shaved bald. She was ripping into her steak, knife in one hand and fork in the other, stuffing it into her mouth, slumped over her meal, chewing. "But compared to other places today, America is the greatest place in the world, thanks to the Freemasons! I joined them once." The woman grinned.

"How, Bellona?" one of the men in black said. "You're a woman."

"I *transcend* gender, you fool!" Bellona said with a mouthful, pointing at Casbolt with her fork. She had a strange oestrous look in her eyes. "You see, this demigod already knows who I am! I find men of war compelling, and America too, because it has fought over ten wars since it was founded – a world record! Regrettably, Julian was … unstable. That Alliance mind-controlled slave wasn't much of a loyalist to Bonner or to me. Julian served nobody but himself. A wife *does not* like that."

"Julian," Casbolt gasped. "You're Julian's wife! That's who you are!"

But how, if she is a man?

Bellona slammed a fist on the table. "Why did you have to say that? You have the Parvus, of course! You piece of crap! That lewd mortal died in combat, and it is *not* my fault that my daughters are ready to be given to the Danavas!

I can be whatever I want to be when I feel like it. Humans do it all the time. It comes with the territory. You get 'em and you lose 'em." Bellona began to chomp on her food again. "Besides, there is *so much* pay for selling chickens."

Casbolt frowned. *So this is the goddess, the mother of the Indigo Children, and she wants to kidnap them and send them to … Who are the Danavas? Child sex traffickers? Chicken is a key word for a child sex slave.* Casbolt shivered. *Christ …*

There was an air of agreement and a few nods among the hideous paedophiles. Casbolt was left with a bewildered array of emotions. Some waiters in white blouses brought food and drink for the men in black. But Casbolt sat inert in the chair, hands bound, his mind remaining the most active part of him.

I failed Julian. He became a victim of these gods – these paedophiles. The pagan gods are paedophiles! Crap! The stakes, everything, have just escalated. I'm trapped by the gods, and what will my family, Meredith and Max Spiers think of my terrible mistakes?

"The New World is great," Kadlu, the child trafficker, said, inhaling her meal. "But the southwest is too hot for me. I like cold Canada and Alaska. The old gods are generally welcoming. I learnt a few things here while in Winslow. It is famous in an Eagles song."

"Sing it for us, Kadlu! Sing!" someone raucous called. A tall man with bleached white tousled hair, who wore a formal suit and a badge on his lapel with the Freemason square and compass. The man's face was covered with burned skin, and his lips were marred by a row of welts all the way around his mouth. His eyes were deep blue and the white around them was azure. Ophidian-like and not human. But something about his mischievous, chiselled face reminded Casbolt very much of Tulugaak.

"Ah, Loki, it might be improper," replied Kadlu. "Singing might cause a thunderstorm. There are many other great and sacred landmarks in Winslow on Route 66 besides the great Crater."

Beauty queen Circe replied with a whimsical smile. "When the people of the Old World came to America," she said with an eloquent voice, "they brought us with them. Their culture with them. The gods and goddesses. We should be grateful, not exploiting them … Most of the time."

"No, the settlers of America were Puritans," Casbolt said curtly. "They believed in one God."

"Ahh," Circe said, tipping back her head haughtily. "Those Reformers of the Tyrant were *failures*. Their own Catholic and Orthodox forefathers excluded them! Forget those pests. The Puritans weren't the first. What about the Freemasons? Hmm? The Vikings? Tell me, demigod! They were migrants from Europe, which is an extremely diverse continent. Columbus had people on his ships who were educated in the Classics. The majority of the population that inherit European culture came from the ancient Celts, Greeks and Romans, did they not?"

Casbolt nodded, dumbfounded. She had a valid point.

"This is our new horizon in the American Wild West. The fire of the West burns in America. The denizen gods of this region are frisky about newcomers, and so should they be, as governments are to refugees. So, we've found our little niche, getting by. We steal, we cheat, we indulge, and we exist in the cracks at the edges of society, where no one is watching us too closely. But most importantly, we thrive with the occult Deep State."

"Why is this important to you?" Casbolt said. "The Crater?"

"It's a grave of one of our great masters – an ancient fallen celestial being," Kadlu said. "You are fooling yourself if you don't believe that the Galactic Tyrant is trying to destroy us. He, Yaldabaoth, will use enemy gods and the Alliance for his own ends. It is time for us to band together against Yaldabaoth. It is time for us to act."

Who is Yaldabaoth? Is that the Galactic Tyrant's name? "Tell me, who are you? Are you the real Circe, then? The daughter of the fallen Titan Helios?"

Grounding her jaw, dawn-eyed Circe pulled her chair out, stood up and removed her glove, brushing the small lamp behind her on the coffee table by the hearth next to Casbolt with her fingers. It became crystal, a shaft of pure, flawless quartz. The light sent a spectrum of rainbow sparkles across the turquoise room through the crystal of the transformed lamp.

Casbolt's eyes bulged. The table hadn't turned into crystal, only the lamp – it *became* crystal.

"You're …" he grunted, causing the woman to stare at him imperiously.

"You have said," she said, flexing her glove back on. "Has the cat got your tongue, darling?" The smug smile on Circe's face was pointed, milky teeth and tar lips, elegant and wonderful. She took a seat, turning her head to examine the crystal pillar that stood on the coffee table – the magic trick had turned everyone's attention, and soon they were all clapping their hands. "I'm sure this wouldn't have insurance costs," said Circe. "This ornament would be a nice delicacy."

"You're in charge of the Carnutes. How?"

"Your questions make my head burn, honey."

"And you hate me because you privilege power rather than honour."

Circe tipped back her head and laughed. It would have been wondrously elegant, as smooth as oil, calm as windless water, if she were not a snakelike child trafficker. "Your scepticism is *adorable*, Aes Sidhe. Don't worry. You're too valuable to become swine." The witch's lambent eyes studied Casbolt hungrily.

"You … You're saying all the gods are real?" Casbolt was stunned. "Zeus? Poseidon? Apollo? They exist? And they're sex-craved paedophiles?"

"Ooooh," the witch gloated. She addressed the Carnutes. "I don't think he knows who he actually is!"

"What? I'm James Casbolt. An Aes Sidhe Chief."

"Yeah, should we tell him?" Loki spoke up.

"Nah. Leave it, hon," Circe said with a flick of her hand. "It wouldn't help for him to know."

What do they mean? I know who I am!

And Michael Prince said, *God. This night is getting stranger by the minute.*

"But my question was, who are you? Are you Circe from the myths? Are the Greek gods real?"

"My divinity shines in me like the last rays of the sun before setting into the sea," Circe intoned. "I thought once the gods were the opposite of death, but I see now they are more dead than anything. They are ground to dust, hard stones devoured. Though unchanging, they hold nothing in their hands. All my life, I have pushed forward, and now I am here at this pinnacle of change. The gods have a mortal's life."

Casbolt frowned at those perplexing words. "Your riddles are not flattering, Circe."

"You claim to be an expert on riddles, then?"

"What? No, I—"

"The Aes Sidhe are renowned poets!" Bellona toyed. "Come on, Casbolt! Entertain us this equinox and tell us a riddle! Let us guess them in under a minute! If you lose to us, then we will tell you our own!"

Casbolt swallowed, the string around his wrists digging deeply into his skin, troubling his circulation. It didn't help when a riot of raucous laugher came from the filthy Carnutes. They were laughing *at* him.

Michael Prince, quick! I need to think of a riddle! Something hard. Something these paedophilic gods would not know. They're not omnipotent …

Thomas Jones. Identity crisis.

"All right! Shut up! Let me speak! Let me speak!"

The gods quieted down. Letting Michael Prince formulate the words,

Casbolt focused intensely on the stained-glass windows of the church saints, as if hopefully seeking blessings from them.

"What is in a mirror that walks?

What is an illusion that talks

And is an enemy?"

The riddle out loud sounded feeble and lame. A dreadful pall of silence followed, faces of deep thought, seething, thinking. Susurrations hissed between the Carnutes. "What is in a mirror that walks? What is an illusion that talks and is an enemy?"

"Yourself?" someone slurred, chuckling.

"Nope." Casbolt wet his lips, hopeful and exhilarated. At twenty seconds, watching the goddesses, the men in black and the Carnutes giggling among themselves, he thought, *I have stumped the* Carnutes.

"Thomas Jones," Loki proclaimed, shooting up onto his feet, chair scuffing the floorboards. "Thomas Jones is a Skin Walker who mirrors you! He walks and talks and is an illusion because he is not you and is your foul enemy!"

"What?" Casbolt bellowed, shooting up from his chair, the string marking his wrists as he tried to pull them apart. The man in black – Khonsu – rose and tackled him, grunting. "How could you possibly know? Thomas Jones is with you all, isn't he? You bloody cursed me, that's what! You bastards! Good riddance. I slaughtered your kind!"

"Impulsive brat," Bellona said in mock aghast.

"I said that riddle to test you! Now I know! Haha! Thomas Jones *is one of you,* for how else could you have known about him?"

Circe's face was blank. "Thomas Jones is all over the news."

"Yeah, but—"

"All right, all right," Loki said whimsically. "It is our turn now to *riddle* you with fear."

"I don't want your games!" Casbolt snarled. Growling, he bumped Khonsu with his shoulder, causing him to fall to the ground with a yelp. The Carnute women giggled and laughed. Khonsu sat on the ground, dusting his suit with his hand, adjusting his glasses.

"What a show this is," Loki said jubilantly, raising his mug of ale in his hand. He took a great gulp, smacking his lips. "Ahhh. Remember the rules, rule breaker. The UN will prosecute you for what you have done. And I will be there, spectating with my mates. You lost, and now you must guess our riddle in one minute. You guess wrong, and time lapses, you will be our surrogate tonight."

Insufferable, Casbolt thought, feeling clammy and hot.

His reptilian eyes shimmering, Loki proclaimed his riddle performatively.

"Heavier than a cat's paw, which cannot be lifted.

Deeper than a jug of ale that cannot be drunk.

Stronger than an old mother, who cannot be defeated.

Of each of these, what are they?"

Casbolt sank back onto his chair. The Parvus burned vigorously, seeking, scrabbling for knowledge, an inference, a play on words, analogies, metaphor, ontology, feline, drink, old mother, heavy, cannot lift, deep, cannot be drunk, strong, cannot be defeated.

"You had to pick an esoteric one, didn't you?" Casbolt muttered.

What was heavier than a cat's paw? *Everything* that was heavier than a cat's paw!

"A tiger."

"Incorrect," Loki said, looking at his watch. "Try again."

Casbolt hissed in frustration. Heavier than a cat … "An elephant?"

Loki shook his head.

Casbolt moved to the next question. What was deeper than a jug of ale? Deep water? "A well is deeper than a jug."

"Close. Deeper than that."

"Uhmm. An ocean!"

"Correct!" Loki clapped his hands quickly. "Now, demigod! Two more to go!"

Prideful, Casbolt thought of the meaning of the next paradox. What was stronger than an old woman? "A warrior is stronger than an old woman!"

"No. Fifteen seconds."

"A giant!"

Loki shook his head.

"A mountain! A … A Fomorian!"

"All wrong. Think existentially."

"Umm. Love?"

"Ten seconds. Hahaha! I'm giving you *too many* hints!"

The Carnutes were cheering, counting down the seconds. Rasping, Casbolt slumped back into his seat, his brain overheating, heart thundering. He got one part of the riddle right. He had an inclination that the last two answers were obvious, but they eluded him utterly. Fear gripped him, sullying his thinking.

"Four!"

Heavier than a cat's paw, which cannot be lifted.

"Three!"

Stronger than an old mother, who cannot be defeated.

"Two!"

Casbolt gave up. He was exhausted, the Parvus dulled, and Michael Prince was silent.

"One! Ohhhhh! Time's up!" A sadistic, devilish, sinister rictus appeared on Loki's scorched face.

"Time … The old … *old* age! Old mother is time! Time and ageing cannot be defeated!" Casbolt shot to his feet, triumphant.

But Loki was unfazed by Casbolt's exclamations. "You still failed to answer the first part of the riddle. Nothing can be heavier than the chaos serpent, the Dragon. Nothing can be deeper than the ocean, the Great Deep of the Abyss. And nothing that exists can defeat the old crone of Time, which brings with her the dance of death and destruction."

Casbolt found hot rage at all these sex-loving Carnutes boiling inside of him. He had been despairingly slighted, proved too incapable to match the scorn intelligence of these people. *I shouldn't have come to America in the first place. I should have left Thomas Jones alone.*

And let the Cabal get away with trafficking Julian's daughters? Michael Prince said. *You're meant to be here.*

Unwilling to compromise his dignity any further, he kept his peace for the rest of the feast, thinking. He ignored all remarks directed towards him and sat in stubborn silence until Prometheus came looming over him like a dark tower.

"The time has come to bring the unseen into the seen," the giant man in black said, yanking Casbolt to his feet.

As the feast ended and waitresses began their ablutions, the Carnutes, led by Circe, issued out of the turquoise room, leaving Casbolt and the three men in black to leave last. It was not to show solicitude at all; for the giants hauled the bound Casbolt out of the La Posada Hotel, taking up their hats and storming into the late unholy night. The moon was completely dark.

Casbolt was hungry, thirsty and too fatigued to care how much time had passed. The singular motive to find Thomas Jones in him dithered, and he couldn't understand it. When the men in black placed him back in the trailer of their truck, they jumped inside the carriage to rearrange stored packages inside crates. Casbolt lay his back on the side, his eyes feeling heavy.

"Camazotz, come here." Prometheus' stark voice drew Casbolt out of his drowsiness. "You mixed the Jiroft items up. Put them in here, you bastard. Leave the Baghdad ones in the other crates."

Casbolt cracked open an eye. "Bagh—" he stopped mid-word.

He examined the crates. They were large, and nine of them were stored at the back of the trailer, stacked two on top of each other. Prometheus, with the two men in black carrying items in their hands, began to rearrange the articles in one of the crates. Khonsu carried a large stone goblet decorated with an embossed relief of a man grasping with both hands the tails of two leopards. Camazotz hauled out a sculpture of dark stone in the congealed shape of a scorpion. A serpent creature coiled around on top of its head, touching the scorpion's stinger. Casbolt knew they had occult significance, but his Parvus Perception was still too feeble to detect any information. Prometheus, helping them, carried a slab in the shape of a man with circular shapes marking his body, his arms raised with feathers sprouting out of them and a helix of intertwined serpents and tail feathers for feet.

Casbolt's heart started to pump. *Oh, you've got to be kidding me. All the stolen artefacts from the Baghdad Museum have been stored right here inside this trailer! God!*

Then when anything couldn't get any worse, behind the crates Casbolt saw two small girls, gagged with duct tape and bound with ropes back to back. He saw them, and the Parvus knew; they were Clarita and Lluvia. Julian's daughters.

"You bastards!" Casbolt fell forwards, crawling.

"Hey!"

"You better not touch those girls!"

"None of your business." Creeping up to Casbolt, the man in black tore off his glasses in the dark – though Casbolt could barely see. But Khonsu's eyes were *gigantic*, thin silted feline eyes that blazed with sharp intensity. "You modern humans are *horrifically* disrespectful to these relics. Instead of using them to bring the unseen into the seen, you store them in museums, advertising them like merchandise. Do you think we fill our pockets doing this?"

Casbolt ground his jaw, hearing the footsteps of Prometheus and Camazotz walking out of the trailer and onto the gravel ground outside. He shook his head. "What about the children?"

"Danavas want to trade," Khonsu said. "These Indigo Children of Bellona are worth the deal."

"What? What is a Danava?"

"It's classified."

"Argh! I'll make it *un*classified as long as I live!"

"You've come to a dead end, James Casbolt. There is nothing you can do." Khonsu, breathing heavily, struggled with Casbolt, shoving him into his box, wrapping the canvas back over and tightening the strings. Casbolt lay in his coffin, groaning in anger at the paedophiles who had won over him and hating himself for not doing anything sooner to save the girls from the demonic predators.

But quickly, he formulated in his head a plan to deliver Julian's daughters.

66

URIM AND THUMMIM

"Blessed is the human
who walks not in the counsel of the wicked,
nor stands in the way of sinners,
nor sits in the seat of scoffers;
but their delight is in the law of Yahweh,
and on his law, he meditates day and night.

He is like a tree
planted by streams of water
that yields its fruit in its season,
and its leaf does not wither.
In all that he does, he prospers.

The wicked are not so,
but are like chaff that the wind drives away.
Therefore, the wicked will not stand in the judgment,
nor sinners in the congregation of the righteous;
for Yahweh knows the way of the righteous,
but the way of the wicked will perish."
—Psalm 1.

One week before the Dulce assault, Joshua Tanrıöver gathered with the marines for a military debriefing. But he didn't expect to lecture to them about ancient Near Eastern myths.

He had been given the opportunity to sit with the colonels at Fort Huachuca to discuss logistics. Working as an assistant at first bothered him, because he didn't want to take part in combat again, but Pounders and Sopher knew he had a tendency to want to separate himself from company, and they thought it would be better that Joshua should choose to continue to work as a field medic. Hearing what they thought about him felt both abashing and accomplishing.

But lingering in his mind, he worried about Ben DePaula missing out. Earlier, Joshua had told Ben in prison, secretly, about two significant visions Joshua had. It wasn't much, but he would be trustworthy in a very small matter.

Before the debriefing meeting, Demos had been kind enough to order from the local store Greek souvlaki wrapped in a gyros pita with chicken, beef and lamb. While they were all eating around the table at the mess hall, Marcus Theis nudged Joshua, saying, "Hey, Joshua, you going to tell us what you learnt about the artefacts Alfred Bonner found at Uruk?"

Great question. About time I told someone. "Well, I discovered that Bonner was breaking all UNESCO cultural heritage laws looking for what is mythical at best."

"During war," Marcus said, oily wrapper clutched in his hands, "the laws don't work. Usually."

"True. But I tell you, Bonner is a leader of a political cult that worships Lucifer. He's not an archaeologist."

"Hmm … Lucifer." Marcus seemed flummoxed. "No one questioned him, though."

"He's a master con man, Marcus. He is a raider and a looter. Not a professional by any stretch of the imagination. Because of him, we could have proof that there was a historical reality to the Epic of Gilgamesh. But no one took measurements or photos or documented anything about this tomb! They just stole the coffin and removed it from its context, robbing us of so much information!" Joshua slapped the table. "Stupid Luciferian morons!"

"We did take photos, actually," Johnny came in, sounding vehement, "but they were either corrupted by some geomagnetic interference or Bonner confiscated them."

"Yeah, Johnny," Joshua said. "It's remarkable what you found, but I'm afraid Egyptologists and Assyriologists will not take our word for it unless the finds in Uruk are published. Unfortunately, that will *never* happen as long as Alfred Bonner is alive. The coffin is most certainly at the Dulce base. And from your testimony and my research, I think it's a coffin for a god-king."

Joshua refrained – he had to do his best to summarise his scholarly work to these laymen soldiers. He needed to demonstrate that, as a pacifist, his value to them was more than carrying and saving the wounded. He also had all the information about the objective of their mission. "During my university semester this year that Judd so graciously paid for"—he slid a thankful smile towards the colonel, who nodded in approval—"I found out the finds at Uruk could be an amalgamation of multiple traditions. The cone-shaped mosaics. False doors. Boat graves. Offerings for the dead. Niched palace architecture and the like. It's claimed to be Gilgamesh's tomb."

"So why go to all the effort to make it top secret?" Jason Laycock said, adjusting his glasses. "Why get this coffin if you're not going to display it at a museum?"

"Do you know why it's top secret?" Joshua said, smirking. "It's because the coffin is *not* just Gilgamesh's tomb. It is also Osiris' tomb. Just like what you said, Johnny, about the Egyptian Freemasons helping you. They were there because *they knew* the coffin belonged to Osiris. After he was murdered by his jealous brother, Seth, Osiris was enthroned as the god of the Underworld to judge the deceased – a role for all of his followers who are mummified. And guess who else has that same role? Gilgamesh. The only people who worship these false gods are magicians, Freemasons and occultists."

"Ohh," Derek Fish said dramatically.

"As great as this may all seem, it doesn't make sense. This coffin that Bonner looted is perhaps the most important archaeological evidence pertaining to the cultural contact of Egypt and Mesopotamia. The first city states were established in Iraq before Egypt, during the Neolithic times. Uruk, and its regional cult centres like Eridu, were where Gilgamesh was said to have ruled. And they are old. I mean, the first cities ever in history."

"What are you getting at here?" Pounders interrupted.

"Bear with me, I'm getting there. I can confidently say, Bonner's evidence is proving what Genesis 10 and 11 and the *Enmerkar and the Lord of Aratta* stories suggest. There was a point in the distant past where all the world had one lip, or one vocabulary, not one language. We know it's impossible for all humans with their different cultures and societies to have one language. One lip or vocabulary suggests one imperial language or ideology, a metaphor for the subjugation and assimilation of conquered peoples under one culture. This was a time where many cities were Sumerian influenced. They had considerable contact with Archaic Egypt, made by movements on both land – up Mesopotamia into Syria and down into the Levantine corridor and the sea – nautical routes connected by Elam into the Gulf and around Arabia.

"So, when the *Enmerkar and the Lord of Aratta* text was uncovered in the ruins of ancient Sumer in southern Iraq, it amazed nineteenth-century European scholars because of how much it compared to Genesis 11."

"The Tower of Babel," Demos confirmed. "When God confused the languages. A story to explain why everyone has different languages."

"Correct. These tales – Gilgamesh, Osiris and the Enmerkar story – predate the Bible by thousands of years, but this *does not* invalidate everything in the Bible. God commanded humans to multiply and spread abroad, but in the Genesis 11 story, humans have gathered together in one place. It is rebellion against a divine order. The plan to consolidate against the divine command to diversify and spread across the Earth is a society without God. It is a society that is a phony peace built off scapegoating a common enemy and gathering the world together to destroy this enemy. If this impulse is nourished, an empire will form, and anything that the leaders plan to do will not be beyond them."

"The Tower of Babel story is an indictment of this human tendency," Demos said.

Joshua beamed at the Greek marine. "Yeah. It is a mockery of Babylon's narcissism. The empire in Iraq thought they were the centre of the whole Earth under their god-king, Gilgamesh. They built a tower, and God responded with justice, scattering them, diversifying them so the creation could be blessed."

"And you imply that the body of King Gilgamesh is what Bonner uncovered," Judd Pounders said from across the room, engaging in the splendid discussion. It made Joshua feel alive, an enraptured sense that he was making a difference to the world. "He wants this same unified society today. He believes we need to create a society that pictures God as a Tyrant, and we must destroy this God and all he stands for if we're to move forward as a human race."

"Spot on," Joshua lectured. "Alfred Bonner wants to *redo* what was done in ancient Eridu before God cancelled the project. He wants to unite the world against the Galactic Tyrant. A world made in Bonner's image with one lip of rebellion."

"To make his name great," Demos uttered. "To become immortal."

"So, this is why I think that the man behind the myths of Gilgamesh and Osiris may have been the rebellious one himself. In the Bible, he is called Nimrod, son of Kush. The Tower's builder. His name in Hebrew means rebel. Pretty fitting."

"Nimrod." Marcus Theis nodded. "Bonner has Nimrod's coffin." Suddenly, he threw back his head and laughed.

"Yeah, Nimrod! According to Hebrew legend, he was a mighty one on the Earth." Joshua toned his voice for a dramatic effect. "He was a mighty hunter before the Lord – a slayer of animals, a king of beasts, like Gilgamesh, wild bull on the rampage. His name was so well known that it got turned into a famous saying, 'who is like Nimrod, mighty one in battle before Yahweh!'"

Just then, for Joshua, a thematic connection in the first book in the Bible aligned with a verse from the last. *And the world will wonder and say of the Beast – who is like the Beast? Who is able to make war with him?*

"Nimrod," Derek Fish, chewing on his lamb souvlaki, said, an impish smile painting his countenance. "What a lousy name. I heard it before! Where have I heard it?"

Marcus just laughed.

Jason Laycock leapt from his chair. "Oh! It's Elmer Fudd!"

"Elmer Fudd?"

"Elmer Fudd from *Looney Tunes*!"

"Yeah, that's right! *Looney Tunes*!" Marcus chortled, holding his stomach. Someone made a silly cartoon sound.

"Remember, guys?" Derek laughed boisterously. "Elmer Fudd was called *Nimrod* when Bugs Bunny outsmarted him. Haha! Remember?"

"Yeah," Marcus beamed, clapping his hands. "*Yeah,* that's it! That's it!"

"Oh man, does that give us the right to bully him?" Johnny said, looking ambitious. "To bully Alfred Bonner, I mean?"

"Are you nuts, Johnny? Of course it does!"

"When we slay Bonner," Demos commented with a mock Bugs Bunny voice, "I dibs saying, 'Aww, you poor little Nimrod.'"

That saying caused an eruption of wheezing guffaws out of the colonels and soldiers.

"Hey, Nimrod!" Derek mocked. "Stop killing those little animals, or I'll whup your ass!"

"Nimrod!" Rubbing his face, Joshua doubled over, chuckling with uncontrollable pleasure. So strange, what had been a grave discourse about the Beast – the Dark Lord of humanity – to these men, it meant an *absolute* joke. A cartoon.

Nimrod was the spirit of Mesopotamian violence and imperialism. His name was likely a corruption of Ninurta – a deity associated with hunting in Assyria. Nimrod was based on Ninus – a legend mentioned in Ctesias' *Persica*, written during the time of the Achaemenid Persian Empire, and Berossus' *Babylonica* in the Hellenistic Seleucid Empire. In these texts, Ninus was a hunter king who founded Mesopotamian cities and was married to the neo-Assyrian Queen Semiramis, who ruled from 850 to 798 BCE. The name of this massive composite legend – Nimrod – became a slew of unsavoury synonyms, and good riddance – it displayed the success of the Hebrew author's polemic against vicious Near Eastern rulers, calling them by derogatory titles to mock their megalomania. The name turned the Sargons, Ashurbanipals, Tiglath-Pilesers and the Nebuchadnezzars into *complete buffoons*.

Until Bugs Bunny took it up.

The Bible is so rad! Joshua exalted.

"Who would be demented enough to call their son Nimrod?" Demos remarked. "It's such a *lame* name!"

"Lame name!" Demos shouted.

"Hey, Nimrod!" Derek said.

Demos gasped. "Did you just call me the Devil?"

"Yeah!"

"Bastard! You Nimrod!" Demos barked back.

"But his name became part of a famous saying," Joshua called, entertaining them. "Imagine this. You are hunting elk, firing a shot from a hundred yards."

"And you nailed it!" Derek added with mirth.

"You nailed it! And you know what they say?"

"What?" Derek said, but his eyes told he knew the answer to the rhetorical question.

"You're like Nimrod," Joshua exclaimed. "The mighty hunter. The man of myth. Gilgamesh."

"We need to start doing that," Derek remarked adamantly. "Every time I nail a three pointer." He used his hands in a mock basketball shot. "*Like Nimrod!*"

A riot of laughter erupted out of everyone.

"Oh my God! That is *so funny!*" Joshua chortled uncontrollably, hand at his mouth. Surprising how much laughter cleared away all his previous worries about the upcoming battle. "Why are these ancient authors telling us this information? It's completely arbitrary!"

"They had nothing better to do," Jason Laycock said, picking at his souvlaki, which had fallen apart.

"Nimrod," Joshua continued, "is ascribed to finding a whole united nation-state. He founded cities like Babylon, Uruk in modern day Warka –

the city Bonner sent you Ageis Unit to plunder. Nimrod also went to Akkad and Calneh, and built Nineveh – supposedly – but that city didn't exist in Nimrod's time. He also built Rehoboth-Ir, Calah and Resen. These are all archaeological sites, real cities found only in the last century and a half."

"Busy guy," Derek said.

"He consolidated all the cities in the east, in the plains of Shinar."

Pounders' eyes lit up as if some epiphany had slammed into him. "Shinar Mission. Ah, *that's why* Bonner named our mission Shinar! It's … Nimrod!"

"Yep." Joshua's muscles were hurting from smiling greatly. "You figured it out, Colonel! Here it is! The truth! Shinar is the Hebrew name for southern Iraq – the Two Rivers." He crossed his arms, feeling triumphant. "It all goes back to Nimrod."

All the marines ogled each other. "Crap! That can't be a coincidence," one of the marines unfamiliar to Joshua said. "You're saying that Bonner had this agenda all along? A plan to dig up Nimrod's tomb and use the Marine Corps as a means to an end to prepare for a phony alien invasion?"

"Apparently, Leo," Judd Pounders said gravely, leaning on the door frame. "The man is *insane* for all I know. He's caught up in a cultic fantasy. He'll kill to get what he wants – he'd caused enough trouble infiltrating the life of one of my men who is no longer with us."

Even the vague reference to Ben cast an ominous shadow over the room, causing the mirth to drain out of all the men. Joshua looked down and realised he had only gotten halfway through his lamb souvlaki.

"Agent Butcher and the FBI have begun to investigate the fringes of Mount Turnbull where Dulce Base is situated," Pounders said. "It's partly above ground, but mostly it's a subterranean base with nine levels. Level nine, being the lowest, is connected by a subway system. The San Carlos Apache and their Chief have also shown the FBI a secret cave where we might have access to the base. They say the passage is sacred."

"Just what we need, sir," Captain Marcus Theis said. "We can split up the units. One combat assault unit can take the base from the hangar above and the other from the cave below."

Pounders nodded. "We know the drill, everyone. We'll deploy our forces by the end of the week."

"Oh, that's sweet," Marcus said, putting his hand in the middle of the table. "Hands!"

Every one of the marines cheerfully tossed their hands in a tight circle, including Joshua and the colonels, one arm on top of the other. The men smelled like deodorant and oil from their meal.

"Three, two, one, NIMROD!"

"Nimrod!" the marines roared, whooping.

"Nimrod! Yeah!" Joshua laughed.

Oh … This raid was going to be the greatest form of divine justice of all time!

———

The best thing – in Ben's opinion, perhaps the only good thing – about being in military detention was the feeling that he didn't care.

He didn't worry that the man was going to get him, because the man of failure had got him. He sank into forgetfulness, doomed to live in his prison cell.

But another great thing – and sad thing – about prison was that Ben had his visions alone, away from the outside world, replete with wretched reminders that he had a daughter who needed saving. None would see his ravings.

Gather them. The First Fruits. Repent.

Those words were ingrained into him deeply. Why would he have to worry about that if he had a daughter still out there in the hands of vile men? Did he really believe in what he'd seen? Did he really think so highly of himself that God had spoken to him? Benjamin DePaula, dishonourably discharged, a narcissist deprived of his daughter and family?

Gather them.

The Church.

While in military detention, Ben had two visions over the course of a single week while in this cell. It might mean that the time of the Jewish holidays had been at hand. But Ben felt tired and languid all the time; eyes half open, he could barely reflect on the visions to figure out what they might mean for uniting the Church.

The first came on Yom Kippur – the Day of Atonement – the holiest Jewish holiday. It was a time of affliction, which literally meant to deprive the throat of eating. It was when the high priest would atone – or as Rob had coined, 'spiritually sanitise' – for the sins of all people.

Ben was a scribe named Shaphan, cleaning and sweeping a luxurious complex lit up by Jewish candelabra lamps. The complex had recessed walls and balustrades carved in the form of colonnettes with petals and voluted capitals of gold. Two prominent palmette pillars resembled fruit trees. Before him, across the golden room, were giant fifteen-foot statues of four-winged sphinxes with lion, bull, eagle and human features. The walls were decorated with vibrant colours, very much reminding him of the ridiculous wealth of the Vatican.

Together with his priestly patron, they found a hoard of old papyri-bound scroll work hidden in situ in an ambulatory behind a series of fabrics within pigeonholes.

Blowing off the dust and rolling out one papyrus, Ben gazed at the fading letters on the scroll's writing in dark ink running from right to left. The leather seams and string bound the papyrus sheets delicately, forming a complete scroll.

On it, he could see they were the lists of commandments. He could *read* ancient Hebrew in this vision, as second nature as reading in English.

Ben was sent by his shocked priest to go out the elaborately rabbeted doors decorated with the head of a pretty woman with an elaborate coiffure to report to the king what he had found. He was asked to seek permission to read it orally because it contained the "Instructions of Prophet Moses". He did what he was told. The king complied.

As Ben read out the Instructions, something happened in the king's eyes. The skin around them tightened; a hallowed-eyed look of anguish. Then he turned away and ran, blindly pushing off all who tried to bring him comfort. Ben felt shocked. He held the scroll in his hands limply, feeling as if he had done some misdemeanour, but his priestly friend reassured him that what he did was honourable.

He'd spoken the words of Yahweh.

The king retreated into his quarters in the cedar palace, a place of great déjà vu. Ben followed the king into the dazzling orange evening sunlit world seeping in from between the arched columned alcoves. He walked to the antechamber, but it was barred by the honour guard carrying spears. He tried to see what had happened to the king, but a sea of curious people brimmed around his quarters to hear and see as well. Did someone get hurt? Was the king ill?

All Ben heard came from the mouth of the king's prophet. She was a tall woman swathed in long enigmatic dark peasant robes. The only colour she wore were four long tassels of white and blue fabric. Striding like a breeze, she received everyone without warmth, tall, lithe and olive-skinned, dangerously serene and beautiful. She made no expression on her face. Everyone admired her for her cultic power and authority. Her eyes were a stunning hazel grey, regarding everyone apathetically, with a high intelligent brow, chiselled chin and a long neck. Her ebony hair was curly and could be seen brimming from her shawl.

The alcoves were silenced at the rising of her hands, and Ben wondered in awe if she were one of the First Fruits. The saints. The remnants of the antediluvian Sages.

She had absolute confidence and poise, speaking with a remarkably elegant diction to the audience. The king was inconsolable, as if he'd lost a son. All along, he'd been zealous for the Almighty, but he was in self-deception and the truth of the Instructions crushed him. He recognised the folly of his fathers, of generations long past, neglecting and culling Yahweh's prophets, their families and their followers, in order to maintain the worship of Ba'al and Ashtart. The king had stripped himself of his garment and collapsed to the floor weeping, covering himself with sackcloth and ashes in repentance.

"The king will remain fasting for the rest of the day," the saintly woman proclaimed. Her voice was not loud, but it overwhelmed every other sound. "All administrative measures are given to the kings' advisers and his relatives for the time being. Leave His Majesty be, for he's interceding and covering for your sins. Disaster is coming upon Yudah, like it did with Samaria and the House of Omri."

Then the prophet's sharp grey eyes found Ben, as if she knew who he was. Her lips were compressed, her eyes incredibly intense. Ben nodded in respect. "Hear and do," she said to Ben. "Gather them."

Five days later, the second vision came.

Linked by chains in manacles, under the scorching sun, dust in his eyes, Ben trudged in line with bedraggled, filthy families filing out of a burning walled city. Towers of burning smoke rose up from that city, turning the sky black, shrouding the sun's strength. The people were forced, led away by soldiers wearing conical and plumed metal helmets, lamellar steel segmented armour, carrying large bucklers, spears and swords sheathed on their hips. Their squinting faces were framed by dark beards.

The slave-refugees stank. They tediously carried their belongings bundled into bags slung on their backs, and some were stacked high on ox-drawn carts. Small children toddled along with their parents, some carried on their father's shoulders. Morbid, dirty families were bunched up on carts. One woman cradled an infant on her lap, while the arms of her older son, sitting behind her, were clasped around her waist.

Among the exiles, Ben wandered across the hilly land, past trees and vineyards heavy with fruit. One grove of the strangest kind had erect stakes carrying hunks of reeking flesh, dangling anthropoid bodies, chests pierced on hooks, flies buzzing like a shadowy halo around the human heads. Howls and groans of agony flung in the air. Families were led by the soldiers, passing the grove of the slain.

Ben felt too exhausted to react to the holocaust. Eventually, he came before a hill with a canopy on top. Under the canopy was a great royal man on an elaborate throne and footstool adorned with ivory inlays of three rows of four figures holding up each other. The king wore royal robes, a royal peaked cap and a wrist band with a circular jewel carved into a rosette. He held a bow and an arrow – symbols of the battle and the victory. Surrounding him were fan bearers. Hatred burned in Ben. This tyrant god-emperor had premediated this disaster.

Then he saw retainers of the emperor bringing a file of men connected by fishing lines. Their hands were bound, their heads raised, beads of blood caking their chins and neck. Ben saw flaming swellings on their lower lips, and he gasped. Fishhooks *pierced* their lower lips. The captured soldiers quivered, whimpering in excruciating pain. Women wept, rolling in the dusty ground, watching their husbands endure agony and humiliation before the emperor, like fish freshly caught slung to the beast.

A war horn blared through the air with a thin peal. Then a voice cried aloud and said, "Men of Hezekiah! Hail Sennacherib, king of the world! The gods of Lachish are in his hands! Now labour and die for Assyria, people of Lachish!"

Suddenly, a great uproar arose, and Ben turned, hearing the refugees, who held their heads, crying in a great crowd of despair. Out of a throng paraded Assyrian soldiers carrying two statues of seated deities – a male wearing a feather conical crown holding a rod – a bundle of sticks – in his right hand, and a woman wearing a leopard-skin flounced dress holding herbs by the stalks in both hands. The statues shone with handsome beauty, shiny metals, precious stones, vivid glazed paints and deep vibrant dyes. Their skin was the ochre scarlet of jasper earth, the hot gold of the sun, the vividness of lapis lazuli eyes, the lush freshness of verdant green garments, the warm black of dark ebony, the rich brown of cedar woods, the resplendent snow-white alabaster and the sharp silver of the moon. And emanating from their bodies, shining out from their skin, was the dazzling radiance of a heavenly aura.

"Yahweh! Asherah," the distressed people cried. "Yahweh! Asherah!"

"Ashur is king, you lousy scum!" roared an angry military general, tall and brawny, cracking his whips. He lashed out at anyone who lunged from the crowd to save their idols. "Get back!" he barked.

People screamed, wailing in horror, as the Assyrian soldiers dropped the idols to the ground before Sennacherib's throne. Sennacherib smirked with delight, watching Yahweh's statue bow before his feet. The despoilation of the divine was fun and games to the Assyrians, mocking, trampling, and kicking dust over the glorious statues, soiling them.

Ben knew what he was witnessing was an ancient war crime. For those who would revile the gods, even Assyria had to capture and respect their subjects. Here, they didn't. The soldiers of Sennacherib were disrespectful louts. Frightened outrage and terror seethed in the exiles.

The king of Assyria rose from his throne. He resembled Saddam Hussein. He looked at Ben, his flinty eyes imperial, austere and cloudy with conceit. Then, with a deep rolling voice, he addressed Ben, gesturing for him to come with a ringed hand. Ben came. The tyrant whispered into his ear. "Gather them." Sennacherib smelled of virgin olive oil fragrance. "The past is perspective. The future is anticipation. The present is responsibility."

Then Ben stood in a dark rocky place.

Where he stood, the ground resembled a barren lava plain. The ground was sandy, cracked with strewn rocks. Farther ahead, the dune-covered rock split open, channelling outwards across a vast plain of ravines and plateaus. Some were so wide he couldn't see the other side – rock formations split and shattered by sheer crevasses twenty or thirty miles wide, shaped as a jagged mosaic of uneven plateaus, some massive, others eroded. In all expansiveness, the plains – barren and parched – looked like a plate that had been broken into small fragments. The farthest he could see, mountains and deep valleys loomed ominously on the black horizon.

Ben looked up and frowned at the rocky ceiling above him. A lacunose ceiling resembling a landscape in itself, with dark green rifts and stalactites.

Out of the corner of Ben's eye, he saw three walkers, humanoid, hiking up a rocky ridge, strewn with six-foot pinnacles of stone. They wove around the pinnacles, wearing strange tight-fitting hazmat suits matching the texture and the colour of the sand and rock. They wore glass helmets resembling those of astronauts.

Their faces glowed.

The strangers with glowing faces walked towards Ben. The closer they got, Ben discerned the light came from bioluminescent freckles on their noses, tiny stars sprayed on their faces inside their glass helmets.

One figure emerged from the company. She was very tall, with a curved feminine form, and halfway across from the ridge pinnacles, she stopped, tilting her face upwards. The woman's eyes were large, suited for the darkness.

Her slanted eyes closed and opened.

A single word came. "Soon."

Ben still remembered the starkness, the vividness of that voice. It shocked him so much that he awoke from the vision, yelping.

The cell was nice. He had a mattress with two pillows, a latrine and a hatch under the door for food. Besides the bars and the small window cut into the brick, he was surrounded by four walls. The prison wardens changed and cleaned his cell before he arrived.

Ben hated it. He found himself sweating, missing open spaces.

What was *soon*? Death? Freedom? His daughter? Soon … That was the most imprecise word in the world!

Ben saw kings of times long past. He saw leaders, and they all failed morally. Ben yearned for righteousness and a pure mind for clarity, but melancholy always clouded it.

A king would take sons and conscript them. They would take women for wives and kill God's prophets and take all the grain, take all the animals and take slaves for labour.

Kings were supposed to be servants, not Sennacheribs. Ben remembered Rob saying that kings were deprived of riches, military power and harem. They were to be scholars of religion.

Soon.

The Omega Plan would culminate; the Galactic Tyrant was coming soon … Ben could sense avid disaster hovering above the prison. During the final week, when the marines mobilised for the Dulce base to defeat Alfred Bonner, he would be alone.

It was on the sixth night after the second vision that Ben heard a sound approaching his cell. His heart leapt in fear, but then was filled with great pleasure when he saw Joshua standing behind the bars, hand under his chin. "I had to show the guards that I was from the Marine Corps to get in."

Ben stretched his hand and cried. In the past, when recruiting this criminal, this con man and fraudster, Ben had called Joshua insane. Now Ben was insane, a criminal, and Joshua the sanest of all, coming to visit him in prison.

And all Ben had done was accuse him.

"I'm so sorry," Ben groaned. "I'm a wicked man."

Joshua had come to him – come to draw him out of complacency. "We are all wicked, in need of love … How are you going?"

Ben shrugged. *What truly happened to this young man that had changed his life? What made him saintly?*

"The most horrible calamity hangs over me. Was it something I did wrong to deserve all this?"

Joshua smiled. "I don't know. I don't believe in karma as I used to. We learn to trust wisdom where we learn from our failings and enjoy good times when they come."

"Thanks for thinking of me. But aren't you supposed to be on campaign?"

"We are leaving in two days. I have time."

"Josh, no one cares about me."

"No. No. People *do* care about you."

Ben struggled to believe that. There was hollowness in his stomach, and he told himself it was a fear of wanting to go back to the world. *Will Joshua free me?* "Why did you come to talk to me?" Ben said.

Joshua didn't meet Ben's eyes. His hand grasped the bars. "There is something I want you to see. Ben, the blood moon omen is here."

Ben's breath caught. *The past is perspective. The future is anticipation. The present is responsibility.* "Yeah. Strange how it is falling around the Jewish feast days."

"It is no coincidence God told his people to keep these Sabbaths. These days may appear arbitrary, but they are not. These times are like sacred places; you go to them, and God will speak through dreams, visions and events. Christians are missing out on *so much*, not keeping the *moedim*."

Ben darted his eyes down. He'd always known something was off about this young Turkish man. Had God been speaking through him too? Was it God that changed him from a loud con man to this honest, kind, scholarly person? Could God do that to Ben too? "The visions have something to them," Ben said. "I had three recently. They *are* patterned, as you said. I know it may sound insane. But … *they're real*. I don't know what else to do with them."

Gather them.

Joshua nodded slowly, speaking gently and carefully. "I believe them."

Ben smirked. "Everyone will think I'm a prophet."

"Maybe." Joshua nodded, smiling on the verge of chuckling. Ben's heart rejoiced. "You're a witness to the past."

"I don't know if I should trust these visions."

"I think you should. Have you studied ancient history, Ben?"

"No. Never."

"So then, it's *very* unlikely you fabricated the visions by yourself." And for a moment, Ben thought he saw Joshua scowl slightly, gazing at nothing. Perhaps he saw something in Ben's eyes that caused him to react in such a way, but as soon as that expression came, it was gone. "I cannot prove with evidence, but if what we are seeing is from God, we should trust in them. We need to have faith. In God, there is no falsehood."

Ben nodded. Could it be that he was misjudging the Galactic Tyrant? No matter of evidence could be used to prove the visions true or false. Yet he couldn't completely believe that he was coming up with these on his own. Ben refused to believe he was having a mental breakdown. How could an insane mind conjure up the Noah visions where it seemed another human being was controlling Ben – Sava-Qayin? But a part of him – the actor – urged Ben to *live* out these visions, to experience them. Embrace them.

Ben began to relate his recent visions. Joshua, leaning against the bars, lowered himself down to sit on the ground.

"Your recent visions, Ben, have a narrative to them," Joshua reflected. "It begins when you read the Word of God. Seeing yourself in it, you make a show of repentance. But you're just playing games. You cry and rent your clothes, but you never actually stop committing sin. You have idols in your heart that must be purged by God's violent enemies, so then, you are broken out into exile, even into the lowest darkness on Earth. But soon … I think *soon* means return to Eden, redemption, resurrection, new creation, trusting in God's provision. Soon, God will save you."

"I think you're right," Ben said, and he hoped so, trying to remain positive. He couldn't evaluate this man; his answer was erudite and professional. How could he, after his display of kindness beyond any person he'd ever met?

"All dreams from God are objective, Ben. They have a singular message to them."

"A singular message? It's about gathering the First Fruits. The giants are returning. The return of the Nephilim. With no Sages to teach mankind this time."

Joshua smiled – an honest, reassuring smile. "Ah. When did you learn about the Seven Sages and the Nephilim?"

Ben shrugged. "My visions are educational. I suspect they were legendary heroes from the pre-flood times, but they sinned."

"Well, the Nephilim are the demigod children of the Fallen Angels,"

Joshua said. "In Akkadian, the Seven Sages were called the Apkallu, and in Sumerian, Abgal. They are cultural heroes, normally depicted as fish demigods, rising from the abyss. They were worshipped and confused for the Fallen Angels and Nephilim in various Jewish texts written during the Hellenistic period. But in reality, they were the sinful patriarchs from Adam's genealogy."

"Yeah, the visions said something similar," Ben said.

"I guess the point was to turn the Mesopotamian hero ethos on its head, to make sure that Israelite and Jewish readers would know that what happened between the sons of God and the daughters of humans was the pinnacle of evil. Mesopotamia had several versions of the story of a catastrophic flood, and they mention a group of Sages, possessors of great knowledge. These Sages – Apkallus – were divine and evil. After the flood, the offspring of the Apkallus were said to be human in descent – having a human parent – and 'two-thirds Apkallu'. Technically, the Sages were confused with the Nephilim."

"I guess that happens. The longer the story is passed down orally, the more distorted it becomes," Ben said.

"Yes. But you know what? The Seven Sages' traditions are seen everywhere across the world. From the Saptarishi in India, the Seven Wise Men of Greece, the *imin.imin.bi* – the seven Heptad of the Hittites, the Seven of the Bamboo Grove in China and the Persian Seven Wise Masters. All these tales echo a truth lost during the millennia. The Seven Sages were not angel-human hybrids. They were the antediluvian saints, first to call upon the name of the Lord. But I digress. You probably don't care about the nuances of obscure legends, do you?"

Ben grinned. "Well, I wouldn't say I don't care, just … I'm ill-informed." In truth, Ben was *fascinated* beyond belief with this discourse. "I'm interested to learn more, Joshua, just … I don't know where to start. I can't start, and I feel that I've spoiled all my chances."

"Have hope. I will give you some of my books and videos."

"Joshua? Are you going to tell me what you saw?"

"Sorry." Joshua got into a squat. "I need to invoke the Temporal Realm. The present is a gate – a liminal zone. I am the future, giving you guidance backwards into the present. And you are the past, cast forwards into the front with guidance to the present. Whether there are seasons, generations, the prominence of empires, royal families or eras that come and go, the arrival of one ends the other, bringing a new beginning." Joshua beamed. "Thus, the pattern of history continues repeating itself.

"Father, I pray according to your character, that you can graciously give

Ben and I the spirit of Sophia and the apocalypse."

——

Joshua took a deep breath and felt revitalised. He felt the portentous embrace of the lovely Holy Spirit gush into his mouth and nose. Wisps of golden oil, richly infused cold freshness of heavenly water and spirit, anointing his anatomy.

He took a step forward, and the ground beneath his feet became colourful glass, spreading from the heel of his shoe. It cracked in a web, growing into a procession of stained-glass windows.

In the fourth dimension, Nefer appeared beside Joshua in his full human form – skin and hair pitch black, shining with an oily irradiance. His features were extremely sharp, too angular to be human, with eyes of pure violet. He wore his awesome topaz, ruby membrane like the draping long-sleeved robe of a Chinese emperor, shimmering with rainbows – thousands of fluttering hairlike cilia, wiry veins and flowery stingers swirling around him, floating and translucent. The glow of his garments shone from within him, a halo of hot pink, bell-shaped, a tangible aura outlining his body.

The gelatinous spirit captured the vision of Ben as it came, so they could study it.

Panels styled like Byzantine icons engulfed the detention centre all around him, phantom light working with the colours, creating a deep-dream effect. Ben wouldn't be able to see this. He called out to Joshua about what he was doing, but he studied the icon, ready to describe it.

"I see you in two visions, Ben," Joshua said. "In the first one, you're a priest serving God in the Tabernacle, bringing an innocent goat to be slaughtered on the bronze altar. You slit its throat and pour out its blood on to the ground. You cast the whole animal into the fire on the altar, burning it up, its glorious smoke ascending with the sweet aroma of obedience. Your garments are white as snow, radiant.

"In the second vision, you are a priest, wearing the same linen garments, but they are filthy and muddy, torn to shreds. You are wrestling an aggressive bison, grabbing one of its horns, pinning the beast to the ground. But the second horn grows larger towards you. One false move, and the bison will buck, and the second horn will gore you."

"Do you know what this means?" Ben said, a shadow barely visible from behind the glass icon depicting him.

"The first one is clear. You could be righteous, humbly serving God by accepting the selfless sacrifice of Jesus Christ, who died so we can be cleansed of sin. But the second one is an antithesis. You're still a priest, but your white garments are spoiled, covered in dirt that represents sin. The bison is – from my studies of the Book of Revelation – the False Prophet. The Second Beast that looks like a lamb but speaks like a dragon – a cult that rises out of the land. The First Beast is a hybrid of all world empires. The second is deceptive spirituality. You're grabbing one of the bison's horns – a human ruler of this cult system – and I'm confident to say that the horn you're breaking is the Alliance. Alfred Bonner himself. The other horn … is a mystery."

"So … You are saying I will finally kill Bonner, and someone new will take his place?"

Joshua shook his head, saying, "You *could*. But that's not the only option. I want you to go by the first. I *strongly advise* you to repent, ask God to forgive you for your revenge and accept his grace and his atoning blood on the cross. As for your second option, you're on your own. Out of God's protection."

"Do you think I'm evil?" Ben said. "God's punishing me for what I have done."

Pursing his lips, Joshua inclined his head, looking at Nefer standing silently by his side, mesmerised by his thousands of hairy cilia and pink aura. "Yes and no. What you have done is grievous." Joshua felt a tightness in his chest thinking about the Damacus prison asylum. "But you are only a human and not God that you should punish people. Evil is the absence of good, and God is goodness. Your actions were evil because you are finite and don't have all the information. You are *not qualified* to punish anyone."

Ben sighed weakly. "I suppose you're right there… But why would God want me? I'm evil."

"Evil is *contingent on good*," Joshua said. "Good is contingent *on nothing*. Evil people twist and steal what is good. Things like the love for your daughter and your father are good, but pursuing that love with a selfish method is evil. Evil, when you examine it, is essentially the selfish pursuit of truth. The intention is off. You *cannot* be evil for the sake of evil, because evil is something *dysfunctional* according to the natural purpose. Make sense?"

"Yeah, actually. But…" Ben uttered, his voice stern. "How can an all-powerful being who is all good, who cares about justice and compassion, allow systematic evil? Why did he let this happen to me and only me if he could have done otherwise?"

"Evil and suffering is *the lot* of all humanity," Joshua replied. "You are not singled out. Suffering is the *contingency* of the creation process. Creation evolved from the death and suffering of many countless beings, but it wasn't arbitrary. God couldn't have done otherwise because death and suffering all results in joy, life and virtue. Evil and suffering are *instrumental* in creating loving souls. Since we are capable of loving, we are *vulnerable to pain.* Evil is not due to weakness; it is the *inescapable cost* of a universe allowed to be free and other from God. His gifts of love and the gifts of suffering are inseparable. Suffering is meant to be a *warning* for someone in sin, living outside Paradise, so they can learn from their mistakes and return."

"My mistake," Ben uttered, "was that I thought the CD was the answer to my problems. But if God just showed me what I did wrong to deserve all this before … I only did terrible things *after* the fact. I tortured Thomas Jones as a *reaction* to the great suffering that came upon me. So, it was *not the cause* then."

"Don't look to causes, but look to the *purpose.* Don't seek reasons, because you will *never get any.* You cannot live for the benefits when reason fails. Trust God, even when all reason and hope are lost. This will mean everything."

Ben nodded in conviction.

"The best thing to do is to become a living sacrifice," Joshua continued. "It *must* suffice. Identify with the goat on the altar. You are the goat that you slay. But you could also become the bison." Joshua swallowed, wetting his throat. "I see different possible futures. I don't know which one is right in God's eyes. He is warning you to repent, Ben. It's not sweet, but it's good. Sometimes, a good, ordered life may not be the life you thought you wanted to live."

He didn't know how this celebrity would react – he'd lost everything, his dreams, his family, his job, his fame. Joshua couldn't see his expression, but he saw Ben's wispy outline of shadow as if he wasn't corporal or real. Less solid.

"I find that … this is a perfectly honest answer," Ben said. "Whatever you are, you are a blessing. You should seriously preach this to more people. You're gifted."

No, he *had* to hide this gift. If churches and institutions found out what Joshua could do, they would be chaperoning him to fortune-tell everyone's future. He would become on demand in the Christian apostate market and become a drug for confident conmen and women. And generally, the people of this secular world had *thousands* of years of training to fear and condemn anyone who claimed to perform miracles, subverting social mores. All the world's a stage, and all the men and women merely players. Cons.

Navigating through the theatre of society as a Christian was a challenge for Joshua. By nature, he was reclusive. He remembered the days of his over-confidence, dabbling in divination. He'd gone through a phase using magical *vibhuti* dust from India – dust made of burned dried wood, burned cow dung and cremated bodies. He placed this dust on his tongue to manifest his wishes.

Ben, on the other hand, navigated through society like an elephant, crowds parting for him in fear and awe. Both Ben and Joshua had to put aside what people thought about them in order to continue living. For Joshua, it was inconvenient but manageable, but for Ben … it was excruciating.

Oh, the depth and the richness of knowledge and wisdom! Nefer worshipped. *How unsearchable is justice? Ways beyond searching out.*

Who has known the mind of Yahweh?

Who has ever corrected him?

For from him and through him and to him are all things. To him be glory forever.

Out loud, Joshua said, "Thank you, Ben. It is a gift, but I don't get the opportunity to speak about these things to everyone. Jesus is among us, and his Holy Spirit, when two or three gather together."

"Yeah," Ben said with wired amusement. "Well … sorry, I was … We are both insane."

Joshua smiled wryly at that. Strange that God operated with the lowly people of this world so often. "We see the ultimate reality."

Around Joshua, the glass icons began to crumble. Swirling golden steam swung across the dimension trying to hold the shards together, and Nefer – producing this same glowing yellow and white steam – used it to re-create them.

Gradually, the fourth dimension faded, and Joshua's world became normal.

Ben was standing in his cell next to him, holding the bars. "I don't know what to do with this information." He stared at his hands, clenching them. "Thank you for looking out for me like a brother."

As Cain was supposed to do. Joshua smiled with joy, saying, "We are called to be each other's keepers."

"I wish you well on the Dulce mission," Ben said. "Next time you have a vision, feel free to tell me, and the next time I have a vision, I will share it with you."

Joshua nodded, grinning. "God has done something, he is doing something, he will do something. Sounds excellent, brother. But before I leave, do you mind saying a prayer with me?"

67

BLOOD MOON RISING

FALL EQUINOX, 3:22 AM

"And y'all, being dead in y'all's transgressions and sins, in which at one time y'all walked according to the age of this world, according to the ruler of the power of the air, the spirit who is now working in the sons of disobedience, among whom we also all used to live by the passions of our flesh, doing the will of the flesh and the mindsets, and we were by nature children of wrath, as also were the rest. But God ... made us alive together with the Messiah."

—From the Epistle to the Ephesians, Paul, Tim Mackie's Literal-literary Translation, c. 60 – 62 CE.

Casbolt awoke with a start. His head hit the canvas, and lying back down, he groaned in pain.

The sound of the rolling door opening the trailer was abrupt, and the canvas was torn away. Khonsu, Camazotz and Prometheus hauled Casbolt onto his feet, nudging him to walk down off the trailer. The men in black slowly began to take out the crates, along with Julian's daughters.

Crickets creaked in the cold darkness as Casbolt stumbled with hands bound at his back, ambling along the cracked arid ground. The trailer had parked in the middle of the desert, with no signs of life or structures. For as far as he could see, there were only undulating hills of dark red rock, small shrubbery and stones scattered across the banal land. The tallest structure in the landscape was to the left – a rising mound of earth, merging into an arete formation.

The men in black led Casbolt up towards that ridge, hiking up the rocky ground. It was not easy with hands bound to his back, tramping up the steep arete. Casbolt crested the arete strewn with piles of stones and rocks of many sizes, his eyes adjusting to the starlight to illuminate his vision.

He was standing on the crest of a gigantic hole in the earth, radius rippling outwards, forming a perfect bowl-shaped impact crater. The earth had been punctured, the valley's ridges swathed in fur bushes and desert vegetation, ringed by rusty red sediment around its brim. So vast was the Crater, it resembled a mountain ring, a dry, bare and bleak wilderness, far from civilisation. Like Antarctica – the wilderness of wildernesses.

Casbolt could see the Carnutes' company miles down by remote viewing with the keen sight of the Aes Sidhe. They hiked down the slopes like ants, zigzagging their way down to the centre of the impact. They were tiny, and he couldn't hear a sound up here. The night was still under the starlit canopy – the purple–blue Milky Way lay strewn across the arched firmament in a band of infinitesimal stars, glorious, twinkling lights and dust of smaller star clusters light years away. It was as if, whenever he looked at the sky before, there had been a haze of light pollution that kept him from seeing the true glory of the stars. This, too, he would have seen in Antarctica on a clear night. Things of the unseen merging with the seen – balancing between two immensities.

"Keep moving," Prometheus' dry voice grumbled, taking Casbolt by the arms down the steep incline, towards the column of people far below. They had already reached the base of the massive hole in the ground.

What meteorite would be large enough to create such a deep crater? Casbolt thought. *And how recently?*

This is the tomb of a fallen spiritual being, Michael Prince replied.

There had to be around a hundred Carnutes carrying crates from the truck heading towards the centre of the Crater. Khonsu and Camazotz walked on each side of Casbolt, and Prometheus brought up Clarita and Lluvia, duct tape covering their mouths. The dark Aes Sidhe, men and women, congregated near the centre of the Crater, which was strewn with boulders. The men in black eventually caught up with the company, who had gathered around a concentric arrangement.

The Carnutes all wore dark clothes, cowls, leather jackets and pants, long and baggy. Mellow wind blew lethargically, rippling their jet clothing, like black streamers in the night. It was hard to distinguish gender, but Casbolt thought he saw someone surreptitious amid the crowd of the gathering, who had a distinctive golden sheen to the eye.

Circe. Her hand supported the arm of an older hunchbacked man dressed in folds of leather and skins, nothing more than a torso and a head, upon whose brow balanced a male elk skull with ornate antlers. This therianthrope disturbed Casbolt, reminding him of the foul rituals when priests wearing animal masks sexually lacerated him. The Parvus inferred from his wear that he was a shaman – people who used drugs to speak to the other Realm and enforce their wills. A man of liminal spaces, straddling two worlds. They shunned materialism, but Cabal materialists lauded shaman as if they were a fun toy to play with.

The three men in black sat Casbolt down as they brought Clarita and Lluvia towards the boulders, setting them down.

"Bring forth the relics of our ancestors," a voice rose from the gathering in the vast desolation. The shaman raised to his mouth a certain substance and consumed it. *A psychedelic drug, no doubt,* Casbolt thought. *Like ayahuasca used by those doing satanic ritual abuse.*

Casbolt sat on the ground thirty feet away from the grotesque group, heart beating, watching the two girls. If anyone tried to abuse them, he would roar and charge into the paedophiles. He didn't care if he died trying to save the children.

A double line of dark-clad figures trudged forwards, carrying from the crates the stolen Baghdad Museum artefacts, including the new ones that depicted scorpions, serpents and animal–human hybrids. As different artefacts were placed around the stones, arranged next to Julian's daughters, a few Carnutes began to shake sistra vigorously, emitting a cacophony of dolorous notes. A group of men and women began to chant in an unknown language. Acolytes accompanied the rattling and chanted with their own cries of ecstatic passion.

With a slender motion of her hand, Circe led the shaman forth. He began to stamp his feet, strutting up and down with swaying motions, performing some desultory dance. The shaman's detestable declamations were repeated, truncated by gusts of eerie wind.

"Tiamat. The Great Deep. The Dark Earth," a depraved oration rang. "The abode of great Inshushinak and the angel of Tartarus Abaddon. Great Architect, foe of Yaldabaoth. Rise up, gather your bones, O Dragon, as the above! Bowstar of Canis Major and Sirius glows, and the fatal head wound heals!"

The shaman waved his arms in a circle, letting out a disturbed yelp.

Julian's daughters flinched in shock, their eyes wide with fear and confusion as they huddled each other for protection.

The shaman spun in the air, lying on the ground with a dusty thud. He lay on his back, eyes wild, drooling mouth flapping, but wordless.

Circe walked up to the circle before the children and the looted artefacts, a censer in hand. With her bare fingers, she picked up a stone and turned it into a flame. With it, she lit up the censer, producing a fragrant incense. The fire crackled, sending out wisps of pungent smoke, ghastly and ribbonlike. Tossing the flame away, she began to walk around the circle, and once she reached the largest boulder, she swathed it in the incense, blessing it. "Shaft of fertility," she sighed, closing her eyes. "Open the pit womb."

Smelling the frankincense, Casbolt tipped his head back, gazing at the sky. The moon was black, but as it bled, a waning crescent of mud-brown hue appeared, looming between a thin band of clouds like tiger stripes.

He looked at the stars congregating even closer than before, like the gods themselves gathering to witness the culmination of a cosmic war.

A lunar eclipse.

"This is the blood of the covenant that the Aeons make against Yaldabaoth," a Carnute called.

Two acolytes stalked towards the drug-induced shaman, hauling him upright. Twin blades of steel winking like stars rose and fell. Fountains of blood spurted out of the shaman's shoulders carefully so as to not kill him. Blood flowed down his clothes and spilled on the ground until it trickled in rivulets. During the entire blood ritual, the wind had stopped. Casbolt watched the girls as they hugged one another, closing their eyes from the gore. Casbolt held his breath tensely.

The three men in black stepped forward, gathering the crimson flow in small cups with scaly patterns, which were certainly Near Eastern and stolen. When filled to the rim, the contents were distributed among the members of the congregation, who eagerly drank.

Casbolt gagged in an undertone. It surprised him that these gore-bellied child-trafficking Carnutes were blood drinkers. *At least they were not physically harming the girls. Or drinking their blood!*

He gazed up at the sky at the moon – a shadowy orange blotch.

When all the attendees had wet their throats, the servile bloodletters raised the swooning shaman to his feet, helping him walk back to the main group headed by Circe.

There was a shaking of the strange sistra for over five minutes straight.

The girls remained frozen with fear and weariness. At some point after the nauseating performance, something, Casbolt detected, moved within the cluster of boulders. Something that *crawled*.

The Parvus screamed with alert, and Casbolt's hairs rose.

A large grey-skinned humanoid clambered out of a hole hidden among the rock formations. Its limbs worked with contorted movements, its head was set low, and its elbows were protruding, as if backwards facing. The horror brought a shocked scream out of Lluvia.

The monster perched on the rock, and then it stood up on two feet before the girls. Casbolt got a good look at it.

It was a giant of nightmarish form. An alien forgotten by science, created by a bizarre divergence of evolution. A species unrelated to humans, a creature forsaken by God.

The creature reminded Casbolt of the Kandahar giant, but in miniature. It was brawny, its skin was mostly pale silver, with small ridges rising from its skin, which stretched tightly like a carapace. It had thick strands of black locks coming out of its head – but ridges of nose and cheeks and scalp looked flinty, capable of deflecting a spear. It had large, pointed ears and a frog-like face, its eyes massive, dark green and slanted.

But unlike the Kandahar giant, this elfish Fomorian wore a tight-fitting suit over its whole body, except for its head. One piece, it was made of some kind of thick dark grey and red leather.

Screams tore out of the girls' gagged mouths, and instantly they began to writhe away, sobbing. The seven-foot creature let out a deep, guttural growl, almost a croak of someone about to throw up. A sound that vibrated the ground.

"No!" Casbolt shouted, his voice echoing across the Crater. "What are you doing?"

"MOOOWW!" the creature growled loudly.

"Danava of Duzakh, warrior of Inshushinak, we come to exchange Blue Blood," beauty queen Circe addressed the giant, walking up to it from the group, fearless and austere. "For voidstone."

The creature calmed, grunting, blinking at the goddess as if under her magic charm. The girls were panicking. Casbolt could see they were breathing heavily, the sides of their necks palpitating. Some Carnutes had to hold them down to keep them from running away from the presence of the chthonic Fomorian. "Voidstone," the creature intoned with a raspy basso vocal cord. It spoke as if the octaves of its voice were gone. "Blue Blood."

"Yes. Blue Blood for voidstone," Circe said melodiously. She held out her hand, holding an artefact in the shape of a rod with a large loop attached to it. Casbolt recalled seeing that same artefact in the basement of the Baghdad Museum.

"Blue Blood," the creature pointed at itself. It took a few seconds for it to comprehend what it wanted. Then it pointed to Circe. "Voidstone."

Circe nodded. "Yes."

The audience stiffened, rapt, as if this moment had been what they were waiting for. Casbolt's breath became short. As the Carnutes hurried the girls to their feet, pushing them towards the creature against their will – they whined and yelped and cried. The creature took the rod and ring from Circe and then, slipping its hand in its pocket, it placed something in her palm.

"No! Bastards!" Casbolt squealed, yelling in frustration at his hands bound at his back. He stumbled forwards, trying to get to the boulders.

Something was in Circe's palm. A dark red gemstone, a garnet quartz that glowed with an ominous dark red-and-violet light.

Casbolt lifted his chin. The moon, like a severed head, a crimson sphere glowing in a cosmic macabre, hovered over the sideways shoulders of Orion. No wind blew.

"Danava," Circe intoned serenely. "The exchange is complete."

The thing – Danava – let out a gargling roar. It lunged, seizing the girls with two hands, using the rod and ring to grip them like a crook. They shrieked along with its cacophonous bellowing. The Danava took and dragged the girls to its hole among the rocks. It lumbered, pulling the thrashing girls into the pit from whence it came. The violence of their struggle and the horror of their screams bore a pit in Casbolt's stomach.

"Nooo!" Casbolt howled, lunging for the boulders, pursuing the monster. "No! No! No!"

The Danava fought the girls and roared deeply on and on like a frantic wild beast chewing its prey. Those rough, snarling, bestial sounds. Enslaved girls mewing to death at the top of their lungs. The purple girl. Devoured by Mac Tíre.

A sacrifice to save the world.

Casbolt froze and fell on his knees.

A grin crept on Circe's face – the Enemy at its pleasure. She looked beautiful with her witchlike golden eyes. But they were conniving like Danu and her little game that had ruined him.

Casbolt screamed until he coughed and spat. Survival guilt … He failed … and …

You're worthless.

He shivered, quivering nonstop on the gravel.

Great *geas* had been incurred on him by the Cabal and the Carnutes. One was obligated to fulfil it, to purify the guilt. Casbolt had promised to protect Julian's daughters from the Cabal. And yet, as he grovelled, bound, he saw no coming back. His promise had been unattainable.

Casbolt thrashed, stomping the ground with his feet in wrath. He sobbed in fury. The girls taken, artefacts stolen and sold, the Cabal succeeded. All purpose – his book, his mission for the last three years – all for nothing.

"No!" Casbolt brayed. "It will not *end* like this! Oh Jesus, *please!* All this time! God! Not like this!"

Geas … the initiative of making right with the world. The great equaliser.

The unreasoning beast – Redlion – emerged. Fire began to burn Casbolt's body.

I'm going to fail again … Don't fail again! Geas! I have striven with darkness to become a better man! I am James Casbolt!

Suddenly, the earth became as unstable as a trampoline. The satanic paedophiles roared, jumping in an avaricious frenzy with the earth as it convulsed violently. Casbolt gasped – the tremors were massive shocks from the horizontal wave and the upwards thrust.

The earth had responded to the shaman's blood spilled upon it and the death of the girls. The earthquake cried out to heaven.

—

Ben sat on his bed, bored, turning over and over in his head the truths Joshua had revealed to him. Ben had come to a sure conclusion.

I will break the horn of the Alliance. Alfred Bonner took my daughter. I will hurt that man just as much as he hurt me.

But he also had another choice: to serve, to deny himself and die on God's altar in surrender to Jesus.

Hatred, loss, grief and passion. Ben was absorbed by gloomy black dejection, nothing pure, nothing right and nothing honourable. The image of his dead father ghastly and murdered was forever before him. Longing for Veronica was dangerous, urging him to take matters into his own hands.

The churn of his stomach. The tightness of his chest. This was what the loss of Veronica did to him. She broke him; she killed him.

When will I kill him? I cannot kill Bonner if I'm stuck in here. How will Joshua's predictions be fulfilled? That was the question.

Tonight would be the night the marines and the FBI would raid Dulce Base. And Ben would remain here, stuck with the paroxysms of anguish. It was a violent struggle to not want to end the life he loathed and to hold on to hope of escaping and run swiftly to Dulce on his own. To run and save his daughter.

Why was God, the Galactic Tyrant, forcing him to give up and die without his daughter? How cruel was that? Or was he taking Joshua's word for it? That was fideism, that was ignorance. Could Ben actually kill Bonner?

Lying on his creaky bed, Ben felt his chest go tight like a boa constrictor, slowly squeezing him. Joshua *teased* him with potential futures.

So manipulative and cunning. A con artist at heart.

Ben groaned weakly and found himself not caring.

That was bad. That way of thinking – to give up – had been his greatest fear in his quest to find Veronica. In those moments, exhausted and horrified in his mother's bathroom with Thomas Jones boxed in, Ben felt the same way. It was *very bad*. He did all in his power to ignore that darkness. It had been hours since his bedtime, but he couldn't go to sleep. Impossible, not with the knowledge of the two choices laid before him.

Life and death. Death by dying to self, or death by facing Bonner, defeating Bonner and saving his girl.

Ben roared, throwing himself off his bed, pacing in the small cell, hands on his head. He thought himself strong. Ben slammed himself against the bars, venting his anger – at the paladin, at Thomas, Veronica, Joseph, Joshua, Pounders, Bonner, Keller, God, everyone. He stretched his hand out, trying to reach the lock, but the door was inches from the reach of his fingers. It was designed just for this kind of tampering. Another tease.

Ben cried out frantically, pushing farther for that lock. *God help me. Don't let the darkness win,* he thought. He ... prayed. *God, please. Please, I can't endure this any longer. Have you punished me enough? Please, not again. I cannot go back. Not again. I don't want this!*

Please!

The feeling of slipping back into that state of apathy engulfed Ben, and he gave up, slipping his back down the bars, pressing his chin against his chest. He crept into his bed and tried to put himself to sleep.

He hit himself hard. This was the end. He lost his last chance. His mind whispered things that betrayed him, whispered things that were ... that *sounded* so true. About Veronica being dead. They should've sounded ridiculous, but they didn't.

Ben waited, lying in his bed for a long time, doing nothing.

He saw movement at the corner of his eye.

Ben slowly stared at the place where the faint light cast upon the bars on the floor. It hid something. Something moved.

Dread quickened his heart, expecting an entity to stir in that still corner. Ben relaxed. *I'm seeing things.*

Then he turned back around and felt the wind glide past his face. The hair on his body bristled. Ben held his breath, heart writhing. There was shadow and silence. Shrugging, Ben lay on his bed to sleep. He rolled over and saw an old man at the end of his bed.

Ben yelped, bounding, raking the sheets off the bed. His privacy, his tomb, had been violated by a supernatural fiend. It was the *pure dread* of being utterly vulnerable.

The fear Veronica would have to feed on for the rest of her days.

The old man turned his head. The light caught his silvery hair and brown buckskin garment.

Ben gasped. This was not a vision – Ben knew he was awake – and yet, he saw a Navajo medicine man standing right there, face to face.

"Chief?" Ben rasped.

The figure had short hair and was corpulent. Not what Ben could remember of the medicine man. He held and leant on a staff of black, white, yellow and turquoise.

"I miss you, son," said the Native American.

What was Ben seeing? A spirit? Ben's blood froze.

The spectre's eyes were polished marble, and his voice was a rumble from beneath the world. "Return to me and trust."

Ben knew the answer intuitively. *Repent and trust in God.*

Joshua said that suffering was a warning to repent from sin. But to become a goat giving up his life, burning on the altar? To trust in God? *He's the Galactic Tyrant!*

Seeming to read his conflicted mind, the spirit sighed, frowning. He opened his mouth, and it was red inside with the flames that burned under the earth. "Your daughter has been given away to another strange people, and your eyes look, and they fail, for your hand is powerless to save her."

The world tipped and spun.

The bars creaked; roars bellowed across the detention centre. The ground wobbled, trembling and bouncing up and down, side to side. It didn't cease.

It went on, increasing.

Earthquake!

The apparition was gone.

The door in Ben's cell twisted apart with a grinding roar. The building exploded. The metal door flung open and slammed into Ben, pressing him against the wall. He yelped in shock and pain.

He felt displaced, until he came to, realising the door had fallen on him, and that the earthquake had stopped.

His entire cell had partly fallen apart. The section of the hallway before him was cracked but had survived, but down the hallway to his right, half of the detention centre had broken into a mound of rubble. Mortar and dust billowed off the pile of brick and metal. The walls had cracked, cleaving out an opening into the late-night air.

"What the hell?" Earthquakes were possible in Arizona, but not common. Ones powerful enough on the Richter scale to cause buildings to collapse were seldom.

Alarm bells rang in the distance. Authorities would come. The prison had been torn apart.

Ben rose to his feet, disoriented. His prison cell was open, and before him, beyond the ruin, was opportunity. The desert, gulches with cacti, and the northern mountains of the wilderness marking the pass towards Dulce.

Ben stepped out of his cell, feeling the cool night caress his face. He closed his eyes, inhaling. He had prevailed, broken out of prison by sheer chance.

Or… God himself decided to act and show himself.

Thank you! Halleluiah! Thank you for doing something in my favour for once!

Ben ran swiftly into the night. Towards Dulce.

—

Praying, interceding and fasting for Ben, Veronica, the O'Learys, Hitesh and his family, and for the marines, Joshua sat a seat away from the soldiers and the FBI combat assault unit inside the subway train, heading to Dulce. Just as he was wrapping up the prayer uttered under his breath, a powerful earthquake struck.

The carriage tottered, lights flickered off, and for a moment, Joshua thought his life would end in a train crash.

"What the heck?" Judd Pounders barked. The marines cried in the dark, the train screeched, and the carriages trembled.

Joshua held onto the seat, prayer and fasting making him apathetic.

Then the lights flashed back on, the train groaned and picked up speed again as if nothing had happened.

"Was that an earthquake?" Leo Urwin asked.

"Earthquake?" Derek Fish blurted. "You got to be joking, Urwin! That was Armageddon, not an earthquake. They're not that strong around these parts."

"That's an earthquake all right, Fish," Marcus said.

"That was mad, man!" Derek called, and the marines laughed.

Joshua picked up his fallen first aid medical backpack and placed the straps on his shoulders, glancing at the only other people on the hijacked Dulce train. A few of the FBI agents wearing black bulletproof vests and Keller Butcher and Brianna DePaula were holding each other tightly in an intimate way.

"Let's get warmed up, boys," Pounders said, a mask of relentless determination plastered on his face. "Any minute now, the train will be coming to a stop. Blocking positions. Combat Assault Unit One will come in with an air attack on the upper levels from a helicopter into the hangar inside the mountainside. We will meet them at the top."

"Colonel, sir," Demos said. "*Semper Fi!*"

"What does that mean, Demos?" Joshua said, smiling with curiosity. "Was that French?"

"*Semper Fi*? It's Latin. *Semper fidelis* means, 'ever faithful', 'ever loyal'. It began to be used in the military since 1660 in the regiments of southwestern England."

Joshua the Envisager nodded in agreement, goosebumps running up his arms. "*Semper Fi*. Ever faithful."

"That's not like you, Josh," Pounders said, smirking friendly. "You're normally the one having to explain."

"Oh, Judd, please. I can't know everything, you know."

"Strange you don't even know the marines' own motto," Pounders said, "but those times serving us, serving me, you've demonstrated more loyalty to your brothers than I've seen in ages. You display what it means to have purpose and belonging. To fight for the lives of all." He turned to the FBI agents. Keller and Brianna smiled triumphantly. "And to your allies, who stand for truth and justice. This is the American spirit. This is who we are. A family. We do all we can for family." Everyone's eyes focused on Joshua – the look that expected him to stand up and be their leader who served.

"Oh, come on," Joshua smiled. "Not in front of everyone. Judd, please.

I'm a follower, not an example. I was a con man, Judd! A con man!"

The colonel laughed. "Those days are gone now. You're a new person, and the only one who doesn't carry a gun going into battle. You're the most courageous and greatest marine I have seen."

"You prepared this, didn't you?"

"May have."

"You should be the one honoured, Judd, not me."

"No."

"I was a liar. A Machiavellian villain. The amount of care and faith you have in me is unrealistic. *You* embody *Semper Fidelis*." Joshua nodded, stepping up to the colonel, embracing him, hands thumping him on the back. "Thank you."

The marines and the FBI clapped and whooped.

Judd's eyes looked red from restrained tears. "Life is short."

"Easy for you to say, old man."

"Hey, young one." He smiled and turned around. "This is our moment. Ladies and gentlemen," Pounders declared, holding up his semi-automatic. "*Semper Fi!*"

"*Semper Fi!*"

68

SEMPER FIDELIS

"Or do you presume on the riches of his kindness and forbearance and patience, not knowing that God's kindness is meant to lead you to repentance? But because of your hard and impenitent heart you are storing up wrath for yourself on the day of wrath when God's righteous judgment will be revealed. He will render to each one according to his works: to those who by patience in well-doing seek for glory and honour and immortality, he will give eternal life; but for those who are self-seeking and do not obey the truth, but obey unrighteousness, there will be wrath and fury. There will be tribulation and distress for every human being who does evil, the Jew first and also the Greek."
—From the Epistle to the Romans, Paul, c. 57 – 58 CE.

The sliding doors opened. Joshua packed in behind the marines and agents, heart thundering.

Greeting them on the station platform were three dark, hairy and tall Australopithecus, Homo erectus and Paranthropus with long limbs and leathery face, looking up at them. They halted, carrying boxes in their hands, intending to place them inside the train – but didn't expect to see the doorway cramped with armed marines and black-vested FBI. Joshua stared, sweating. Two of the hairy hominids had large bushy beards. The other had a cranium deformation like Akhenaten or the Paracus skull in Peru that showed signs of dolichocephalism, where the newborn's skull was malleable for head binding.

Jason Laycock took a deep breath through his nostrils.

Then, with a loud voice, he bellowed at the top of his lungs, "NIMROD!"

He pressed the trigger, and the three stunned hominids were corpses. Revulsion struck Joshua, watching the giant primates die.

The Marines fired along, bullets roared mindlessly, exterminating unexpectant hominids in this underground station, sheering them in a blender of destruction, leaving behind a shower of blood, husks and hair. They howled and shrieked. The sound was horrendous.

"Nimrod!" the marines roared through the barrage. "NIMROD!

"Whoo!"

"Yeah!"

"For Dan!"

"Nimrod! Hahaha!"

The laughing drowned out the panicked chanting and bloodcurdling screams of the dying. What Joshua noticed in the carnage as the marines and agents pressed on was the giant Neanderthals and Paranthropus were not off one beat. Their song was in harmony. They knew what to sing as they died; they kept on grunting to a song until they couldn't sing any longer.

Though covered in hair, with deep-set eyes, they were too human, anatomically. One had too much hair, too much muscle around the temples. One had smooth, round black skin with prominent breasts and nipples. A female. She reminded Joshua of a character from the *Planet of the Apes*, or even worse, a kidnapped human slave. It formed a lump in his throat as he watched her die.

This is terrible! he thought, outraged. *Why does Alfred Bonner keep human-looking primate slaves?*

"Hell's bells," Derek Fish exclaimed. "What's up with all these apes?"

"They're not apes," Joshua blurted out. "They're Neanderthals."

Jason Laycock scoffed, reloading his gun. "What? Bullocks! I just killed a bunch of bad guys in monkey suits!"

"I ... wouldn't joke about that," Johnny Best said.

The sheer amount of taking the piss out of killing apes repulsed Joshua. It was not long until human security reinforcements began flooding into the station, joining the hominid foray, carrying guns. They engaged with the FBI agents, taking cover behind dividing walls and staircases that led up to levels eight and seven.

Joshua backed against the wall, following Pounders, Marcus and Johnny Best. Guns crackled, ringing in his ears, the soldiers bellowing in the maelstrom. They ducked, taking cover, then popped up again to fire. During the shootout, Joshua saw Brianna take a shot in the leg from an enemy – Keller saw it, and howling, he ordered the agents to fire back at the security guards mercilessly. As soon as he saw Brianna arching back her head in pain, holding her lower leg, lying against the staircase wall, Joshua, watching for a lull, blundered as fast as he could over to her.

"Josh!" Pounders called amidst the gunfire.

"Saving lives," Joshua muttered to himself, slumping low, swiftly reaching Brianna's side. Ben's ex-wife was pale faced, but it didn't wipe off that confident smile when she saw Joshua.

"How bad is the pain?" Joshua said. "Can you walk?"

"It … it stings. Should be able to limp," Brianna said, and she was chuckling, taking a sharp breath. "Oh … I'm okay, Josh. Just … shocked."

"Why are they not surrendering?" Keller shouted, firing, ducking and standing back up, expression wild with fury and determination.

Joshua tended the wound with antiseptic, then pulled out bandages and dressed her lower leg to staunch the excessive bleeding. He bound the cloth hard, applying adequate pressure. Brianna was sweating profusely. She endured the pain, hissing and breathing deeply.

He observed the battle and the zipping bullets. The marines and the agents fortunately had the upper hand. When the last Alliance soldiers were shot dead or retreated, Keller Butcher scrabbled from his blocking position behind the railing towards Joshua.

"Is the wound bad?" he said hastily.

"Just keeping pressure on it," Joshua said. "We'll call medical support. I'll stay here and keep her safe. Keller and the others, speak to Pounders, and continue the raid to meet up the ground crew from the aircraft hangar."

Pounders nodded as the marines discussed a plan among themselves, then split off.

Demos hunkered down at Joshua's side, looking strangely joyful.

"Jesus, brother, you're really crazy going in there without a weapon," Demos said, smiling.

"Somebody's got to care, and somebody has to serve."

Demos smiled. "Arete. Means in Greek, 'excellence of any kind'. You got that too in you, and I like it."

"I know. Leave us here," Joshua said to a stubborn Keller. "I have Demos and Pounders here. Complete the mission." It felt strange to command an agent around, but that man looked torn, suggesting he was in love with this woman.

"Keller," Brianna said. "Listen to him. I'm in good hands."

Reluctant to leave Brianna's side, the agent nodded, swiftly gathering his men, and joining the marines, continued the assault.

"NIMROD!" the marines called, whooping as they charged up the stairs, leaping over bodies of men and apes.

—

Blundering through shrubs, scaling ravines and hills, Ben finally saw the spangled lights of a military installation on the side of a mountain. He wheezed, out of breath, leaning against a tree trunk, mopping sweat from his forehead.

He'd been sure the police were behind, vigorously hunting for him, but what did it matter? He was going to find his daughter at last.

Ben hobbled down a narrow gulch towards a cluster of tall grass, where a small stream barely deep enough to submerge his feet trickled lethargically down the incline from the mountain. Lights in the distance showed copious gates and stations leading into a hollowed-out maw of rock, fitting factories of grey stone.

The area between Ben and the base was populated by thick small trees, giving way to a large hanger of rigid linear roads winding outwards, closed off by gates. On the peak were tall radio towers with a boxed station at the top, and Ben saw a helicopter there, blinking red and green lights, thundering loudly. Crickets chirped, and the moon was nowhere to be seen.

Something moved.

Tense, Ben scanned the grass in the darkness. A night bird?

Relaxing, Ben approached the creek to cross, but then something behind him rustled. He tripped on an unseen root and stumbled onto the stones into the freezing water.

Getting to his feet, Ben spun and came into the presence of a shadowy human figure.

Reflexes taking over, Ben skipped to his feet, trying to trick the attacker, but it evaded to the side swiftly. It punched Ben, but he blocked, gripping the assailant's arms. They grappled, tugging and spinning around, grasping shirts, heels digging into the riverbank.

Ben realised he was fighting a woman. And she was strong and skilled.

Raising his right arm, bending it back and twisting it by the elbow, she brought Ben to one knee, but using his other knee, he brought her down with him. They rolled and tumbled into the shrubs along the uneven ground and into the tiny stream.

Bruised and soiled, they wrestled on the ground. The woman mounted him. Worming, Ben tried to get on top of her, got to his knees by grabbing a small tree trunk, then heard the distinct sound of a knife drawing out of its sheath. He felt the blade hovering at his throat.

He looked into the woman's eyes – she looked vaguely familiar – that fierce dark ice in her Mongolic eyes, her grim, determined face, hair tied up. Squatting, she wore a tattered and worn working uniform.

"Who?" Ben managed. The blade pressed coldly against his neck.

"You're more demented than I thought!" she whispered with sharp fury.

I've seen this woman before! Ben thought. *Pays to know names!*

"Get the hell off me!" Ben resisted, but the woman slammed Ben back into the freezing water with her other hand.

"You should really turn back. There isn't any shelter for miles, and this base is under attack." She gave Ben a rictus smirk, her hair stinking with an oily odour.

"Who are you?" Ben whispered harshly.

The woman jeered, laughing in derision. It was then that the most brutal pain erupted in Ben's groin. A heavy blow struck him. Ben roared out a gasp, arching his head. He hissed and groaned, tears in his eyes. He found himself hyperventilating, his hip throbbing.

The woman stood over him. She had punched him directly in the groin, and the pain was insufferable. It made Ben's stomach and bowels churn as if he would throw up. He rolled on the ground, gasping. Pain, so much pain! Ben began to chuckle, trying to kick at the woman.

"Look at you," the woman snarled. "I will *never* forget what you did to the innocent boy at your mother's house!"

Ben stared at her, shocked. Yes, *that's* who she was. She was the Aes Sidhe – a victim of elite child sex trafficking rings – and she had come to his mother's house and threatened him the same way, telling him the brutal truth of the Galactic Tyranny.

Ben found himself grinding his jaw in frustration. "I'm doing this because I'm the only one who can save my daughter."

Ben noticed a subtle change in the woman's stone-hard countenance. She twitched, blinking, slanting her head slightly.

"You're from Dulce Base, are you?" Ben hissed.

"You shut up," hissed the woman. "I thought you were awake. That you could understand …" The woman swallowed hard, abruptly lowering her glance.

"Please," Ben begged calmly, raising his hands in surrender. "If you're a slave from Dulce, tell me where I can find Bonner. I need to find him."

Ben felt tears leak from his eyes. He really didn't prefer to beg weakly before this woman, or anyone, but he was *desperately* in need. He wasn't sure if he could walk normally now because of her!

The woman's head nodded slightly, her eyes staring up at him. "People used to look up to you." The knife touched Ben's throat.

"I'm not the enemy." Ben hovered his hand over the blade. "I'm trying to do the right thing. To kill Alfred Bonner. He took my daughter and killed Zoe. How did you escape? Tell me, and I will get you out of here. You're one of them, right? Trafficked. Don't lie to me."

Suddenly, Ben saw the woman's knife hand slacken, her mouth dropping, eyes twitching.

"Bonner has abused you too," Ben said passionately. "I see it in your eyes. Come on, don't waste my time. I'm trying to prevent what happened to you from happening to my daughter. You know why? I care. That's why. *I am* awake – bloody *darn* awake! I *know* the truth; I know I can get answers! I'm *not* like the others! I care! Me! I care that you survive, so tell me where Bonner is so I can do it! Tell me now!" Ben took a deep breath, calming his outburst. He really shouldn't be making such promises, but he had no choice now that he had arrived at Dulce. "I cannot fail now that I've come so close. Tell me, please. Where is Alfred Bonner?"

"There is *nothing* you can do," the woman rasped. She met his eyes. They were glazed with moisture. She removed the knife completely, but Ben still lay on the bank. In the heavy stunned silence, the liminal stream trickled to his left, slithering and weaving in sand and rock. "It's too late." She stood up, ghastly in form. "They are all going to die, Ben. Everyone you love."

"Stop," Ben said, voice small. He locked up. The numbness set in, flaming embers of darkness that never disappeared.

"There is no hope." The woman was forlorn, gazing listlessly at the creek. "Veronica … Bonner has already got her."

Your daughter has been given away to another strange people, and your eyes look, and they fail, for your hand is powerless to save her.

Ben's breathing became labored. He clenched his teeth.

Thomas Jones … Patala.

The woman glared at Ben in pain. He froze when he watched her … Watched Veronica in the shadows slip out of his grasp. Watched as a procreating dread that made Ben unable to fight – unable to do anything – take over. *Your eyes look, and they fail, for your hand is powerless.*

Ben whined as the morbid woman continued. "Your pain is not new to me," she said, placing a comforting hand on his shoulder. "I know the darkness as much as you do. I want you to be the man that everyone wants you to be. They cannot see you like this."

"Tell me where Bonner is."

"Give up. You've tried and tried, but nothing gets better. You've lost everything. Just like me, you will learn to accept that this is normal. If God loves you – if God loves all – why hasn't he shown everyone the truth? The truth only *you* want?"

You will find the Truth. The paladin promised. The cursed paladin who cast Ben into this nightmare.

No family. No purpose. No friends. No acting. Ben blinked tears out of his eyes. Everything withered and withdrew, wanting to stop hurting.

The woman drew her lips in a grim smirk. "Let me do you a favour." She slowly got to a squat, and holding his chin, gently nicking the knife against his skin. Ben winced, feeling the cut sting. "If I dig it deep enough, your life will end. We are born in this cursed life to lose everything. The only sole victory in life is to abandon the pain. Stop wanting to *force* things the way you want. You have control over *nothing*. Liberate yourself, Ben. From suffering. From craving."

Ben felt everything around him darken. Funnelling.

"Veronica is dead," the woman said finally. "There is nothing you can do."

There was nothing he could have done …

God! There isn't anything I can do!

"Why are you doing this?"

"Because you don't understand what Alfred can do, for I'm his …" Choking, the woman slumped.

Ben blinked. "Alfred's what?"

"Alfred." The woman's voice was wooden. She stepped back, holding her throat, knife hand at her side. She walked in darkness, enduring torment. "We children have been slaves for too long!" Then the woman groaned, tilting her head, raising her arms, fists clenched, knife raised. She cried, exclaiming, "If only I was big as you! If only … If only I would have *fought them off!* I would have beaten them up! If only *my father* cared for me!"

Ben stared at the abruptness of her outburst, touching his stinging wound. "You're a slave to your … father." He trembled despite himself. This unfortunate girl was a tool used by dark secret societies run by sex traffickers. This was the reality before Ben of what his Veronica could potentially become if he did nothing.

Ben slowly got to his feet.

"You are something else, Ben. You are something else. I wish I was as strong as you." The woman seemed timid, so uncharacteristically shy now. She took a step back, dropping her knife.

"Promise to show me, woman. What's your name?"

The woman was silent for a while, staring at nothing. "Marcell. Yeah. It's Marcell."

"Marcell?" *Wasn't that a boy's name?* "All right, Marcell. Can you show me inside?"

Marcell nodded and, turning around, took a few furtive steps over the stream towards the mountain. "I'm going to die," Marcell whispered, groaning back to Ben as they navigated through the shrubbery towards the mountainside.

"I'll promise Bonner dies first." He grabbed the discarded knife, holding it in his hand. It was a well-crafted weapon, callow silver in the starlight. "Lead the way."

Picking her way towards the sloping rocky mountainside, Marcell reluctantly led Ben to a small cleft in the stone – a hole cleaved into the rocky roots of the mountain – and began to ease herself down into it.

The Underworld. Marcell confirmed that Veronica was to be sent to Hell by Bonner's will. *That is what Thomas Jones' maze is, right? Patala is Hell.*

Ben exhaled and knew he had found the way, standing at the entrance of the cave, astonished. His emotions were contorted and twisted in an unidentifiable mess.

"How can I know you are not leading me into a trap?" he said, his breath tight with pain.

Marcell didn't respond. She led Ben deeper. It was hard to limp on unruly ground. The cavern smelled of dank dust, and the only faint light was the incorporeally present yet mysterious light that came from the other side of the sloping cavern.

The woman stepped fluidly over the fallen rubble stones with balance and ease, and with elegance, she gingerly ambled along – such a contrast to her curt belligerence.

It was once they reached the corner that was about to turn towards the light, where industrial sounds echoed through the cavern, Marcell grasped the dark slate wall, slumping as if weighed down by a heavy burden. She groaned. Her skin perspired. "I cannot do this." She was sobbing.

Ben snarled. "Do what? Help me? Come on, you're a strong woman."

"No, no." She shook her head, twitching and trembling. Her face was pale as a ghost. "I need to escape."

What had gotten into this woman? One minute she'd been all tough and confident, telling Ben to die, and the next, she was inept, paranoid and broken. *What did Alfred Bonner do to her? Bastard!* "Yes, you can. I will let you go free from here."

"No. No. You don't understand. He will find out. He knows. He will send the Wild Men." Marcell groaned in distress, placing a hand over her mouth. "I cannot face him. Please, you begged me to show you where my father is. But now, I return the favour."

"We keep on failing. But I'm not in the mood to give up now." Then he paused. Ah, there, that was Noah's words, Noah – the Sage who survived the dying world. "The door of mercy is open."

Marcell lowered herself to the ground and leaned on the wall, her legs twisted under her. She gazed up at him, looking exhausted. She wore tattered shorts, her shins and thighs exposed, grimy and muddy from the fight. Suddenly, she appeared to gain the dregs of her repose, becoming grimly austere, back straight. She nodded, tears leaking down her face. "Then do me one last favour." She sounded like a different person. Strong and confident. "If Veronica exceeds your grasp, I beg of you, give me a blessing so I can live."

Ben stared, shocked. "No …" *Marcell just told me to kill myself. She accused me, and now she expects me to be kind to her?*

"Please," she begged.

Ben frowned, and suddenly, he *understood*. This woman, a traumatised girl, had been promised that she would be protected from evil. Ben could be that swift-footed hope of good, that inspiration for her now, as if he'd done it for Veronica.

Dark in thought, foible, pale, longing for death, Marcell sought for a blessing, but it kept exceeding her grasp.

Ben knew too well that same despair of failure, the curse that cleaved to him. Marcell and Veronica would have to live with this dread.

He stared at Marcell, the poor and frail girl. She'd been defiled.

Veronica, his offspring, his only family that survived.

Alfred Bonner, the implacable enemy.

Ben brandished the combat knife in his hand, and the Actionman – long dormant – arose from the depths and stepped into the light. Alarm bells in the base warbled.

Justice is what men deserve, Ben thought. *God, I pray you have mercy on me.*

"May God bless you, Marcell, from harm. May God bless Veronica. May God have mercy on us all, suffering gratuitous evil. May we survive what we must face next."

This molested girl he would protect. In Veronica's name.

—

Honour must be rectified. *Geas* must be restored.

And only James Casbolt could do it.

Red rage filled him as he lay in the dust on the ground, incapacitated, radiating heat.

Then the wind stirred. The dust crept along the Crater. The moon, a bloody head – hung over the dangling corpse of Orion embedded in the black firmament.

In his desperation, a long strenuous scream gushed out of the Redlion. Rising slowly, he strained, pulling against the bonds around his hands.

Then a Spirit of berserker wrath thrust upon Casbolt. It rushed into him from an intake of deep breath, filling his lungs. The power *pounded* in him like the clapper of a bell. His muscles burned with energy, desiring to move. Redlion, clenching his fists, pulled his hands apart, and the ropes snapped, his bonds melting off his hands as wax catching fire. He stood up and saw an aura around himself, white-and-yellow smoke-like fire streaming off his arms. Against stellar darkness, he was a shining star of the heavens.

For a moment, he was both confused and exhilarated by the light radiating out of him. The flames of wrath. Of judgment.

Quivering with rage, the Spirit of power erupting, Redlion rushed towards the Carnutes, splaying out his right hand, summoning his Curruid Spear from the Otherworld. He felt a tugging – a pull of the materialising weapon.

Four paedophiles – those dragons, those snakes in human skin – on the fringes of the company saw him, and with loud cries, they charged.

Gáe Bulg formed from smoke in his fingers, just as he swung in a great arc, slashing the weapon through the four men. They slumped to the ground instantaneously.

Redlion moved in to attack. More wicked Carnutes assailed him, and he swept them away like chaff.

"Kill him! The Redlion is unleashed! Kill him!"

Getting into Orca on the Wave – a vicious wide-arching strike, slashing downwards – Redlion roared, rampaging with fiery anger.

—

Gun to his chest, Marcus Theis navigated through the forlorn base, leading his combat assault team and the FBI through winding corridors. They reached an industrial tunnel that had caved in, ruined rubble blocking the way.

To the side of the tunnel was a large, heavy door with a green escape sign, and Derek, peeking inside, raised a hand gesture for everyone to halt. Johnny Best skulked behind Marcus like a shadow, jaw tight, eyes determined. This kid had come a long way – he'd persevered admiringly and held his chin high after Drill Sergeant JJ Girgos castigated him publicly. Now he served an honourable purpose.

"Door's locked, Captain," Derek said. "We need to blast the bastard down."

"Affirmative," Marcus said. "See where it leads."

Johnny looked down the cold and silent industrial tunnel, dark with faint sterile lights on the ceiling, some in the distance flickering eerily from earthquake damage.

Blasting the lock on the door with a few rounds, Derek swung it open, and Marcus, his marines and the agents poured inside, preparing for security guards.

It led to an empty control room.

"Where is everybody?" Jason Laycock said.

"Evacuated," Keller said, gun raised.

"Keep your eyes peeled for a trap," Marcus commanded.

The controls had displays of security footage on monitor screens, control panels, knobs and other technical devices.

"Who would leave all the monitors on like this?" Keller grumbled, but his FBI colleagues didn't respond.

Marcus frowned at the videos. Fuzzy security footage showed various sections in the base, some flickering with static, black and white, but clear enough to know what was going on. From various angles and perspectives, the footage revealed child test subjects in gowns. They looked as if they had been operated on, drugged by the scientists who were leading their gurneys out in haste.

"Guys," Marcus said. "I think our combat assault just became a rescue mission."

—

Charging into the howling chaos, Redlion assaulted the child-loving Carnutes swarming around him. He swung Gáe Bulg, and the supernatural metal cut through flesh and bone so easily, it felt as if he was cutting through smoke. He swung and thrusted in a maelstrom of death, cleaving bodies apart. Leopard Seal Snags the Prey. Orca Tosses the Calf. Iceberg Breaks off the Glacier.

He had to get to the men in black, to Prometheus and Circe. The children of Satan. He wanted them dead at the end of his Spear for sacrificing Clarita and Lluvia to Fomorians.

A deranged Aes Sidhe woman with dishevelled hair, leather vambraces and a knife attacked. Redlion tripped her, but she broke her fall with her arms, using her legs to twist Redlion's body, pinning him to the ground on one knee. Punching the woman, he grabbed her knife, breaking her wrist, and plunged the weapon into her neck.

Carnutes jumped towards Redlion, and he rolled to the side, grabbing his Spear, raising it. It skewered the two men, and they thrashed in agony, their screams inhuman.

Very quickly, the fight became close range. Redlion didn't have enough room to swing the Spear. Growling in vexation, he dismissed his Spear into smoke and began to bludgeon bodies, clouting them with his bare fists. They glowed orange and yellow with the strange smoke infusing him. The Spirit of wrath sent them hurling to the ground in a single strike. He pulled in arms, breaking noses, back-fist punching and jabbing his opponents. Smashing, thumping, pounding left, right, centre, under, and back, counterattack.

The energy that burned within him raged like a hurricane in his chest. He didn't know what it was, but it was supernatural strength, so much so he was barely able to keep it from ripping him apart.

Redlion saw the Carnutes standing back into a fanning circle, trying to preserve space for the battle. Redlion grabbed a woman's hair in his glowing fist and leapt into the air, decking her onto another enemy, hurdling her over his shoulder, snapping her arm.

Redlion felt cold metal slice his shoulder. He grunted as a Carnute man slashed his knife back and forth. Redlion cudgelled him, arm barring the attacker, blocking his other hand, twisting the wrist.

Suddenly, gunshots addled the calamitous air. Redlion dashed away as Carnutes chased him. On this claypan, there was nowhere to hide. He grabbed a fallen Carnute and used her as a shield from the pursuers. Bullets thudded her flesh. One bullet peppered her body, gashing Redlion's thigh. He bellowed, and the pain numbed. He burst forwards, charging, raising the fallen body, ramming into the firing Carnutes. Tossing the body aside, he gripped the gunman, arm barring his stiff elbow as far as it would go, cracking it. The man howled.

Redlion aimed the gun and fired, spinning around at his ring of enemies, muzzle flashing.

The sky lit up with fire, and Redlion only had a second to spare as he threw himself to the ground. A column of flames arced downwards, barely missing him. Smoke blistered Redlion's nostrils. The orange-red glow of the power around his eyes didn't go away. It burned constantly, immunising him from the burns.

Parting the smoke, Circe strode forwards, a single flame burning in the palm of her bare hand, her teeth and black lips a rictus snarl. Next to her was Prometheus, brandishing his great and terrible sword on his shoulder.

Carnutes swarmed Redlion, and he thrashed them with fist and Spear. He went for the joints, breaking them.

A knife bearer swung. Redlion dodged the hissing blade three times, the fourth barely deflected by his Spear haft.

Suddenly, a flying side kick struck Redlion's stomach, sending him to the ground on his back, and he dismissed the Spear. Two lean figures loomed over him, one with a knife raised. Redlion, getting into a V-sit, kicked the knife bearer. Shifting, he kicked the second Carnute. The Carnute evaded and lunged, backhanding Redlion in the face.

His vision clouded, but the orange-red steam around him lingered.

The knife man swung, and Redlion jerked. Hot pain raced through his arm. He growled, throwing his elbow into his face. The second Carnute lunged again, but he kicked him back down. Redlion kicked his leg up, knee connecting with the man's face. Pulling the knife out of his shoulder, Redlion got up, walked towards the attacker, hauled him up with one hand and stabbed him in the neck. The man whined and sobbed. Redlion pulled out the knife and stabbed the neck again, blood splashing everywhere. Redlion stabbed and stabbed repeatedly, then tossed the dead thing man into the Carnutes.

Redlion would kill them all. He was a fire storm of justice that couldn't be stopped. He summoned his Currid Spear and continued the rampage, nonchalantly cleaving through Carnute after Carnute after Carnute. There were hundreds of them.

Redlion crashed into Circe. She clawed his face as the Spear rammed through her gorgeous body. She dropped the stone, emitting an un-light – violent dark red – of congealed red shadows. Redlion crushed it under his boot. He disengaged, leaving the beauty queen witch cleaved in two.

Redlion spun in a fluid motion. He had to get to Prometheus. Tunnel vision and singular in motive, the divine spirit that rushed upon him burned on and on, like charged electricity.

Carnutes replaced fallen Carnutes, and they all died, screaming. The Redlion waddled in a wake of destruction – cairns and mounds of bodies of dead, crimson belly spear Gáe Bulg soaking in their blood, bits of their flesh snagged on its razor-sharp points.

Casbolt was not surprised by the massacre he had committed.

Prometheus stood by the altar of rocks, the cleft where the Danava had taken Julian's daughters into the Underworld. The Titan was tall and strong. He had taken off his glasses, revealing his huge feline reptilian eyes glowing teal blue. With his hat discarded, he was bald, pale as the moon, his cranium elongated like an alien. His scalloped blade with its vestigial cross-guard hung in his hand.

Casbolt pushed forward, marching towards the man in black, wrath imbuing him.

"Yaldabaoth's breath," Prometheus cursed, raising his sword. "A pawn of Übermensch created by people in power. You're a beast."

Casbolt tucked the shaft of Gáe Bulg under his arm, narrowing the distance between them. "The men in black are Titans who fell from Heaven and raped human women. You, Prometheus, have incurred great *geas* upon me *and* humanity! Fight me!"

"Idiot," Prometheus chuckled, twirling his sword. "I'm not an Anunna. I'm not what I seem."

Casbolt remembered now something mentioned in the Turquoise Room; something about Skin Walkers. Shape shifters. Fomorian forces of deception.

Casbolt lunged, swinging the bloody Spear upwards. Prometheus evaded with wind-like fluidity, battering the Spear with a flick of his sword. Casbolt pulled back, twirling the Spear, shaft slapping against his back, getting into Starfish Caught in a Brinicle.

"You glow like the heroes of old!" Prometheus called.

"I'm no hero. But I will not let evil flourish." Casbolt smiled, the thrill returning. His shoulder and thigh throbbed with mild pain, warm blood slowly leaking from the wounds. Each step was burning. He had to make this fight quick. "Sons of Danu don't leave without a fight."

"Vanity," Prometheus intoned. "We both wield indestructible weapons – you carry the Curruid Spear of the Tuatha Dé Danann, and I, Adamantine

– metal forged by the gods of Olympus." Haughtily, the asura swung a flurry of strikes, Casbolt using the length of his Spear to his advantage to deflect them all. God-metal clanged against god-metal, resounding like peals of high-pitched thunder, singing a cathartic rhythm.

Prometheus skipped backwards, flourishing and pacing. "You're a fool, James Casbolt. You're hardly my equal."

Then Prometheus, with a zigzagging baulk, sprang into the air with a gliding strike, jabbing his sword downwards. Casbolt dodged, barely, raising his Spear to deflect. He swung, and Prometheus leaned back, Spear cleaving the air. He twirled around, backhanding the Spear.

Casbolt barely caught the Adamantine blade with the back of his Spear haft, and like lightning, he landed a flurry of furious twisting attacks upon the asura blade. Gáe Bulg's tip slid into the vestigial cross-guard. Twisting his blade, Prometheus got both weapons into a bind, bending Casbolt's arm backwards, locking him up.

He yelped in pain. Prometheus grinned – he had thousands of years of experience. Laboriously breathing, Casbolt strained, but the Fomorian pulled away, evading. Completely calm, Prometheus kept disengaging. He flourished his blade as a way of taunting.

Glory! Kleos! Redlion resounded throughout his being. *Attain it! It's ours!*

Sucking in his pain, Casbolt's long red Spear jabbed, but Prometheus batted it away, lunging back at him, great sword flashing. Casbolt evaded like a flittering skua, Prometheus hunting Casbolt like a leopard seal.

Then, with a sudden jolt of speed, Prometheus became a blur, moving inhumanly fast, faster than any super soldier, faster than a buzzing fly.

Pain and power threw Casbolt to the ground. The next thing he knew, he was on the ground, his head throbbing, shoulder and thigh spasming.

Prometheus stood over him.

Getting onto his feet, he threw Gáe Bulg as Prometheus swung his blade, nicking the projectile, but the Spear gashed his shoulder. Prometheus gasped, stumbling backward. He grabbed his wounded shoulder, dropping the sword, which turned to smoke.

Casbolt roared from his pain. Blundering like a bull, ramming into the asura with his body, dust billowed around him. He pushed and shoved, landing on top of the man in black.

"Please," the man in black rasped, his plaid face pearled with moisture, wildcat eyes gapping. "You cannot take me back."

"You fear," Casbolt rasped, grinning. "Some Titan you are."

Prometheus' mouth formed into a rictus. His massive eyes glowed a vibrant teal. "The voidstone is dangerous, you Chief of mud creatures. Take your victory. But I warn you, your end is coming. I foresee when the Heralds of the end come, death shall find you. You shall be betrayed by the one love of your life."

Casbolt hesitated, his mind overwhelmed by those strange words. "I may die, but dying while facing darkness alone is what makes me better than you."

—

Tara came forward because stupid Marcell kept on procrastinating, humiliating her. She twitched.

She castigated herself for being honest about her feelings towards Ben. He misunderstood. Clearly, her honesty had failed to make the impression that she wanted. To him, her words were poison, feeling sorry for her schizophrenia as she begged for mercy when, in reality, Tara was being honest, her only hope to bear the frustration of living as an abused sex slave.

Why did she plan to escape Dulce, and then, in her weakness, she made a promise to help Ben?

She felt clunky – a worthless muddle of a woman – backing against the wall as US marines and FBI agents stormed the base, freeing test subjects. Panic seized her; hearing gunfire brought back unpleasant memories. She hunched, dwelling in the shadows behind ennui grey walls. She knew the marines and agents were saving her, but she felt unworthy to be saved.

"I have to get out." And break her promise?

Cold gripped her, and she looked up. A zigzagging fissure split the ceiling above. A fresh crack from the stress of the earth tremors. She felt the ground under her with her hand. It was wet from leakage.

The military had got to Dulce – had it been Ben's doing too? Ben had never mentioned the military would accompany him on his selfish revenge quest for his daughter. The Devil was in that man's eyes.

But a deep part of Tara wanted Ben to succeed, wanted his marines to end her father, Alfred Bonner. At last, justice was at hand.

Tara placed a hand over her mouth in dismay.

She couldn't face the carnage before her. Something inside adamantly refused. Dulce Base, which had broken her, had been broken, rendered into chaos by the earthquake. Parts of the roofing structure had fallen apart, the mountain rock disgorged in strewn piles here and there on the concrete ground.

Would it end like this? Would it end with the marines finding her wretched, undignified body? No, marines may be men, but they had to be different. They were disciplined, trained men of honour. Not like the Alliance guards.

Tara convulsed, letting out shuddering breaths. Her mind, her body, burned as if a black flame were scorching her inside out, slowly roasting her over the years as she decayed as a human being. She had promised herself to never trust men. Men like Ian Mastemah had traumatised her – he promised to give her sexual pleasure for wisdom, then sold her to Alfred Bonner as a gift. Could she trust the marines to save her? Could she ... hope again?

No ... I failed, then failed again. I always fail.

She slumped, burying her face in her hands. Why had she not escaped as Ben had suggested? "It's because I'm a coward. I'm gutless."

What could she do? Suffer endlessly? Let Marcell procrastinate? She'd been berated and browbeaten for doing that too when she was about to shoot up a school. Marcell tried to give some of Tara's humanity back. The handlers had known he was a liability when she became a boy. When had that nonsense started happening?

Marcell was a fantasy, a lie. Tara was a senile angry woman – a hater of males – but weak.

Tara arched her head, staring at a deft crack in the ceiling. Water trickled from the cleavage, dripping in a puddle at her feet and on her head. Cold water. Mountain tears.

A couple of times late at night, unable to bear the gazes of the guards who slapped her ass when she passed by, she snuck out near the secret passageway to hang herself. But one of the workers – the timid one, who remained aloof, blushing at his friends' actions, found her in the process of trying to tighten the noose and cut the ropes. That man was young. But like the rest of them, he was a mere delivery man for the Alliance. He coerced her. Even in this sacred moment, he did something no different from the rest. Could not *one* man just respect her rights and wants?

But did Tara need help then? She was supposed to be Aes Sidhe – they had to fight, to be strong.

The second time she sought death was three days ago, when she heard the terrible vulgar language of the drunk Alliance Aes Sidhe next door, keeping her up at night, and unable to bear the anguish, she tried drowning herself in the bath as one last effort. She closed her eyes and drifted in silent peace.

The next moment, she was hugging Alfred Bonner. Her father had come to save her, and she broke, all sodden and humiliated.

Even her *father* prevented her from death.

Shivering, Tara sank into a ball, chin to chest. At this point of overwhelming distress, she knew she had to act.

And defy her father.

Everyone had been defiant at some point in their lives or experienced the defiance of others. Acts of spite, deliberate choices to forge one's own path. Many found ways to resist restraints, patriarchy, expectations, and child sex traffickers, to defy what may seem insurmountable odds to achieve something meaningful, or simply relish the opportunity to rebel. But for Tara, it was right to fight back, yet it could cause more anguish to herself the more she tried.

Barbelo's curse got to her.

Tara groaned, hands wet in the puddle, staring at her sorrowful reflection. Her eyes bulged as she felt the mark on her forehead.

Pain racked her, causing her vision to spin. Arching her back, she collapsed on the floor, twitching, flapping her hands, splashing in the puddle, yelping shrilly. She tried to clamp her teeth shut, but her endless shriek filled the room. It was one scream among many in the battle around the corner. She felt as if she had been beaten from head to toe, every stroke landing at once. Tears leaked down her cheeks shamefully. Crippling darkness plundered her.

She saw someone standing over her. Gasping, she spun and saw a boy standing next to her.

It was Marcell. A pretty primary Mexican schoolboy of nine in uniform with long socks pulled up his lower legs. She had never seen him like this before, hands clasped in front of him, brown hair and … that face. He looked like one of the boys she wanted to murder in her attempted school shooting. He stared down the corridors, towards the tunnel that led straight to the ninth-level station, expression horrified, eyes wide and sorrowful. A face of a child watching a brutal murder, stealing his innocence.

Tara stared down the way Marcell was looking. Down there, a guttural groaning belch vibrated the walls. A male Sasquatch, mighty and vitriolic.

Suddenly, the marines behind her were responding to distress calls, begging for reinforcements. But the marines saving the child slaves were still firing at their adversaries, the Dulce guards marking and shooting at the marines.

Tara twitched – she knew those feelings. Hearing them twisted her heart. Soldiers were down there; Ben's men were fighting to save the enslaved children just like her, and now they faced a monster that served Barbelo and the Aeons alone.

"No!" one of the men shouted. "Brianna's down there!"

"Pounders, what is your status? This is Combat Unit One. Over!"

"Reinforcements, now!"

"Hey! Stay with the prisoners, Keller!"

"Wait! What are you doing?"

The man Keller bellowed in desperation, clanging bullets escalating.

Her opportunity. There was a woman in the rescue raid.

She's probably wounded down there, Tara thought. She couldn't watch successful women fail and die. It was *so* cruel, *so* unfair. "Go. Do something good for once." Despite herself, Tara feebly stood up on damp bare feet. But when she stared at Marcell, she gained his strength.

She listened to the howling cries and the rapidly blitzing battle. "You led them into this, DePaula." She spun around from the tunnel.

A shower of water, a steady stream, splattered on her face. She looked up at the leak in the ceiling from the crack and let the liquid dampen her hair and clothes thoroughly. Baptising her.

Marcell stood next to the leakage, facing the tunnel. It made her very soul contort in knots, seeing the despair on his little cute face.

Tara could hear the sounds of gunshots cease. Or was that her mind playing tricks? Instead, she heard the moaning of the dying. The weeping.

"I have been here before!" she said, turning around. "I can prevent a massacre! I have full control!"

Freedom … It was just her – herself. Freedom … How sweet and good was it?

She gazed down that dark tunnel, towards death, the American men and woman amid them. Stark decision seemed to crush her. What if she was too weak to save them?

"No, I can," Tara said. "I can. *I can.* Someone has to save. I will protect those who cannot protect themselves."

And how relevant was that for her, for she had been the one who couldn't protect herself? At that moment, for the first time, the pain in her forehead vanished. She could think clearly.

I'll lead myself to death doing what is right.

———

Ben stopped in the middle of the abandoned base, his limp blinding with pain that sapped his strength.

At last, he could find the truth.

It was inevitable. Divinely sanctioned, revealed through Joshua's seeing. The horn of the beast would break as Ben sinned and saved his daughter.

He felt nothing but the need to obey the impulses of a darker agency.

Ben raised his chin high, watching the lofty stairs. He bound up them madly, trying to not put much pressure on the bad hip. He sulked like a wounded predator into the elaborate, expansive office where stark banal lighting cast over the chair of a golden-blond cranium, back facing him. Ben hid behind a pillar, his skin crawling with pleasure.

Holding his breath, Ben closed his eyes, leaping around the chair, knife pointed at Alfred Bonner.

"Sit down!" He clawed at Bonner's collar, throwing him back in the chair. Bonner ogled up at him, shock in his azure eyes.

"How did you—"

"Shut up," Ben spat.

"Don't threaten me, Ben."

"Why her?" Ben's throat tightened. "Why her and not me?" Bonner's icy-blue eyes knew what that inferred. "Answer me!" Ben bellowed.

"You're special, you know." A jeering smirk split Bonner's treacherous face. "We're both special."

Heart palpitating, Ben leaned inwards, directly into the giant man's face, knife pointed at his eyes. "Why?"

"Look at me." Bonner sounded thoughtful, with a lofty firmness. "Dulce is a foster centre for lost children and a prison for paedophiles. I do not take. I *receive*."

Then Bonner struck. Batting Ben's knife hand away with great strength, getting to his feet swiftly, he shoved Ben sideways. Ben collapsed, bracing for the table, hauling himself up, and charged.

Bonner pointed a gun. Ben gasped, slamming into Bonner, but the man pushed him back to the floor again. Grunting, Ben scrabbled around and froze, eyes keen on the cocking gun.

"Put your hands behind your head," Bonner growled, deep as an earthquake.

———

"I'm all right, really," Brianna said tartly, refusing any more treatment of her wound. "Keller needs me." Joshua tried to stop the woman, but she mulishly hopped up the stairs where Keller had gone.

It only took a few minutes for Joshua to realise that what Brianna had done to escape the train station platform was sensible. Over the corpses of hairy creatures, a guttural moaning, a strained siren of a furious beast, echoed from everywhere. A trumpet declaring the eschaton.

"What was—"

"CAT 2!" Pounders hissed. "We need reinforcements, now!"

Joshua listened, ears straining from the deafening silence of the sound that had reverberated sonorously . His heart thumped as Pounders and Demos, with a small squad of marines, readied their weapons. In silence, they mobilised into blocking positions, poised to fight.

First came a smell wafting into his nose. It was like an old banana left to rot in a trash can that had been salvaged by a skunk. It had a greasy, hairy feel to it.

Then the horror swung from the other flight of stairs Brianna hadn't scaled. It flew with remarkable speed – a hurling mountain of fur and muscle – crashing to the ground, landing on all fours. The hairy hulk stood up – posture not slouching; it was shockingly humanlike. It stood on two flat feet that gave the creature its infamous name. Bigfoot.

It was a male – an alpha, perhaps. It was nine feet tall, gazing at the dead of its kind, attuning to a hooting rhythm of wrath and annihilation. Its pudgy nostrils were flaring. It had an orangutan look with brown-orange hair swaying thick like jungle vines along its long arms cupped with lanky fingers. Those fingers grew into claw-like nails. It stomped forwards across the platform, feet like thunder beneath the earth.

The way it walked with large strides resembled someone striding through snow wearing a pair of skis. The strangeness of the high gait, its movement as if gliding with no head bob, was demonic. Its face was pitch black – as if painted black – and its almond eyes were polished jet.

The marines opened fire. Colonel Pounders led them bravely.

The Gigantopithecus bowed over, barking, leaping to the right with astounding speed. Bullets missed him. The marines aimed, firing again. But the Gigantopithecus was too quick. It swung with one hand around the staircase with a grumping *whaph!*

Fire ceased. A marine shouted into his com kit for aid asap. Pounders turned, and Joshua thought he saw on that senior face a smile, glinting with sweat-wrinkled lines extending from the corners of his eyes. Despite hopelessness, the smile seemed strikingly maternal.

The Gigantopithecus bulled from out of nowhere. Stretching out its nails, a hideous grin formed on his face. The beast dared Pounders to fight. It was unfair – Pounders and his three men were hobbits compared to the King Kong rippled with muscle bulk.

Without warning, with one single nonchalant sweep of his powerful arm, the Gigantopithecus felled Pounders.

"No!" Joshua bellowed.

He beheld his true father hanging in the air, dashing against the concrete like a rag doll, tumbling off the platform and onto the train tracks, out of sight. Numbness gripped Joshua – ice compacting his chest. He let out wails of despair as he ran towards the train tracks.

The Gigantopithecus roared in victory, beating his thick chest.

Judd was dead. A surreal verisimilitude.

"Josh!" Demos screamed. Joshua ran to where Pounders lay.

The rest of the marines opened fire – none shrinking back despite the truth they were going to die. Bullets pelted the Sasquatch's body, but it lunged into the barrage. Slashing at two marines, nails amputated one man's right arm, sending him shrieking in anguish. He was quickly flung to the ground, skull cracking on the concrete. The other man was slashed and trampled flat. The third fired, and the Sasquatch kicked him upwards. He flew, screeching, gun flying from his arms. When he landed, the beast stomped on him.

Joshua ran, and the Sasquatch hissed, marking him. It didn't fear pain; many bullet holes marred its chest and arms, blood caking its fur, oozing down its body in dark smears.

A bugling *whoop* piercing the ears, vibrating the bones, caused his eye to throb. Joshua reached the platform edge and saw … a mangled body on the tracks, unmoving.

Roaring to the end of himself, Demos opened fire as the Sasquatch charged for Joshua. It stopped and turned around. Joshua looked back at the beast, dangerously close to him, as it faced Demos.

"Hey!" Demos screamed, offering up his life for Joshua. He fired at the monster's head.

The giant grunted, stumbling back in shock, covering its face from Demos' bullets. Demos stood in the gap of life and death, as the creature got onto all fours, taking shelter behind a pile of Sasquatch corpses.

Then a low frequency vibration – a shockwave – assailed Joshua. His ears stung with pain, making him hiss, hands clasping the sides of his head. His sternum rattled from the buzz.

It even affected Demos across the platform. The man went stiff, his neck bulging with strain. He dropped his gun, falling onto his knees.

Something was happening, as if *sound* was attacking them!

Nefer let out a cry of anguish in Joshua's spirit as the rampaging Gigantopithecus turned to Joshua, its black face blank.

"COME ON!" Letting out all his agony, Joshua stood against the Nephilim standing on his feet.

It sprung spryly. Joshua embraced his death.

A flying projectile collided with the giant. An ear-ringing explosion that sent Joshua hurling over the edge, dropping onto the tracks, bruised and battered. He grazed his forehead, bruising his arm perilously on the rail. Stinging pain kept him writhing on the ground, but the anxiety of being on the tracks when the train came was stronger. Rising up on all fours, he growled at his agony, reaching Pounders' body. He felt for a pulse and wasn't shocked to find none.

Dead. Done.

Joshua exhaled. Numbness gripped him.

All of what this man had done for him in his life was … spectacular. If a man could be a miracle manifest, Judd Pounders was that man.

Human footsteps brought Joshua's head up, and he saw a mean-looking young girl standing over the edge of the smoking platform. She parted the smoke with shoulder-length hair, tattered jeans and muggy clothes, grasping an RPG launcher in her hands. She had a savage look to her – grim of face with intense eyes, brow scowling. Tattoos marked her bare thighs. She was gleaming with moisture, and her hair was dark and damp, strands splaying over her shoulders and neck. She could have been an attractive type, but from the hard lines around her eyes, Joshua knew she was one of the child slaves of Dulce who'd escaped.

She was low in spirit.

"Get ready," the girl said. "Off the tracks, unless you have a death wish!"

Joshua grimaced, reaching up. "I didn't ask for any of this …" He slumped.

The girl nodded in respect, then got on her knees and helped Joshua and Pounders off the train tracks.

—

Panting, Ben rose slowly off the ground, hands rising behind his head.

He stared at Bonner – an angular, handsome Nephilim, untouched by age. He was no simple-minded senior politician; he had the muscular build of a heavyweight champion, with keen eyes and a wise, knowing face. Bonner motioned him to move towards the desk. "Open the drawer."

Ben obeyed unwillingly, scowling. He opened the draw. Inside were handcuffs.

"Put them on."

Ben put them on.

"You don't deserve your daughter."

"No," Ben muttered, unable to believe his misfortune. "Just let me see her. You have her."

"I do, DePaula," Bonner said. "I have her safe with me. I will show you."

Uncertain whether Bonner was telling the truth or not, Ben glared as the man led him at gunpoint down the corridor towards a storehouse with a large metal hatch at its centre. It resembled a sewer or a well with a circular door capping the shaft down below.

Accomplishment tried to soften his heart, but fear and panic hardened it more. Even at gunpoint, Ben would fight his war to the end.

Ben gazed at the hatch inside the mellow room, with a weak neon light hanging through cobwebs dangling from the metal ceiling beams. One section of the wall had a continuous crack reaching from floor to roof. There was nothing in this room except for discarded tools, worktables, a garage roller door and the central hatch.

"Making children disappear is the way the secret societies wage war with the Galactic Tyrant," Bonner said dryly. "It makes people lose their faith. Your child was taken away from you to reveal that you're not a father. You're a devil of Babylon."

Ben felt his chest cramp with pain. He closed his eyes, swaying. *He deceived me!*

"I just wanted to let you know," Bonner said. "Casbolt never took the girls. The Manicheans of Light did."

Ben opened his eyes, looking up sharply. "Ian?" Bonner was now standing before Ben, gun in one hand, the hatch between them.

"Yes. I never steal children. I give children who are kidnapped by the Cabal refuge. Take a look. Perhaps your daughter is in there."

Ben snorted, falling to his knees, cuffed hands grasping the wheel knob. He was trembling, his throat constricting.

"Only one way to find out," Bonner intoned.

Jerking, Ben turned the wheel with all his might. "Veronica." The wheel squeaked, like his voice, turning until his muscles tensed. At last, battling against the wheel, the hatch opened. "Veronica?" he gasped. "Veronica! Veronica!"

The only sound he heard was his own cries coming back up to him from within the deep maw of death and neglect. Notwithstanding, Ben peered, feeling his daughter was down there.

"You see, Ben DePaula," Bonner said. "You may have saved a child once, but you lost your own. The kidnapped children have nothing. I need to send them to Patala. The Galactic Tyrant is coming. To fight him, we educate the children in the high culture of the asuras. It is the next small step for mankind to face our apocalyptic threat. The words of the dying show us the asuras are important and that Jesus Christ … is evil." Bonner's eyes grew distant, and Ben thought he could see remorse in them. "On the ocean of life and death, the dying say something is coming. The children I take will save us. I know I cannot escape karma." He lowered his gun towards Ben's feet. "But neither can you."

Growling at his odious fate, Ben shot up to his feet. He doubled over from the sudden fiery pain in his leg and the disorientating bang of the gun. "God!" he blurted, stumbling until his legs dangled over the edge of the pit. He gasped, his strength depleting quickly. He gazed at his leg, saw the concrete ground blotched with his crimson blood. He felt nauseated, slipping towards the pit in the ground. *I'm dead. Just … go in there.*

Ben fell and writhed lethargically into the pit. He gritted his teeth, his breathing short and rapid. He hadn't felt in this much writhing pain since earlier this year when he had broken his L2 vertebrae at Haditha.

It was black inside, the dimness devouring Ben, besides a shaft of light from above. Ben grovelled, his cuffed hands trying to feel the rocky wall. Was he blind? No, the pit was cramped. As he pushed himself to sit up against the wall, his leg screamed with pain.

He smelled the iron of his blood. *I have to make a torniquet or something.*

"Better for one man to sin than the whole world be destroyed," Bonner said serenely above. "Goodbye, Ben the Actionman." Mouth a smug grimace, Bonner grabbed the hatch door and closed it shut.

The light vanished. The trapdoor squeaked and groaned, and Ben was entombed.

He tried to cry out – this was not what was supposed to happen! Joshua's visions of the future …

Liar!

Ben couldn't see, only feel. Presently, he placed a trembling hand over his wound. The air in the pit was musty. Breathing would be difficult.

"Oh." Ben made a weak whimper. The darkness was solid and oppressive.

A part of Ben thought he'd deserved this. It was an act of justice, what Bonner had done; he knew about the crimes Ben had committed, and he simply did the right thing.

Excruciatingly slowly, Ben wormed on his stomach and began to probe, to touch, to smell, to feel. Ben used his hands and his body to sense his surroundings. He felt things, using his hand to get a general feel of their shape. Plastic water bottles. Shoes.

Then his hand felt something furry, soft and round. He slid closer, applied pressure, and the toy squeaked weakly.

Ben gasped haggardly. He wanted to sob, but he couldn't. In his hand, he held something so precious, but he couldn't see the darn thing. But feeling it and hearing it was more than enough to impact him.

In his hands, he held Pip. Veronica's favourite toy.

Long ago, he'd promised Veronica and himself that he was strong and brave enough to protect her. He'd said that to the unknown child he saved at Haditha. That was the reason why he became the Actionman. A role model for the next generation.

The Actionman wasn't dead. He didn't even exist.

The Actionman was a lie. He'd always been a lie.

Numbness claimed him. Hollow darkness that was so much worse than the pain in his leg. He couldn't think. Didn't want to think. Ben had been given *exactly* what he deserved. There was no paladin, Navajo, or Judd Pounders to pull him out of it this time.

Ben rested his head on the wombat. His fingers tenderly touched the toy. Pressed, it let out a sad, forlorn sound, a deflating sigh.

"I'm so sorry, Veronica. I couldn't protect you." Ben wept, curling into a ball.

———

Alfred Bonner peered at the hatch, hands folded behind his back, nodding.

The foolish enemy was trapped away, judged like the Dragon in the Bottomless Pit.

Hearing gunshots echoing in the base, he turned the gun in his hands.

Time was running out to abandon Dulce once and for all. Alfred knew and anticipated Judd Pounders would come with a combat assault force to make right after being used. Gilgamesh of Kush had warned him about this before, so he had time to prepare. During the night, the god-king's *ba* travelled to spy on the senior as he made his plans and returned during the day to report back to Alfred, telling him the truth in his thoughts.

Alfred had a secret escort assembled on the summit of the rocky outcrop of the mountain above, where the satellite dishes, radar station, and his aircraft were. Perseus Euergetes safely stored the voidstone from Ellora and took it away in the helicopter. Bhairava and the other Aes Sidhe had also taken with them the coffin, the Mycomantic fungi, Augmenters and the *Baidi* Pearl of the West.

But there was one last thing Bonner had to do.

Alfred stalked around into a second corridor splitting off from his office towards the unconstructed region of the Dulce base. There, the walls were pure stone, the bedrock of Mount Turnbull – a sacred mountain that contained a Gateway into the Underworld.

This was why the base had been built here by FEMA (the Federal Emergency Management Agency) during Truman's presidency – it housed the Apache Gateway. The cave symbolised the gate through which their ancient ancestors first emerged into the present world. The first and primeval Gateway, which held the Dragon Pearl in the Grand Canyon region known by Albert the Navajo, was one of many Gateways.

Gateways were portals into the Underworld – Patala. Alfred gave trafficked children to Patala so that the denizen asura would become familiar with humans. This was the promise they made with Nicholas Roerich, who discovered Patala in the twentieth century. *But we are already programmed to be prepared for aliens from movies,* Alfred thought. *When Patala comes to us, the world will be prepared and will know what to do when the ships arrive. Then ... we will have educated humans who have lived with the asuras, ready for the Kalipolis to thwart the Tyrant.*

Turning into the cave, Alfred stood on the railed metal landing that hung over a high drop above the concrete floor, gazing upon an unusual circular formation in the earth at the end of the landing. Under the hanging rock was a round hole carved into the stone, which the Natives called a *kiva* – the place of human sacrifice – and within the *kiva* was a small depression called a *sipapu* to drain the blood.

The Gateway to Hades was made of living rock, naturally formed with its ridged arch inscribed with rock art. Alfred walked up towards the rock, hovering his hand over a motif in red pigment – an outline of a horned figure with a round head, akimbo arms, decorated with a single diagonal line. The arms were shown with elbows slightly raised and the forearms bent down. An energetic appearance, as if the figure was lifting itself over a cliff.

A symbol for entering the Netherworld.

Was it a shaman wearing a buffalo-horned headdress? An *Uhepono* – the Puebloan for an asura (an Underworld creature)? Or a powerful underwater spirit said by the First Nations People to inhabit the watery abyss below?

As Alfred descended two steps into the *kiva*, he lay a hand on the motif. Next to him, lying in the *kiva* over the small depression, was Veronica. She had to be given general anaesthetic to avoid harm. Alfred had his servants bath her, clothing her with white, pure clothes, ready for the Washukarni to take her as their own kin.

Preventing Veronica from falling into the hands of the entertainment industry, Alfred saved her from Ian Mastemah's "business" clients wanting to audition Veronica and Zoe for modelling photoshoots. Alfred had seen the video files – the ones where Veronica and Zoe were undressed and raped in bed by Ian's friends. Eventually, Veronica and Zoe would have become porn stars of Hollywood, which, ironically, was the very place Ben worked.

Alfred chuckled. There were too many risks to send her back to Ben after what that man did to Thomas Jones. Ben had to die first in order for Veronica to be free. While the Actionman failed, Alfred, under his own jurisdiction, sent his homeland security Aes Sidhe led by Bhairava to Colombia disguised as a vaccine doctor to recover Zoe and Veronica, hunting for paedophiles in a village in the jungles of Narino Province. As the girls slept in the huts and the paedophiles – the Nahash – were outside around the campfire getting drunk, Bhairava went to save the girls. He hid under the bed when the paedophile leader arrived. Just as he was about to take off his pants, Bhairava struck and slew him. He took the girls and ran off, just escaping the Nahash's chase, bringing the girls back to Dulce to safety.

I did you a massive favour, Benjamin.

Alfred Bonner pulled out from his pocket a red voidstone infused with animal Pnuema – glowing blue and white. He knew the Native American tribes had special rituals and songs to open Gateways during their ceremonies without the use of Pnuema, but Alfred didn't know the rituals, so he had to cheat.

Commanding the energy within the voidstone by chanting a mantra to Maitreya, the stone leaked out of the stone, smearing the horned motif. The strata all over the hanging rock began to glow blue-white light from the seams.

The earth around him hummed and vibrated.

———

Keller Butcher snuck gingerly through the industrial corridors, one hand clutching his gun. His keen eyes scanned every corner, every crevasse as he crept, looking for Brianna.

A humming sounded down the corridor. *Earthquake aftershocks?*

Keller slipped behind the corner, both hands on his gun. He followed the strange low sounds, back against the wall. A glowing faint blue light cast across the floor from the corridor beyond, over the bare rock walls lined with crystalline veins of quartz. The humming grew intense.

Taking a deep breath, Keller took a step, his heart thundering. Swinging around the corner, he aimed his gun, beholding something he didn't expect.

The corridor was a cave, accessible by a metal catwalk lined with a railing to the right, where a sheer drop led to the concrete floor below. At the end of the catwalk, lowered inside a circular pit, was a tall blond-haired man standing with his back to him, before a rocky archway, rock art inscribed on the stone.

And these inscriptions were *glowing*. Emitting a soft and eerie radiance that infused the minerals of the cave. The light cast a giant shadow of the man, spreading across the ground, touching Keller's feet. Next to the man, a young girl lay on the floor.

"Show me your hands right now." Adrenaline raged inside Keller. He took ginger steps across the catwalk. *Oh God, that's Veronica!*

The man didn't turn. He seemed to be holding something in his hands.

Veronica lay on the floor, still, as if dead.

"Don't move! Show me your hands right now!" Keller raised his voice, heart palpitating savagely. He did it. He had to aim, had to kill this bastard once and for all. He couldn't miss. "Stop right now! Show me your hands! Do not move and show me your hands!"

The tall blond man calmly raised a hand. He took a step backwards, turning side on, slowly moving up steps onto the catwalk. The eerie blue-white light made his angular, sharp features stark and grim. A lean scar ran down the side of his face, from left cheek to his lip.

There was something in his clutched fist.

"BOTH HANDS!" Keller bellowed. He was trembling. "Open them! Open your hands! Drop it!"

The man, not saying a word, opened his right hand. Out dropped a small dun stone, which skated across the floor.

"BOTH HANDS! RIGHT NOW!"

The languid man raised his left hand. A gun.

Keller fired as the man fired.

In a blink of an eye, Keller skirted a breath's width. The popping bang and the biting pain at the side of his head disorientated him. He stumbled, clutching his head.

He felt the side of his head. It was only a terrible gash. Warm rivulets of blood oozed down the side of his face from his temple. He swore. Blood trickled into his eyes, and he desperately smeared it with his sleeve. If he'd been a second slower, he would've died.

The six-foot-six blond man clutched his left ear, face tight with anguish. He recovered, then bounded towards Keller. Keller faced him and charged.

Ramming into the man, Keller grasped his left gun arm, restraining it. The man was strong; he shoved Keller with one hand, and with his other bloody hand, struck him with a blow to the neck, twisted his arm and snatched his gun. Dizzy, Keller elbowed him, shoving him, sending him stumbling, dropping the weapons. He grunted, fighting Keller.

The two struggled for advantage over the guns, twisting and turning aimlessly. In their brawl, they hit the railing, an endless fall spanning below. Keller screamed, slamming the man's chest and face with his fist. The man pulled his hair, yanking Keller's head back.

Keller roared in pain, gasping. Blood rolled into Keller's vision, stinging his eye. His neck felt that it would break. He thrashed, he kicked and he fought with all his being. His mind disjointed with pure rage, his muscles trembling. The man resisted his attack, hands pressing against his arms.

With a final desperate throe, Keller kicked the blond man's shin as hard as he could, then kneed him deep in the groin.

The blond man let go of Keller's arm and hair. His legs went slack, as if something yanked him off the ledge, and he slipped. The man thumped onto the ground, headfirst, sliding off backwards, underneath the railing, plummeting off the catwalk and to the ground below. Three seconds later, the body hit the ground.

Keller stumbled into the circular pit, bilious and dizzy, blood reddening his vision. He fell on his knees before Veronica's body.

"Veronica," he grunted. He'd done it. *Praise God!*

But Keller had pushed too hard. He'd *almost* died. He'd *almost* failed.

The shock of it stunned Keller. His body vibrated, tingling from the very rock. "Veronica." He was struggling to breathe. She looked beautiful, lying there asleep. Then his hand, blotched in blood, stained her pure garment as he touched her feeble pulse.

"Praise God," he rasped. He had to take her out of there. Rush her back to the men. Call an emergency vehicle. But … *time.*

I'm going to fail her. I'm going to lose her. It's probably—

No. Go. Carry her. Run back. Get Veronica to the medic. Go to Joshua!

Keller would have smiled, but the head wound afflicted him, his sight doubling, head throbbing. He picked Veronica up, handprints of crimson smearing her garments, staining them with his life, shed for her life.

—

Following the sounds of the thrumming and the gunshots, Brianna entered onto a platform before a glowing cave and saw Keller, half his face smeared in dark blood and Veronica in his arms.

She roared out a gasp, leaning a hand on the rock wall, clutching her wounded thigh. The dark rock lit up with a fierce light, vivid white tinged faintly green-blue. "Keller!" Brianna howled, tears brimming her vision. "You found her!"

"Yes!" Keller trumpeted. "Praise God!"

Veronica! It couldn't be!

The sounds of the portal were nauseating now, having just opened. Keller turned and looked at her, exhausted. He then looked at Veronica with maternal empathy. In the light, Brianna's daughter looked angelically peaceful amid the surging chaos.

Brianna tried to get to Keller, but her thigh felt like it had solidified into metal. She arched her head, sighing in pain.

Keller just stood there, trancelike, holding her daughter. Behind him, the portal coalesced in aggregations, complex oblate forms, turning into the familiar shape of …

A fractal. A maze.

—

"Keller!" Brianna screamed. "Get out of there!"

Keller moved towards Brianna, but he could hardly take a step, as if he was moving within water, moving within a dream. *What's ... what's happening to me?* He pushed against it, gritting his teeth, frustration boiling within his loins, as he took three ginger steps towards his love. The farther away from the portal he got – having already been caught by it, standing on its threshold – the more his body and mind seemed to gradually disassociate as the portal began to suck him in. Like a black hole, the closer he was, the harder it was to escape.

Dread assaulted Keller. The expression on Brianna's face reflected his terror. He made one last final attempt to move, but his mind swam and spun. He fell on his side, carrying Veronica.

"Keller!" Brianna shrieked in desperation, her hand outstretched. "Come on!"

"No! Don't come any—"

Vicious light kept Brianna back. A dazzling armed spiral swirled in haunting symmetry, grabbing him, flaring lines churning through its mass, intricate repetitions twisting down into infinity.

Keller and Veroncia were pulled backwards into the nimbus maze. Brianna vanished in the light. Cell by cell, fibre by fibre, radiance and sound plucking them apart. Re-forming. Transferring.

—

Casbolt sat down, tending his terrible knife and bullet wounds, watching Prometheus' corpse disappear into writhing white translucent goo, undulating like muscles, bubbling and boiling. The mass vanished into thin air as if the manifestation hadn't been real. The demonic Fomorian been sent back to his prison in punishment.

Exhausted and worn, Casbolt stood and began to pick his way through the corpses of satanic Carnutes, feeling no sympathy for them because of their paedophilic acts. The eclipse had long passed, and the night was lit by pure moonlight and starlight. He would begin the long journey across this claypan – an arduous journey. Up one of the ledges was an observatory where tourists could safely stand and gaze over the edge at the immense formation in the Earth, and he made it his objective to go up there. The squalls of wind were brutally cold, beating against him as he hiked.

Then something moved. Parvus Perception, keen in awareness, had Casbolt spinning around, marking a lanky human emerging from the pile of fallen bodies. The face of the man was pale, caked in grime and dirt – a distinguishable look likened unto to Casbolt's own form. The double fled like a deer.

Casbolt broke into a sprint. "Thomas!" he bellowed, his thigh pain throbbing.

They ran across the ancient claypan of stones and dust. Thomas blundered in pure panic, but Casbolt, with grinding breath, surged after him. The air roaring in his ears caused tears to brim in his eyes. "THOMAS!" What had happened to his incredible surge of strength and power when he needed it most?

Straining greatly, Casbolt reached for Thomas Jones, dragging him down. Thomas fought back. With a strained yell, they fell forward, skidding across the stones and rolling in a swath of dust. Thomas screamed, an extraordinary wail of bewildering fear. Both of them wrestled against one another, clawing at forearms and clothes, two sweating, fighting men on the edge of panic.

Casbolt managed to get on top of Thomas. He pried at his face and looked into the eyes of the Ophidian. It was himself in pure dread, and it amused the Redlion, a small part that was completely, utterly and irrevocably enraged.

Thomas' eyes had an even and subtle glow. Lapis lazuli blue irises like Casbolt's stared at him, but the whites around them were light azure. The pupils shrunk, becoming tiny slits. Blue within blue eyes.

Then blood gushed down Thomas' nostrils in torrents, dripping down his upper lip and over his mouth and chin.

In that microsecond, Casbolt was completely persuaded Thomas Jones was a Fomorian shapeshifter too.

The demon snarled, pulling a knife on Casbolt. Casbolt grabbed the wrists, gripping it hatefully, breaking it, pulling the weapon free with a grunt.

The Fomorian let out a horrible warbling roar that wasn't human. His eyes were of a serpent – turquoise evil. Casbolt slammed the Fomorian's head back on the stones to daze him and trembled as he plunged the knife towards Thomas' face, but the shapeshifter managed to grab Casbolt's wrist.

Casbolt grunted, struggling to breathe. He forced the knife closer, clutched in his off hand. He used his right hand to press his hand against Thomas. Sweat pricked his brow as the knife tip touched the edge of his left nostril. Casbolt pushed harder. He would not find rest until Thomas Jones was dead.

"No one consumes me," Casbolt snarled, quivering from the wounds of his body, sweat from his nose dripping down the knife. "Snake."

Thomas whimpered, his trembling grip waning.

With a surge, Casbolt forced the blade up past Thomas' nose and into the eye socket – piercing that reptilian eyeball like a ripe blueberry. The knife rammed right through into the brain.

Thomas convulsed so violently that Casbolt almost lost his balance, but he held on to the hilt, with his legs on the husk, and twisted the knife deeper.

Then suddenly Thomas' body changed. Just like Prometheus' body, it bubbled, stretching, growing until it was an enormous tremoring white shadow with dragon-like blue eyes and a peaked, nondescript head. The white mass writhed, bulging horribly like firing oil, and within the bubbles appearing and then vanishing were the faces of many people, objects and animals. Casbolt stared, disgusted at the random things bubbling in the pool of seething white muscles.

A second later, an eerie wind slithered around Casbolt, and the phantasm left, the white mass vanishing completely. The knife dropped to the dusty ground.

Casbolt stumbled back and collapsed, weak and exhausted. He lay famished, his thigh and shoulder throbbing excruciatingly. His mind swam – and only then did he realise how thirsty he was.

Once he regained his strength, Casbolt trotted up the hill, barren, abundant with rocks, dust and feeble hispid shrubs. Only his bitter saliva tried to satisfy this thirst.

Clambering like a weary beast, mind disjointed, Casbolt climbed the hillside, his mind going black, groaning, tongue cleaving to his throat. He didn't move except for the steady rising and falling of his lungs.

Rest …

The air began to stir, infused with the scent of diesel. Rumblings of a helicopter roused louder and louder until the beating sounds of the rotor blades vibrated in his sternum.

Light appeared before his shut eyelids. Slowly, wearily, Casbolt pushed his head up, as a man appeared in his vision. He hauled Casbolt up the last stretch of the Crater, taking him up into the open doors of the blaring vehicle. Casbolt swayed, head slumped, feeling as weak as a newborn Emperor chick.

Patrols. Had Max Spiers finally had enough and sent a government squad to escort him back to Antarctica? At this point, Casbolt didn't care. He was so emotionally destroyed it was hard to even walk, but the soldiers carried him into the helicopter. He'd killed Thomas Jones, but Meredith, his friends and family were awaiting him …

Casbolt felt dread and sorrow engulf his apathy for his selfishness. It pained his heart when he thought of Meredith now, and his mother's words pleading for him to come back from America – the land of exile. The only thing Casbolt could do was feel sorry about his sins and harden his heart; in that way, it made him feel better about himself. Feeling bad about what he did meant he could have the potential to do right.

Once inside the helicopter, as it flew away from the land, Casbolt was given water to drink. After sculling it, he drowsily leaned towards the nearest officer and said, "Where are you taking me?"

The man shifted in his seat as his wounds were checked. "Aes Sidhe, by the command of the Terra Nova Central District, you're to be taken back to Antarctica to face charges for breaching UN protocol."

"So … I'm not arrested?"

"Placed in detention until further notice from the United Nations."

Casbolt blinked, lying back. That would be right.

"You have anything to say about yourself? For refusing your duty? For the massacre and the penalties held at your account?"

"It is by might to make right," Casbolt mumbled.

Funny. This was how strict and important Antarctica had become for all governments. Climate change. Natural history. The secrets of the Fomorians and the Galactic Tyranny. Aes Sidhe flashpoints. The frontier of secular scientific research, Antarctica needed him *now*. It had taken him a whole two years out in this Babylon, that Antarctica itself had finally caught up to him, to take him back home. His reckoning.

Back to face his sins, his crimes against the Aquarians. Casbolt had been cowardly to try to escape them. It filled Casbolt's heart with traumatising dread. The Carnutes could have killed Casbolt easily, and it would have been the most terrible punishment. But now he had to live to face his evils.

Casbolt cursed Yaldabaoth, the Galactic Tyrant's Spirit. Whatever power had saved him, Casbolt started to detest it.

With his guilt and remorse, the wretched, lustful James Casbolt would be part of his life forever, a reminder for the rest of his life. But he resolved in himself after Thomas Jones' death that he *could* have control over himself and the weakness of his moral actions.

James Casbolt was to be a slave, and he accepted it. All leaders were ultimately slaves to their responsibilities. Casbolt would be able to fulfil his new life's mission to find evil and remove it. It was the only reason why his life had been spared.

The world doesn't need saints, Casbolt thought. *It needs antiheroes – flawed people who have touched the darkness, who are strong enough to face the darkness.*

Casbolt lay on the stretcher, closing his eyes, feeling the despair over his life subside as purpose hardened his heart. Equivalent to the same sense of passion he felt when he began to write his book *Agent Buried Alive,* it felt refreshing committing to his new life, and controlling his alters more efficiently, like horses on a chariot. He felt this empowerment because of his decision to formulate the intent of every action with the meaning of doing good. To do justice. Ultimately, his actions at last manifested and mirrored his initial intent from the start.

He could actually do it – he could fight evil with good without making the same failures of the past.

James Casbolt reflected deeply on what seemed right in his own eyes, embracing the most amazing apocalypse. He might be a better man – and in fact, he thought, with a bittersweet smile, he was.

69

MARANATHA

"The kings of the earth and the great ones and the generals and the rich and the powerful, and everyone, slave and free, hid themselves in the caves and among the rocks of the mountains, calling to the mountains and rocks, 'Fall on us and hide us from the face of him who is seated on the throne, and from the wrath of the Lamb, for the great day of their wrath has come, and who can stand?'"

—From the Scroll of Revelation, John the Apostle, 95 – 96 CE.

Joshua watched the strange girl who called herself Tara – just Tara – trying to bind up the wound in Johnny Best's biceps.

All around on the station platform were hundreds of local children and young people who were test subjects and patients delivered by the marines and FBI, ready to be rescued by the authorities and transferred to rehab. Such a dramatic sight would surely expose the Alliance's secret society on the news. Marcus and the other marines aided the survivors, made escort calls, status reports, and helped in any task at hand to respect the dead and to help the wounded.

Brianna returned limping to her FBI colleagues, distraught and woebegone. Joshua didn't see Keller Butcher in their midst. He started to worry when he saw the FBI agents embrace Brianna, who buried her face to weep, for a long, long time.

Subdued, Joshua thought about their failure to find the Uruk coffin. Had it been destroyed in the battle or earthquake? Or had it been smuggled away by Alfred Bonnor? It fostered disappointment in Joshua. He could have discovered something great.

But it's not about discovering something great to become renowned, is it? Joshua thought. *It's not about uncovering the next sensation – Damascus and the sadness of not being there alongside Johnny Best and Marcus excavating Uruk. It's about being patient. Not wanting what is right in my own eyes. One thing philosophy has taught me. One thing the Words of God taught me.*

But no one cared about the coffin anyway. The base was secured, the Alliance had escaped to fight another day, and the marines had saved the kidnapped children.

But Judd Pounders' death left Joshua hollow with shock. Judd's corpse was placed inside a mortuary black bag, and people in white masks, gowns and gloves hauled him away.

The purpose of being human is to reflect God's own Presence and character into the world. Pounders embodied it. Nefer sent – a timbre of words wafted through Joshua's body, loosening deep knots in his muscles.

What makes you sorrowful about this? Joshua thought back.

"It is a very relevant thing for the Servants of Yahweh to feel sorrow," Nefer said, appearing as a gelatinous glowing sea jelly in the air before him. "When we limit ourselves in creation, we participate, we experience and we have sorrow. Behold, I love the earth – it is for all the fairest creatures. Sorrow and loss to me are interesting, but death is foreign. The hearts of men stray often, not using their gifts amid the turmoil of the world. There is a great divide between humanity and divinity. A stark divide that will be finally amended. This is one gift, one promise, humanity in Jesus will all share with the gods. Ultimately, it is within us all to make a choice: will we receive the gift to become stewards of love or risk perverting it, ruining kinship? Whereas the gods and spirits remain until the end of days, our love for the universe is singular and more poignant than yours. Therefore, as the years lengthen, we grow more sorrowful. Gods don't die until the world dies, and we are not recreated unless the world is recreated. But unless we leave our first estate, we die, becoming death, subjecting ourselves as an enemy of life itself. Nothing can slay us – age does not make us mortal, but unless ten thousand centuries grow weary, we can waste away with grief."

"Is Judd in Paradise?" Joshua said mournfully.

"He did not love his life unto death. He gave his life for you and for his men. He's a victorious warrior."

The truth. The smile Judd gave Joshua before death was the reassuring smile of divine peace and joy.

"Thank you, Nefer." Joshua smiled, then went to check on Johnny, inspecting Tara's work. Joshua helped her, refining her techniques, which he'd learnt from field medics earlier this year at Haditha. Techniques on how to clean wounds, how to treat the patient and how to bind wounds. It took a long time; authorities had been called to investigate the base, and ambulances from the nearest military installation in Arizona would be on their way.

"You're a fast learner," Joshua said. "You're very driven."

Tara simply nodded, her expression taut.

"So, what's your story?" Joshua asked, feeling he had to ask her something to make her feel as if she belonged.

Tara looked up at him, haggard and smelling of body odour, but something was alive in her light grey eyes. The skin around her eyes looked pink, as if she hadn't slept in days. "You will not believe a word I say."

"I promise I will not discount you. Please. I'm in your debt."

Tara sighed, but when she spoke, her voice was strong and almost quivering with emotion. "I'm a woman." She nodded, staring at nothing. "Yes. I *am* a woman. I've been molested by traffickers." She hesitated and swallowed. "All is darkness. I want to give up, but I must not despair. I am a woman. I know where I have been. I know I am safe. For now, that is enough."

———

Joshua strolled, exploring the chthonic Dulce base, and saw the prison cells that, according to the FBI, held paedophiles and sex offenders arrested by Alliance Aes Sidhe.

This world he lived in reeked of evil. Children, millions of them, were enslaved right now by perverted, porn-loving men and women. Such leaders of the Earth could not have done such wickedness unless they were influenced by demonic powers.

It partly made Joshua grateful that he'd been called out of the systematic darkness and also powerless that he could do nothing about it.

But the Kingdom of God would soon conquer the Earth. The demonic powers had lost.

As Joshua walked, he understood that in this complex, the supplies … everything about it indicated the truth. Dulce was both a base and a bunker, an ark for a remnant to be protected from annihilation by a so-called 'alien' invader.

The second appearance of Jesus Christ on Earth.

Joshua saw half of the base had been marred by the earthquake. An earthquake of biblical proportions. An apocalyptic transfer of power. The end of one rule to begin another.

The Earth convulsed in zeal, and Yahweh, the Creator of Earth, remained supreme.

Joshua was surprised to see how many investigators were hurrying through the tunnels and industrial warehouses and alcoves in block buildings, taking out the criminal paedophiles from their old prisons, allocating them to new ones. There were over one hundred paedophiles locked up down here. It appeared Alfred Bonner's Alliance was an independent anti-sex-trafficking organisation.

But how if the Alliance are Luciferians? Joshua thought, perplexed.

The problem in Satan's kingdom of slavery was the fact that people scapegoated other people. No matter how genuine the prejudices were, the slaves of Satan insisted criminals had to be stopped. They treated sinners as if they were a virus to humanity, as if they were sub-human. The world didn't give chances for these depraved people to rehabilitate. To lock up a paedophile in prison, in an asylum, in that pit, with no intention of redeeming him, was only making his impulse darker. There was no healing. No restoration. No repentance. The Alliance destroyed who they saw as criminal and rescued those who they saw as innocent. They took justice into their own hands and blamed God for all the evil. But they never blamed themselves.

Ah, but what if there was a world where no one scapegoated each other and no one harmed and used each other? Joshua thought, stroking his chin. *This, to many, is the apocalypse. This is the Truth.*

But there were always survivors. Always a remnant who could find life and truth.

The darkness hadn't been kind to Tara. She was very young, Joshua realised – not even twenty years old. She inferred that she had been kidnapped from her family and sold to paedophiles and sex traffickers in Asia at a very young age. Her entire existence was living in uncertainty, from man to man, apartment to apartment, hotel to hotel, country to country, travelling the world for sex and money. She was one of the lucky ones; only the children who impressed traffickers the most were more likely to survive to their teenage years, because they were sold and "looked after" by their handlers for longer periods of time. For years upon years, all Tara knew was despair and resentment. It made Joshua sweat and shudder.

But now she had found the Light. A way out to freedom. She was smiling and laughing when she mentioned that she'd found freedom.

Freedom. Salvation. New life. Resurrection life … Joshua knew what that was like. Earth wasn't just under Satan's rule; Yahweh's kingdom too was here on Earth.

There was opportunity.

Joshua struggled to compose himself after he let Tara have a genuine conversation. He could tell she trusted him; she could tell life and light were within him, but Joshua didn't have the pride to tell her about it and witness Christ …

Joshua idly followed the investigators examining the base to see the laboratories, thinking about Tara sympathetically in his mind. Her peril had a familiarity to it – it reminded Joshua of the land of the Middle East. A land of scapegoating, crisis and tyrants, where he suffered his lunacy in the asylum of Damascus. The land of his father and the incredible words he gave to him after he graduated from high school.

Go, my son. Be something different. Here, I went to the pains to give you this lucky chance to escape from this cruel world. Go, do something with your life. Make your dreams come true.

Freedom. Joshua dwelt on those words, smiling. *Be something different.* He had. He'd always wanted to stand out, to be set apart, distinguished from everyone else and succeeding. He loved niched things, because he felt that it had meaning in his life to contribute.

Father, you will be proud, Joshua thought blissfully. *After this, I will buy tickets and fly to Crete to meet you and bless you.* A thought occurred to him, then, if he should take Pawani with him on a holiday to see the Minoans … The ecstasy of it made his cheeks burn, and he smirked.

He entered into a utilitarian sterile corridor, lights dim and derelict. The expansive banal concrete with the metal doors reminded him of Haditha Dam. It gave him a sense of wholeness and competence as he walked through the familiar corridor.

Haditha, Joshua mused as he walked down the eerie aisle. The shadows. The apparitions, the flickering lights and the smoke. *Was that why Bonner chose Haditha Dam for a mission? Demons are bound in that river …*

"Haditha Dam … It has demonic forces …" Joshua paused, and at last, figured it out. "Ah! Yes, that's *exactly* why Bonner sent my unit to the Dam! Fallen Angels are *bound* in Haditha Dam! The entire dam is built over a Gate! The Sixth Trumpet of the Book of Revelation speaks about this! Four demons are bound in the river Euphrates, and when it dries up, they will be unleashed to slay the third part of men. Oh God, saving lives as a pacifist actually held the Fallen at bay!"

The marvellousness, the brilliance of God's perfect love and timing, had Joshua overflowing with praise.

If Joshua hadn't killed the Iraqi boy, what alternative possibilities of the future could have transpired? What if he'd never raided the *Magharat al-Ju*, or if the jinn had killed him? He would have never become a saint in the first place. He would have *never* gone to Haditha Dam, and Joshua would have *never* chosen to become a pacifist. He would have *never* saved Pounders' life from poltergeist attacks. And ultimately, he would have *never* been able to hold back the four Fallen Ones from breaking free from their prison.

So many factors and serendipities.

If the future remained so open with infinite variants, the present outcome was therefore intrinsically valuable for factors not yet known or could be never known by Joshua's present temporal part.

"I know God has middle knowledge about actualising feasible possible futures, while working with humans in their freedom. I *could have* become an ordinary soldier, but instead, I chose to become a medic, and by doing that, I saved the world from experiencing Hell at the hands of four demonic gods. This reveals that whatever future event is actualised is *always* the best. A world that includes life and suffering is a better world than one with no life and no suffering. Theoretically, there are *no possible worlds* where we are free and evil doesn't exist. The greatest outcome of all possible worlds is the possibility of great evil fully rejected. Father, I pray a time like that could come quickly. Maranatha… Ahh, I see it now! Yes! Yes, it is foreknowing, therefore, that the four gods bound in the Euphrates will be unleashed … at some point. I only delayed it!

"Oh great, I'm talking to myself again." He sighed. "Well done, Josh. What a novelty."

Feeling enriched and graceful, hands in his pockets, he prolonged his walk, then suddenly, a cold wind engulfed him.

"Joshua, walk into that room, please."

Joshua stopped, stunned. "What? Nefer?"

The spirit was invisible, his voice disembodied. "Turn around now."

"Oh great. Now I'm being forced to do something *against* my will! But what is turning around to have any intrinsic value to the universe? It's not significant. Come on, turning around, as if that will have great consequences. I could easily do otherwise!"

"Come on, bumpkin, obey me just this once! There is something *very important* you need to find in the other room."

"How important?" Sighing, Joshua turned. "Nefer. I beg of you, don't become a determinist."

The spirit laughed, not at him but at something funny that Joshua failed to understand. "Please follow that corridor." The scholar's imperative carried desperation. Whether it was the coffin of Nimrod/Osiris/Gilgamesh inside – and Joshua hoped it was – he freely stalked down the industrial hallway, passing machines and glass vats. He entered a large garage at the end, with a large metal hatch at its centre, domed with a circular door capping the shaft below.

"There's nothing here, Nefer."

Then he heard something. He ceased the scuffing of his feet, listening. The silence laid heavily upon him as he waited … for the sound.

A faint muffled squeak. A toy.

Joshua gazed at the hatch in the ground from whence the sound came.

70

OF GIVING WHAT ONE DOESN'T DESERVE

"For I consider that the sufferings of this present time are not worth comparing with the honour that is to be revealed to us. For the creation waits with eager longing for the revealing of the children of God. For the creation was subjected to futility, not willingly, but because of Him (God) who subjected it, in hope that the creation itself will be set free from its bondage to corruption and obtain the freedom of the honour of the children of God. For we know that the whole creation has been groaning together in the pains of childbirth until now. And not only the creation, but we ourselves, who have the first fruits of the Spirit, groan inwardly as we wait eagerly for adoption as children, the redemption of our bodies."
—From the Epistle to the Romans, Paul, c. 57 – 58 CE.

Ben was standing up in a place of smoke. The only source of light was his phantom form. He glowed like a chemical glow stick, a smooth cobalt blue colour, a very dense light emanating from him.

I am … dead.

The sky was dark and deep, and Ben stood as a single solitary light in a field of shattered, brittle, bone-white rock, dull and jagged, broken plateaus and chasms extending boundlessly. Amorphous shapes made of curling grey vapours rose from the ground in the shadowy distance. Ben thought he saw a congealed human form, mouth open, rising lethargically towards the black sky.

What is *this place?* Ben thought.

"CINVAT."

Then he was hit by the force of a truck. He was plucked off the chalky ground, mounted on a horse and into the lap of its rider swathed in shadow.

A neigh filled his ears. Ben looked down. He could hear the deep demonic whispers of the dark rider in his ears speaking an ancient tongue. The sounds held him captive.

He gazed upon the equine head of the horse, flecked with black spots of disease and corruption. Maimed skin, sickly pale and mottled, mucus cleaved around its bones, spine and skull, bloated and melted like wax. Grotesque things dripped around the hollow eye sockets, steaming with smoke. He saw the throbbing arteries undulating within the neck fat and muscle, decaying into a pale green colour.

Ben should've gagged and vomited, but he didn't.

The Black Rider spurred the undead horse onwards. It snorted, running through the endless field of shattered plateaus and smoke, flying over chasms.

I'm going to Hell, Ben thought with dread. *And it's my fault.*

"No!" he yelled in defiance, but the grim spectre whose lap he was in let out a shrieking wail worse than any film he'd heard. A clawed hand gripped his shoulder.

Ben howled incoherently at the advent of terrific scalding that coursed through him, everywhere in his body. There was no brain to isolate the intolerable pain in this place. From the top of his head to the bottom of his feet, that same burning fire made him spasm. No pain receptors. No brain. No nerves. One hundred per cent *pounding pain.*

The pale undead horse ran at a very fast velocity, impossibly fast, through sheets of smoke. Bleak wind battered against Ben, blinding him.

I have … to … gather them.

Of course he was going to Hell. This was what he deserved. It was what he wanted.

He failed his father.

He failed his mother.

He failed his daughter.

He failed his wife.

He failed his sister.

He failed his colonel.

He failed his soldiers and friends.

He failed his fans.

He failed himself.

He'd lost everything, one by one. He was just rags … just rags. Stone wore thin. The evil of it …

Evil is contingent. Joshua. *Good is contingent on nothing. Evil steals good. Trust in Truth and Wisdom.*

Only then did Ben realise how evil he was. The Chief of chaos. Of nihilism, impotence, madness and pride. Redemption couldn't be possible, locked forever in a universe of pure hatred and torment. Ben *loathed* it.

Where … He needed confirmation. *Where is it taking me?*

"IT'S TAKING YOU TO SHEOL," rasped a malevolent voice.

Where is Sheol?

"IN THE BOWELS OF THE EARTH."

Sheol? Confusion brought him back.

He felt uncertainty writhe within him. Then remorse for all his foolishness and guilt for what he had done in his life. It became so obvious, and so filthy. The sin of life became, in this place, as distant and blurry as his experience as a toddler. The horrors of it, the wickedness Ben committed, were just, as it was unthinkable for an adult to chew on poison. He knew better.

But what was ahead, he felt, would be far worse than the anguish he'd endured already.

The thrashing hooves and huffing horse became a gushing, lulling sensation. The black flame – himself – blocked and clogged Ben's hearing.

What have I done?

Ben opened his eyes. A reliable solution came, and it all made sense. He *longed* to be damned. He wasn't afraid of Hell, because he'd endured it already in life. Ben had become nothing because he built his life on things that had been taken away. A wilful self-inflicted judgement. Hidden from God's face, cursed with the ground, an outcast.

Ben laid his eye on the slithering flames. The dragon within him.

Numb dread replaced his pain.

No … No! I don't want to!

"Gather." For the first time in an endless deep, a small husky sound parted Ben's lip. "God." There was no room for self as a sacrifice.

I have done this to myself! I can change!

Then returned the death pain that traumatised his being.

Ben hissed, bearing it all willingly. His pain … it was like a wall of ice crashing into him. He pushed himself into it, forcing himself slowly away from the numbness, feeling the resistance of consciousness. He wanted to give up. To let oblivion take away his pains and sorrows.

"Gather them!" he screamed, pressing into the incredible pain. His voice sounded strange – it formed bubbles as if he were speaking underwater. Yet, he could breathe.

A white star appeared in the void.

"*God, I want you to be my life! I give my all!*" He bellowed, bubbles exploding from his mouth. He no longer feared Death behind him, because he saw the star of hope and purity in eternal blackness.

And *desired* it.

Then, with the speed of lightning, radiance *exploded*. The horse, rearing up, hastily stopped, shrieking. The Black Rider's claw dug hard into Ben's shoulder.

Ben howled. From that light came life, joy, love, long suffering and peace.

Out of the white-pink liquid light rode forth a winged aurochs, brawny white with curved silver horns on its head. It lunged out of the dazzling glare. Above it, a hand of polished bismuth reached out.

Reflexively, Ben *grabbed hold*.

Everything froze. The pale horse screamed as the albino aurochs' horn pierced its ribs. The horse reared from the collision, and Ben would have fallen over if the hand hadn't saved him.

Mounting the iridescent winged aurochs was a lithe voluptuous body completely covered in black and red interlocking plate. A knight, mighty and strong, had its right arm raised, its body blocking the green horse and Death, and its left held Ben. The starburst breastplate was a steel wall, glistening with golden decorations, sparkling magically, so vibrant, like a tessellated illusion – the polished bismuth had a three-dimensional illusionary look with spectral iridescence dancing in auras. The powerful knight had an iridescent chrome helmet and a threefold curvaceous crown, with an angular face plate, Optimus Prime-like. A plasma veil of orange and hot pink emanated from a rosy-gold moisture around the armour, floating in the pelagic current.

Ben hung between two cosmic principalities, immensely powerful. He stood at the *epicentre*. He knew that the Black Rider holding his left shoulder could rip it off and the angelic knight holding his right hand alone could crumple him into a ball.

A wrathful demonic growl rattled from Death, a sound of confusion and odium.

"MOT THANATOS! HE IS RANSOMED!" a tremendous voice reprimanded from the knight. It sounded feminine, but it had great power.

Then, in a blink of an eye, the knight's right fist punched Death's cowled face. The air *cracked* with a surge of power. Death flew off the pale horse's back, gushing away at light speed.

The undead horse, however, remained, skittishly released from invisible bonds. With supernatural speed, it galloped away.

Ben lurched to his feet, staring at his saviour riding the winged aurochs as it lowered him to the ground … more like cloud than a solid surface. Ben stared, bewildered and enraptured.

Was this the paladin who whisked Ben away from Haditha Dam?

Then Ben saw the helm shimmer pink, the plate becoming transparent – barely visible – revealing the stoic face of a woman, a strong innocent girl with immortal maturity. Her face was olive, Middle Eastern, shimmering, for the helm was still there as a light-brown nimbus. Ben looked upon her and couldn't put any age on her at all. The light of the stars was in her light eyes, blue as the ocean, but queenly, for power and wisdom was in her glance. Dark sepia tresses bound in a bun with dyed strands of silver grey. She had a natural curl to her hair, and the strands flowed like waves, as if Ben were seeing her underwater.

The Eve dismounted from the back of her aurochs, noble in her bearing, inspecting him with serene longing and sadness. Her lips were parted, her teeth milk and stark – she wasn't smiling, nor was she frowning.

"Who are you?" Ben whispered. Suddenly, he was overwhelmed by the scent emanating from her, and it shook him. It was the smell of flowers with overtones of gardenia and jasmine, unmistakably his grandmother's perfume. He had already been perched precariously on the precipice of emotion, and now the flooding scent and attendant memories staggered him. The scents of love and peace and nostalgia and affection embracing him when he didn't deserve it … Ben broke. "Why did you save me? Leave me! I'm a sinful man! I don't deserve this!"

The woman knelt, her arms outstretched as if they were the very arms of his true mother. He felt the presence of love in her. It was warm, inviting, melting.

Ben looked up. The lady's armour was gone, replaced by a well-cut prismatic white-light dress with a filmy gelatinous train flowing like jellyfish tenacles behind. She was barefoot, and the light dress didn't cover her nakedness, only suggested it, for she was not ashamed. Her fit, muscular form was wonderful, with thick bulging legs and strong dark arms, and above her brow was a crown of silver lace netted with small gems.

Gradually and intentionally, she moved her face closer to his, and just when he imagined she was going to kiss him, she stopped and looked deep into his eyes. They contained an aqua universe. Excitement bubbled in Ben. He knew he recognised this woman, someone he had passed by many times long ago but never met.

She smiled, and her scents embraced themselves around him. "Peace be with you. You were vigorously invested," her divine pristine voice sung.

"Who are you?"

"Atargatis. Lady of the Sea and Herald of Yahweh. Ben, find wisdom and walk in it. Come. I will show you the Truth."

Atargatis turned her swanlike neck, sweeping her arm outwards to show Ben something. He followed her gaze.

At first, he thought he saw himself and the goddess travelling towards a vast column of colour, vibrant clouds of violet-gold and flaming vermillion burning brilliant sprays of radiance that pulsated out towards them, flaming against the immediate darkness, only to subside and return to their source. They extended from innumerable heights to innumerable depths. The colour of sound, the colour of scent and taste. They reminded Ben of Hubble's Pillars of Creation, but *alive*, glittering balls of infant stars being born.

But when Ben thought he beheld one thing, it was something else entirely different. Ben knew that the nebula was no longer a nebula made of gas and helium. It was, in fact, a high and lofty pyramidal mountain running with streams of living waters.

He was on Earth. A pure, new Earth.

Along the mountainsides were lush jungles and structures merging with the trees – a gigantic arcology that *grew* from the jungle flora. Mushrooms like geometric mansions and buildings soared to great heights and widths, with swanlike decorations decked with jewels, radiance and mycelium membrane structures. The curved walls glistened with crossed polarised light.

The megacity extended in six directions in arches and skyrise bridges. Vast gorges with gardens and waterfalls formed a great wonderland in the arcology. It resembled Thailand – shimmering majestic rivers fructifying the landscape with a remarkable opulence of fertility and green trees. Archipelagos dotted this vast land, turquoise water carving limestone karst formations covered in dense virgin jungle.

A great bay stretched out before Ben in the middle of the two great golden streets of the city. The bay expanded for kilometres in the middle of the arcology from horizon to horizon, shimmering with the brilliance of a pink sunset. The water was clear as crystal, where pods of whales breached the surface, flaying about their tails happily, their flippers waving in applause. Spinner dolphins flew, arching in the iridescent air acrobatically.

Romping, prancing, gliding, crawling, waddling, slithering; Ben saw a whole variety of animals and birds of all sizes and plumage, reptiles from small to great dinosaurs, to synapsids and megafauna – extinct and alive. They played and celebrated in the golden streets to a tune of praise.

"Oh my God!" Ben rasped in wonder.

In the centre of the Garden grew a colossal glowing date palm and a colossal glowing fig tree.

No shadow existed here in the kaleidoscope of abject goodness. The scents of sweet perfume and sharp spices, of delicious foods and magnificent flowers, floated in the air, as if every good smell in the world were gathered here.

Then the formations of the garden city became a nebula. A cloud of swirling gas, light and colour dancing and weaving a tapestry of love, transformed into what Ben could describe as bodies and entities and a large riverine valley filled with emerald vegetation, flowers and light.

And then Ben, through a watery veil, saw an army of children. Little radiants, their bodies and distinctive garbs glowing with auras of individual colours and breathtaking hues and textures. They were mainly white, and wispy light rippled from their bodies as the children giggled and played with one another.

Then, emerging into the clearing were armies of adult humans. They flooded out of the forests, out of shelters and dwellings made from the large roots and thick trunks of trees. The dwellings were of various cultural styles and of diverse designs, roofs made of rich webs of leathery material. Moss and yellow-coloured lichen bearded the eaves, and vines of tropical fruit and exotic mushrooms decorated the houses like spangling lights. Many of the shelters were part of the trees and branches, rising many stories high into the canopy, interlaced with buttresses of living branches. Each unique dwelling place enhanced its forested surroundings, blending in naturally. Manmade habitats and the environment were in harmony.

These human armies were without number, a sea of glorious gods and goddesses coming out of their verdant dwellings, wearing garments of various flames with unique bits of other colours embedded in each one. Many carried palm branches and leaves, waving them ceremonially and playfully.

Ben gasped as he saw they were his families, extended families, cousins, close friends, aunties and uncles, his grandparents and their families and relatives over from Italy. All his friends: their children, loved ones, and their relatives. He saw people of different cultures. A great multitude that couldn't be counted. Native Americans from Alaska, the East Coast, the Great Plains, the Pacific Northwest to Mexico and Peru. Africans, Europeans, Middle Easterners, Chinese, Japanese, Indians, indigenous Australians, Filipinos, Pacific Islanders and everyone in between. *So many* differences. *So many* people.

"COME!" It was an eruption of pure delight and affection, a song of elation. In response, a celebration, a wordless yodel, roared from the sea of a trillion people. In harmony. All the humans from all tribes and nations, each in turn for as long as they needed, bowed; they began to embrace and sing. Some were crying out words of love, while others simply stood with hands lifted and eyes closed. Many of those whose colours were the richest and deepest were doing the sign of the cross and lying flat on their faces. Everything that had a breath sang out a song of unending love and thankfulness.

The godly humans were worshipping, hearty love pouring from them with the force of a supernova. Ben was sobbing. This was *the most beautiful thing …*

The goddess Atargatis squeezed Ben's hand. She was smiling, but her eyes were glazed with tears. Together, they floated down the transparent waterfall towards the ground below. Ben saw Atargatis' tender, winged aurochs with bulk and brawn lie down with her like a pet, chewing on emerald grass.

Ben stared out from the waterfall in the direction of the symphony of children's laughter. Playing with the children at the banks of the clear river, playing splash with a diprotodon, a baby mammoth and a lamb was Zoe and …

Ben gasped. Moving towards them, he pushed up against an unseen force, invisible but in front of him.

As if she saw him, Veronica ran down the trail that ended directly in front of Ben. She was many years older, a teenager, but Ben couldn't deny her features in full bloom.

"Oh my God! Veronica!" he yelled, trying to move forward. To his consternation, he ran into a power that would not allow him to get closer, as if some magnetic force repelled his effort.

"She cannot hear you," Atargatis intoned.

Ben didn't care. "Veronica!" he screamed. She was so close. So lovely and healthy, her dark tanned skin glowing with lean muscles. Veronica stood strong-boned and splendidly gorgeous, her gaze not focused at him, but at something that was in between, larger and obviously visible to her but not to him.

Ben ceased fighting and half-turned to Atargatis. "Can she see me? Does she know that I'm here?"

"She knows that you are here, but she cannot see you. From her side of time and space, she is looking at a beautiful waterfall. But she knows you are behind it. She is waiting for you to pass through into eternity to join her and our Lord."

Ben watched every move his precious Veronica was making. To be this close to her again was painful, to see her stand in that Veronica way, holding her hand at her hip, all slender, swaying, all grown up and mature. "Has she forgiven me?" he rasped. "I failed to save her."

"Her previous life was a dream," Atargatis said. "She's awake and doesn't believe the lie that there is someone to blame."

"You mean ..." Ben rasped. "It's not my fault?"

And Atargatis uttered, "You must forgive yourself, Ben. This is where new creation begins. Grief is a sign of love, and love is God. Veronica's love is *much* stronger than your fault could ever be. The living, dynamic activity of love has been going on forever."

Someone called Veronica's name, and Ben recognised the voice. She shrieked with extraordinary delight and ran back barefoot on the grass. Abruptly, she stopped and ran back with excitement to her daddy. She made a big embrace, as if she were hugging him, and with eyes closed, gave him an affectionate blow kiss.

Ben wept uncontrollably, tears flowing like the waterfall. From behind the barrier, he hugged her back and blew her a return kiss.

And now Ben could clearly see who had the voice that had called his Veronica. It was his dad, Joseph, embracing Veronica in a hug, and then she went to hug another man next to Joseph ...

She embraced a glowing man ignited like a star. He had supernatural strength, swinging her around twice before putting her back on her feet. Veronica's hair flew with joy, and she tipped back her head, laughing.

Then the glowing man let go of Veronica and walked towards Ben. He walked into the stream as if the waterfall didn't bar him. He had eyes as orange as twin red giants blazing majestically in space. His eyes appeared asymmetrical; his right eye seemed slightly larger than his left. The right eye looked unfocused, as if gazing *through* Ben, knowing Ben better than he knew himself.

The man's warm smile was on the verge of laughter. He wore an ornate priestly vesture with a white turban and a white-and-blue garment reaching his ankles and hands, clasped with an elaborate vest with the shape of a breastplate of embossed gold woven into fabric. The breastplate pulsated with twelve cross-polarised gemstones of different colours, inscribed with Hebrew names.

The man was brawny and slim, skin burnished bronze, glistening brightly. His grey beard dripped golden oil. His hair was short, curly, and he looked

Middle Eastern, perhaps Arab or Indian. His hair was white as snow, and the skin on his face was marred with many scars, scourging lacerations, ripping across his temples down his large aquiline nose and towards his chin. One slashed down his left eye.

Beautiful Atargatis bowed to her knees, kissing the man's hand, saying, "The Lord be magnified! Second Adam, who was, and is, and is coming! You are worthy, and by your blood, you redeemed humans and made them into a kingdom, and they will rule the Earth!"

The man chuckled. It was friendly, casual and simply incredible. The laugh made Ben delight with a silly joy. "Ash," he said perkily. "I'm especially fond of you."

The solar flares of the priest's eyes met Ben. "Brother Ben, you are exceedingly blessed."

Ben, exhausted from suffering, struggled to breathe. His jaws were quivering. Tears blinded his vision of the man. The aroma that radiated from him was the camphoraceous scents of eucalyptus, the petrichor of a spring shower in the mountains and the delicate, smoky smell of lavender.

"Vengeance is mine, brother." This priest's voice was gentle and friendly. It had a strong Syrian accent. "Am I deaf and blind that I cannot see and hear the cries of pain that rise up to me? The violence, the tyrants, the extremists – they'll all fall. I am coming to rescue, for I have completely reconciled all to myself everything on Earth and in Heaven.

"There are those who have undergone tribulation that cry out to me day and night. I ask of you, Benjaman, when you return, say to Joshua that the Lord said he is a magnificent scholar. Thank you for loving me in prison."

Ben had no idea what he meant by returning to talk to Josh … Why return? There was no return. Return to where? His dreams? "Who are you?" Ben asked. "Are you the source of the visions?"

Second Adam didn't respond. He took a step forward towards him, and appearing in his hands was a luxurious, starry, bright-white garment, shimmering with a thousand diamonds.

Ben touched the opulent robe. Surprisingly, it was soft and smooth, yet heavy in its thickness, and it had the slight reflective sheen of polished mother-of-pearl iridescence. Perhaps it was just the moment between life and death that Ben had thought he had never seen colours so vibrant and so beautiful as celestial white. "Th – thank you—"

"It is not for you," Second Adam said, withdrawing the garment. "Ephraim, you try to make sense of the world in which you live based on a very irrational and incomplete picture of reality. Now you see reality. If you knew I am goodness and that everything—the means, the ends, and all the processes of individual lives—is covered by goodness, then while you might not always understand what I am doing, you would still trust me. But you *don't*."

What? Ben stared, shocked. "Who … are you?"

The man with the oily sheen said, "You will return. Someone has to gather the Church. My wife."

"I will." The words just came out.

"I am the source of creation and the firstborn from the dead. Gather them."

"I will do it. But I am vile. I … I can't even look at myself. The way I lived was wrong! I'm not worthy!"

The priest with outrageous battle scars frowned sympathetically for a moment. Then he spoke in a clear voice. "My *precious* brother, I have *already* forgiven you. Let the one who does wrong continue to do wrong; let the vile person continue to be vile; let the one who does right continue to do right; and let the holy person continue to be holy. Walk again in the covenant teachings; the Kingdom of God is here. This is the burden and the patience of the saints: that they have faith in the testimony of the Lamb and keep the commandments of God."

"I don't understand how that can be done," Ben said.

"I make all things new. Gather them. The First Fruits. Prepare for the Nephilim. Repent."

Ben frowned at those familiar words. "Who *are* you?" he asked again. And yet, he thought he knew already.

"I Am . . .... dead," the man said. "I Am . . .... alive. By my death, the head of the snake was *crushed*. Authority is given to me, in Heaven and on Earth."

Then Second Adam offered a right hand to touch Ben. The sleeve exposed, he saw at the joint between wrist and forearm a hole in the flesh. Pierced by something that had bored through tendon and muscle.

The crucifixion nail.

Ben clutched onto that hand, fingering the wound of God. "Why now? Why did you wait all this time to show me who you are *now*? You could have prevented *so much!*" Ben cleaved to Jesus, bawling into his ornate garments.

Jesus hugged him.

—

Returning to the world from eternity in Christ, with Christ, was like falling to sleep and entering a dream.

Ben sniffed, opening his teary eyes, and the world became a sterile, banal room – the real dream world. Empty, quiet, lulling and mellow … filled with death and despair, he lay in an unfamiliar, dim hospital room.

And he was not dead … He'd been so surprised and drenched by transcendent joy and hope and love that death lost its grip on him. And this time, there wasn't a father there to be on his side as much as Ben hoped.

He'd run from the Father and stumbled into the Son. The one who drew all darkness out, consuming it. The very wounds of the Second Adam revealed this, the violence that the world inflicted upon him. And in his death, he was reconciled again with the Father in the embrace of the Spirit.

Gather them. Two becoming one. Ben felt a loss and a longing, and even a little sadness, but satisfied all the while, knowing that he had another chance to live. To fulfill his vocation.

"Oh my God," Ben broke out. "Father, Jesus Christ, Holy Spirit. Bless your holy name. Your blood has cleansed me. You have restored me. I know now that I can live and forgive myself for the wickedness I have done. For killing myself over Veronica … You *saved* her! Hahaha! You watch over her … Thank you … Oh thank you! I am wretched, and I cannot do anything to help myself. Only you found me, Father, and I know my evil. It is because of your kindness I can become a better man. I can repent." Ben laughed. "I repent! I confess! I will do everything you say! I will gather the Church! I will construct the city of God! I submit my life to you, oh Lord my God! Oh God, you have revealed to me who you truly are! *The Truth!*"

He sobbed again. Strange that by giving up his whole self, he found his real self where joy could be found. Not keeping back, Ben instantaneously submitted his ambitions, love and wishes and every fibre of his being to Yahweh. He burnt wholly.

In the end, Ben had been wrong to choose independence. For years, Ben had looked to himself for meaning, purpose and success: it brought him loneliness, rage and ruin. But when he gave Christ a chance and looked for him, Christ was there, at the door of his heart, and on him was everything Ben had loved, transformed and redeemed. Hope beyond death. Life itself. Jesus Christ. Yahweh in the flesh.

Victorious.

"I have conquered …"

The hospital door opened, and the lights switched on. Coming into the room were Joshua and the Navajo family.

Ben wanted to cry in gratitude. But he only laughed, bouncing in bed in ecstatic, childlike joy. He hugged his Navajo friends, from Chief medicine man Albert to his son and daughter-in-law.

"Benjamin," old Albert said.

Ben gasped, "Albert!"

Then Albert laughed, and the sound was like music, Edenic rivers watering a parched land. And as he listened, the thought came to Ben that he hadn't heard laughter, the pure sound of merriment, for days upon days without count. Laughter, like that of the divine Presence, echoed upon his ears from afar – all the joys and fulfillment he could have ever known. Ben burst into tears. As sweet rain that had passed away to give space for sunlight and rainbow, laughter welled up. Laughing, he sprung from his bed and hugged Albert. He felt mended and well, all his strength returned.

He turned to Joshua and found the Turkish man beaming affectionately, arms crossed.

"Josh," Ben cried. "Wow! Yeah, man! You believe what happened to me?"

"What happened?" he said.

"I touched God's glory! God is building a city out of people! I saw Heaven!" Strange, now he thought differently after the fundamental Second Adam, who had been with him from the beginning, had revealed his true structure and identity. The rational order where all things hold together. The uncaused cause of emergent matter, space-time and information. Ben demanded answers, and *this was his answer*. The Truth.

Now Ben knew the right thing to do. He was partly worried, yet hopeful, he would find stability in time as he lived. The white garment was ready, and Veronica was waiting for him in Paradise. He would see her again as an automatic result of living a life to the fullest, but the otherworldly glory *didn't matter* in his mind. For opulence wasn't the point, and gain wasn't the goal, but rather, it was the *journey* to reach the destination.

Joshua chuckled. "Ben, that sounds like you experienced the new heavens and the new Earth. Paradise in the eternal now."

Ben chortled, saying, "Josh, God said something to you!" Ben stopped, lost in his memories for a moment.

"You spoke to God?" Joshua said, smiling, accomplished. "What did he say?"

Ben paused, grasping for the words. "He said that Joshua is a magnificent scholar. Thank you for loving me in prison."

Ben stopped and watched his friend's jaw tighten, puddles of tears filling his eyes. His lips and chin quivered, and Ben knew his friend was fighting hard for control. "You'll have to tell me all about it later," Joshua said, rubbing his eyes, leaving Ben to wonder and to remember. "But man … When I carried you to the paramedics, you were dead. How did you return?"

Ben smiled plumply. "I tell you, Josh, the DePaulas are tough oxen. But God is tougher. He was dead and rose again from the dead." Then Ben paused, and addressing everyone in the room around his bed, he said, "Thank you for being there for me when I had … no one." Ben slumped as waves of memories of his sin entered his heart. "I need sanctification. I can't believe I did what I did …"

"Ben," Albert said kindly. "The present state of the world is despair and chaos, but the whole outlook of humankind can be changed. It is possible if we believe that the power of the Great Spirit is eager to be our friend. But sin has made us prideful and self-conscious, dethroning the Great Spirit. When the human being comes to the point where they cannot go on, where they give themselves over, and give space for Nihitaa', Nihitaa' acts. His grace towards us is enough. It is sufficient. Even in your affliction, Ben, Nihitaa' is afflicted. Like a structure in an archaeological mound, what has always been will be made clear. The reign of Yeshua is the already but not yet."

"I know now," Ben said with confidence, nodding. "My eyes have been opened to this slowly. The Seven Sages. The Israelites. The saints. They may have failed us, but what is coming … The Nephilim – the violence, the children of evil – are returning, and the Church needs to wake up. We *need* to gather the saints! I need to gather the Church all over the world. I have to unite the churches in a common cause, not to dissolve their differences, but to make their diversity *valuable* and not a hindrance to harmony. There are saints to be found everywhere. I have no idea how this will actualise, but I have full trust that God will *somehow* make this happen. If he can save me, then he can unite the world."

"Ben," Joshua said with shock and awe. He grinned, on the verge of laughter. "Ben! There are over forty thousand denominations claiming the Truth, with so many cultural differences that are near impossible to bridge. This … oh God, this calling is *ambitious*."

"I will make sure I work with you on your mission to unite the assemblies," Albert promised. "Nihitaa' willing."

"But for now," Ben said, "I want to learn more about the Bible in an *academic* way."

Joshua nodded curtly. "All scripture is God-breathed for what is necessary for salvation. The testimony of the Lord makes wise the simple; the precepts of the Lord are pure and true, rejoicing the heart. A cohesive story of the beginning and the end that leads to Jesus' life, suffering, death and resurrection."

Suffering was normal. Plight was the condition of the world. Ben wanted to walk in wisdom, to learn more.

Because Ben knew Veronica was all right and at peace. His selfish agony had fled, giving him space to open his heart.

From nihilistic despair to hope, Ben realised that God was *so deeply* invested in the renewal of all things, not destruction or cruel ruin. And there was much peace in this. There was comforting peace and completeness, realising the truth that God's vengeance and reckoning of evil and abuse was active. He wasn't merciful at the expense of justice. He was instead a *perfect balance.*

Ben wanted to honour Joseph and Veronica by preparing others for the flood of judgement before it was too late. Becoming *a* judgement – driven by angry, vengeful intent – even if for a noble cause, didn't matter. It was the grace that found Noah, the grace that found Joshua, the grace that found Ben, which was *much more* powerful than judgement when shown to others. God loved him, and God deserved to be loved back.

Albert bowed his head and prayed with Ben and the Navajo. The Chief spoke, saying, "Nihitaa', Son and Spirit – our Creator, Redeemer and Sanctifier. You will bring us life and raise us up on the third day. Keeper of the sacred fire, kindle within us the trust that you'll comfort our friends in the Underworld. As we part in sorrow, may the warmth of your mercy gather us together in your kingdom. In the name of your son, Yeshua, console us."

"Amen," Ben said, beaming. "Thank God for you, Albert."

Gather them. The heirs of Christ in the new world. Spread the Good News. Keep the Commandments.

"I'm ready. Where is the nurse? Tell them I am better." Ben closed his eyes. More pain and loss were coming. More depression, more anxiety, more loneliness. More wars. It was daunting, terrifying, but Ben had hope. The cosmic battle began with the struggle of life. But Ben *mattered*; he'd found a cornerstone, something he didn't have before. A rock-solid foundation to stand on as he battled against chaos.

Just as his father Joseph had won in the end, Ben could too. Via selfless suffering and servitude, the tyrant's last weapon of death had failed against all those in Christ.

Above, before, through and in, God was the *Galactic Creator*, the source of order through which all things cohere and came into being. The secret societies wanted to gather together to kill God for all the evil he had caused, and yet, they never realised that God had *already* been served his sentence. The tidal wave of evil crashing upon him, he overcame.

With triumph and with glory.

Victorious and powerful, God – through the woman warrior, an angelic deliverance, an ally to Ben – had saved him. Unafraid to bloody his hands for the sake of his love, the depth of God's love was the love Ben had for his daughter and more. It couldn't compare to anything else. By enduring the worst fate any human could suffer, the self-giving victim of violence and hatred overcame death. No god or goddess had done what Jesus had done, forgiving his enemies and then conquering death by resurrecting bodily.

God wanted to be loved as much as Ben wanted to be loved.

He understood that mentality so much! It was the love a father had for his daughter! *God* is a parent! *And he has adopted me!*

The police came, took Ben and sent him away to an unknown prison in Phoenix.

He prayed that his confidence and steadfastness in Christ would not deteriorate over time. He prayed for humility to obey authority, for the strength to gather the Church. Above all, he prayed for forgiveness for calling God the Galactic Tyrant.

Ben missed his daughter, he missed his father, but he had Joshua and the Navajo to console him. God's images.

But above all, Christ had given him a revitalised potential to become a new man.

A new Benjamin DePaula. He had stripped off his old self and put on the new, genuinely free.

New creation!

Peace flooded into Ben's heart, and here, he fully understood what Noah in his visions had meant. "For justice is without *khesed* to one who has shown no *khesed. Khesed* triumphs over justice," Ben reflected in the back seat of the police car, driving away from the hospital.

Time had been renewed. The grace of *khesed* restoring a new beginning.

—

Sitting in the hospital lounge room, Tara watched the police arrest Ben

DePaula with jealousy and envy.

Ben was alive and smiling like a saint! The unfairness of a sordid, evil man receiving such hope filled her heart with black fog. She was too exhausted to fight it.

Tara shook in anger. Such worthlessness, the jealousy, the frustration, the shock, the uncertainty of what to do with her life besides being a prostitute … Now she *loathed* the brothel. She had grown out of it. Too good for it.

Free … but with nowhere to go. Tears leaked from her eyes as she wept silently.

Freedom wasn't enough for her.

Tara was that bad. Just when she thought she had achieved rest and peace and fulfillment, it meant nothing. Ease was an impossible blessing. She couldn't stand; the lights were dim, no one paid her attention, not even the doctors asked her if she was okay! No one went to check on her, acknowledging that she was sexually abused! She could feel Cabalistic ingredients: the bitter factions among the staff, frustrated by their circumstances working late in the morning, focused on their own duties, the barely disguised superiority and disdain, the patronising personal righteousness barely concealing the brutality of therapy. The electric shock, the probing of the body, surgery, the manipulation of thoughts and behaviour. The dehumanisation – every day herding patients, the pompous coldness of doctors distancing themselves from their death fears.

Tara was cursed. Tara had been forgotten. Her father was likely dead or arrested. Her mother … gone. She desperately wanted someone to remember her in the shadows of death. Like Joshua … What a *gorgeous* young man. Where was he?

But then, in her dismal state, a prudent, tall and fit teenage Navajo around her age noticed her and approached her. He wore a necklace made of turquoise, which to Tara glowed like crystallised life.

"Are you okay?" the young man said, his voice deep. Tara studied him, groaning. He had dark hair, an olive complexion and a chiselled chin. He wore a leather vest. His face had no reproach hidden in it; his eyes were solicitous. But she curled up.

Please, please! Not again!

Tara couldn't trust men. They took advantage of damsels in distress. She twitched, her mouth contorting, holding back the emotional anguish. "Leave me alone," she snapped tartly.

"I'm not leaving until you get help. Sister."

That remark made her mouth twitch. "What are you talking about? I am no one's sister!"

"Look up."

Tara frowned in shame.

"Yes, you are. You need good medicine." It was a sure statement. Truth. The First Nations People were known as healers. They could heal *any* illness.

Tara felt her face contort, muscles twitching, raw pain and raw emotion swelling inside. Sister … Her brother Vayden … Was he still alive? What about her mother? Where was she? "Go away …"

"You're my sister," the young man said. He was sad. It was as if Vayden was in this young man in spirit.

Tara looked up. His eyes *recognised* her.

Tara smiled passionately. The men in her life were black holes, annihilating and sucking in everything. But this young man was a wellspring of potential, life and redemption, like Joshua. If only she could, for a change, drink in this man's words and believe them without hurting!

A sister. A family. What a *ridiculous gift!*

"How do I trust you?" Tara rasped. "Sorry, but you could either fix me, or you are afraid of me. Make sure you know what you are about to get yourself into, man."

"I don't fear. I just care about you," the Native American boy said. "But I know someone who *can* fix you."

Tara squinted as the golden light from the rising sun burst into the room from the window.

"Sister," he said, gently. "The fight you fought was *so long*." Tara closed her eyes and began to sob in strained silence. "You *are not* alone. You *are not* wretched. You wanted to give up many times, but Grace found you at this very moment. You must be …"

"Exhausted," Tara finished, sniffing, tears dripping down her cheeks and chin.

"It's just the wet season, okay? The encroaching winter doesn't last forever. The rains have passed and ceased."

The boy beamed, snuggling into her. She let him. He smelled of aftershave and wore a leather vest over a cardigan of wonderous Cherokee weavings of fawn beige colours and zigzag patterns she could get lost in.

A wash of power rushed through her veins, and the darkness stilled.

"You're awfully kind." Her jaw suddenly quivered, chattering uncontrollably. Her vision blurred, complete with tears. She couldn't believe that he hugged her, such an impossibility that she could love … Extraordinary. It was like … like …

A rising from the dead.

A *spiritual* resurrection.

The young Native American smiled, placing a caring hand on her shoulder. It sent warm waves through her body. "Darkness and death will not endure," he whispered tenderly. "My people believe in the return of the sun's warmth and the renewing rains. From death and desolation comes life." A lean smile appeared on his face. His teeth were very fine white, and something in his expression made it impossible to fear him. "The winter has passed; the rain has ceased. The flowers appear on the earth, the spring trees produce their fruits, and the time of singing has come. The shadows flee at spring."

Tara knew, from those strained eyes, he'd endured much harassment and disrespect in his life. But this boy had the courage to make himself vulnerable to her. Never had she met a single man who was capable of doing this!

"I am Tara."

"Yes. Tara." He nodded, his expression deeply troubled for her. "I saw you helping the wounded. Now you are free."

Truly free and loved. Tara could trust someone for a change. She could be part of a family. Where people valued her worth and treated her the way she *longed* to be treated. For years, she'd been cast away, treated like a toy that had been broken – and then cast away by her family because she paid allegiance to the Cabal by force.

Now this person was her brother. Love radiated from him. She didn't do anything to deserve it. It just … happened.

So strange! So beautiful!

Whimpering, she slipped her hand into his, and he clasped their fingers together. "Help me." Emotion flowered in her dead heart, and she felt the passion of it overwhelm her soul. Tara wept, sniffing in silence. He consoled her. She eased her head onto his chest, so she could hear the steady life source that was his heart beating in his chest. The young man rested his chin on her head, and for the first time in what seemed like forever, Tara felt celebration in her heart.

Healed by the good medicine. Tara composed herself. "What is your name?" she said, leaning into his embrace.

"Declan. Declan Summerhill," the accepting young saint said, breath the warmth of the bronze summer sun on her face.

It made sense. This was who Tara had become. She could choose now to become a trusting woman, a woman of strength, a woman of nobility, valour and freedom. She felt that she would fly over the hill, the evil subdued.

Love existed. She saw it in Declan, and he saw it in her grace. Tara was glad her impression was wrong. It would take *years* to be restored, but with Declan, the journey would be worth it.

And that journey began with a simple request to go out to the café. "Come with me, Tara. You want to have some breakfast?"

71

GO TO ONE'S KA

"Concerning the coming of our Lord Jesus Christ … Don't let anyone deceive you, for that day will not come until the rebellion occurs and the man of lawlessness is revealed, the son of destruction …

For the mystery of lawlessness is already at work. Only he who now restrains it will do so until he is out of the way. And then the lawless one will be revealed (apokalypto), whom Yahweh will kill with the breath of his mouth and bring to nothing by the appearance of his coming. The coming of the lawless one is by the activity of Satan with all power and false signs and wonders, and with all wicked deception for those who are perishing, because they refused to love the truth and so be saved. Therefore, God sends them a strong delusion, so that they may believe what is false."

—From the Epistle of Second Thessalonians, Paul, 51 – 52 CE.

Alfred Bonner lay on a medical bed, completely bandaged, hooked to a life support machine inside his helicopter. He opened the box and stared at the metallic spheroid, the Pearl of Power. He desired it to define him, for healing; for such was its power to make the bent world straight. To make what was loose, fixed.

Seeing clearly what he must do, Alfred took the mysterious, precious Pearl out from its box, and in his bandaged hand, he stroked the gem. Affectionately. He'd almost died, but his worth as a catalyst of healing saved him. For Gilgamesh, Osiris, Maitreya was with him.

The world was full of successful yet unethical satanic people and paedophiles, but the mission to save the children and arrest the depraved would continue. The Alliance had many bases all over the world.

Why had the Navajos safeguarded the Pearl of Power for thousands of years only for him to find it? They had demented dogmas that prevented them from seeing that their religion was infected with egotistical moralism.

I almost died. Alfred felt paralysed. He could barely move except for his eyes, and only his hand and mind gently. He clutched the White Pearl, knowing it helped his thinking, strengthening his cognition.

Veronica was on her way to Patala. Keller had gone into the Gate with her. He would die in minutes – Hell's heat caused one to drown internally if not in a coma or in an aqua suit. But the Washukarni should be expecting an arrival on the other side of the Gateway. Veronica would be sent to the Washukarni, and Alfred had peace that she could be of great potential to help the cause against the Tyrant.

Five Pearls of Power … not of the flesh, but over flesh. Gather them. Restore me.

The disembodied voice of the dingir lugal – god-king – chanted, whispering in German.

The *ka* – the inherited life force of an individual, an undying part of one's persona – was only a part of the god that often interacted, much like the *ba* did with the living.

You restored me from death? Alfred thought. *Or was it the Pearl of Power?*

Both. For I am dead, and yet I am the one who was and is not; and I shall ascend. I am regeneration and fertility.

Voices from the past. The archaeologist dug so the dead may live again, for that which was in the past may not be forever lost.

Alfred had more. He had the past *embodied*. When he had written the Dynamics, he had the burden of recognising the relative importance of gods, ghosts and grave goods as keys to help save a dying humanity twisted by Yaldabaoth, the greatest scam of all creation.

The five-part soul spirit of Osiris was the first rising and dying god. His coffin had the extraordinary initiative and plan from the past not yet realised.

Alfred stared at the Pearl – the endowment of worth, of raw power, energising the mind.

Then he looked at the niched palace façade coffin, set against the wall to the far side of the room in the gloom. He had something of power and note – the coffin from Uruk. A coffin inscribed with the name Bilgamesh in Sumerian. Oral legend remembered him as Gilgamesh.

The elaborate input into the funerary rituals performed by the Sumerians did not celebrate death, but it was a testament to how the ancients avoided the destruction death brought, since life expectancy back then was very low.

Burial was major and a standard expenditure – especially for the Egyptians. The god Osiris was said to set the example of this through his death, burial and resurrection. His cult-influencing mortuary customs came from the Early Dynastic deity Khentamentu – a form of the funerary god that assisted the dead through the Underworld – inextricably linked with the guarantee of the imperishability of the body, seen in the practises of the wrapping of the linen and the application of resinous substances, dating back as far as the fifth millennium BCE. The dead needed the living to offer offerings for the mortuary cult to preserve the deceased's memory. To become immortal. Gilgamesh's dream. That was the role of the *ka* – to mediate with the living and create bonds of friendship with the community.

Strange, every time Alfred held the Pearl, he felt *extremely* erudite. His mind racing and brimming with wisdom that he would have normally forgotten. Perhaps that was one of its powers? Cognitive potential?

I should use this more often, Alfred thought, enraptured.

But such erudition could have also been a result of his bond with Osiris – the original un-emasculated Christ. He'd *overcome* death.

Most of the world was not ready for this apocalypse.

"Although death destroys man," Alfred said, "the idea of death saves him."

And I wish I'd understood that when I lived and died, the *ka* of the coffin replied in English. *I did not see I was worthy enough to live on. I was wrong. I am worthy of eternal life to make my name great. As are you. You ruled with me in a life before your birth. You are a king.*

Indeed. Alfred's vocation all along was to save this coffin from museums where it would go to no use. In sad galleries and storerooms, there were things that the public were never meant to see that could be seen. This was why Alfred had to, without Saddam Hussein's regime's approval, secretly sneak the coffin out of Iraq from under his nose. The power in the wrong hands would mean destruction.

The only person he could trust with the Pearl's and coffin's legacies, lore and potency was no one but himself. Only Alfred was a protector of the dignity of the ancients. Only Alfred was the forerunner of a new world to come.

The gods had *chosen him.*

One problem remained – Alfred's own body was like a mummy; he couldn't move his legs, his face felt numb, and he worried, dreaded, that for the rest of his life, he would be confined to a wheelchair.

"Can the Pearl heal me? Can it work miracles?"

One can, the *ka* intoned telepathically. *The Pearl of Heart. But I am afraid its location is lost. We will need more time to hunt for it.*

Time … A wave of bleakness consumed Alfred's heart. *I may have handicaps, and my life extension is decreasing, but I have Osiris.* "You are the true and living Christ. The Five pearls will reknit your five parts. I will gather the Pearls of Power so I can restore you, restorer of limbs. What must I do next as your simulacra?"

Alfred's eyesight *enhanced.* The room suddenly appeared to be lighter. The darkness not so dark.

Then the lord of death and regeneration intoned, *We'll deal shrewdly with the peoples. Gather as many allies as possible until the Restrainer is removed, to quicken the Return. It will prepare us for the good city to rule.*

When will the Restrainer be removed?

Very soon. One god alone cannot hold the chaos of Tiamat at bay forever. The torment will break him. He's breaking now, and my servants will return to the Earth. As we wait for the Restrainer to break, we must unify the Earth, gather the people, lest our Enemy exposes our plans and the Cabal and the Galactic Tyrant come down to war against us.

Infatuated by those promises, Alfred stared into the White Pearl, cupping his hand around it. The world was about to change; the spiritual will rule over the material. To maintain order out of the chaos unleashed by the Tyrant's Restrainer, four more Pearls of Power needed to be found.

He *needed* to find them. To gather them.

Alfred Bonner chuckled to himself. "Five Pearls of Power. Not of the flesh, but over flesh. Gather the Pearls. They have the power to restore you. We will persevere."

I see … Ben DePaula has aligned himself with Yahweh. The traitor.

"What?" Alfred exclaimed aloud.

Some mud creature freed him! Ben has become a scion of the Galactic Tyrant and an Enemy of the gods. For now, the military has imprisoned him. His plans to unite the Enemy will be stalled, giving us more time to await the removal of the Restrainer, to gather the Pearls, and to rally the Lahmu to reclaim the ancient forms. Once the Lahmu return with the storm, the Enemy will crumble. In this, the Lahmu will bring back my dearest love. My Enkidu.

Ah … Enkidu. The Wild Man equal of King Gilgamesh. Strange how one god could be another at the same time. Osiris, Gilgamesh, Apollyon, Maitreya. Who else?

How many gods inhabit this one power?

But to kill Ben … Alfred would ceaselessly resist terrorist-bent attempts to unite the world. They had to be cut, sullied. Unfortunately, the Dynamics said *nothing* regarding the presence of a born-again Christian liability following Ben.

Alfred would make sure the Alliance impoverished him and his movement. He *would*.

72

FREE FROM DESIRE

"I saw in the night visions,
and behold, with the clouds of Heaven
there came one like a Son of Human,
and he came to the Ancient of Days
and was presented before him.
And to him was given dominion
and glory and a kingdom,
that all peoples, nations, and languages
should serve him;
his dominion is an everlasting dominion,
which shall not pass away,
and his kingdom one
that shall not be destroyed."
—From the Scroll of Daniel, 605 – 165 BCE. A Messianic prophecy.

Bhairava, Just Son of Danu, walked into the bustling bazaar. The capital of Iraqi Kurdistan, compared to most cities in Iraq, Ebril was uncharacteristically peaceful.

It was boring. The Kurdish city's booming economy was thanks to a combination of tight security and oil wealth. In this absence of conflict, Bhairava could be in his element, to act with a zero balance of karma. He had to be a master, not a servant. He had to make his act based on the intention that it was his duty as an Arhat of the Fourth Initiation. Bhairava, now a member of the Alliance and its new branch called the Great White Brother and Sisterhood, made it his earthly duty to be a master of higher vibration.

He was *not* of this Earth. He was stuck in the carapace of a body, ready to be shed.

Ahead loomed the high walls of the Ebril citadel. It emerged from the surrounding landscape one hundred feet high, a rare surviving example of a fortified settlement that had grown up on the top of an imposing ovoid-shaped tell – an archaeological mound – in the heart of the city. The maze of alleys and cul-de-sacs radiated from the main grand gate with Ottoman-period urban forms and street patterns. Once, this citadel had been called Arbela, an important Neo-Assyrian centre.

There, Bhairava heard that Adel Rasheed Wahab's main informant, Sheikh Ibrahim, was a Hezbollah sex trafficker.

Karma would get him … Bhairava could hesitate … he had *all the time* in the world to go into the bazaar and … walk.

Each person chose his own fate. There was no arbitrary suffering in the world. If one was miserable doing one's duty, one had hope and expectation of fulfilment in future lives. Bhairava's miserable fate was his duty, for duty's sake – Just Son of Danu.

A slave to existence.

He looked upon the greedy merchants and sellers. They were forces of karma without knowing it. They made people like Bhairava fail to attain moksha – nonexistence and escape from the cycle of rebirth. *The wicked, reaping what they sowed,* he thought. *I will be that cause. I will be the agent of their bad karma. I must escape existence.*

Every time Bhairava closed his eyes, he could hear the screams of the people he'd killed. The screams grated on his soul. He longed to shed this body … why did he agree to extend his life?

It's because I let people use me, Bhairava thought. *That's why I've lost all motivation ever since the Nindingir gave me a life extension.*

The blame game was a shame. After he decided to spend time in Iraq to earn his wages for the Alliance, after being robbed by an insurgent in Baghdad, after he abandoned Ian Mastemah's Zionists and joined the Great White Brother and Sisterhood, he'd survived multiple assassination attempts by Adel Rasheed Wahab.

After the fall of Baghdad, Iraq had become a polarised country without Saddam. Everyone and every city estranged one another. The country in the hands of the Shi'ite majority was an unbearable reality for the Sunni minorities. And then there was the Syrian civil war just next door to the west.

The Kurds, too – also Shi'ite and oppressed by the Ba'ath – now had control over their capital of Erbil.

Yet, shadows of unrest lurked. Could Bhairava survive another close-call bomb? If not, he could be reborn again into the next life as a god to try to attain moksha and nirvana once more.

He had nothing to lose.

He sighed protractedly at his tedious life. Each time he carried out an assassination, he found himself hating the victims. He hated them, not just for molesting young children, but for not being strong enough to kill him. And Bhairava could go right now and kill Sheikh Ibrahim.

No … He'd rather not … kill. Do nothing. Acting meant pain. Pain meant his life was meaningless. Conflict was chaos and undoing. Boredom was the Ascended Master's ideal. And naturally from boredom came conflict to satisfy desire. And with desire came action, and with action came … pain.

One step in front of the other, Bhairava thought in shame of his hypocrisy. *Don't think. Attain the Void –* sunyata.

Bhairava dusted off his hands, wearing a long white kurta robe over a red garment, sauntering through the bustling bazaar, towards the citadel. He needed to be seen doing menial things, as the Kurds here were suspicious, looking out for men wearing dishdashas. Arabs they deemed to be part of the former Ba'ath regime would be lynched, beaten up or thrown out of windows.

He passed a television screen at a vendor that caught his eyes.

Calling for the withdrawal of troops from Iraq – from the bad war – President Barak Obama spoke to a crowd on a replica of the Great Altar of Pergamon. Yes, Bhairava recognised the structure. The original was built around two thousand years ago by the Attalid Dynasty of the empire of Pergamon on the coast of Turkey during the Hellenistic era to rival the culture of Alexandria and Athens. There had been a time when Bhairava used to love art history, especially classical art from Greece and Rome. It made him emotional of times long past. *Ah, the past … A release.*

All desire caused suffering. Suffering happened when one desired and took something impermanent as if it was permanent. Hankering after things that were not the same over time. Function without attachment to anything was how one attained moksha and became an Ascended Master. You did not even desire the urge and fruit of an action. One acted for nothing. One lived for nothing.

People around Bhairava in this mediocre sea of merchandise just wanted more and more, feeding their desires. But Bhairava stood in stasis, in a sea of suffering. Mechanical acting, melancholy existence. Desire frustrated. Mind and senses purified; an Ascended Master free from desire and … bored. Pitiably painful.

Bhairava looked at Obama on TV. He had seen the Altar in Berlin for his art projects. Before his wife and baby died … Before Alfred Bonner … Before the Aes Sidhe and the Nindingir. Before his life turned upside down.

The paragon of Attalid piety, the Great Altar had been built when the Greek rulers had taken a simple gory altar of animal sacrifice, scaling it to the size of a temple, adorning it with friezes of the gigantomachy. He recalled it was the Seat of Satan in the Bible.

Obama … following the example of Albert Speer of Zeppelinfeld. Pathetic tyrant.

Save children for the sake of saving children, Bhairava thought. *That's why you will go up to the citadel and find the paedophile Sheikh Ibrahim.* Bhairava wandered along dejectedly.

He climbed up the stairs passing under the citadel gate, crowned by six flapping red, white, green and gold Kurdish flags. The citadel streets resembled an archaeological site. The walls were sandy bricks, devoid of people. Large pithos, façades, arches and dirt filled these ancient streets. Arbela survived, and even thrived, while other great cities such as Nineveh crumbled.

He entered a small house with a sign that said "The Turkman" – but the Parvas Perception told him that this was a cover. The entrance was decorated with wooden spoons, baskets, tea pots, knives and weaving work.

Bhairava hurried inside to the back of The Turkman, through the back door and along a track towards abandoned buildings. He climbed the back stairs, slipping through an opened window into a laundry. Luckily, Ibrahim had a tight schedule. Muslims prayed five times a day.

Bhairava slowed, listening, hearing nothing behind the door. Slowly, he turned the handle.

He walked into a room with bookcases, leather-bound volumes and displays, and a few feet across from him, a large ornate desk.

He walked onto the prayer mat with a dead body on it.

Someone had already killed the sex trafficker.

"*Uhrzeit gleich endzeit,* Michael Oppenheim," a deep, saccharine voice sounded. The Parvus Perception told Bhairava it was an American accent speaking German.

"How do you know my name?" Bhairava hissed, hand gripping his knife. "Who are you?"

"Haha. I know many things." The chair behind the desk turned. In it was a dashing Asian man, with his fingers in a steeple, elbows resting akimbo on the armrests. He looked very young, perhaps late twenties, with black straight hair and a smooth, round face. He wore a light brown suit and matching pants with long pattern socks, legs crossed over each other. "Things are not what they seem, son of Danu," he said with a bright, smug grin.

Suddenly, people began pouring into the room. Five men and two women. Yet one of the women looked familiar. She wore a *tilak* on her forehead like himself, and Bhairava knew immediately who she was: Alfred Bonner's mistress, Deirdre! The Nindingir! Bhairava began to panic, knowing what this might entail. Subjugation. *No! This is negative karma for following Ian Mastemah and not stopping Joseph DePaula's murder!*

"What the—? Vale, who is this?" One tan-skinned bold man with glasses wearing simple jeans and a shirt asked peevishly.

"Hey, Binoy, I'm just opening doors of opportunity here," the Asian man named Vale shot back, then turned to Bhairava. "I am your unseen master. I have been watching you. You're a Platonic Kantian, Michael Oppenheim. You're so ... *odd!* Wonderfully odd you know that, Michael? You, the master of Pneumaurgy, who owns the truth. The truth that your life"—his enthusiastic expression became stern—"is utterly redundant."

Bhairava twitched hearing his wretched name again. It reminded him ...

Valentina. His one-year-old.

"What?" he rasped. "How do you ...?"

The man smiled mirthfully. "I know many things, but there are many things that I do not know. It seems to me that Ian Mastemah and Metatron are willing to join me for a greater cause. You can only become a friend with your enemy if you become an enemy of their enemy. So Metatron let Ian and I have freedom to do whatever we wish, and Ian failed. Not my problem. You don't need to be afraid now. You're in incredible hands, Bhairava. This crew is a fellowship. You'll be loved very much. We are the Bodhisattvas, and we can show you the way to freedom. I can be your guide to self-mastery, to become an Ascended Master of the Sixth Initiation, attaining nirvana and having power over everything! You have worked hard towards the principle of asceticism. I want to help you on that journey."

"Where should the line be drawn between security and freedom?" Bhairava said.

"Interesting question. Why do you kill?"

"It is my punishment. For bad karma in my early life supporting the Axis powers. I fight because I have no choice. I am forsworn."

The voices accused him … The spirits of the Underworld …

"Forsworn." The Asian man nodded, stroking his chin. "Morality is not how we make ourselves happy, you know. It is how we make ourselves *worthy* of happiness. You get the trick? You, Michael, you have *no guile!* You have no drive, no goals, no agenda. You're boring, to be honest. But guess what? You're ready for the Rapture! No human distracted by the world can attain divinity. Only the boring ones can do it." He gestured at himself. "Like me."

Bhairava let out a shuddering breath. His knees began to shake, and he willed himself to stop them. "You're … my master now."

The man at the desk made a grimace. "It's just so simple, is it? I am not your master in the bad karma sense."

"What do you want me to do?" Bhairava said.

The man pulled from out of his bag a three-and-a-half-inch-tall figurine of a lioness-headed human made from ivory with no legs below the knees. She was a marvellous work of art. Three and a half inches tall, she had an extremely muscular body with her knuckles pressed together across her chest. "Tell me, you have a brother, Michael?" the Asian man said.

Bhairava stared at the man, incredulous. "Yes, sir … One. He died in the trenches."

"I'm sorry," the Asian said, examining his lioness figurine. "How old was he? Older? Younger?"

Bhairava blinked, frowning deeply. "What …?"

"I'm making a point," the man said, raising his voice, cocking his head.

"Younger," Bhairava muttered, lowering his gaze from the people looking at him. His brother … He could barely remember that sweet boy.

"Did he ever tell on you?" the Asian man asked.

"I … don't understand, sir. Sorry."

"The Cabal sent Carnutes to rob the Baghdad Museum," the man said. "Just when I went in to find something, I stumbled upon something powerful. Ancient. And now the Cabal are telling on me for causing the damage to cultural heritage, like a meddling little brother. He's right now sabotaging our mission in the Middle East." The man raised a glance at Bhairava. Mischief and pride glinted in his eyes. "I need the Aes Sidhe's endorsement if I am to gain what I need. What I wanted wasn't in the museum, but, like James Casbolt – that baffling creature – I wanted to help restore the stolen artefacts. So, I brought this with me for safe keeping."

He lifted up his hands to show the figurine of the ivory lioness-headed human with a body-builder physique. "This goddess came from Baghdad. Her name was Inanna in Sumer. Ishtar in Akkad. Aphrodite in Greece. This figurine is Elamite, I believe, Early Bronze Age. There used to be a temple dedicated to Inanna here called Egasankalamma, you know? This is her kingdom. This land belongs to her."

"Why … is this important?" Bhairava intoned.

"She represents the Bodhisattvas' mission. My crew's mission," the man said, his voice clipped, eager and assertive. It dripped with conceit. He met Bhairava in the eyes, serious and stern. "We need to attain a special stone."

"The Voidstone?" Bhairava rasped, panic quacking his heart. *This is my agami karma.*

The Asian man shook his head. "The Chintamani Stone. Agartha rises, Bhairava. The Dynamics foresee this. The Cabal is already ahead of the game. They're making inroads, finding Gateways into the Underworld. Now all I need is to find my own." Then the man placed the figurine away. He sat cross-legged on the chair, like a meditating Buddha. "Conflict with the West and the East will come to pass. Everything is in place. Trade can transform quickly into war. And from it, Agartha will emerge to support our world in the Great Reset."

"You're insane," Bhairava said.

The man guffawed. "Oh! You don't even know who I am yet! Let me introduce myself. I – Valentine Xin – I have survived the traumatic hell of Patala and returned to tell the tale. I was afflicted unjustly by a god-king of the Underworld who is the mafia of mafias. This god-king, Inshushinak, is behind all, if not most, of the child sex trafficking rings. I'm going to save millions of children he has enslaved. Would you care to join me?"

Bhairava's knees felt like buckling, but he stood there on the prayer mat, numb. Why had his "guide" revealed himself now? Defeat a paedophilic god? Could it be … Could it be possible that Bhairava could see Agartha again?

"Do you know what the city of Babylon was called during ancient times?" Valentine said.

"No," Bhairava said, bewildered by this difficult man.

"*Eskiri-tabba-anki.* Babylon, which grasps the bridle of Heaven and the Underworld. Eridu – Babylon, the pleasant city. A Gateway mustering the gods. Lalish is one of these Gateways. You will go there before the Cabal do."

"Why?"

"Lalish is a portal into Patala." Business-like, Valentine dug into his bag, pulled out a document and handed it to Bhairava. "Read this document. It will explain what we are all about, and it will give you an idea of the mission and our purpose." Then Valentine stood up, smiling. "Think about it before coming back to me with your decision. Have a great afternoon! All right! Who's hungry? Falafel, anyone?"

"Me," a gruff Gaelic man with red hair and Aes Sidhe blue eyes intoned. "Bloody love falafel!"

Valentine and his happy entourage retreated from the room, leaving Bhairava deserted and horrified. To be in the hands of one who understood his abilities could be the potential ruin of himself. He stood there for a time, with a dead Arab.

Bhairava, the wretch, looked at the paperwork, four pages printed on both sides, describing the mission of the Bodhisattvas. Their plan was backed by the Alliance; the plan to rescues the sex-trafficked slaves in the Duzakh Empire in Patala. Bhairava was surprised that he had the strength to remain calm as he read.

The last three pages were Valentine Xin's transparent CV: raised between Beijing and New York by the House of Aisin-Gioro, he was a champion at Olympiad math, with a degree in computer science at Colombia, and an entrepreneur, founding Metatron. He had a second degree and a masters in philosophy, and he attended the Ralston Collage Masters in Humanities tour to study the classics and ancient Greek. Valentine was also a Buddhist practitioner, a Pak Hok Pai red belt, the Délok from Naraka and Sporeward extraordinaire, revered by Ascended Masters and Aes Sidhe alike.

Bhairava reverently folded the paper, shocked that his hands were steady. He should have trembled.

For soon, the whole cosmos would quake.

EPILOGUE
THE BRIDGE OF MEGHALAYA

5615 BCE

"And they shall build houses and inhabit them,
they shall plant vineyards and eat their fruit …
For the days of my people shall be like the days of a tree,
and my chosen ones shall enjoy the work of their hands.
They shall not labour for nothing,
and they shall not give birth to horror,
for they shall be offspring blessed by Yahweh,
and their descendants with them."
—From the Scroll of Isaiah, the prophet's disciples, future promise of new heavens
and a new Earth, c. 740 – c. 540 BCE.

Noah looked towards the top of a rubber fig tree – the tree spanning bridges. Fruits and orchids sprouted from its trunk, vanishing into a tangle of lianas in the canopy. A golden-crested hornbill flapped above off its perch with a croak, and the chorus of hoolocks dripped echoes. The sound of the gushing Son of Creator weaved through the opulent screen of blue-green, where a previous tree-shaped bridge collapsed by flooding from a storm.

The rain of the Weeping (the wet season) had just stopped. Drizzle dripped off Noah's wide reed hat, sweat darkening his trousers. The leaves above shed heavy drops from the humid skies. A low mist hung over the ground. The Weeping coincided with the windy storms, where the deluge of torrential, unstoppable rain, tumbling down the mountains, created lethal torrents. The storms were capricious; they brought insurmountable challenges for the animal and human communities. Sometimes, the rains got chaotic enough that Noah's family had to learn to swim in case their village was engulfed. Earthquakes were not uncommon.

Fig tree roots wound outwards from the base of the trunk, rising over the surface of the soil, forming a long tree bridge, breached by the storms. Stepping meticulously over a bed of writhing roots, some formed to create stairs – one could not tell where God and human work ended here – Noah found a suitable grove, branches hanging with lichen, filtering the moisture from the clouds hovering over the mountains. Noah used his staff to tap the ground for snakes. A huge moon moth, mimicking a quivering yellow leaf, fluttered away. Noah knelt, feeling his hand across the damp grey woody bark to find the filamentous infant roots. The ground hummed and crackled. A rich fungal smell drifted upwards.

Noah found the strands of tress-like roots.

Links must be renewed. These bridges had to be very strong, *living* bridges formed out of strands of fibrous roots. And after one or many had been completed, they became a part of the laurel forest, where human-made constructions melded into creation. The bridges aided the villagers' mobility to reach their terrace farms.

The people had built these perfect bridges out of fig trees for generations and generations. His family were pragmatic, and Noah would continue to cherish the pragmatic tradition. Humans and plants giving to each other, growing, growing every day. Large towns imposed *on* the landscape, but the tree bridges *were* the landscape. They were the long-lasting traces of Noah's munificent ancestors: the first custodian Life Bearer – the woman from whom sprang species.

The rushing river hissed mightily over the broken bridge, tearing through plant roots, wearing down boulders strewn in a rocky causeway.

The key here to overcome this flood was to plant fig trees by the riversides, carefully. And once they were mature enough – plenty of water came in the wet season – one would use the voracious aerial roots. They were the best kind for grafting, these strands of young roots, they combined and grew into a living bridge.

A young strong bridge represents my kin, Noah thought as he wisely weaved strands of aerial roots around each other, perpendicular from the boulders. They built one another. They gave to one another. They couldn't grow stronger than the other roots tangled around them if they didn't have one another. They received life and they gave life simultaneously. A regenerative bridge that spanned the river was impeccably strong enough to hold foot traffic.

As Noah shrewdly guided the strands of young roots away from the riverbank through hollowed halves of bamboo tubes he'd cut back home, a frantic rustling brought his instincts to high alert. A boy flung out of the ferns, laughing, playfully trying to climb a tree.

"Get down from there, Premyi!" Noah called to his little brother.

"I just saw pink dolphins! Pink dolphins, Noah! Look!" He'd been as happy as the time when Lamec, their father, had taken them on swimming lessons in the river during the hot season, despite Dhara – his mother – refusing adamantly. She would've thought her husband was teaching him to drown rather than to swim. Noah also recalled riding Milsila's pet elephant Yaphet with Premyi, waddling through the swamps when the Son of the Creator broke its banks, when the fields were inundated up to the elephant's ankles. The animals learnt to cope with the constant moisture, and, during those days of the cold season giving way to the hot, Noah would also weave farming shells – oversized hats – for the rice farmers. In this wet world, flexibility and practical wisdom were crucial for all things that had the breath of life.

Emerging out of the green screen of damp ferns behind his little brother was smiling Milsila. She was fourteen years old, like Noah. She was of the Tynrai – renowned mahouts – wearing a wide straw hat like Noah, her skirts tied up as a loin cloth, bare legs and arms tanned, using a staff for balance. Her hair was frizzy and damp.

She laid her intelligent light eyes on Noah. "Why didn't you tell me your mother wanted you to become a healer?" she said.

"We have the menagerie, the farm, the bridges." He made a loop of four strands. "But I'm also a bridgeman, Milsila. Everyone's got their purpose."

"Yeah, well." Milsila leaned on her stick. "You go out and be a hunter for me. Hunting Nephilim. Like everyone else."

Noah shrugged, raising the bamboo to reinforce the framework. This frame would rot over time and become the energy for the process of inosculation, so Noah had to reinforce it. He studied the sprawling web, aerial branches dangling like grasping hands over the destroyed shape of silver roots forming the old bridge. Cataract current gushed around it.

Hunters of Nagaland lived by the spear. They killed. They, like the Sages of old, like Yared, the descended spirit, removed bridges when they could've built bridges that would grow. They were deluges of foolish people, ritualising their killings of people at random for initiation. The Naga, like the Sages, came about to kill off the Nephilim, but they became Nephilim themselves through their viciousness.

Hunt the Nephilim. Why would Noah be deceived by this lie? Hadn't the Sages failed humanity to be faithful to U-Blei, abandoning the Khesed Bond? The pact to serve humanity during times of tribulation? Couldn't humanity live without such pride? The Sages recruited by U-Blei and his spirits imbued the Sages with special powers to fight Nephilim. But they sinned, becoming prideful. They had won the world and yet lost the world. The Sages were an old bridge, deceived and dead. Crumbling, they were forgotten forever, grown over by vegetation.

But the ancestor Hanok, son of Yared the traitor, pleased U-Blei by being a witness of right relationship. Noah's family greatly honoured Hanok, for he was his ancestor, directly connected to all the tribes of Meghalaya.

Milsila rubbed Noah's shoulder as he wrapped gentle knots. Noah stopped worrying about what would become of his bridge, staring at her face. Milsila was more than his friend. She was his other, exhilarating self. Who else in the world could be like her? "I'm worried about you," she said, her voice alive with exuberant personality. "You're too dedicated to work. You need to go out into the *real* world and have some fun. In Meghalaya. But build this bridge for me first. It connects my village to yours. You're the best bridgeman that I know."

Noah smirked. "Thanks, Milsila."

"All right," Milsila said happily. "Down there, I'm going to find the pink dolphin before you do."

Noah didn't like pink dolphins; they had snouts too long, needle-like teeth and bodies that appeared deformed, swine-like. But his favourite animal had to be the hoolock gibbon. Slender, agile and wise, their arms were longer than their legs, and Noah loved them because of their nature. They looked the most human of all animals and yet were not human. His *kiaw* (grandmother) Edna kept a family of them in her menagerie – a paradise forest – that Milsila named Meghalaya.

Every weekend, Noah would have something to look forward to. Walking across the bridge into this dark mysterious land brought warm liquid oozing through his body. He felt graceful, wiser and stronger crossing into mysterious Meghalaya. Light could barely penetrate the canopy where he built tree houses. There was an abundance of resources for the kingdom – riots of good trees, plants climbing in profusions, all with their own rainbows of colourful fruits.

The animals were the people. The gibbons would swing, and Noah and

Milsila would chase after them. One time, they both gained a gibbon's family's trust, and they even reinforced their bonds by grooming their fur for dirt and lice. During such sacred moments, up in the fig trees, as king and queen, Noah and Milsila had the most intimate and funniest times of their lives. They rose high into the clouds together, sharing the Creator's voluptuous provisions with the gibbons and with the stars of spiritual beings.

The Sages failed in their quest for Paradise, but Noah and Milsila found it. This was very good.

"Wait until I finish making the frame," Noah said, pulling out an axe from his belt. Grabbing one of the tall bamboo stalks nearby, he hacked it with the precise measurements he'd learnt. He placed the truncated bamboo inside his cane cone-shaped basket that slung over his back. He continued the process again, splitting the tubes in half horizontally, manipulating the fig tree rubber roots across the interior of the bamboo, closing them, tying them, aligning them across the old bridge.

Once the frame was done, Noah had to wait a year. He crossed the old bridge, climbing meticulously down the tree roots, and sat down by a mossy rock on the riverbank. Milsila and his brother had gone down to his left – it was slippery – so he took off his sandals, using all fours. He took a sip from his waterskin, sitting on a boulder.

The sky was cadaverous. Often, Noah let dull weather dictate his mood, a constricting melancholy that numbed him often. The Weeping came in a ceaseless cascade of sullen drops for days. Never furious, never passionate like the storms. It was slow, like the blood of a year dying on its way to the cairn.

Noah sighed protractedly, closing his eyes. He said a quick prayer to U-Blei, the Creative Creator, feeling his heart stir with love.

He would *never* become a hunter of Nagaland. He would *never* follow in the path of the Sages, those cursed creatures. If there was one to follow, it was Hanok, just a man, just a teacher. An aesthetic who vanished in the Himalayas. Hanok – simple and humble.

"Noah, look what I found," little Premyi said, on the verge of laughter. "Look, look!"

"Hey, watch your step! The rocks are slippery!"

Wet and grubby, Noah's little brother climbed up the boulders, opening his wet, grimy hands to reveal a small round stone. "Look at it." Premyi's voice was affectionate.

"What is it?"

"A fossil," the eight-year-old replied giddily. "But look, it has rainbows!"

Noah studied the little imprinted spiralling ram's horn. Premyi was not fancying. It really *did* have colour to it. Extraordinary that a simple rock could shine with an impossible nacre. Noah managed to grin.

Upon seeing Noah looking inexplicably better, Premyi bloomed like a flower. "I found it for you. To make you feel better." The kid was a runt, looking half his age with flushed cheeks, a smooth, round face, cute slanted thin eyes and long brown hair reaching his shoulders in curls. He was missing a few of his front teeth, making his smile adorable.

"Rainbows ..." Noah whispered gently. "It is beautiful, Premyi. Thank you."

—

"They found Milsila's body. She'd drowned this morning down the river."
Blameless Milsila had slipped and hit her head.
No, everyone here could swim!
"You're lying! She's not even dead!"
Noah ran to find the bridge shattered. The storm had passed, and the winds had been violent. Milsila had a sleepover at his place after playing with the Meghalaya animals.

It began to rain in the morning when she departed. She'd been washed away by the cataclysm. The rubber fig roots died, snapped, dangling in the current flow.

Noah's jaws were rattling. His bridge couldn't fall! It was mature enough!
Milsila. Dead. You. Bridge. Flood.
Noah ran until he almost slipped, but he went on, flying as a gibbon. He ran in the cool of the day, fighting his uncle, who found him, trying to carry him home like a baby.

—

Noah lay on his bed inside his mother's earth-worked terraced house at the farm growing rice, ginger, turmeric and betel. A shake here, a sniffle there, persistent tears rolling down his cheeks, his throat constricted as he sobbed. He'd blocked the door. It was drizzling, and the skies were grey.

How could he have prepared for this? Milsila – frozen forever on the boundary between youth and maturity ... The image of her, running before him into Meghalaya, turning her neck to look at him, head tilted, smiling rapturously, laughing, arms swinging. The image of his heart. Her joyous imagination brought *such vivid salvation.*

Gasping, Noah let hot, angry tears drop down his face. Before, he saw the adults crying in the village – they were crying for themselves, not for Milsila! They didn't know her! They treated her death as if they all lost their *kiaw's* property inheritance. But Noah's stomach churned. He could fix broken bridges, but he couldn't figure out how to stop hurting himself.

The door opened, pushing aside the buckets. The Nephilim had followed him!

Noah cried out as someone embraced him.

"My Noah," Dhara said. Noah trembled despite his mother's warm bosom.

"Ma, is U-Blei sending Milsila to Damnation?"

"No, my son. U-Blei would *never* send that incredible girl there."

"Then I will go instead of her." Noah glanced at his hands. "It's my fault she's gone."

Milsila had slipped onto the rocks; blood shed over the rock of Son of the Creator. The crimson blood that covered his hands contained her life.

Noah began to break again. He bounded unconsciously, but Dhara had already grabbed his arm.

"Noah," she said forthrightly, pressing him into her robes. "It's *not* your fault."

"It is," he sobbed.

"Noah, you need to learn to let go," Dhara intoned. "Letting go could be what it means to live."

And ... that's a good thing to let people die when I could've saved them? Noah thought. *Milsila had tricked me! She just wanted to walk my new bridge to show that she was no coward. Why? She probably would be somewhere right now, laughing at me.*

"But," Dhara said, "I can tell you the most important thing to do now is to honour her memory."

Everywhere Noah looked was red. He wished he could wash it all away. Milsila's blood. Blood was one of the most colourful parts of the body – but why did the colourful parts have to be hidden unless something went wrong?

Blood. It determined your inheritance in this world. Blood. It was like the greenery all around him, but blood was different. Both covering and polluting, it was life. It needed to be cleansed before it cried out. Washed and cleansed with water, blood cleansed what water could not.

Red Human, from dirt we came.

Milsila no more, to dirt she became.

"I don't want to be a bridgeman," Noah muttered, gazing at the shimmering sea of the setting sun. Why was the sky vivid with orange, pink and purple bows when the sun was about to set? Was it angry at being forced to drown below the horizon? His farm was at the top of the valley; it seemed the sun had sunk under the surface of the clouds every evening.

"Noah." Dhara's voice was a calm pond. "Many things that I don't understand happen." She placed a fond hand on Noah's shoulder. "I will always be with you."

Noah *had* to give something back to honour Milsila. But did he expect to receive anything in return? That was the question. The eyes of those elephants, gibbons, and other creatures he'd watched die … had been so colourful … What had been the point of beauty when it always faded? What had been the point of fruits that always decayed? What was the point of bridges when the deluge kept violating them?

He looked into his mother's hazel eyes, thinned with an epicanthic fold. "I regret I ever made bridges."

"Noah," Dhara said, voice gaunt. "Do you know why I named you? Do you know what your name *means*?"

"I do not know …"

"*Nuakh*. Rest." Dhara's consoling voice became melliferous chimes of wholeness. "Rest. Settling down. During your *Gerkhun*, your father sung, 'We shall be comforted from our labour and toils of our hands, from the ground which U-Blei has cursed.'"

If only Noah could rest from the incredible duty to maintain this Garden kingdom, Meghalaya, that he ruled as a king. How could he nurture Meghalaya with the ground that consumed Milsila? His other?

Rest. The rhythm of creation and the universe sought to this ultimate rest at the culmination of time, resting on the Seventh Day after work was done.

Yet how that would be restored, and how the greater semblance of order could take place, was difficult to deduce, but Noah trusted that it was taking place, somehow, some way. Perfection was his craft, but the rest was an art.

Working, walking, wounded.

The unstable bridge caves in.

The Sage, filled with sickness and determination, envy invades.

The Sage lives on, with toilsome fists, scrabbling hold.

A ruined bridgeman, holding on.

But better is one palm, open hand, full and patient.

Burdened with responsibility, yet tranquil, not leaning on the toil.

Milsila had died just when Noah needed her the most. She died, so Noah could return to the kingdom of Meghalaya, walking over the roots on the ground, under the protective cover of fig trees, the choir of animals swishing, braying, the colour artistic. Noah would construct a memorial for her: a basket raft tied with her toys, make the bridge larger, out of the fibrous fig tree roots. *That* would be honouring her.

"I am … You think I am …" Noah swallowed. "The Chosen Seed?" The Chosen Seed promised by U-Blei to Life Bearer. The Chosen One destined to crush the head of the Snake Enemy. The Sages lived by the promise of the Chosen Seed. Yared – the founder – thought he was it. As their leader, he called for a return to the Creator. But the Snake Enemy set his seat in his heart, and in the hearts of all the Sages, and then, Yared became the snake instead of the snake crusher.

"You are our peace. Our hope," Dhara intoned, and getting up, she promised Noah a visit to Milsila's clan to attend her cremation.

But Noah thought about all these things. About the Sages' pride and Hanok's humility. About his raft that he shall build for the girl in his life who gave him life. And above all, he thought about being at rest. Being hope for others. Completion.

Caws of waterbirds and hoolocks echoed from the tops of fig trees, mourning for Milsila along with the sighs of the rain.

END OF BOOK ONE OF

THE ERA OF THE END

ACKNOWLEDGEMENTS

My literary journey began in 2018 with an idea to write an epic sci-fi fantasy mythopoetic saga based on the Book of Revelation and conspiracy theories. James Casbolt was the first character I envisioned, who would serve as the main protagonist in a TV show script I wrote. By 2020, I finished the script and realised I had created a nightmarish monstrosity.

During the 2020 festive season, I began converting the *Omega Plan* script into a fiction novel. By the start of 2022, I had the first draft of the novel done, but it was peppered with plot holes, info dumps, awful tangents, filled with on-the-nose preaching and cringeworthy episodes that made no sense. *Omega Plan* draft 1 was my greatest failure and at the same time, my greatest success.

But I couldn't stop there. From 2022 to 2023, I rewrote and edited the story so many times, weaving in new ideas and plots, tightening the story, refining the narrative into the form that you have before you today. I cannot explain how it all came together; I honestly believe the whole process was providential for the people in my life that helped the book come into its final form.

All this would not have been possible if not for the people who supported me. Firstly, I want to thank my family and extended family for believing in me from the start. I express my deepest love and gratitude to my father and mother who have spent countless hours and money to help guide and fund me through the five years of writing, editing and publishing this work. Thanking them here will not do justice. My parents are utterly remarkable. I want to thank my amazing friends excited for the story and for all those who prayed for the story. I want to thank my lecturers and teachers from high school, Monash and ACU for instilling within me the passion for academia in history, theology, literature and philosophy—the wisdom that reinforces this series. You know who you are if you're reading this. I want you to know that I would have never produced this labour of love without you. May God bless you all abundantly.

I also want to express my sincerest thanks to Kathy Betts (Element Eds) for her wonderful editing, proofreading and patience, Ludmila for the character POV artwork, my beta readers Ayebai-preye Iwowari, Harry Stone, Ifeoluwa Olorunniyi and Chizitere Godwin and Damonza for the Volume I cover design. I also wish to give a special thanks to Tahlia Newland (managing editor), Rose Newland (book designer) and the rest of the team from Alkira and Escarpment Publishing for helping me publish this big book.

I give thanks to all the people that inspired me and influenced me over these five years. I will also like to acknowledge the scholars and research I consulted for this book and the creators who helped shape the story: Brandon Sanderson, Jeremy Duncan (Upside-Down Apocalypse: Grounding Revelation in the Gospel of Peace), Tim Mackie (The Bible Project), Richard Bauckham (The Theology of the Book of Revelation), Greg L. Bahnsen (Victory in Jesus: The Bright Hope of Postmillennialism), Matthew Bogdanos (Thieves of Baghdad), Lawrence Rothfield (The Rape of Mesopotamia: Behind the Looting of the Iraq Museum), Nicola Crusemann (Uruk: First City of the Ancient World), Holly Baglio, Carmen Imes, John Walton, Tremper Longman (The Lost World of the Flood: Mythology, Theology, and the Deluge Debate), Michael Jones (Inspiring Philosophy), Michael Morales (Who Shall Ascend the Mountain of the Lord?: A Biblical Theology of the Book of Leviticus), William Paul Young (The Shack), René Girard, C.S Lewis, Brian Godawa, Denis Villeneuve, Ian Shaw (The Oxford History of Ancient Egypt), Jeremy Black, Andrew George, Amanda H. Podany (Weavers, Scribes and Kings), Wally Brown (Navajo Traditional Teachings), Chief Joseph RiverWind, Dr. Laralyn RiverWind, David Duchovny, Chris Carter, Joseph Blenkinsopp (Creation, Un-creation, Re-creation: A discursive commentary on Genesis 1-11), Michael LeFebvre (The Liturgy of Creation: Understanding Calendars in Old Testament Context), Michael Heiser, JP McMahon (the Way Biblical Fellowship), Dalton Thomas (Days of Noah), Gabriel Said Reynolds (Exploring the Quran and the Bible), Peter Berresford (Celtic Myths and Legends), Alejandro Gómez Monteverde (Sound of Freedom), Tim Ballard, Amar Annus (On the Origin of Watchers: A Comparative Study of the Antediluvian Wisdom in Mesopotamian and Jewish Traditions), Martti Nissinen and Risto Uro (Sacred Marriages: The Divine-Human Sexual Metaphor from Sumer to Early Christianity), Gregory Mobley (Samson and the Liminal Hero in the Ancient Near East), Fr. Stephen De Young, and Jonathan Pageau (The Symbolic World).

Literature cited directly within *Omega Plan*:

- *Holy Bible*, (quotations from the ESV and NIV with changes by the author. Tim Mackie's Literal Literary translation for Bible Project used with permission.)
- *The Birth of Civilization in the Near East*, Henri Frankfort, Project Gutenberg, Doubleday Anchor Books, 1956, (public domain).
- *Paradise Lost*, John Milton, 1667, Global Language Resources, Inc, (public domain).
- *The Book of the Dead or 'Book of Coming Forth by Day'*, Translated by E. A. Wallis Budge, 1895, Sacred Texts, (public domain).
- *Desiring Divinity: Self-deification in Early Jewish and Christian Mythmaking*, M. David Litwa, New York, 2016, (used with Litwa's permission).
- *The Sumerians: Their History, Culture and Character*, Samuel Noah Kramer, University of Chicago Press, 1963, (used with permission).
- *The Deir Alla Inscription, Jordan, 8th Century BCE.* Translation by Baruch A. Levine, from *The Context of Scripture Volume Two: Monumental Inscriptions from the Biblical World*, William W. Halo, Leiden: Brill, 2001 (used with permission).
- *The Treasures of Darkness: A History of Mesopotamian Religion*, Thorkild Jacobsen, Yale University, 1978, (used with permission).
- *The Babylonian Gilgamesh Epic: Introduction, Critical Edition and Cuneiform Texts*, Andrew George, Oxford, 2003, (used with permission).
- *The Oxford History of Ancient Egypt*, Ian Shaw, Oxford, 2002, (used with permission).
- *The Treasures of Darkness: A History of Mesopotamian Religion*, Thorkild Jacobsen, Yale University, 1978, (used with permission).
- *Death of Gilgamesh*, translated by Jeremy Black, The Electronic Text Corpus of Sumerian Literature, Oxford, 1997, (public domain).